MECHANICS-
MERCANTILE
LIBRARY.

GORGEOUS EAST

ALSO BY ROBERT GIRARDI

Madeleine's Ghost

The Pirate's Daughter

Vaporetto 13

A Vaudeville of Devils:
7 Moral Tales

The Wrong Doyle

GORGEOUS EAST

EAST

ROBERT GIRARDI

ST. MARTIN'S PRESS NEW YORK

GORGEOUS EAST. Copyright © 2009 by Robert Girardi. All rights reserved.
Printed in the United States of America. For information, address St. Martin's Press,
175 Fifth Avenue, New York, N.Y. 10010.

"Let's Face the Music and Dance" by Irving Berlin
© Copyright 1935, 1936 by Irving Berlin.
© Copyright renewed. International copyright secured.
All rights reserved. Reprinted by permission.

www.stmartins.com

Book design by Kathryn Parise

LIBRARY OF CONGRESS CATALOGING-IN-PUBLICATION DATA

Girardi, Robert.
  Gorgeous East / Robert Girardi.—1st ed.
      p. cm.
   ISBN 978-0-312-56586-2
   1. Soldiers of fortune—Fiction.   2. Brotherhoods—Fiction.   I. Title.
PS3557.I694 G67 2009
813'.54—dc22

2009016756

First Edition: October 2009

10 9 8 7 6 5 4 3 2 1

For my creatures: Charlotte, Ben, Samantha

CONTENTS

Once did she hold the gorgeous east in fee;
And was the safeguard of the west . . .

Men are we, and must grieve when even the Shade
Of that which once was great, is pass'd away.
—William Wordsworth

All civilizations have their sufferers. In every country in Europe, and without doubt in America also, live men for whom life is a penance. Some of them have been stricken down by misfortunes or by unforeseen happenings, and the sight of the places where they have been unhappy has become unbearable for them. Others have suffered by their own mistakes or they have committed some act for which their consciences reprove them; they know that they can reconstruct themselves only by escaping from their pasts. For all those beings, for all those whom Dostoevski calls the "Insulted and the Injured," the Foreign Legion offers a refuge.
—André Maurois

AUTHOR'S NOTE

❦

The French Foreign Legion, the famous mercenary corps founded during the reign of King Louis Philippe in 1831, endures to this day as a last resort for any man stupid or desperate enough to join its ranks. Though an anachronism, a relic of nineteenth-century warfare, the Legion is a living relic: Legionnaires served in the first Gulf War and in Bosnia, and are now deployed in Afghanistan.

Legion headquarters, once located at Sidi Bel Abbès in French Algeria, were removed following Algerian independence in 1961 to Aubagne, Bouches-du-Rhône, in southwestern France. Only foreigners (that is, non-French citizens) age eighteen to forty are accepted as volunteers there, at the Fort de Nogent near Paris—open around the clock, 365 days a year—and at several other recruiting stations throughout France. Officers are selected from among the top graduates of the French Military Academy at Saint-Cyr. Legion commissions are eagerly sought. No ambitious young officer can re-sist the chance to mold soldiers out of such unpromising human clay as the Legion provides—traditionally, the worst of the worst, criminals and run-away husbands, alcoholics, sociopaths. But to these lost men the Legion still offers a unique privilege called *l'anonymat*: a new identity and an assumed name affixed to their uniforms via Velcro tags that may be discreetly removed in the presence of television cameras, journalists, or police detectives. This is, in effect, a chance to start broken lives over again.

The political situation in the Western Sahara, fictionalized in these pages, is roughly as I describe it. Though there exists at this writing no such thing as a Marabout Insurgency, it is not beyond the realm of the possible. Meanwhile, the war between the kingdom of Morocco and Polisario—the armed faction of the Saharoui Arab Democratic Republic (SADR), a phantom state also known as the Non-Self-Governing Territory of Western Sahara—drags on. Now entering its fourth decade, it remains one of the least known conflicts in the world, perhaps because phosphate deposits and fishing rights are not as pertinent to the global economy as oil. The UN Mission to Western Sahara (MINURSO) has been involved in negotiations to end the conflict since the 1970s, but—to no one's surprise—its efforts have proved ineffectual. Hundreds of thousands of Saharoui refugees are still housed in hardscrabble camps in the Algerian desert, not far from the town of Tindouf.

Fatal familial insomnia, or FFI, a hereditary condition caused by the same type of mysterious infectious proteins (prions) responsible for mad cow disease, is rare but well documented by medical research.

My efforts at verisimilitude end here. This volume is a work of fiction, offered as an entertainment; certain details of life in the Legion and elsewhere have been manipulated for dramatic effect. The characters described in the following pages are not meant to resemble anyone now living or once living, now dead.

GORGEOUS EAST

1

SARABANDE FOR
A SUICIDE

1.

Phillipe watched the pale young woman coming down the Grand Degré from the abbey, slowly, past the knickknack shops and the kiosks selling holy water, in the midst of a crowd of tourists in the rain. She gleamed like an apparition against the gray afternoon light. It was late July but wet and cold, as is often the case along this stretch of the Breton coast. A perennial gloom emanated from the abbey's dark, medieval stones; low-lying clouds obscured the pinnacle of its famous spire.

The tourists were Americans, big and ruddy and loud and badly dressed in their usual array of sports paraphernalia and baseball caps—one of the package groups off the buses parked in an endless line along the causeway to the mainland. The pale young woman, clearly French, didn't belong with them, wasn't a part of their group, but seemed in the grip of a lethargy that prevented her from breaking away. Perhaps she had allowed herself to be drawn along at their shuffling pace rather then fight through the crush to the Gothic gates, to the causeway and the car park and the salt meadows and the tidal flats beyond, to France, a misty blue outline in the near distance. The Americans looked warm in their thick sweatshirts emblazoned with colorful logos. On their feet massive, elaborate sneaker boots—some with bulbous protrusions and lights that flashed with every step. The young woman wore only a thin cocktail dress made of a black, silky material, the sort of thing better suited to an intimate party in Paris, an evening at Soixante-Sept, or any of the other fashionable nightclubs in the Marais. The complicated straps of her sandals glittered with faux jewels; her toenails were painted gold.

The guide in charge of the American tour group raised his umbrella and began to speak, gesturing at the overhanging story of a half-timbered house from the fifteenth century. In the next moment other tour guides up and down the street raised similar umbrellas at similar houses and began to speak in their own languages, and an international cacophony echoed off the ancient, dripping facades. Phillipe heard snatches of German, Spanish, Japanese, Greek.

Meanwhile, the Americans had advanced a bit and now shuffled in place just across the railing from where Phillipe sat beneath the striped awning on the terrace of Aux Trois Ancres, sipping a cognac and going over his notes. He was writing a monograph on Erik Satie, the avant-garde composer—one of the most eccentric and whimsical figures of those bright decades lying across 1900 that the French call la Belle Époque—which he intended to submit to *Revue du Musique Français.* But Phillipe had been writing this particular monograph for a couple of years; writing was only a hobby for him, one of many. And now he rose out of his seat beneath the awning and let his notebook fall unheeded to the wet ground.

The young woman stood there, shivering in the rain, behind the broad backs of a couple of middle-aged American ladies. To call her beautiful missed the point. She possessed a kind of flickering quality, like a flame seen through a rice-paper screen. Her pale skin, nearly white, as if she lived entirely by moonlight or bathed exclusively in milk, seemed illuminated from inside. She was probably in her early twenties, and clearly Parisian—her dress and glittery sandals, her glossy black hair cropped short, all in the latest style—but this veneer of sophistication could not conceal the obvious from Phillipe: Here was someone in a great deal of trouble.

Now, the young woman's blue eyes, close to the color of Phillipe's own, though far more vivid—a kind of indigo blue—flashed toward him. Their gaze met for a second or two; she didn't seem to register his presence. Then, she turned away, and the tour group shuffled on, and somehow Phillipe knew she intended to commit suicide. More, he knew how she intended to do it: She was going to follow the Americans to their buses along the causeway, climb over the rocks and onto the mudflats with the tide rushing in, and simply give herself up to the relentless surge. She might be dashed against the breakwater, or washed out to sea, to England across La Manche. Either way, it wouldn't matter much to her, though she probably hoped they wouldn't find her body afterwards.

Phillipe gasped, certain of the annihilation he had seen in the depths of her eyes. But he also recognized this death wish as a kind of fatal caprice, a passing psychological squall. Two or three days from now, he knew, if she survived, thoughts of suicide would be gone from her. She might not even remember this desperate afternoon so far from familiar Parisian boulevards, with the rain coming down and the lumbering tourists and the gargoyled silhouette of the Mont-Saint-Michel acting as a suitably dramatic backdrop for her death. He watched her move off toward it now, the fatal tides already rolling in. She was through the l'Avancée gate, through the Porte du Roi, the Americans bearing her away like a crowd of gaudily dressed pallbearers—and yet he hesitated. How could he know what he knew? Was this some kind of macabre fantasy on his part? No! He had seen it! And he knew he didn't have much time.

Phillipe tossed a few bills down on the table, more than what he owed, and, leaving his notebook on the ground, dashed after the young woman, pushing pedestrians out of the way, crashing down through the causeway gate. She was already on the other side. He caught sight of her glossy black head, moving along about twenty meters up the causeway. She passed the first bus, then the second, and Phillipe's pace flagged slightly—could he be wrong about this after all?—then she sidestepped into the gap between the third and fourth bus and disappeared. He dodged around a clutch of Danes lined up to board a bus painted with a huge Danish flag that would take them back to Copenhagen, and came out on the narrow strip between the buses and the breakwater just as the young woman climbed down over the rocks exactly as he had imagined she would. In the distance, a white wall, advancing.

Phillipe leaped over the rocks without thinking about the possible consequences and slogged out as fast as he could, but he didn't seem to be making any progress. The wet, gummy sands of the flats sucked at his handmade leather boots; each step weighed a kilo. The young woman, barefoot and much lighter, glided across the surface, head down, oblivious to the doom rushing to meet her at a rate of about one meter every second—the speed, as Victor Hugo once observed, watching the rising tide from the battlements above, of a horse at fast gallop. Phillipe fought against the sand, lost one boot and kicked off the other, and somehow reached her no more than five seconds before the wall of water hit. He grasped her shoulder and swung her around and their eyes met for the second time that day. This time, she registered his presence as an outrage. She came back to herself with a shudder, and she came back angry.

"*Non!*" the young woman screamed. "*Le salot!* Bastard! Don't touch me! Let me go!"

"Not this time!" Phillipe shouted over the roar of the waves, then the water smashed down over them, hard. They were thrown back onto the sand, submerged and picked up and whirled along together in the current, like the damned lovers Paolo and Francesca in the hot wind of Dante's *Inferno*. Phillipe kept a hold on the young woman's shoulder, got an arm around her waist, and pushed off the bottom to surface for a breath of air. As the current lessened, he swam with one arm, pulling her along toward the causeway and the buses, their steely sides gleaming ahead like the gates of heaven.

The Foreign Legion emphasizes an utterly rigorous regime of physical fitness, even for its officers, musicians, and cooks; fortunately for Phillipe, the ability to swim a hundred meters in full combat gear was a mandatory part of basic training. Phillipe reached the causeway, was dashed against a sharp protrusion, cutting a gouge in his cheek; then he grabbed on to a rock and managed to pull both himself and the young woman to safety. He dragged her around the buses into the road as she coughed and choked out the seawater she had attempted to swallow. The swift-running tides had torn the thin dress from her pale skin and she was naked except for a pair of midnight blue panties. Phillipe bent her over and pounded on her back with the flat of his hand as tourists stood around gaping. The Americans seemed shocked, not by the violence, of course, but by the nakedness. A few Japanese snapped pictures with expensive digital cameras.

"Is she all right?" one of the Americans asked in English.

"What the hell's going on?" another one asked.

"Maybe someone should go get the police, whattya call them—the ghendarms. . . ."

The young woman crouched there, arms clutched about her nakedness, shivering violently, blue lips drawn over her white teeth.

"Your shirt!" Phillipe shouted in English at a tall man wearing a Chicago Bulls sweatshirt. "Can't you see she's freezing?"

"Here ya go, buddy," the tall man said, and he drew off his sweatshirt and tossed it to Phillipe. "Keep it."

The young woman still fought against him, but weakly now. He managed to get the huge sweatshirt over her head—it reached nearly to her knees—and Phillipe pulled her up and marched her back up the causeway toward the grim edifice of the Mont, looming like the prison it had been for a century or so of its thousand-year history, the prison it was again today for one shivering, stunned young woman. The prison of this life.

2.

They sat by the fire in the empty parlor of Phillipe's hotel drinking Calvados, the potent stuff warming their insides. The young woman— her name was Louise, this much Phillipe had managed to get out of her—now wore one of his expensive silk shirts and flannel pajama bottoms borrowed from the concierge's son, printed with cartoon figures from the Asterix comic books: There was Asterix, the pint-sized Gallic warrior in winged helmet, bottle of magic potion in hand; there the obnoxious bard Cacofonix playing his lyre; there Obelix hoisting a menhir, his little white dog at his side.

Louise, eyes lowered, studied her cartoon pajama pants with some intensity. The white dog, bone in its mouth, appeared to be headed for her inner thigh. She hadn't uttered more than a word or two since she'd been pulled from the sea. Phillipe had ordered a *bifteck en sauce au poivre vert* for her from the concierge, and when it came she ate hungrily, plate on lap, without comment.

When she was done, she wiped her mouth on the sleeve of Phillipe's shirt and studied him, a frank hostility in her eyes. No doubt he represented everything she'd been taught to despise: from the severe military cut of his hair to the conservative, tailor-made civilian clothes he wore, to his steady, serious demeanor. He was at least twenty years older than her and not exactly handsome. But he had the sinewy thinness that comes from rigorous field training, from an intimate familiarity with the Manual of Arms—coupled with an aristocratic demeanor that women found attractive. More, he had a kind of self-possession unavailable to ordinary men. There is a perfection to

be achieved in matching oneself exactly to one's capacities; here was someone who was always quite successfully himself. A startling lock of pure
white his ex-wife Celeste had derisively called the Flame of the Pentecost
shone from the center of his dark scalp.

"*Eh bien*," Phillipe said, at last. "How does it feel to be alive?"

"Don't expect me to thank you," Louise said, thrusting out her lip like a
child. "I won't."

"How was the steak?"

"Not too bad. A little lacking in flavor, maybe."

Phillipe nodded. "I see."

"And don't get any ideas about going to the police. If you go to the police, I'll tell them . . ." She hesitated, scowling. ". . . I'll tell them you were
bothering me and I jumped in the water to get away from you."

A long silence followed this ungenerous threat. But Phillipe could see her
point: Suicide was still a crime in France; anyone who attempted it might be
legally incarcerated, either in a mental hospital or a jail. Really, he ought to
call the police. The rain had picked up in the last hour and the dull sound of
it drumming against the diamond-paned windows echoed in the little parlor.

"You're not going to believe this," Phillipe said at last, keeping his voice
calm, affable. "But my family name is de Noyer"—literally of drown—"don't
you think that's an odd coincidence?"

"No."

Phillipe tapped his fingers on the arm of his chair. He had dealt with
many recruits like this—sullen, aimless young men who had joined the Legion as the result of a drinking binge or because they'd run out of money
to buy hash or cocaine, or because they'd never heard of any world where
promises were kept; each bunch worse than the last as the years went by.
They were cynical beyond all reason to be so, had no respect for tradition,
no ambition, no faith, no real desire for anything except reckless sensation.
No honor. His own adjutant Caporal-chef Pinard had been one of these;
now he was a Legionnaire. But there existed an antidote to pointless nihilism, as simple as it was unexpected: high standards and extremely harsh
discipline, impartially applied.

"You know I could have killed myself pulling your ass out of the drink?"
He sat forward suddenly, an edge in his voice. "As it is, I lost my new boots
and cut my cheek"—he touched the swollen place beneath his eye—"not to
mention the price of that steak. Why did you do such a stupid thing?"

"That's my affair!" Louise spit out. "*Fiche-moi la paix!*"

At this, Phillipe reached over and without warning slapped her hard across the mouth. She gasped and fell against the wingbacked chair.

"*Canaille!*" she cried, outraged. "*Espèce de merde!*" Tears began rolling down her cheeks. She leaned forward and put her face in her hands and began to sob. Phillipe watched impassively for a while. Then, he got up and wet his handkerchief in the water jug and handed it to her. She pressed the cool fabric against her eyes, against her cheeks, and her tears gradually subsided.

"I was in a new club last night, in Paris," she said, still gasping a little. "We waited a long time to get in, we were all pretty high. Ecstasy, some cocaine. I was there with my lover and his girlfriend—mine too, I guess, since we were both sleeping with the cheap little whore—then more of my friends came and . . ."

"Go on," Phillipe said gently.

"Suddenly everything and everyone seemed horrible. Just horrible. I can't explain it . . ."

"An attack of misanthropy," Phillipe suggested. "Depression. Disgust with life, with all the sordidness. Or perhaps just the drugs."

"I don't know. But I fought with everyone, viciously. I fought with my lover; I slapped Chantal and she pulled my hair and I slapped her again very hard and she cried, then I couldn't take it anymore, I just turned around and walked out. I left my purse on the bar, with everything, my papers, my keys, my coke, my money. I realized this outside when I got into a taxi—but I couldn't go back. *Mais jamais!* So I told myself if I could get all the way to the coast like just that, with nothing, then I'd drown myself in the sea, and then the horribleness would be completely finished. I took the métro to the gare d'Austerlitz without a ticket and I got on the TGV without a ticket and the conductor just walked by me. It was like I was invisible, already dead. I rode all the way up to Rennes on the train, then I got on a tour bus with some Americans and no one asked me anything. No one said a word. So I reached Mont-Saint-Michel and well"—she paused—"it seemed stupid not to go through with it . . ." Her voice trailed off.

"Then I found you"—Phillipe couldn't keep a proprietary note out of his voice—"and I stopped you. Thank God."

"*Alors, c'est ça!*" Louise jerked her head up, sharply angry again. "You saved my life and that means I'm yours. *Et maintenant tu veux sans doute me baiser*—now you want to fuck me! Well, stand in line, asshole. They all want to fuck me, every man I ever meet and half the women! It's the afterwards they don't know what to do with."

"The thought of making love to you has occurred to me," Phillipe admitted, amused. "For obvious reasons. Very well, I'll say this—only if you want to. And I can assure you that I'll know what to do afterwards."

The possibility of sex suddenly hung in the air between them. A ludicrous impulse—and yet somehow the perfect answer to the watery death that had nearly engulfed them both.

Louise studied him frankly, heat rising in her indigo eyes.

"You're not too bad-looking for an old bastard," she said softly.

"*Merci, ma petite,*" Phillipe said, and he smiled.

3.

They went up the narrow stairs to Phillipe's room on the top floor. It was very small, taken up almost entirely by a double bed, a small sink, and a large, old-fashioned armoire. Louise stepped into the armoire and closed the door, a whimsical gesture—though for an alarming second, Phillipe thought she might be busy hanging herself in there—then the the door creaked open and she emerged completely naked, having peeled out of his tailored shirt and the concierge's son's Asterix pajamas, and her own midnight blue underwear. She paused there so he could admire her body, her arms resting casually on the clothes bar, her profile reflected in the long, tarnished mirror on the inside of the door.

"You reeled me in from the bottom of the sea," she said, her voice a whisper. "Like a dead fish. There's nothing left of me now. *T'as raison*—you're right—I'm entirely yours. Anything you want . . ." And she lowered her eyes, a charming and unexpected flush reddening her pale cheeks.

Such an offer does not come twice in a lifetime. There were all sorts of reasons—psychological, moral, religious—not to have sex with a young woman who had just attempted suicide, but just then none of them mattered to Phillipe and he reached out for her and drew her down on the bed. There was no artifice to what then transpired between them. What's the point of subterfuge if you've been swept together to the gates of death and back again?

Outside the round window over the sink, seabirds wheeled, even at this late hour. Slate gray clouds slid across the sky. Mont-Saint-Michel loomed over the tidal flats and salt meadows, an ambivalent deity. The stone corridors of the ancient abbey stood empty now, utterly silent; they hadn't rung with the footsteps of the Benedectine monks who built the place in more than two hundred years. Phillipe and Louise lay side by side atop the sheets in the chill, small hours, a false light glimmering over the sea, toward England, and she sought to explain herself to him, to describe more accurately the frigid sense of absence she'd felt in Paris the night before.

"It seemed there was nothing left in my life but an icy loneliness," she said. "My head filled with emptiness, my heart with sorrow."

This statement sent an odd little frisson dancing up Phillipe's spine that had nothing to do with the cold in the chilly room. He leaned down and pulled the bedspread over their bare flesh. Satie had written almost the same phrase in his diary a hundred years ago after being dropped by the only woman he ever loved, the tempestuous painter Suzanne Valadon.

"You know Satie!" Phillipe said. "Those are his words."

"Satie?" Louise said, confused. "You mean the composer—Erik Satie? I believe he lived in Arceuil. Isn't there a statue of him near the Hôtel de Ville?"

"So you don't know this phrase?"

"Not as a phrase," she said. "I know it because it's written here." She touched her breast. "But I am ashamed to admit I don't know French culture, my own culture, as well as I should. My father sent me to an international boarding school in Switzerland and then university in the U.S.A. He wanted to get me as far away from France as possible."

"The U.S.A.!" Phillipe said, aghast. "Why would anyone do such a thing?"

Louise sighed. "He was"—she struggled with the words—"an unusual man, a difficult man. A celebrity. He did not marry my mother, so for a long time, my existence was kept secret. . . ."

"But who was this person? François Mitterrand?"

Louise told him and Phillipe couldn't help being impressed: Everyone in France knew her father, Hector Vilhardouin—the famous singer, the bad boy of the *chanson français*, and one of its greatest practitioners. Hector was an icon—like Aznavour or Piaf or Jacques Brel—but more combative than these, loved and reviled until his death from a heroin overdose at age fifty-eight. During the sixties he scandalized France by reinventing himself, trading in his Gauloises Bleus cigarette, Sinatra-style Borsalino hat, and *Bob le Flambeur* trenchcoat for Nehru jacket, love beads, and marijuana. He then became a spokesman for a variety of radical causes, crossed the line to sing jazz and rock, hobnobbed with Bob Dylan and Mick Jagger, Hendrix and Miles. It was a brilliant defection, shocking at first, that made him even more famous in the end. After his death from the overdose in the bed of one of his mistresses— the gory details covered for weeks in literally every organ of the French media—it came out that he'd fathered several illegitimate children with a variety of women kept quietly in separate establishments in Paris, like some kind of Oriental potentate or Picasso. His only legitimate daughter, Alphonsine Vilhardouin, a film actress well known in France—she'd been twice nominated for the Palme d'Or at Cannes—was just starting to get work in Hollywood.

"Well, well!" Phillipe said. "Hector Vilhardouin! Is it true?"

"Yes, it's true." Louise sniffed. "You can see this has made things difficult for me."

"Of course." Phillipe stroked her hair.

"They brought me a paper to sign when he died," Louise continued. "I was to renounce the name of Vilhardouin for a certain sum of money. I refused. I threw that paper back in their face."

"Good for you." Phillipe ran his hands over her breasts, along the curve of her hip. He was getting hard again.

"Easy to say, but now there is no money at all, and I must work. But I can't find anything I really like to do. I've been fired from four—no, five— jobs in the last two years. I'm not stupid, you know, I'm really quite intelligent."

"Yes, I see that."

"My problem is I don't care about working. What's the point of working just to get money? You work, you come home, you eat, shit, sleep, get up again to go to work and come home again and so on and so on and maybe you go to clubs on the weekend, and the cinema every now and then and maybe the beach in August and the years pass like that and then—voilà— you're dead."

"That sounds about right." Phillipe suppressed a smile. "You've definitely hit it on the head."

"But what I really want to do is learn, understand. Take Satie—tell me, why do I not know his music? Because there hasn't been enough time for me to read all the books I want to read, to listen to all the music. To live."

Phillipe pulled her close and they made love again. Then, it became too late for sleep, or too early, and they put on their clothes—Louise wrapped herself in the American tourist's enormous Chicago Bulls sweatshirt—and they went out arm in arm along the ancient battlements of the Mont. The sun rose to the east, over France, sparkling yellow off the receding tides. Phillipe spoke to her in a low voice, utterly assured, his mouth close to her ear, his hand on the small of her back. He told her what would happen next, tomorrow, in five years, in ten, and she listened, twitching faintly from time to time, like a moth stuck to a screen door.

First, they would get married. He would install her in his château, which was not far from Honfleur up the coast. She would have all the time she needed to read, to listen, to learn, to garden, to raise dogs, to do whatever the hell she wanted to do. They might even have children, but at her age, she would have years to decide about that. He also had an address in Paris, a house, actually, near the Sixteenth Arrondissement; an apartment in the south, in Béziers, which was not as fashionable as Nice or Cap d'Antibes, but still a fine little town, and the weather was very nice and you wouldn't believe it, they had bullfights and a fiesta there twice a year, just like in Madrid. . . .

Louise listened, astonished. After he stopped talking, she stared at him, wild-eyed, the fresh morning light in her face.

"*Mais, t'es fou!*" she cried, nearly shouting.

"Not at all," Phillipe said, a faint smile on his lips. "Or at least not at the moment. I'm afraid some of my ancestors were definitely crazy. I might as well let you know that now—it's a calculated risk. Tends to skip a generation or two, but when it comes, it hits hard and usually later in life. So there's always the chance I'll go crazy someday. But at this moment, I'm completely sane."

She looked up at him, her eyes wide and sea blue in this fresh light. Suddenly, she didn't feel tired at all.

"You really have a château?"

"Modest in size, but yes. The de Noyers have been part of the landscape around here for at least seven hundred years. There's the ruins of a twelfth-century keep on the grounds. I have my car in the car park, I can take you right now if you like. It's not so far."

She threw up her hands, exasperated. "This is ridiculous!"

"Of course." Phillipe smiled. "But not more ridiculous than suicide."

"I can't marry you! Absolutely not!"

"Why not?"

"For one thing, your age."

"I'm forty-four—how old are you?"

"Twenty-four."

"That's not so bad, is it?"

And it wasn't, in France. For the French, such an age discrepancy was entirely acceptable. But Louise, who had perhaps spent too many years in the United States, wouldn't answer him.

They walked along now in silence, the tide sparkling below, the seabirds fighting one another for minnows in the surf, and stopped again at a small guard tower. They had reached the end of the public ramparts, as far as they could go without mounting to the walls of the abbey itself, and the way was blocked from here. They stood for a long time staring out over the sea in silence, but were really looking out with breathless trepidation over the uncertain vistas of a shared life.

"I know nothing about you," Louise said, her voice hoarse. "You've let me talk and talk and you've said practically nothing—" She stopped herself. "You see? It's impossible."

"What do you want to know that you didn't find out in bed last night?" He grinned. "Just marry me and find out the rest later."

"So, would I have a title?" she said, trying to sound cynical. "Madame la Duchesse, perhaps?"

"There was a title," Phillipe admitted. "Vicomte de la Tour Grise. But the tower is long gone and the title no longer exists, as far as I'm concerned. We haven't used it since the Revolution."

"*Merde, un aristo!*" Louise very nearly spit.

"I'm a citizen of the Republic, just like you," Phillipe replied calmly. "I work, I have a job. I'm in the army. Doesn't pay enough to live decently; it's more of a family tradition with us. A vocation. One of my ancestors fought with Turenne at Sinzheim, another with Bonaparte at the Nile. And so on."

"*Militariste!*" Louise jabbed a finger in his direction, belligerence rising in her voice. "Fascist! You'd probably vote for Le Pen! *Eh bien, moi*, I'm a creature of the Far Left. You might as well say I'm an anarchist, antiglobal, antiwar. So you see, it would never work out with us. I must have someone of my own politics." She was looking for anything, desperate for any reason to turn and walk away.

"Good." Phillipe nodded, refusing to be discouraged. "Because I usually vote Left—Socialist Party. Depending on the candidate, of course—the important thing is character. But . . ." He hesitated. ". . . You should hear the whole story, everything. I went to Saint-Cyr, you see. The top five officer candidates out of every class have the honor of applying for a commission in the Foreign Legion—though very few are accepted, since first you must endure the same harsh basic training as the men who will be under your command. But I applied and so—"

"*Non!*" Louise gasped, interrupting. "*Putain!* You're not with the Foreign Legion!"

"I am."

"They're the worst! A bunch of brutes! Criminals! I've seen them beating each other in the bars in Pigalle in their ridiculous white hats! Drunk and bloody, just beating people up with their fists! Just for the fun of it!"

"There are no saints in the Legion," Phillipe admitted somberly. "Only desperate men from every nation, men with no place else to go, men who need a second chance."

"You mean mercenaries, hired assassins . . ."

"I mean foreigners who have volunteered to serve France to the last drop of their blood. It's an ancient tradition. Louis Philippe gave the Legion its first standard, which has since been carried to every corner of the earth."

"Oh, very nice!" Louise said, disgusted. "Spoken like a true imperialist!"

"If it makes you feel better, think of me as a musician," Phillipe offered brightly. "I play the piano, like your father. I'm not famous, of course, but I am second in command of la Musique Principale. We're very well known, one of the best military marching bands in the world. And there's le Chorale du Légion, which is my direct responsibility. Singing is one of the great traditions with us. Last year, in the competition at Moscow, we took the silver medal. If we only had a decent top tenor. But good tenors are hard to find—"

"Enough!" Louise cried suddenly, clutching her head. "Stop!"

Phillipe stopped himself, abashed. He had already said far too much. The thing that separated Satie from every other composer of his era—from Debussy and Ravel and Saint-Saëns—was his exquisite silences; the long, melancholy pauses between notes. Now, Phillipe played out one of Satie's somber sarabandes—that courtly, complicated little dance—in his head, leaving plenty of space for the reverberating silences, and when he had finished, he took Louise by the arm again and they went back to the hotel, to the dining room, just open for breakfast.

Louise ate like an American, which is to say heavily, ordering an omelette, *spécialité de la maison*, usually reserved for dinner, more like a soufflé than an omelette, and a platter full of homemade goose liver sausages, and ate every scrap. Phillipe ate a few crumbled pieces of a croissant and drank several cups of coffee. His stomach felt unsettled, sour, though he appeared completely at ease, an ability that might be attributed to battlefield training or an aristocratic disposition, or both. They finished eating; the bill came and Phillipe paid, but neither of them stood up to leave. The waiters clattered around impatiently, clearing dishes. The lovers didn't speak, they didn't say a word; they hardly looked at each other across the starched white tablecloth.

2

GATEWAY TO
THE AGE OF THE
HIDDEN IMAM

1.

From the air the Saharoui refugee camp at Awsard in the Algerian Sahara looked like a heap of dirty clothes tossed onto a pile of sticks. Scraps of canvas, blue plastic UN tarps, striped bits of native fabric all flapped and billowed from improvised tent poles in the steady desert wind known by a woman's name—Simoom—unbearably hot and pregnant with a nagging, sandy grit.

The Russian-made Antonov C-160 circled the camp in the teeth of the wind in the yellow desert light, lowering toward the uneven airstrip below, flecks of mica hissing against the scarred glass of the cockpit. As they banked for the approach, dark stains revealed themselves between the dunes at the southern perimeter. These couldn't be mistaken for anything else, even at this altitude: great mounds of trash and human excrement, the refuse of the refuse.

"Poor miserable bastards," Phillipe said, half to himself, staring out the scratchy window. "Living in the middle of all that filth for generations."

"Since 1973, Colonel de Noyer"—came a voice at his shoulder—"during the first Polisario war. That's when the Moroccans drove them out of the coastal districts."

The voice—nasal, self-important—belonged to Dr. Hanz Milhauz, the man from MINURSO, a befuddling acronym that somehow described the UN Mission to the Non-Self-Governing Territory of Western Sahara, to which Phillipe had just been sent as an observer by the French government. French military observers are almost always drawn from the officer corps of the Foreign Legion; Phillipe had observed multinational peacekeeping forces at work all over the world in the last five or six years: Bosnia, Kosovo, Cyprus and the Comoros, Somalia, Kosovo again, Afghanistan, Iraq.

"It was the necessity of fighting on two fronts that brought Polisario to their knees," Dr. Milhauz continued. "With half their forces besieging Nouak-chott, they couldn't hold Laayoune against the Moroccans. The evacuation was terrible, a botched job. Thousands died of starvation, the trail of bodies stretched from the Atlantic to the mountains."

"Yes, I know all the history—" Phillipe began, but Dr. Milhauz made an impatient gesture. The little man acted as if Phillipe had stepped onto the plane at the UN Mission Compound in Dahkla that morning with a copy of *Paris Match* under his arm and nothing but the latest celebrity gossip in his head.

"You may know," Dr. Milhauz said, "but you don't truly understand. How could you? No one in Europe understands. They see refugees and say 'Well, let's find a way to send them home.' But in this case, the home in question does not exist. The Saharoui Arab Democratic Republic is a fiction. It has been eroded, wiped off the map, not by wind and rain but by international politics. This is a very intricate situation. Extremely complex. One must first take into consideration the web of tribal affiliations, then the influence of the mullahs—they're called Marabouts out here, and they're more like magi-cians or miracle workers than holy men"—a breathy pause—"simply put, we've got to do our best to avoid the kind of disastrous mistakes the Ameri-cans are making in Iraq."

"Which mistakes are you referring to exactly?" Phillipe stifled a yawn. "I was there, you know."

"Oh, well—" Dr. Milhauz frowned. "Everything they've done has been a mistake, hasn't it? A direct result of unilateralist arrogance!"

Dr. Milhauz was Swiss-German, a doctor, not the medical variety, only a Ph.D., one of those self-important economists who infest the UN and insist on introducing themselves to everyone as Dr. So-and-So. He had nervous hands, constantly in motion, and was as round as a person could be, like a walking egg—which somehow made his imperious conversational style all the more ridiculous. His black round-framed eyeglasses—in the style of Le Corbusier—only emphasized his general roundness. He wore the kind of great-white-hunter khaki outfit favored by UN functionaries and television journalists in desert places, the vest and pants covered with inexplicable flaps and pockets, some zippered, others buttoned, all filled with nothing in particular.

"Look—over there, to the west." Dr. Milhauz poked an insistent finger at the window. "You can just see the Moroccan Berm. You've heard of the Berm, haven't you?"

"Yes, I've heard of the Berm."

"Well there it is, take a good look. The enormity of the thing can only be appreciated from up here."

Phillipe squinted into the yellow light and saw two parallel lines inscribed on the desert in the distance as if by a giant hand. The Berm was a defensive wall of sand sixty feet high and two thousand kilometers long, backed by a corresponding sixty-foot-deep trench, undulating over dune and guelb and dry wadi, side by side across the desert floor like two snakes into infinity. It had been built by the Moroccans in the early 1980s to separate the desert-dwelling Saharoui refugees to the east from Moroccan occupied territory along the coast that had been the most inhabitable part of the Saharoui homeland. The Berm was one of the only two man-made constructions visible from space with the naked eye. The other was the Great Wall of China.

"A human rights disaster." Dr. Milhauz wagged his head up and down like a bobblehead doll. "Took six years to finish. Convict labor, you know."

"Yes, I do, actually, Dr. Milhauz," Phillipe said, no longer concealing his annoyance. "But thank you so much for reminding me."

"Just trying to be helpful," the little man said stiffly. He returned to his seat and his laptop, its screen fading for lack of battery power.

In two months, Phillipe would deliver yet another report, this one on the Saharoui refugee crisis, to the Committee for African Affairs of the National Assembly of the Fifth Republic in the Chamber of Deputies in Paris in closed session. He had read the committee's MINURSO dossiers thoroughly before leaving France. He had pored over maps, talked to every Saharoui refugee he could find, read at least twenty books—the best being *Never-Ending War:*

The Gutting of Western Sahara, written by a British journalist, since killed in mysterious circumstances at Laayoune in the Saharoui souk, a kind of walled ghetto imprisoning those Saharouis who had remained behind in what was now an overwhelmingly Moroccan city.

The book contained a gripping account of the Saharoui revolt against Spanish rule in the early 1960s and the chaos that followed Spain's withdrawal from the phosphate-rich colony. Before the victorious Saharouis had a chance to establish their Arab Democratic Republic (SADR) or design a flag, they'd been invaded by the Moroccans from the north and the Mauritanians from the south, both hungry for territory and what wealth there was to be derived from phosphate deposits and fishing rights. The Saharoui rebel army, called Polisario—another befuddling acronym—which had defeated Spain, quickly defeated Mauritania, bringing the war to the very gates of Nouakchott, the Mauritanian capital, before a treaty was signed.

But thirty-odd years of fighting hadn't been long enough for Polisario to drive out the powerful Moroccans in the north—who were, at long last, winning. Not through guns and bombs—as Dr. Milhauz might say—but through economic policy. The Moroccan government had poured millions of dirhams into developing the territory stolen from the Saharouis they now called the Southern Provinces of the Kingdom of Morocco. They had irrigated fields, beefed up fishing fleets, built soccer stadiums and office buildings, and paved over Laayoune's parched, dusty plazas with blinding white flagstones.

And so the SADR existed now more as an idea than a genuine nation. The unfortunate Saharouis—450,000 of them, one of the largest refugee population in the world—waited for an increasingly elusive victory, for the order to return home to Laayoune, no longer their capital; waited to bring their boats back to the rich fishing grounds off Cape Juby, now trawled by fleets of Moroccan vessels. Hopeful, angry, deluded, living on UN protein crackers and logs of tasteless UN cheese and vats of distilled water in the squalor of a dozen camps strewn around the Algerian town of Tindouf like a handful of *crottes*—camel droppings—tossed into the desert sand.

2.

An hour later, they still hadn't landed. They were in a holding pattern, waiting for a signal from the ground crew—sometimes camels or a herd of goats wandered across the airstrip—the Antonov C-160 circling the vast tent city fifteen kilometers out as dusk came on, a dim blue flush in the sky from the east. Or maybe the air-traffic controller was merely taking his siesta in the sweltering heat. Phillipe closed his eyes. His sleep had been troubled lately, uneasy—as if there were, generally speaking, something he'd forgotten to do, or something he'd done that he shouldn't have—though he couldn't say now what these things might be, and not knowing gnawed away at his subconscious.

Just two days ago, he'd been in Paris with Louise, going out to dinner for their anniversary. The hard pavement of the boulevard Raspail shining in a spring rain, the crowds coming out of the cinemas in the Place de Clichy, limousines three deep to the curb at Trebuchet in Montparnasse. Reservations on Trebuchet's trendy back terrace had been made weeks in advance, but Louise decided she wasn't in the mood for a scene and they ended up at Chez Manon in their usual corner booth. They ate lightly and exchanged gifts: a beautiful necklace of eighteenth-century Venetian glass flowers for her; for him a pair of black velvet Hermès slippers stitched with his monogram in gold thread. Then back early to the house in Neuilly. There they pulled at each other's clothes in the entrance hall with startling avidity, eager as a couple of teenagers, even after seven years of marriage: The taxi idling at the bottom of the steps, the driver counting his tip on the front seat just visible through the pebbled glass of the street door, and Phillipe tugging up his wife's tight skirt as she bent over the heavy Directoire table, the shadowy pattern of the ironwork grille falling across her bare back in sinuous arabesques.

Later, in bed, they made love, gently, face-to-face. Afterwards, Louise shuddered in his arms and admitted she was very worried. She'd had a disturbing dream like Caesar's wife before the Ides. In it she was falling from a great height, perhaps from the walls of a massive fortress, into complete darkness. Western Sahara—where the hell was this place? Hot as hell and dangerous, no doubt. The ass-end of the earth!

"Africa is here"—Phillipe drew an outline in the air with his finger—"Western Sahara's here"—jabbing the South Atlantic coast about halfway down. "Mauritania's here, Morocco here. All this is mostly unpopulated desert, except for a few tribes of Berber nomads. That's the Sahara part. The Western part—"

"Oh, shut up." Louise made a face. "What if you get taken hostage by terrorists? *C'est possible, non?*"

"No," he said. "Al Qaeda's got nothing to do with it. This isn't jihad, this is Moroccans versus Saharouis. Muslim versus Muslim, an old-fashioned battle over access to natural resources. The UN's on the ground there only as a negotiator—respected by all parties—with a couple of thousand troops to keep order until a deal can be worked out."

"And how long have they been there working out their deal, your UN?"

Phillipe grinned. "About thirty-five years."

"Idiots!" Louise exclaimed. "So they take you away from me for a puppet show!"

"You can't blame the UN, I'm afraid," Phillipe said. "This is a French affair. I'm being sent at the request of Madame de la République."

"To hell with that bitch!"

"Spoken like an aristocrat. Congratulations. But if you could only see the condition of the refugees—"

"Enough!" Louise cried. "They're boring, your refugees! Send someone else! Send your adjutant. What's his name—Pinard."

Phillipe laughed at this.

"If you knew Pinard . . ."

"Why not?"

"He's a great hulking Canadian, a hard-luck type. Uncomfortable in his own skin. He plays the oboe in the Musique Principale. A good oboe player, even very good, but let's be honest, the oboe is a ridiculous instrument. I can't say what kind of officer he'd make, he's never been under fire. But I can tell you one thing—he's definitely not diplomatic material."

Traffic boomed from beyond their bedroom balcony, racing madly around the circle at the rue de Rennes. Now, Louise indulged herself in a few tears and held him close.

"I really wish you'd quit, Phillipe," she whispered, sniffling. "You're away from home too much. Afghanistan in February and Iraq last fall and Aubagne half the year and now this terrible place. It's difficult for me, being alone so much. And you know"—she kissed him—"maybe it's time for us."

Phillipe swallowed hard. "You think so?"

"What do you think?"

He paused, considering his answer: They'd had seven good, busy years alone with each other, dividing their time between Paris and Brittany and Béziers (they went for the bullfights twice a year) with frequent side trips to England, where Phillipe had aristocratic friends vaguely connected to the royal family. Louise gardened and listened carefully to music and took Russian and

Italian lessons at the Sorbonne and read the classics—she was particularly fond of Flaubert's *L'Éducation sentimentale*, which she'd read to Phillipe twice out loud—and made sheep's cheese from her own little flock of six sheep each spring at the château, playing at country life like Marie Antoinette in her mock-rustic village at the Petit Trianon. Louise had also learned the viola passably and could accompany Phillipe on simple pieces. They had many friends, a busy social life: Happiness attracts others—to paraphrase the *Maxims* of La Rochefoucauld—as a rose the hummingbird.

But Phillipe was over fifty now, Louise over thirty. She was right, it was definitely time.

"Children . . ." Phillipe's courage faltered at the word. What would it be like? Was he fit to be a parent—or too selfish?

"Child. Let's start with one."

He smiled at her in the darkness. New life, new hope. "*Bien.* I'm ready."

She pressed herself against him and they embraced.

"It's the damned pill," she whispered. "I've got to get off it. It takes about a month for my body to adjust."

"When I get back, then . . ."

"*Oui.* When you get back."

3.

They landed at last in the boiling red light, the sun a hard vermillion orb falling to the west. Great clouds of dust billowed up as the Antonov's four prop-jets spun to a halt. The rear gangway lowered on its hydraulics and Phillipe descended into the stifling air with a small flight bag slung over his shoulder; the extent of his luggage, it contained a couple of changes of clothing, the usual toiletries, and a draft of his monograph on Erik Satie, still unfinished after all these years.

He was closely followed by Dr. Milhauz, juggling two large bags destined to join his trunk and other odds and ends on the tarmac. The man traveled like a nineteenth-century naturalist, like Charles Darwin circling the world on the *Beagle* with brass instruments and leather-bound tomes. These bags were piled to one side and this seemed like a natural place to congregate. A Quonset hut hangar on the other side, apparently abandoned, loomed like the mouth of a robbers' cave, filled with shadows.

Phillipe didn't like the look of the place. His reaction was immediate and felt like a premonition. The desert wind blew steadily in the red dusk; the stench of nearby refuse piles assailed their nostrils. Soon night would drop temperatures fifty degrees, but for now the heat lingered. Dr. Milhauz collapsed on one of his crates, mopping his forehead with a handkerchief. The red light of the dying sun shone in his face.

"This isn't good," the little man murmured uneasily. "Where are the Pakistani troops?"

"Did you tell them we were coming?"

Dr. Milhauz looked up at Phillipe through his owl-glasses. "There's supposed to be a UN transport waiting. The Pakistani contingent of our forces have been assigned to this camp. Sixty-five men, not counting medical personnel."

Phillipe didn't say anything.

Besides the flight crew of the Antonov, hurriedly preparing for the return flight to Dahkla, they were alone. The dunes loomed all around; the tent city, about thirty-five kilometers off, couldn't be seen from the airstrip. It seemed they were as good as abandoned in the absolute middle of nowhere. Soon, the big Russian plane taxied down the runway, its takeoff lights blinking, gathering speed for the assault on the night sky. As the prop-jets screamed into full power, Dr. Milhauz put his hands over his ears. Then the plane was gone, its wheels folded into the fuselage, the sound of its engines fading into nothing.

"By the way, let me do the talking," Milhauz said presently.

"There's no one to talk to," Phillipe said.

"I mean tomorrow. When we meet the Saharoui Camp Committee. As a gesture of respect, I like to speak to them in the Hassaniya dialect and not Spanish or French. Do you speak Saharoui, Colonel?"

"I speak only French and English," Phillipe said. "And also Spanish, German, Portuguese, Swedish, Italian, and a little Russian."

"Aha!" The UN representative raised a finger. "You do not speak Hassaniya! I do!" But this moment of triumph instantly dissipated. He took a step closer to the colonel, his shadow elongating. A fenec fox, its ears trembling, watched him from the darkness of its burrow beneath the lip of the dune.

"I shouldn't tell you any of this," he said in a low voice. "I mean you're not one of us, are you?"

"Aren't we all engaged in the same cause, Herr Dr. Milhauz," Phillipe replied, "world peace?"

"Yes, yes"—the little man wagged his head impatiently—"as are all beauty queens and socialists and children under ten. But let's be realistic. The United Nations is a country unto itself, with its own laws, it's own hierarchy and chain of command. In some sense, it's like a perpetual motion machine, feeding on self-generating energy and rarely going forward. It responds to a crisis, but inevitably becomes part of the crisis by refusing to act, by maintaining its own status quo. Understand me, this isn't necessarily a bad thing—merely the way things are."

Phillipe looked at the little man, astonished. "Well, that's deeply enlightening, Herr Dr. Milhauz!"

"We negotiate endlessly, we produce reams of paperwork, just to produce reams of paperwork," the little man continued. "As I say, our interest is in the status quo. If we keep things the same, they can't get worse, don't you see?" He licked his dry lips. "But now, I think events are getting ahead of us. There have been odd rumblings. Conversations overheard in the bazaar at Dahkla, rumors from the Saharoui souk in Laayoune, a place all but impenetrable to Westerners. Even the Moroccans can't get in. And there's this symbol—"

He inscribed a crude hieroglyph in the sand with the heel of his boot: an eye shape, with a sharp point at one end and crossed over the middle by three parallel lines:

"It has appeared everywhere very suddenly. On walls, on street corners."
Phillipe leaned over to study the odd marking.

"Some say it's an eye, others"—Dr. Milhauz swallowed—"a bee."

"I don't see that at all." Phillipe frowned. "Looks more like a fish to me."

"This part"—Dr. Milhauz indicated the sharp point coming out one end—"is supposed to be the stinger."

"But what's it a symbol of?"

Dr. Milhauz shrugged. "A secret society, a conspiracy, who knows. Perhaps an uprising—"

"Against whom?" Phillipe said, perplexed.

"Against the Moroccans. Or against Polisario. Or perhaps against us, against the West. Against reason, you might say, against the sciences. Against"—his voice descended to a frightened whisper—"economics."

"*Du calme, mon ami,*" Phillipe said, smiling to himself. "There will always be economics."

"Or it may be nothing," Dr. Milhauz continued. "Maybe just a kind of joke. In any case, I urge caution. Watchfulness. Can you be watchful, Colonel?"

"Yes, I think so," Phillipe said. He studied the little man critically in the red light. Perhaps he was insane.

4.

Night came, and with it utter blackness. The temperature began to drop. Dr. Milhauz reached into one of his many suitcases and drew out a knit woolen ski cap and scarf. Phillipe shoved his hands into the pockets of his Hermès blazer. Hours passed. He smoked the Gitanes he'd brought from Paris, winnowing the pack to one. Dr. Milhauz turned the pages of a book beneath the slowly weakening beam of a flashlight. Neither spoke. Just before midnight, a truck engine sounded in the distance. They waited and the sound came closer and soon they saw the white throw of headlights wavering, bumping over the dunes.

"Ah!" Dr. Milhauz exclaimed. "Here they come. There must have been some sort of miscommunication . . ."

The truck pulled up in a swirl of dust. But it wasn't the Pakistani military vehicle bristling with soldiers the doctor had expected. It was a battered Méhari pickup—little larger than a Volkswagen Bug—with one door missing. Up front, two dark figures, a young man and a boy, veiled against the dust—though the effect of their covered faces was sinister, banditlike.

"Where are the Pakistanis?" Dr. Milhauz demanded. He did not speak Hassaniya as he had promised, but Spanish.

"You come," the driver replied, his Spanish rudimentary. "And you"—he gestured—"in back."

Dr. Milhauz looked down at his pile of luggage, aghast, and then back at the truck.

"But I can't fit even half my gear—" he began.

"We go!" the young man insisted. "Now!" And the truck began to roll off. Phillipe tossed his cigarette in a trail of sparks into the dune, shouldered his bag, and jumped aboard.

"Come on, Doctor."

The little man, confused at first, grabbed a bag and ran after the truck, which gathered speed. Phillipe held out a hand, but it was no use, Dr. Milhauz failed to grasp it and fell behind.

"Help!" he squeaked, running along, panting for breath. "Help!"

Phillipe turned and pounded on the roof of the cab. The driver didn't seem to hear him, or heard him and didn't give a shit. The doctor receded in the vast night of the desert, waving his arms, wailing—who's to say what would become of him out there alone? Phillipe took off his Hermès blazer, wrapped it tightly around his elbow, and smashed it into the small oval window at the back of the cab. The glass shattered in three large pieces and fell into the front seat, where it crumbled into shards. Phillipe shoved his arm through and crooked it around the driver's throat.

"Stop!" he shouted in French. "Stop! *Now!*"

The driver, swearing in Hassaniya, clawed at Phillipe's arm, but Phillipe squeezed harder and at last the little truck skidded to a halt. The boy in the passenger seat stared, his eyes frightened above the dark veil.

"Back up!" Phillipe ordered.

"Let me go!" the driver gasped. "I kill you!"

Phillipe reached into the pocket of his trousers and pulled out the ebony-handled Italian switchblade he always carried—another Legion tradition; everyone, even the officers, carried a concealed weapon—and brought the point to bear against the young man's throat.

"You don't understand," Phillipe said through his teeth. "I am not a member of the United Nations Defense Force. I am not a Pakistani. I am not Dutch. I am an officer of the French Foreign Legion. You've heard of us?" He pressed the point into the driver's skin until a drop of blood appeared. "I asked you a question!"

"Yes," the young man said. "Imperialist jackals! Murderers of women and children!"

"Exactly," Phillipe said grimly. "So understand that it is I who will do the killing if you don't reverse gear and pick up my friend!"

The driver shouted something in Hassaniya, perhaps appealing to the boy who didn't move.

"Reverse gear," Phillipe said, his voice full of military authority. "Do it."

The driver reached for the gearshift and the truck bounced backward over the veined asphalt of the airstrip. The pitiful figure of Dr. Milhauz was revealed in the amber glow of the tail lights, sitting on the ground in despair. Phillipe withdrew the knife, but he did not release the pressure from the driver's neck.

"I would help you up, Doctor," Phillipe said. "But I'm otherwise occupied."

Dr. Milhauz lifted his head and stared. Then he took off his glasses and wiped them on his shirt. Tears had streaked the grime on his face.

"This is very bad," he muttered as he climbed into the truck. "This does not bode well for our mission here."

Phillipe released the driver from his grip. "After you take us to our quarters, you will return for the doctor's things. Understand?"

But the driver didn't respond. He shoved the truck in gear and sped off, just as the moon appeared, round and red between the clouds.

5.

The way station was a large, tattered tent that had once been part of a mobile UN hospital unit, its Red Cross insignia scrawled over with overlapping graffiti—Phillipe saw the slogan POLISARIO VIVA! SADR VIVA! peeling now, and in several places, apparently fresh, the odd bee hieroglyph Dr. Milhauz had inscribed in the sand. Worn but magnificent Berber carpets covered the canvas floor within. These, a couple of storm lanterns, a ten-gallon tub of UN protein crackers, and several gallon jugs of stale water were the only furnishings. They slept fitfully that night atop the carpets. Dr. Milhauz snored so loudly, he woke himself up several times; Phillipe, plagued by sand fleas and uneasy dreams, rose before dawn.

In the morning, the young man in the Méhari truck returned, its bed full of Dr. Milhauz's gear. A cohort in the back kicked the stuff out of the bed, shouting obscenities in Hassaniya, and the driver roared off to the east, which was the direction of the camp at Awsard. High cirrus clouds streaked the sky just beginning to blaze. The suitcases and trunks had been broken open, rifled through; everything of value and half the doctor's clothes, gone. His books remained, but they had been defaced, the pages torn.

"This is an outrage!" Dr. Milhauz cried, outraged. "I'm going to report this to the council!"

Phillipe watched placidly, munching on a cardboard-tasting UN cracker—his breakfast—as the little man went through the tatters of what was left, gathering his clothes into heaps, discarding his destroyed books, burying the rubble in a sandy hole.

"But they missed something," he said, smiling weakly. "These!" He pulled up a hidden compartment in the bottom of one of his trunks to reveal two bottles of Johnnie Walker Red—this stuff as good as currency in some parts of the world.

"I would be careful, Doctor," Phillipe cautioned. "From what I've read, the Saharouis consider alcohol an abomination. A crime against Allah."

"I've often thought a drink or two would solve these people's problems instantly," the doctor said, adjusting his round glasses. "Join me?"

"Too early." Phillipe shook his head.

The doctor, clutching the bottles to his belly, disappeared into the tent and could be heard in there all afternoon, drinking whiskey and muttering to himself.

6.

Two days passed. Phillipe spent them not unpleasantly, chasing the shade around the tent, writing long letters to Louise and working on his Satie monograph. His cell phone, useless out here, showed no signal, only the smiling, animated mussel graphic of the French wireless network Moulignac.

When Satie died in 1925, his brother and a few close friends broke into the small, single room in Arcueil, the dingy Parisian suburb, where the eccentric composer had lived for the last thirty years of his life without receiving a single visitor. There, they found an incredible rat's nest of fantastic stuff, a lifetime's worth of creative detritus. Two broken pianos (one of them chalked with the cryptic phrase *this house haunted by the Devil*), both stuffed with bundles of unpublished compositions, several masterpieces among them; the dozen mauve velvet suits Satie had worn in his Velvet Gentleman years around the turn of the century, when he had refused to wear anything but mauve velvet suits; every letter, every scrap he'd ever received from his only lover, Suzanne Valadon, including images of himself that she'd cruelly snipped from those few photographs showing them together and sent back to him—these kept in a somber black envelope, its surface splotched with the tears wrung out of Satie's broken heart. Also, carefully arranged in cigar boxes, thousands of neat squares of paper covered in the most exquisite calligraphy: drawings of imaginary Gothic buildings, poems written in an unknown language, illustrations for novels that didn't exist. And a series of absurdist advertisements Satie had placed at great expense in the major Paris newspapers:

*Glass Castle for rent—needs curtains, reasonable rates. Talking cat for
sale—bores easily, plays "Chemin de Fer." Puppets of God made upon request.*

Not long after Satie's room was cleared for its new tenants, several of his
friends were visited by the same strange dream. They were walking on a
wooded path in the Bois de Boulogne on a dark day, storm clouds brewing
above the tree line, when they met Satie coming along in the opposite direction. There he was, in evening dress, wreathed in his own sunlight, smiling,
trademark bowler hat raised, beard neatly trimmed, pince-nez sparkling, his
teeth gleaming like pearls, and a pair of pink wings neatly folded against the
back of his cutaway.

"Tell me something, my friend," asks the glittering, pink-winged Satie
(the same question in each dream!), "does everyone still suppose I'm dead?"

It was pleasant for Phillipe to think about Satie and the beautiful, lost Paris
of 1900 all the way out here in the barren wastes of the Sahara. Thoughts of
Satie and Paris were inextricable from thoughts of Louise. Phillipe had brought
along a CD player and two discs of Satie's music; they contained, among other
compositions, *Mémoires d'un amnésique, Messe des Pauvres, Trois Morceaux en forme
de poire.* But the machine's batteries had exhausted themselves, forcing Phillipe
to reconstruct these complex compositions in his head, a strenuous and time-
consuming mental exercise. Hours passed like this in the devastating heat, with
Phillipe squatting motionless in the shadow of the tent but thoroughly occupied on an imaginary piano, scrupulously trying to recall every last note, his
fingers moving across a keyboard sculpted out of sand that kept blowing away.

7.

On the afternoon of the third day, Dr. Milhauz emerged from the tent
flap, terribly hungover, having privately consumed both bottles of Johnnie Walker. He padded around to the east side of the tent in his socks and sat
next to Phillipe in the sand, contrite and smelling strongly of alcohol. For a
while neither of them spoke.

"I'm afraid I drank all the whiskey," Dr. Milhauz confessed.

"And how do you feel now?"

"Terrible."

"Ah."

"What have you been doing all this time?"

"Nothing much." Phillipe shrugged. "Thinking. Writing letters. Do you know the music of Erik Satie?"

"No," Dr. Milhauz said. "I'm an economist, not a musician." He paused. "And basically a coward, I might as well admit that. I have been rude to you, Colonel de Noyer. I apologize."

"Don't mention it."

"I'm beginning to think we won't get out of this," Dr. Milhauz continued, his mouth turned down, grim. "Clearly, something's going on in the camps. I have my suspicions but . . ." His voice trailed off.

"What kind of suspicions?"

Dr. Milhauz shrugged. "They're trying to teach us a lesson, I think. They're softening us up."

"For what?"

Dr. Milhauz looked at Phillipe, tears brimming in his eyes. "For a terrible blow of some kind. Actually, I think they're going to kill us."

"But we're neutral, you and I," Phillipe said reassuringly. "We're here to help them. Get them better drinking water, more food. Medicine. Why should they want to kill us?"

"It's too late for all that now," the doctor said. "Thirty years too late. The Saharouis hate the UN and they hate MINURSO for maintaining the status quo. For failing to act." A pause. "Are you married, Colonel?"

"I am," Phillipe said.

"You're a lucky man." Milhauz studied his socks, a fine grit now caked into the weave. "I have no wife"—he interrupted himself with a wordless exclamation, then—"I have wasted my life in the desert among people who hate me! I should have stayed in Zurich, gone into banking, gotten married. That's what my mother wanted me to do. She's very old now, and she's alone."

Phillipe stood, brushing sand from the seat of his pants. "We won't sit around waiting for this blow to fall. We're going to start walking."

"To where?" The doctor threw up his hands. "We can't go to Awsard, not after this. The next camp is seventy-five kilometers away!"

"That's nothing," Phillipe said. "An easy three-day march, even in these conditions. We'll go by moonlight, sleep during the hot hours. I've got a compass and plenty of training in orienteering, believe me, so we won't get lost. Contrary to popular belief, not a single Legion patrol has ever been lost in the desert, not in a hundred and seventy-five years. We'll carry water and as many crackers as we can hold. We'll get there all right."

Dr. Milhauz looked up hopefully, shielding his eyes. "Do you really think so?"

"Ever bet on the horses, Doctor?"

"No." Dr. Milhauz shook his head. "I don't gamble. Economically speaking, it doesn't make sense."

Phillipe squinted toward the heat shimmer of the horizon.

"One of the places we love to go, my wife and I, is the track at Longchamps," he said. "It's a beautiful green place with all the crowds on a Saturday and the horses, just magnificent, going over the jumps. Really, there's no finer sight. Do you know"—he paused, remembering, suddenly—"last time we went, my wife put down a single bet on three horses and hit the *tierce* in disorder? The woman won five thousand EU and some change! All this is to say that she's damned lucky and I know—I'm absolutely sure!—some of that luck has rubbed off on me."

He looked down at Milhauz sitting there helpless. He felt sorry for the man.

"Courage, Doctor. You're safe with me. I'm going to get a couple hours sleep inside. We leave at moonrise."

And he went into the tent and lay down on the carpet and fell asleep instantly, to the sound of a Satiesque piano pleasantly tinkling from a pleasantly appointed room, its tall window overlooking a charming private garden somewhere off the Place des Vosges in the Paris that existed always at the back of his mind.

❦

Phillipe woke up long past moonrise. Doctor Milhauz was gone. He walked around the tent, calling the doctor's name, and was answered only by the wind. He climbed the nearest dune and stared into the gloom of the desert but couldn't make out any sign of the man, not even a trail of footsteps in the sand. A cold, queasy feeling began to spread in his gut, that might have been the result of days of eating nothing but UN survival crackers and drinking stale water, but wasn't.

He hurried back to the tent, made a sling for two plastic gallon jugs of water out of his blazer, stuffed his pockets with more crackers. But when he stepped out of the tent, compass in hand, to orient himself to the bleak horizon, he found them there waiting for him, as if they had sprung up, fully formed, from the cooling sands: six dark figures, dressed in the long hooded robes called djellahs—dark blue or black, hard to tell. Their faces were veiled. Only their eyes gleamed in the darkness like the yellow eyes of desert cats.

8.

They went by Toyota Land Cruiser, fast, slamming painfully over the rough terrain, the remaining twenty-kilometers to Awsard. Blindfolded, Phillipe sensed the evil presence of the camp hanging in the air—a spiritual pressure that was the weight of despair, a thick brown stench that was the odor of the waste pits, of thousands of hopeless human beings densely packed into a couple dozen square kilometers of corrugated shacks and ragged tents with no sewage facilities or running water and nothing to do except wait for a salvation that would not come. Phillipe's hands, tightly tied with abrasive nylon cord, went numb.

The Toyota stopped abruptly. Phillipe, shoved out of the back, was forced to trot along at a quick pace through the warren of alleys between the hovels. They had fixed the rag around his eyes carelessly and he was able to wiggle it loose by moving his ears up and down—an ability inherited from his father, a natural comedian, who used ear wiggling to great comic effect at the stuffy Sunday dinners of Phillipe's childhood. But, even without this blindfold, the darkness was such that Phillipe couldn't see much of anything: only the faint green glow of a kerosene lamp burning from an open tent flap; the white bones of an animal left to rot in the middle of the sandy path; the dark shapes of the hovels like termite mounds. Veiled faces peered out at him once or twice from the shadows—uncurious, hollow-eyed—then fell away. A dog whimpered from somewhere.

At last, they reached the central area, a sandy plaza the size of a soccer field set behind a perimeter of barbed wire. This was the nucleus of the slowly expanding amoeba that was the Awsard refugee camp. Here stood the UN administrative buildings, square, ugly cinder block constructions; the supply depots; the communal showers. Banks of electric lights glared down on UN food reserves left out in rotting mounds in the open air.

More veiled men in long, hooded djellahs—clearly blue, Phillipe saw now—guarded the gates with Kalashnikov assault rifles. A few words were spoken, the gates slid apart, then one of the men noticed Phillipe's blindfold had come loose. He tied it around his captive's head, this time very tightly, and Phillipe was led through the gates and across the plaza and into one of the buildings. He could sense the closeness of walls, the presence of a ceiling. Someone forced him to his knees and removed his blindfold. He was in a low, featureless room, staring up at a trio of blue djellah-wearing veiled men. They stared down at him as if in judgment.

"What have you done with my colleague, Herr Dr. Milhauz?" Phillipe demanded in French.

When no one responded, he repeated the question in Spanish, then in English.

"That odious nonbeliever has been dealt with," one of them responded in Arabic-inflected English. "He has been judged according to our laws. He was a known drinker of alcohol, which is an abomination to God."

The veiled man in the middle removed something from his robe—an empty bottle of Johnnie Walker Red—and threw it hard at Phillipe, who ducked out of the way as best he could, but not before a corner of the square bottle caught him sharply on the forehead. Phillipe saw a painful flash of light, felt the welt rising on his skull; then his vision cleared and he got a better look at his attacker: The one who had thrown the bottle was shorter and stockier than the other two but clearly held authority over them. His hands and the only other visible square of flesh—the narrow margin between veil and hood—showed the intricate, spidery webbing of a design done with henna. This surprised Phillipe, as such decorations were usually reserved for young women, especially brides. On his feet, just visible beneath the hem of his robes, the blunt toes of ugly orthopedic shoes—also unusual among men who usually went booted or barefoot.

"You mean you've killed him," Phillipe said quietly. "You've murdered poor Milhauz. He was harmless, he was afraid."

The hennaed one turned to his companions and spoke a few rapid words in the Hassaniya dialect. Phillipe was blindfolded again and a dry wadding stuffed into his mouth so he couldn't speak and they dragged him back out of the house none too tenderly, over stones and around corners. At last, they stopped and Phillipe's blindfold was removed: A heap of severed heads, crawling with flies, the skin stretched blue and rotting, the eyeballs gone, rose before him. Phillipe nearly vomited, but such a reaction with the gag in his mouth would have proved fatal. To stifle his revulsion, he counted the heads. He reached thirty-five before the nausea subsided.

These were the heads of the Pakistani soldiers Milhauz had been expecting. This, clearly, was why they hadn't arrived on time. Phillipe rolled his eyes toward the sky, but couldn't see a moon. He was now in a sandbagged enclosure, flanked by the burnt-out husks of several off-road vehicles bearing charred blue paint and UN markings. Then he saw that the flies swarming around the heads weren't flies at all, but bees—odd, because bees were generally not indigenous to this part of the desert. In the absence of flowering plants, these industrious insects were busy gathering their sugars from congealing blood and rotting flesh. Off to one side lay a mound of packed earth taller than a man and twice as much in diameter—which Phillipe suddenly recognized as a hive of monstrous proportions. The sound that came from this hive was unmistakable, like the metallic grumbling of a powerful electrical dynamo that would never be turned off. From a small opening at the base of the hive extended the legs of a man perhaps stung to death, his exposed flesh covered with bees.

A bee landed on Phillipe's wrist and stung him. He gagged, choking—he was mildly allergic to bee stings—as the histamines from the sting caused his sinuses to fill. In a moment he couldn't breathe at all. When it became clear that he was suffocating, one of the blue-robed guards pulled the gag from his mouth. Phillipe doubled over gasping and released the contents of his stomach on the bloody ground. The hennaed one had been watching from a safe distance. Now he hove into view, stepping carefully over the blood and vomit with his clunky orthopedic shoes.

"I will tell you who I am," he said in French, spoken with a hard accent—perhaps English or German. "I am the Anointed One, the Arch-Beloved. My first name is I Am. My second name is Most Beneficent. My third name is He in Whom There Is No Harm to the Blessed."

"No," Phillipe gasped. "Your name is *putain de merde*. And you are a ridiculous lunatic!"

"To the infidel, the unbeliever, I am He Who Is to Be Feared," the hennaed one continued, his voice rising. "To them, I bring death and destruction. I remove their heads and feed their bones to the unclean beasts of the desert. This is the uprising, the jihad that has been foretold! I ride the wind at the head of an army of Marabouts, magic-working warriors of God, who will sweep this land clean so that fruit trees might grow where there are now only rocks and stones and sand, flowers bloom where the ant and the scorpion now find their home. This army will be called the Holy Marabout Army of the Gateway to the Age of the Hidden Imam. I offer as my frontline

soldiers the bees of Paradise"—he gestured to the hive—"to scour the unclean land. The Saharoui people have suffered too long in captivity. I will
redeem their exile. I will lead them out of the wilderness of sand to the sea.
I am the enemy of all who are unclean. I am the enemy of the Moroccans,
who shall fear my wrath. I am the enemy of the Algerians, who have given
us this miserable patch of ground as you would give a dog a corner of earth.
I am the enemy of the SADR and of Polisario, who are lukewarm, I spit them
out! I am the enemy of the United Nations liars who give us tasteless crackers to eat and terrible cheese and endless years of waiting. I am the enemy of
MINURSO, who will do nothing to alleviate the sufferings of my people. I
am the enemy of all in the West who are unclean, of men who lie with men
and the women who lie with women and the women who do not cover their
faces and who are whores!" He rose and spread his arms wide, as if to include the entire desert in his grasp, the world itself. "My fourth and final
name is Al Bab"—shouting now at the top of his lungs—"the Gateway to
the Age of the Hidden Imam!" Then, after a pause, in a normal tone: "That's
my speech. I'm still working on the details. What do you think?"

"I understand completely," Phillipe said. "You are a fraud"—once he said
this, he knew it to be the truth—"you are an imposter. You—"

He was not allowed to complete this statement. One of the veiled guards
stepped up behind him and struck his shoulder with the stock of a Kalashnikov so hard it dislocated the joint. Phillipe felt the pain of this dislocation
like an electric shock. He fell to the ground and tried to keep himself from
screaming, but couldn't. The guard stepped forward now and kicked him in
the gut, which had the effect of jarring his dislocated shoulder. The pain
from this final blow was so acute, it drove him over the edge into the dark,
merciful state of unreason and he passed out.

9.

Phillipe awoke some time later in a rickety prison cell dug into the desert
sand, with a corrugated tin roof and scrap-wood walls. The pain from
his dislocated shoulder blotted out everything—courage, honor, love—and
he lay on the sandy ground in the grips of this blackness, moaning weakly. He
felt himself becoming unmoored, he felt something inside his head tearing
off and falling away. He knew now he was going mad as his ancestors had
gone mad; and he lay there for a long time, completely out of his head, rid-

ing with them over endless plains covered with asphodel on one of the huge
piebald warhorses of Brittany, but riding toward a blankness, a vacancy—as
night gave way to dawn and gray slivers of morning light showed through
chinks in the walls of his cell.

Then, something pierced the clouds swaddling his brain. A few hesitant,
plaintive notes like brilliant rays of light, interspersed with long, melancholy
silences. It was the opening section of a piece by Satie; the *Gymnopédie
No. 1*, which the composer had written in 1887 after wriggling his way out
of mandatory National Service in the French army. The notes sounded
again, stridently, and soon the whole piece followed, unfolding like a rose in
sunlight, and Phillipe found himself able to shake off the shadows and rise
to his feet.

He leaned against the wall and forced his shoulder into it and rolled back
and forth—the sharp, stabbing sensation nearly causing him to faint again—
until he heard a kind of popping sound, and the shoulder joint snapped
back into its socket with LEGOlike precision and the pain lifted in an instant
and was gone. A sense of euphoria filled him now as he worked himself out
of his bonds, though every bit as crazy in its extremity as the radical un-
mooring he'd felt earlier. But this was not the time to think of such things:
Phillipe saw now that he'd been sharing his cell with a pitiful round something like a soccer ball that was Milhauz's head. The little man's Corbusier
glasses were gone; his eyes, half open, showed a kind of surprised look, while
his mouth and lower jaw were frozen in an exclamation of terror.

Phillipe examined this sad object. No longer revolted by the sight of a
severed head, he took it gently by the ears and held it up.

"I'm very sorry about this, Herr Dr. Milhauz," Phillipe whispered. "I'm
afraid I'll be leaving you behind, contrary to article seven, section two of
the Code of the Foreign Legion. But I'll be back, I swear it. And I'll take
your head to your mother in Zurich for a proper burial. You have my word
as a soldier of France. I also swear on the tombs of my ancestors, the lords of
la Tour Grise, that I will seek out the archimposter Al Bab, I will find him
and I will cut off his head. You will be avenged!"

Not surprisingly, poor Milhauz didn't respond to this bellicose declara-
tion. Phillipe set Milhauz's head down in the sand and looked around. His
cell was hardly secure. A bit of the corrugated roofing, missing in one corner,
made a narrow opening to the outside. By wedging himself into the angle of
the walls, Phillipe managed to shinny himself out and onto the roof. His

prison turned out to be nothing more than a kind of storehouse in the middle of a densely packed neighborhood of tents and hovels. The camp spread away on all sides, looking almost exactly like a garbage dump. Goats foraged for trash in the alleys. It was just after dawn; night still held sway in the east. No one stirred. Below, guarding the door, one of the Marabouts slept, Kalashnikov cradled in his lap.

Phillipe dropped down quietly, lifted the Kalashnikov from the guard without waking him, and began to walk, not furtively like an escaped hostage, but head up and brisk, as one might walk along the Champs-Élysées on a Saturday afternoon. He kept walking toward the west, stopping only when he reached the perimeter wire and open desert spreading beyond. The Algerian town of Tindouf lay about fifty kilometers to the south-southwest of where he stood.

He turned back and hunted through the neighborhood until he found something he could use: a 175cc Husqvarna dirt bike, half hidden under a plastic tarp, its camouflaged tank nearly full of gas and stenciled with the markings of the Pakistani army. Phillipe slung the Kalashnikov over his shoulder and rolled the bike out toward the desert. There, on the rim of the emptiness, watched only by a curious lizard, he kick-started the little engine and puttered over the dunes and down a trail that fed directly into the Tindouf road.

No one followed, no shots echoed after him through the desert air. Ahead, only blue sky and yellow sand.

10.

That night, in Tindouf, Phillipe told his story to the Algerian authorities. The next morning, five hundred Algerian soldiers, Phillipe with them, rolled into the camp, fully armed, only to find the hennaed one and his Marabouts had vanished.

No one in the camps would admit any exact knowledge of what had happened to the Pakistanis. There had been some kind of a fight in the UN compound, someone said. You could hear the echo of gunfire, see the flames and the black smoke rising up. All they knew was that the Pakistanis, who had recently raped some of their women, hadn't again emerged from their barbed-wire enclosure and cinder block buildings. No one knew anything about an earthen hive full of bees or an uprising of Marabouts. Meanwhile, inside the depot, the only trace of Al Bab and his cohorts was the pile of Pakistani heads and the remains of the hive, which had been doused with gasoline and burned into a shapeless black pile. The scorched carcasses of many bees crunched like spent cartridges underfoot.

Phillipe searched for hours, but couldn't find the hovel where he'd been kept a prisoner, and so wasn't able to locate Milhauz's head, which he had promised to repatriate. This inability haunted him on the plane all the way back to Dahkla, where throughout the course of the long debriefing with MINURSO command, he saw in his mind's eye the gaping mouth and sad eyes of the unfortunate economist.

11.

A week later, after a slapdash medical examination at the Legion hospital in Aubagne and several debriefings with representatives of various branches of the French government, including the Sûreté and the Deuxième Bureau at the Fort de Nogent, in Paris, Phillipe found himself on recuperative leave wandering the rooms of his beautiful house in Neuilly.

An August evening, high summer, heat coming in through the open windows. Paris was empty except for the tourists, the better cafés deserted, everyone, even the taxi drivers and the waiters, at the beach or in the mountains. Louise had probably gone down to Saint-Jean-de-Luz, the unfashionable but pleasant seaside town where they had recently bought a small vacation cottage. Phillipe hadn't tried to contact her since his return to France, though she was easily reachable via cell phone. He tried now, dialing her number twice, but hung up both times without leaving a message.

He dragged himself up to the large bathroom on the second floor, with its elegant gold-framed mirrors and Napoléonic-era alabaster eagle-foot tub. He had often made love to Louise in that tub, but this thought—he couldn't explain it to himself!—now injected a darkness into the core of his being. He disrobed, dropping his uniform in a crumpled heap on the tile floor and studied himself naked in one of the long mirrors. He had changed. He was not the same man he'd been just a month before. His body, formerly muscular and pink, looked emaciated, slightly yellowish, and showed the scars and bruises of rough treatment. More remarkably, his hair had gone stark white during the course of the single night he'd suffered the captivity of the Marabouts. The little patch of white that had been called Flame of the

Pentecost by his first wife had now ignited his entire scalp. But his face looked oddly smooth, younger perhaps, as if unusual suffering had worn away the wrinkles and lines, given him the smooth complexion of the marble statues of the saints in Saint-Germain l'Auxerrois.

That night, lying clenched and rigid in the big bed, Phillipe couldn't sleep.

It had been this way since Awsard. He hadn't slept more than an hour or two a night in the last couple of weeks, sometimes as little as fifteen minutes out of every twenty-four hours, although he couldn't really say he felt tired. His brain seemed in the grips of a kind of frantic electricity that was not entirely unpleasant. A letter had come for him the week before, mailed to Legion headquarters in Aubagne, now passed on to agents of the Dieuxème Bureau for chemical analysis. The envelope, covered with colorful Moroccan stamps, had been mailed from the disputed city of Laayoune in the Non-Self-Governing Territory of Western Sahara; a single sheet of flimsy blue paper lay within, scrawled over with terrible, ungrammatical French in a spidery, childish hand:

We let you live, you who is our bloody Ishamael. You one have survive alone to tell all, to warn all of the coming slaughter of the evil smelling nonbelievers. Al Bab, he called Gateway to the Age of the Hidden Imam, he an Hidden servant of the Hidden Imam, who will clean and sweep the earth so a beautiful and fragrant feet of the Hidden One might trod upon it without fear of corruption or dirt, without stepping in the offal of dogs and women. He has Peace Be Upon Him! come down from the mountain's cave where he been to sleep for a thousand years. Tiny angels, resembling bees, sting him awake and now he speaks this warning to the whole world, beneath the mighty sign of the bee! All unbelievers in Western Sahara will have their heads cut, unless they return to their own lands or to hell like the excrement-eating dogs they are. But yea, we shall pursue them even there! I beat them with my shoe! I beat them all with the heel of my shoe! The Holy Army of Marabouts is raging and raging, their hands turn against all. Heed my many warnings of Al Bab! Who am also called He Who Leans at the Gateway to the Age of the Hidden Imam, and Exceptional Righteousness. Who am called Sharp-Edged Weapon of God, who am called . . .

And so on, page after page.

Phillipe found this letter amusing, mostly for the strident, pseudo-Koranic style and purposefully bad French of the imposter who wrote it. Still, he couldn't sleep, though not from fear. He would never sleep again, he knew this now, and for him it was an end: the doom that had preyed on his family since the days of Saint Louis had at last found him.

This condition, a creeping kind of violent madness, was the peculiar curse of the males of the de Noyer line. Records documenting its effects went back hundreds of years, the pattern more or less always the same. The afflicted male stops sleeping and after weeks of relentless insomnia begins to hallucinate. He is possessed by freakish manias, hears voices, sees unspeakable visions. These visions drive him to commit terrible crimes—usually murder—or in some cases prompt a spectacular suicide. The history of the curse of the de Noyers—long, tragic, and bloody, but relieved by occasional episodes of low comedy—mirrored the history of modern France.

The dastardly Ravillac, a bastard son of the family, was chained to four horses and pulled limb from limb for the regicide of Henry IV in 1558. In 1620 another one of Phillipe's ancestors, believing the Bishop of Rennes to be a wild pig, and believing himself to be out hunting in the woods, shot the prelate dead with an arquebus during mass at the cathedral and for this was burned at the stake. A hundred years later, Phillipe's great-great-great-grandfather, an amateur naturalist and friend of Voltaire's, tied stones around his neck and jumped into the murky waters of the Vieux Port at Honfleur during the Blessing of the Fleet. He left a note saying he intended to investigate the secret lives of fish and, not to worry, was adequately prepared for a long stay at the bottom of the sea. Another great-grandfather, a famous soldier who had fought at Valmy, sat out the entire fifteen-year run of the Napoléonic Wars because he suddenly conceived the notion that God intended people not to wear clothes and they wouldn't let him fight naked. And there was Phillipe's own grandfather, killed charging the German guns at the Somme during the First World War, carrying nothing but a toilet plunger and a scandalously pornographic novel written by the poet Guillaume Apollinaire. (These awkward items were changed in army dispatches to an officer's sword and a copy of the Gospels. Subsequent newspaper editorials made the man a hero of both church and state; he was posthumously awarded the Légion d'honneur and interred in the Panthéon near the tomb of Maréchal Lannes.)

Horrors similar to these, as yet barely visible, were coming toward Phillipe slowly through the ancestral mists. It remained for him now only to choose his particular form of madness; a choice—the last act of his rational mind—in which lay the essential difference between murder and suicide. But Phillipe, summoning all his mental discipline, chose neither. His act of will, existentially perfect, was in keeping with the best traditions of the de Noyers: The ancient motto of the family, engraved on the armorial shield hanging over the family crypt at Saint Marie's church in Honfleur—*Tantum Transiere Probi*, Only the Righteous Shall Pass—suggested just this kind of heroic denial of an unalterable destiny.

So, instead of murder or suicide, Phillipe chose the two things he loved most, sacred objects to carry along with him as he entered his personal twilight: Satie and the Foreign Legion. Satie, whose music exuded peace and humor, for the peace denied him at night. The Legion for its order, for the beauty of men marching in lockstep to the sound of the kettledrum, the bass oboe, the Chinese chimes—difficult instruments completely unknown to any other marching band. Only this kind of order, both military and musical at once, might withstand the irruption of unreason Phillipe had experienced in the desert. Choice made, fate settled. But Phillipe still couldn't sleep. He got out of bed at 3:00 A.M.—the high noon of the sleepless—and went downstairs to the piano and played from memory Satie's *Trois Morceaux*. Playing Satie was nearly as good as sleep. It soothed the raw, torn-away places in his brain, quieted the electric buzzing in his mind's ear. As he played, he closed his eyes and viewed scenes from the Legion's last Bastille Day parade in Paris as if watching 3-D slides through one of the precious View-Master *visionneuses* of his childhood.

There they are, the ten thousand, assembled on the Champs-Élysées, la Musique Principale in the lead. Then, the opening notes of "Le Boudin"— the Legion anthem—played on a single cornet, high and clear and sweet. The whole band picks up the tune a moment later and the battalions, moving in unison, begin their march down the famous avenue slow as a funeral cortege at eighty-eight paces per minute, always at the back of the back, behind the Mechanized Artillery and the Armored Cavalry of the Armée de Terre, beneath the streaking blue, white, and red contrails of the Mirage jets of the Maritime Airforce. They are in no apparent hurry to reach the draped grandstand full of foreign dignitaries and generals, politicians and movie stars. But they arrive at last and there, they halt, and the heels of ten thousand boots strike the cobbles in unison with a precise, martial clatter. Silence. Every eye turns toward the central dias beneath the vast tricolor flag. But instead of the President of the Republic in his elegant dark suit, flanked by cabinet ministers and Isabelle Adjani, there sits on a pillow in the place of honor poor Phillipe's brain, a pink, spongy mass full of tiny holes, its very cells being eaten from the inside out by hideous, invisible little creatures like dust mites, eating away until everything, every last memory has been eaten up, digested, defecated.

Phillipe's eyes snapped open at this horrible vision, his pajamas soaked in a cold sweat. But he continued to play, he didn't miss a note. Satie would quiet the creatures, put them to sleep, make them eat his brain more slowly. This was his secret weapon against them. And so, Satie's plaintive, melancholy *Trois Morceaux* echoed in the empty town house, absorbed by the beautiful carpets, the paintings on the walls, by his wife's expensive clothes hanging in the closets upstairs. Poor Louise. The thought of her peerless flesh filled Phillipe with revulsion now. He still loved her, but what was love? A concept invented by idealists to palliate certain uncomfortable requirements of human nature for the continuation of the species. And in France, as someone once said—was it La Rochefoucauld?—love was merely the exchange of two whims and the fleeting contact of one skin against another.

Out in the garden a pear tree swayed somberly in the breeze, in time to the music.

3

RAPUNZEL

1.

Kasim Vatran's house stood at the top of a narrow pedestrian street off Istiklal Caddesi in the Beyoglu District of Istanbul, not far from the old monastery of the Whirling Dervishes. The cable cars of the Eski Tramway hung suspended above the dark mouth of the funicular tunnel just a few blocks away. Heartbreaking afternoon light shone now on the Lower Galata, on the blue-green waters of the Golden Horn, crowded with shipping.

The house, painted gray and pale green with dark green shutters over the sharply arched windows, was one of the few remaining Ottoman-era buildings in this increasingly developed neighborhood. A traditional onion dome crowned the square tower that ran up the front, but Vatran (Yale Architecture; AIA, Frank Lloyd Wright Notable Design Winner; First Place, Prix Viollet-le-Duc) had brutally deconstructed the once elegant facade. He had ripped out the third floor, tower and all, to install a spare, postmodern interior behind a wall of tinted plate glass, its smooth, greenish surface interrupted with a complicated arrangement of stainless-steel pins and cables, like a set of braces on otherwise perfect teeth.

Smith hid in the shadows across the street as sunlight crept up house by house until it shone directly on Vatran's monstrosity, glinting off the cables and pins and illuminating the aquariumlike box of the third floor. From this vantage Smith could make out every detail: the barely functional stylized furniture, the austere lighting fixtures, the asymmetrical wall hangings made from shredded pop cans interwoven with strands of pure, beaten gold, bought by Vatran and Jessica at the Gagosian Gallery, Mayfair, during their last junket to London. Who could live in such a room? Smith thought bitterly, even though he knew the answer. Who could rip out one-hundred-and-fifty-year-old hand-carved cabinets and crenelated alcoves and install this postmodern bullshit?

Then, a black metal door opened and Jessica, fresh from the bath, entered carrying a large-format fashion magazine and Smith's heart missed a beat. Her gold-blond hair was wrapped in a blue towel. She was still wearing the plush, expensive terry-cloth robe he had bought her at Barney's two Christmases ago, when they were still in love. She folded herself onto the uncomfortable sofa in sunlight reflected as green shade through the tinted glass, shook her still-damp hair from the towel and opened the magazine. Long minutes passed as she turned the pages slowly. Smith could see, or perhaps only imagined he saw, water droplets drying on her flesh in the sun, the blond strands of her hair curling as they dried. Desire and pain twisted in his gut; he became conscious of an uncomfortable stiffening in his travel-stained khakis. God, he wanted to fuck her. He'd thought about little else, all throughout the slow, miserable train ride from Paris—across Europe second class, then down through the Balkans on rickety locals, stopping at every sad, one-goat town, the sullen platforms full of half-starved Gypsies and hard-eyed ethnic cleansers in surplus military fatigues, rusty rabbit guns slung over their shoulders.

Without knowing how it started, Smith felt tears on his face. His emotions in charge suddenly, his heart racing. What the fuck's wrong with me? he thought desperately. Why am I such miserable bastard? Then control, motherfucker, get control!—these words echoing in his skull like the shrill warning bleat of a diving submarine—but he couldn't control himself or didn't want to, and his tears fell to splotch the cobbled pavement. He was thirty-two years old, physically fit, attractive, a moderately successful actor/singer/dancer with ten years of stage experience under his belt—he'd played Freddie for LORT A scale in an Equity production of *My Fair Lady* at the Guthrie in Minneapolis just a couple of years ago—how many working actors could say they'd done LORT A?—the only place to go from there was

Broadway, name-in-lights stuff. And yet he felt finished, spent. Weak as a child with leukemia. And now the tears wouldn't stop.

Meanwhile, Jessica basked up there in the warm aquarium sunlight, still turning the big pages of her magazine. The Tünel-Taksim tram rattled along Istiklal Caddesi, packed to the doors with Turks on their way home to the working-class tenements of Dolapdere as the high, thin wail of the muezzin called all pious men to evening prayer.

2.

A few minutes later, an old Turkish man, wearing a ribbed woolen cap on his head and a dirty tweed jacket full of holes, clanked up the steps from Istiklal. Strapped to his back was a strange apparatus—a tin-lined wooden box with various brass domes and pipes attached, like a crazy homemade version of a scuba diver's air tanks. From beneath his left arm protruded a long spigot; tin cups dangled from hooks on the thick belt around his waist. He saw Smith standing half hidden in the shadows and stopped.

"*Iyi aksamlar,*" the Turk said. "*Nasalsiniz? Çay? Su?*"

Smith knew enough Turkish to know the Turk wanted to sell him a cup of tea. The old man was one of a dying breed—the itinerant urban tea peddler. They used to wander the byways of Istanbul by the thousands, selling tin cups full of Turkey's favorite beverage for a few lirasi, less than a penny, a little extra for the fresh mint that they carried around in fragrant leather bags. There were maybe a dozen left now, maybe twenty, in the entire city of ten million. Running into a tea peddler in Istanbul was like catching a cab in Manhattan not driven by a Pakistani or a Somali—what were the odds?

"*Hayir, mersi,*" Smith said—no, thanks, a kind of knee-jerk American tourist reflex to peddlers of any kind.

"*Çay?*" the tea seller persisted gently, holding out a cup. He was a small man, hunched from carrying his tin-lined tank of tea around for thousands of miles over these steep and windblown streets. His face, dominated by a scraggly gray mustache, was deeply lined but kindly; he might be sixty or perhaps eighty, hard to tell with Turks.

"*Hayir!*" Smith said again, but he realized suddenly that he was very thirsty, that he was dying of thirst, that nothing had passed his lips, not food or water, since before noon. "Well, O.K. *Tamam*—" He went fumbling in his pocket for change.

The tea peddler reached for his spigot, then caught sight of the tears still wet on Smith's cheeks. He touched his own creased visage and put a concerned hand on Smith's arm.

"No, I'm fine," Smith began, "just a piece of dirt in my eye . . ." He tried to say more, but found himself giving way to emotion again; it was no use. "Shit!" he said in a choked voice. "This is really fucking stupid!" And he tried to grin, but couldn't and bowed his head and found himself heaving with sobs.

The tea peddler clucked sympathetically, still patting Smith's arm. Then, something, a flash of sunlight off the stainless-steel cables above made the old man glance up, and he caught sight of Jessica in the aquarium window, engrossed in her magazine, her golden hair throwing off light. The thick terry-cloth robe had fallen away from her legs and a wide swath of creamy flesh shone there like the marble thigh of a goddess.

"*Eh-eh!*" the tea peddler let out an exclamation. "*Genk ksiz, cok pahali. Sini cekmek!*" He looked from Jessica's exposed thigh to the tears on Smith's face and back again. Now he understood. Here was a scene from a storybook: the golden-haired princess in the tower; the lovelorn palace thief weeping from a broken heart in the alley below—though in the old Turkish stories it wasn't a golden-haired princess at all, but a dark-eyed page boy with lips like rose petals and soft, fawn-colored skin.

The tea peddler clucked again and filled a tin cup with tea and handed it to Smith, who drank deeply, not bothering to wipe the rim, slightly green and worn thin by the passage of many lips. The stuff was sweet and strong and cool, despite sloshing around the tank on the man's back all day, and soothed Smith's dry throat. When he tried to pay for it a moment later, the tea peddler shook his head. He wouldn't accept a single coin.

"Come on," Smith said. "Here, take it—"

The tea peddler only smiled sadly and began a speech in Turkish in a low earnest voice—advice for the lovelorn, Smith guessed—though he couldn't understand a word.

"*Türkçe bilimiyorum,*" he interrupted, a phrase from the guidebook—I don't speak Turkish.

The tea peddler nodded, thinking. At last he held up a finger and plucked at Smith's sleeve and did a little pantomime that meant come with me, come with me, and descended a few steps toward Istiklal Caddesi.

Smith hesitated, then let himself be drawn down the slope and into the crowds along the busy sidewalk. The tea peddler kept hold of his arm as they came up the steep grade to Karakoy, talking all the while, a soothing monologue. Maybe Smith was being taken somewhere dangerous where he might be robbed, held for ransom, murdered, his body dropped in pieces into the Bosphorus. No. The tea peddler seemed like a straightforward kind of guy and Smith trusted his instincts. Anyway, he had lost something crucial over the last year of struggle, self-indulgence, failure, and depression: curiosity. He no longer cared about what would happen next.

3.

The pillared arcade where the Whirling Dervishes once performed their ritual dances stood empty except for a few cats asleep on the cool paving tiles. At the far end of the arcade, near the street entrance, a fat man sat at a small table reading a newspaper. Crowding the table, an old typewriter, piles of dingy writing paper, pens, a few tattered paperback multilanguage dictionaries. A sign bore inscriptions in five languages, the last one English:

PROFESSIONAL WRITINGS—LETTERS PERSONAL & ROMANTIC—PETITIONS, ETC.—TURKISH, FRENCH, ITALIAN, GERMAN, ENGLISH. TRANSLATE UPON REQUEST. M. AYAK, PROP.

Here was the public letter writer of the Tünel District; most city neighborhoods had at least one, a necessity in a country where nearly 30 percent of the population couldn't read.

There were no chairs for patrons so the tea peddler unstrapped his tank and squatted down and began speaking to the letter writer in rapid Turkish, all the while gesturing at Smith, who stood there awkwardly, hands in his pockets. Smith saw that the typewriter was a 1940s-era crackle-black Remington Rand Noiseless and wondered where the hell you'd get ribbons for a machine like that in Istanbul, then noticed that it had no ribbons at all. It was rusty-keyed and just for show, a symbol of the trade.

At last, the tea peddler stood back; the letter writer motioned for Smith to step forward:

"You are English?" he said in a decent facsimile of the language.

"American," Smith said.

"So"—the letter writer nodded—"I also write very good American. You want me to scribe a letter of love to the woman with the hair of gold in the window?"

"No," Smith said. "Thank you."

The letter writer paused, disappointed at losing this bit of business. Then he indicated the tea peddler: "Such a man here, he is from the country, from a place called Caltilibuk, which is in Bursa. Do you know Bursa?"

"No," Smith said.

"A very beautiful area, many trees, many flowers. The people of Bursa are plain people, but honest."

"*Tamam*," Smith said. O.K.

"*Iyi, tamam.*" The letter writer nodded. "So this man wishes me to say to you some things because he cannot say them himself, having no American to speak. With your permission. *Evet?*"

"Yes, go ahead," Smith said.

"First the man say you make him sad because he think of his son, who was a foolish young man so much like you."

Smith didn't respond to this.

"He also say you must forget this woman who has a rich husband in the window—"

"She's not married," Smith interrupted. "Not yet."

"Perhaps." The letter writer nodded. "But she is the woman of another man. So much so true, yes?"

Smith allowed that this was true.

"Aha!" The letter writer wagged a finger. "Such a woman is bad poison for you. This good fellow"—he indicated the tea peddler—"wishes me to say something private about his only son, Hasan. Many years before today, his son was good, handsome, strong. But he throws himself under a railway carriage in Bursa for the love of a girl whose parents had betrothed her to another man. This is very terrible, but more terrible is that the boy did not die from such foolish act but he cuts off two legs at the knee. So now, he begs alms on the street in Bursa and is a very sad person and consistently remains unmarried."

"I'm really sorry to hear that," Smith said.

The letter writer translated these words of condolence and the tea peddler bowed his head.

"So our good gentleman"—again the letter writer indicated the tea peddler—"wishes me to say you must not waste tears like so on this woman. That there are many other womans for a handsome young man like you, so strong and with such beautiful hair . . ."

Smith's hair, blond and thick and nearly as lustrous as Jessica's, had been one of his chief attributes as an actor. In addition to his work on the stage, he'd done a couple of shampoo commercials; he'd been the "after" example in a national print campaign for Rogaine.

The letter writer went on for some time, translating the tea peddler's unsolicited advice, and Smith stood there and took it, moved by this concern from a total stranger. But they were wasting their breath. He'd already squandered everything, emotionally speaking. He had— —to use an old-fashioned phrase—ruined himself. He'd let his show business career, already tenuous, slide further into the professional Dumpster while he moped and drank heavily at dive bars in Brooklyn. He hadn't sung before an audience in a year, hadn't gone to an audition in months; he'd fought with his manager at Tycho, Dunston Talent and been dumped by that venerable agency. He'd alienated all his friends in New York by his self-indulgent whining and monomaniacal obsession with all things Jessica. And now this ill-advised trip to Istanbul: the precious rent-controlled apartment in Brooklyn Heights sublet to an African student, nearly everything he owned sold to pay for tickets and travel expenses—to what end? Did he really think Jessica would renounce her gilded life with the very successful Kasim Vatran and come back to him? Just now, he couldn't bear to answer that question.

Shadows grew between the tombs among the fig trees in the old Ottoman cemetery visible on the other side of the tumbledown courtyard wall. Smith checked his watch—a classic old Rolex that had belonged to his father, one of the few things he hadn't sold—and noticed with a surge of panic the lateness of the hour. He had to get back to the hotel, shave, bathe. Prepare himself.

"I appreciate all your help, guys," Smith interrupted, and he shook their hands warmly. "But I've really got to run." He extracted a few thousand lirasi notes from his wallet and handed them over to the letter writer. The tea peddler protested—such advice as they were giving should not be paid for— but the letter writer, a more practical man, folded the bills quickly into his pocket.

"*Sagol*," he murmured. Thanks to you.

"*Teşekkürler,*" Smith responded, backing away. But the tea peddler found time for one last question.

"You go to her now?" the letter writer said, translating.

"I'm afraid so," Smith admitted. "I'm sorry."

"*Kotu*," the tea peddler said, shaking his head, wearily.

"He said this bad for you," the letter writer said. "He also say if you might need our help, so you come, you find us . . ."

"You're very good people," Smith called to them. "I won't forget your kindness." Then he turned and hopped the courtyard wall and ran off through the tombs to the street, already forgetting them both.

The tea peddler and the letter writer watched him go.

"The boy is running to his doom," the tea peddler said in Turkish.

The letter writer agreed. "But what can we do?" He shrugged. "He's an American and not a Muslim and therefore misguided. And possibly, like most Americans, addicted to drugs and alcohol."

The tea peddler made a gesture that meant such matters were beyond him. He strapped the tin-lined apparatus to his shoulders and followed Smith's path out into the street, leaving the letter writer in the courtyard, dusk fast descending, with his ribbonless Remington Rand and a few sleeping cats for company.

4.

Smith showered quickly in his cavernous not-quite-clean bathroom at the old Stamboul Palace Hotel and dressed in his best shirt and jeans and a soft cashmere tan blazer and slipped his feet into the comfortable down-at-the-heels cowboy boots he always wore when traveling. His room, also cavernous and not quite clean, had fancy plaster rosettes molded into the walls, the whorls and petals trailing long, spidery strands of dust.

The Stamboul Palace had been the hotel of choice in Istanbul in the 1920s and '30s—Garbo once stayed here for a few days and Graham Greene for the three months it took him to write one of his lesser known novels. Turkish schoolchildren trooped down the main hall on Smith's floor twice a week to have a look at the room where Kemal Atatürk—the Father of Modern Turkey—stayed for a single night in 1922. This room, its doorway blocked by a thick glass panel, hadn't been touched since the day he checked out. A rotting towel hung in shreds on the brass bedstead where the Great Turk had tossed it; a scrap of paper bearing his hasty scrawl lay yellow and curled beside the ancient two-piece phone on the nightstand.

Smith knocked back a couple of shots of raki in the bar downstairs for courage, set his iPod on shuffle, and worked his way through the crowds up

Mesrutiyet listening to an unlikely combination of the thousand eclectic tunes stored in digital memory: This included himself singing a sea shanty from the score of *Behold Me Once More* (he'd done that popular all-male review off-off Broadway back in '02); the pounding house of Academy 16; Frank Sinatra from the Nelson Riddle era (a phrase jumped out at him: Hey jealous lover!); the Jam; Fred Astaire; Sisters of Mercy; Hank Williams; the Decemberists; one of Ástor Piazzolla's experimental tangos. It was like having old friends around him, friends from home.

He arrived at Vatran's house at a quarter after six. Soft green light glowed from the fish tank of the third floor, empty now except for its uncomfortable furniture and bad, expensive art. Smith rang the buzzer twice and waited. After what seemed like a long while, a servant answered the door. He was a short, barrel-chested man, powerfully built, with a square, thuggish face. On his feet, red Turkish slippers with the toes curled up like elf shoes.

"*Iyi aksalam,*" Smith said. Good evening. "*Isti yourm Hamm Jessica.*"

The servant looked up at him suspiciously through scraggly, owlish eyebrows that desperately needed trimming.

"I speak English," he said at last.

"Great!" Smith said brightly. "Jessica is expecting me."

The servant brought him into the foyer; the traditional Ottoman interior of hand-carved wood and mother-of-pearl inlay was gone here too, replaced with vinyl, rubber, polished granite, and steel. The walls had been taken down to bare brick, the central stairway gone to make way for a stainless-steel elevator. The servant ushered Smith into the elevator and pressed three. As they ascended slowly, he continued his appraisal, studying Smith frankly and without embarrassment.

"So, what's shaking?" Smith said.

"You are her brother?" the servant said.

"No," Smith said.

"You look much alike."

"People say that," Smith said, slightly annoyed. "But it's just because we're both tall and blond. You've got to get past that. Take our skulls, for example. Totally different—she's round, I'm more of an oval. And our belly buttons—she's an innie, I'm an outie."

The servant frowned. He didn't understand. But before he had a chance to inquire further, the elevator doors opened smoothly to reveal a large room, its floors composed of smooth marble paving stones robbed from the rubble of some other luckless old building. There was no furniture to speak of, only a few large cushions strewn about. Two priceless eighteenth-century kilim rugs hung suspended in shadow boxes on the wall.

"Hamm Jess," the servant called, and in the next moment, Jessica stepped out of a concealed door from another room that looked like the kitchen. She carried two glasses of red wine and wore a white silk shirt, vaguely Turkish, and flouncy tan pants embroidered all over with tan paisleys, so subtle you could hardly see them. A gold mesh belt slung low around the waist matched her gold chandelier earrings. She had turned Turk, Smith could see—it was not an outfit she would ever wear in New York; still, she looked great. She had put on a little weight, but looked healthier for the extra pounds. Her skin, nicely tanned, held a faint golden luster. She had just returned from a private beach resort on the Black Sea, where she'd gone with Vatran and his parents (so she'd said in her last e-mail) rambling on at length about the luxurious hotel where they'd stayed in separate suites for the sake of Vatran's mother: its polite, efficient service, its white courtyards and deep green awnings, everything surrounded by high protective hedges of thornbushes and brambles. And the beach itself, not sand but small, glossy stones, guarded by men carrying submachine guns. It was becoming increasingly dangerous in Turkey for men and women to cavort together in public wearing bathing suits.

"Hey, Jessica honey," Smith said in the casual tone he'd practiced for months now in front of a mirror. "You look really great!"

He flashed her a fond smile and kissed her on both cheeks. All his acting ability would be required to pull off this role, the most difficult of his life: the easygoing ex-boyfriend, who just happened to be traveling in Europe and thought he'd drop by. After all, weren't they still good friends?

Jessica pulled away from him quickly. It seemed she could smell his desperation, but maybe not.

"Here," she said, pushing the glass of wine into his hands. "We're going to need this. Well, Johnny"—she raised her glass—"success to crime!" It was one of their old toasts, something Bogart says to the cops in *The Maltese Falcon*, and they clinked glasses and both took a long swallow. "Hey, Ahmet! *Iyi gunler, tefeci!*" she called sharply over Smith's shoulder. He turned, startled, to see the servant malingering obstinately by the elevator door, thick, muscled forearms crossed over his barrel-chest like an opprobrious genie. Apparently, she wanted him gone and he refused to go.

"Out, old uncle!" Jessica called again. "*Rahat* fucking *burakmak!*" The servant, grumbling, reluctantly left the room.

"What is he, the butler?" Smith said.

"That's Ahmet," Jessica said. "He's Kasim's creature. Loves the man like a, like an I don't know what. Sort of like a slave, if you ask me, been with the family for years. Thinks he's got to stick around just in case I decide to drop to my knees and give you a blow job."

Smith grinned at this. She was as endearingly foulmouthed as ever. "Sounds like a good idea to me," he said in a jokey tone, but his spine tingled at the thought.

"Ho-ho," Jessica said. "Don't you fucking wish."

Smith followed her into the kitchen, a long narrow galley fitted with the latest European appliances and an island of beautifully grained rose-colored wood, a single solid piece like an oversized balance beam that must have come out of the heart of a large and very old tree. The kitchen was thus far the coziest room in the house. Smith knew from e-mails that Jessica had designed it herself with a little technical assistance from one of Vatran's engineers. She pulled up a stool at the beam end and handed over a small plate of meze—marinated olives, stuffed grape leaves, pickled tongue, fried cheese encased in flake pastry.

"Wow," Smith said, taking a stuffed grape leaf. "Very impressive."

"Don't get too excited," she said. "I just bought this shit at a little place around the corner."

An uncomfortable silence followed. They were catching up with themselves quickly, with the awkwardness of seeing each other after nearly two years and everything that had happened. Jessica picked olives out of the dish daintily one by one and popped them into her mouth. She deliberately kept the beam between them, one arm crossed over her breasts. Smith didn't want to eat, wasn't hungry, his stomach burning from stress, but he made a decent show of it. Desire sounded in his heart like the booming of a great brass bell. He stuffed a handful of olives into his mouth and almost choked on a stray pit, which he spit out after much coughing.

"Jesus, you all right?" Jessica said, alarmed.

"I'm fine," he said, an unintended tremor in his voice. "It's the pits . . ."

Then he looked at her and felt himself weakening, and pain and resentment shone in his eyes.

"Oh, God," Jessica moaned. "Here we go. I knew you shouldn't have come. I mean you hate Istanbul, right? All you did was whine and complain the whole time we were here."

"I was sick," Smith said hotly. "Remember? Anyway, I don't hate Istanbul! How could anyone hate Istanbul? It's got all that Byzantine crap, all that Ottoman crap, you name it, utterly fascinating. What I hated was you and him. What I hated about Istanbul has nothing to do with the city itself, which is beautiful. I hated that this was the place where—"

Smith stopped himself just in time, gulped down the rest of his wine and poured another glass. The place where that bastard stole you from me, he wanted to say. The place where my heart is buried, where my life started to go off a cliff.

5.

Two years before, Smith and Jessica visited Istanbul at the tail end of a monthlong Mediterranean vacation—Athens, Crete, Rhodes, and Turkey—blowing the money he'd saved from his lucrative League of Regional Theatres gig at the Guthrie, singing "On the Street Where You Live" ten times a week for overstuffed, sweater-wearing Minnesotans. They hung out in the city for three days, took a side trip to Hisarlik and the ruins of Troy, and were in Istanbul a second time for the final two days before their flight back to the States.

It was a Saturday, sunny, but with a sharp, stinging wind blowing off the Sea of Marmara. They got up early and visited the Topkapi Palace, paid extra admission to see the Harem of the Sultans along with an unacceptable number of tourists, shoving their way through the narrow hallways, through the Room with a Hearth and out into the courtyard of the Valide. They'd been bickering all morning, nothing serious, the inevitable result of being constantly together for almost a month; then Smith came down with a case of diarrhea caught, he guessed, from a bad pastrima roll bought off a street vendor near the Hippodrome. He decided to stay in bed that night; they had a small, airless room in a cheap hotel not far from the Hagia Sophia. Jessica did nothing but bitch about the accommodations—particularly the roaches she found crawling in the bathroom sink—and just after nine o'clock threw aside the Candace Bushnell paperback she'd been reading and announced her intention to go dancing. Something about her fevered, erotic energy (she was, Smith imagined in his diarrheal delirium, throwing off visible pheremones like electrical sparks) made him swallow two more extra-strength Immodiums and drag his sore, sorry ass along to a series of dance clubs with expensive covers where a horde of beautiful Turks—pop stars, soap opera divas, gay, straight, the gilded youth of Istanbul—danced the night away.

The pounding of Euro-Turk techno only gave Smith a headache that seemed to reverberate in the depths of his tortured bowels. While Jessica danced in the crush at Babylon, Cubuklu, 2C Club, Laila, Smith got to know the crudely appointed bathrooms of these otherwise opulent establishments. They ended up at Gomku, a mixed/trans/gay place in the Karakoy district just after midnight. Jessica plunged into the omnisexual crowd on the dance floor—a gyrating swirl of club kids, preop transsexuals (their balloonlike silicon implants flopping out of tight tank tops), and the quasi-straight cartoonishly macho men who loved them. Meanwhile, Smith slumped down on a stool at the bar, glass of soda water in hand, clenching his anus to keep the bile inside. He held out as long as he could, then couldn't hold out any longer and ran for the bathroom, there interrupting an outrageous scene: two transvestites giving a third a blow job like something out of a shemale porn film, in full view, right against the sink. When he returned to his stool ten minutes later, though he didn't know it yet, his world had changed beyond recognition.

Jessica, now at the bar, beer in hand, stood shouting over the pounding beat into the ear of a well-dressed Turkish man, his silk suit jacket impeccably tailored, his black hair slick as a beaver pelt. When he responded, Jessica held her own ear a little too close to his lips, laughed loudly, touched his arm. She introduced Smith as "my friend Johnny," even though they'd lived together for three years in Brooklyn and were considered by her parents to be more or less engaged. The Turk's name was Kasim Vatran. He wasn't typically handsome—the nose slightly crooked, the eyes a little bulgy—but he possessed a direct forcefulness, a natural authority that was at the same time controlled and aggressively sexual. He was, he said, an architect who had studied in New Haven; he often traveled back and forth between Istanbul and Manhattan, where he did consulting work for the well-known architectural firm of Stern, Potts. All this was very impressive, Vatran's manners were above reproach, and he insisted on paying for everything, but his attitude toward Jessica was one of carnivorous intensity. Smith just wanted to go home.

They left Gomku about 1:00 A.M. Over Smith's objections, Vatran took them in a cab to a taverna in Cihangir overlooking the Bosphorus. A more romantic spot couldn't be imagined: the immortal dome of the Hagia Sophia illuminated in shades of gold and green across the strait of dark water, wind tousling the tops of the cypress trees. They drank raki and beer and talked; rather, Jessica and Vatran talked as Smith sat by, ignored, his bowels boiling. At about 3:00 A.M., after several trips to the taverna's rudimentary facilities—a mere hole in the ground—Smith insisted Jessica return with him to the hotel. Jessica refused, and they argued as Vatran sat by, coolly smoking a cigarette.

"Look, it's my last fucking night," Jessica said. "I want to stay out."

"No, tomorrow night's your last fucking night," Smith countered.

"Whatever. I'm having a good time, I'm meeting people, and I'm nicely buzzed. I'm not going back to that shithole right now and that's what it is literally, a shithole, because you're going to be in there shitting your guts out 'til who knows when."

"Great," Smith said bitterly. "Thanks for your concern. I'm sick and this is the kind of—"

"I'm not your mother," Jessica interrupted. "I think you can take care of yourself."

At this point, Smith pulled Jessica aside, beyond the Turk's earshot. He took a deep breath—how would he put it exactly?

The moon, nearly full, hung just overhead. The Bosphorus gleamed splendidly in the moonlight, which shone also off the spires and minarets of the ancient city that had seen titanic seiges, chariot races, opulence beyond imagining, vast corruption, triumphs, massacres, the rise and fall of a thousand generations. Just then none of it looked beautiful to Smith, but hostile and barren and alien. He suddenly felt that awful vertiginous feeling, the same dizzy sensation of the ground slipping away from beneath his feet he'd felt when told of his sister Jane's death from a misdiagnosed case of meningitis. She'd just turned thirteen. (All these years later Smith could still hear the approaching clack-clack of leather-soled shoes down the waxed corridor at Herbert Hoover Intermediate; then the principal, grim-faced, at the classroom door: *Excuse me for interrupting, Miss Woodward, but John's mother is waiting in the office. . . .*) Smith was an orphan now—if such a term can be applied to a man in his thirties: His father dead from nothing, from depression and grief three years after his sister; his mother dead in a four-car pileup on I-80 during the murderous ice storm of '00 that had caused twenty-seven fatalities across the Midwest. The life of an actor, necessarily itinerant, often impoverished, didn't allow for the formation of many close friendships. Smith had no family except Jessica.

"We don't even know this guy—" Smith began desperately.

"I know him," Jessica insisted. "I met him."

"Well, I'm going."

"Fine. Go."

"He wants to fuck you. That's obvious."

"Bullshit!"

"He does. Ask him."

"Well, I'm not going to fuck him!"

But she did.

She fucked him in the backseat of a cab three hours later, at dawn, with the meter running as the driver, heavily tipped, stood off at a safe distance, pulling on a cigarette. This betrayal was confirmed in a catastrophic manner two months later, back in New York: Vatran, in the city for one of his consulting gigs, called the cell number Jessica had given him in Istanbul and took her to lunch at the Yale Club and then back to his room at the SoHo Grand, where they made love vigorously for hours. When Smith got home from work that afternoon—a tedious, poorly paid voice-over gig at a recording studio all the way out in Montclair—Jessica was already packing to leave with Vatran for Istanbul.

Smith stared at her, stunned, openmouthed, as she explained herself tersely: She'd been in love with Vatran since Istanbul. While she still loved Smith, she was no longer *in* love with him.

"I don't know what else to say," she concluded, a surgical *froideur* in her voice. "I'm sorry, but I'm Kasim's woman now. I belong to him."

"This is c-completely c-crazy!" Smith stuttered. "You can't just, just . . ." He couldn't say any more. He felt like tearing his hair out. He felt like a beetle, pin through its thorax, stuck to a card. He trailed after her out of the apartment in shock, stood speechless by her side as she waited for her cab, waved stupidly as she got in the back and the door slammed. It was like she'd suddenly died. There was the hearse taking her away.

"We can e-mail," she called through the open window. "We won't lose touch, I promise. Anyway, you need to know what to do with my stuff . . ."

6.

Now, Smith stood in the kitchen of Vatran's house in the Beyoglu, in Istanbul, face-to-face with Jessica for the first time since that terrible afternoon. He lifted his second glass of wine to his lips and put it down again. He still couldn't say what he had expected to accomplish with this foolish mission. Did he think Jessica was going to throw herself into his arms? Drop to her knees, as she said, and give him a blow job? Still, there had been odd hints in her last few e-mails, intimations of discord, vaguely delineated fights with Vatran. . . .

"Look, Jessica, let me ask you something straight-out," Smith said suddenly. "Are you happy? I mean here in Istanbul, with him?"

She hesitated for a long moment and Smith's heart did a crazy jump.

"No one's happy all the time, moron," she said, and she looked away. "That's just not the way it works, so don't get any funny ideas. This is my life now, I'm practically a fucking Turk, O.K.? I'm starting to think like a Turk. Last week, driving back from Ince Burun, from the beach, Kasim asked me to wear a headscarf, I mean the rednecks out there"—she made a gesture that meant the rest of the country, the vast, Anatolian hinterlands where the peasants still used oxcarts to get their produce to the market towns—"they see a woman's hair uncovered, especially a blonde, first they cream their fucking panties, then they take out a big knife and cut your throat."

"A headscarf?" Smith managed, astounded. "What's next? A veil? A burka?"

"Oh, fuck you! Turks don't wear burkas. That's an Afghan thing."

"O.K. A chador."

"That's, like, Iranian, shithead. Here it's a hijab. And fuck you!" Suddenly, she tilted her head back and laughed, showing a row of orthodontically perfect white teeth. "God, why am I swearing so much? I don't swear anymore. It's your goddamned fault! Kasim says it's ugly and unfuckinglady-like and blah-blah-blah. But it feels good to say fuck again. *FUCK!*"

She shouted this last explicative at the top of her lungs and stepped around the beam and gave Smith an unexpected hug. He hugged her back and caught the flowery scent of her hair—different from the way it used to smell, some new Turkish shampoo, he guessed, but also the same. She pushed him away after a moment, an affectionate shove that nearly sent him crashing into a rack full of expensive copper pots and pans.

"Come on," she said. "Kasim's waiting."

"No way." Smith shook his head. "I don't want to see him. Absolutely not."

"Too bad, fucker." Jessica smirked. "He wants to see you." And she finished her wine and went for her jacket.

7.

They caught up with Vatran at seven thirty on Nevizade Sokuk. It was just dark, and in Istanbul people eat very late, but tonight, perhaps because of the excellent spring weather, the terraces of the *meyhanes* were already crowded with diners and a cacophony of live, instrumental *fasil*—like klezmer, only more so—pumped out of the brightly lit restaurant interiors up and down the narrow street.

Vatran sat talking emphatically on his cell phone at the VIP table outside at Boncuk, the table farthest from the curb, elevated on a narrow platform six inches above everyone else. Clearly, here was a successful man (pin-striped Savile Row shirt, tailored cream sports jacket, neatly pressed dark trousers, Italian crocodile loafers) doing very important business over his cell phone. He saw Jessica and Smith coming toward him out of the crowd and jerked his head away quickly, as if offended by the sight. Jessica stepped up and kissed him on the cheek and sat next to him and put a hand on his thigh. Smith stood by hesitantly, for a moment. Did he really want to break bread with this bastard? But he sat down anyway.

"*Evet,*" Vatran was saying into the cell phone. "*Evet, lazim . . . gitmeliyim . . .*" Then Smith heard the phrase "*budala geri zekali,*" which he knew—from the little Turkish phrasebook he kept in his pocket—meant stupid idiot or cretinous moron and which he assumed referred to himself. Meanwhile, the waiter hovered. He wore a white coat with blue epaulets and a blue and white military-style cap like a soldier in some two-bit road production of *Carmen*.

"*Raki, lutfèn,*" Smith said, ordering the booze, a command for which he didn't need to consult the phrasebook.

"*Hamm?*" the waiter bowed to Jessica.

"*Bardak beyaz sarab.*" She nodded, ordering a glass of white wine, and the waiter went off smartly.

Vatran snapped his cell phone shut. "Hey, I don't want you getting drunk!" He turned to Jessica.

She rolled her eyes. "Give me a break, Kasim," she said. "Having a glass of wine and getting drunk is not the same thing. A glass of wine is good for you. All the doctors say that."

"Drinking is bad, period," he said. "It adds weight here"—he tapped two fingers against the underside of her chin—"and here"—he pinched her thigh roughly.

"Oww!" Jessica said. "Fucker!"

"And I told you not to swear!" He pinched her again and this time, she pinched him back, and they tussled more or less playfully for a long minute, pinching and tugging at each other until the waiter set down the drinks.

Smith watched this display of rough affection with a jaundiced eye. He mixed his raki slowly with water and the potent stuff turned milky in the glass and he drank off the top half, the sharp, anise-flavored liquor warming his throat on the way down. It was true, he and Jessica looked like brother and sister; they were both from Iowa, of similar Midwestern English-German stock, and perhaps their relationship had been, in some fundamental way, slightly incestuous. It was also true that Jessica and Vatran seemed the perfect complement: her big, blond Midwestern good looks; the Turk's Levantine complexity, olive skin, and sleek dark pelt of hair, his sideburns, architecturally perfect. These two will make exotic, beautiful offspring—a rueful thought that occurred to Smith like a stab in the heart.

Food arrived somehow, a dozen oblong plates, the usual meze—peppers stuffed with rice and meat; small, deep-fried sardines sprinkled with coarse salt; a selection of strong cheeses; spicy vegetable dips and *pide* bread; unknown pickled items in small white bowls; a variety of olives—more of the same kind of stuff Smith had eaten back at the house.

Vatran ate heartily, crunching the sardines whole between his teeth, bones and all, bent over his plate like a truck driver, elbows on the table. Jessica also ate well, but, as if she had taken Vatran's admonishment to heart, barely sipped her wine. Smith ate almost nothing, nibbling on a little bit of this or that, but ordered two more rakis for himself.

"Be careful, son." Jessica winked at him across the table. "You don't eat, you're going to get yourself drunk."

Vatran grunted at this. He didn't talk much; when he spoke, speaking in

Turkish and only to Jessica, he pointedly avoided meeting Smith's eyes. Smith didn't try to make conversation. He knew now why Vatran had insisted on meeting for dinner—the man wanted to humiliate him in front of Jessica, to let her know that this old boyfriend was nothing, a nuisance, to make clear that Smith's presence didn't matter one way or another.

At last the coffee arrived, along with a plate of Turkish sweets drenched in honey. Smith felt himself to be drunk suddenly; his ears burned, he saw little drunken squiggles out of the corners of his eyes. He drank his coffee and ate a sweet in a vague stab at sobriety.

Jessica stood up. "Got to go to the little girls' room," she said, and she wagged a finger at Vatran. "I don't want to come back and find you boys at each other's throats." She walked around the table and into the bright, humming interior.

An old woman in a voluminous skirt came up from the sidewalk a moment later peddling silver earrings off a piece of cardboard covered in black velvet.

"*Cok guzel kupe,*" she said in a singsong voice, pushing the board at Vatran.

"*Kakmak, fahisehise!*" Vatran snarled and knocked the woman's board to the ground; other diners looked over, startled, then looked away. The earring peddler gasped and let out a stream of invective, but Vatran ignored her and she gathered her spilled earrings and went away, cursing. Now, he leveled a hostile scrutiny at Smith; it was the first extended eye contact all evening. Smith, just drunk enough for a confrontation, stared back.

"Hey, Kasim"—he gave a little wave—"what's up?"

Vatran nodded to himself, muscles in his jaws tightening angrily. "So tell me, buddy," he said. "Why the fuck are you here?"

Smith flinched, taken aback by the naked hostility in the man's voice.

"Vacation," he said.

Vatran nodded. Then he lunged forward and jabbed a finger in Smith's face. This time, Smith didn't flinch, though the finger came a bare half inch from the end of his nose.

"We both know why you're here," Vatran hissed. "You're here to fuck Jessica! You think maybe you fuck her, she's going to come crawling back to New York with you. Is that it?"

"Not exactly," Smith said, and he scraped his chair back, away from the accusing finger, trying to keep calm. "I was in Paris, in the neighborhood, so to speak. Thought I'd drop down to Istanbul, see how you two were getting along."

"That right?" Vatran grinned mirthlessly. "Paris is two thousand kilometers from here—"

"Actually, it's a pretty easy deal," Smith interrupted. "You get on the Orient Express at the gare de l'Est, it's a nice ride, the food's great, and you catch up on your sleep. Wake up a couple of days later in Istanbul."

"You took the Orient Express," Vatran said like he didn't believe it.

"You bet," Smith said. "Man, what a great ride!"

Of course it was a lie. He'd flown into Paris because flights to Istanbul were prohibitively expensive just now and he got a deal to Paris; those rattletrap local trains through the Balkans were the cheapest way after that. He had exhausted his savings. He didn't have much money left; barely enough scratch to make it back home.

"The Orient Express costs something like five thousand U.S." Vatran waved a hand. "Jessica told me you were a bum, some broken-down hack actor without two fucking cents in his pocket. That you still live in the same piece of shit apartment in Brooklyn, that you don't—"

"Jessica says a lot of things that aren't exactly true," Smith interrupted again. "First of all, I'm a great singer. All the critics say so. And I'm a pretty damn good actor. I sing, I dance, I emote. Classic triple threat."

"—don't know when it's time to quit the acting bullshit and get a real job. Is that right, buddy?"

"Utter crap," Smith said, though it was all true. "I just did *Les Miz* off-Broadway." Then: "And I guess she didn't mention my trust fund."

"What?" Vatran seemed startled by this.

"Oh, yeah," Smith said, improvising freely. "At the moment it's just interest off a couple of million. That is, until 2010. Then I get the whole bundle, which amounts to a lot more."

Vatran sat back and crossed his arms. "Lies," he said. "Hack actor lies."

"I'm from Iowa," Smith said. "Know what they've got in Iowa? Timber. My great-grandfather, Carstairs Wellington Smith, cornered the timber market back in the 1880s. You should see my parents' place. They call it Smith Castle, a huge Victorian smack in the middle of town, right across from the courthouse. Got our own lake out back, stocked with carp . . ." He grinned. "And you gotta admit, carp's a pretty tasty fish."

This was getting good. Iowa was rolling prairie, practically treeless, except for the occasional windbreak and along the rivers, which were mostly full of trout, not carp, but how would a Turk know that? Smith's real great-grandfather, also named John, had been a dirt-poor farmer, mostly barley and rye, an original Iowa sodbuster; his grandfather, the same, though a little more successful, diversifying into soybeans, alfalfa, and corn. His father had broken the mold, finished high school, done two years at Iowa State in Ames and ended up as postmaster in Montezuma—which as everyone knows is the administrative hub of Poweshiek County—and there Smith and his sister were born and raised.

Smith's mother, after a quick night-school course in shorthand, worked for years part time and underpaid as secretary to the dean of the English department at Cornell College, an hour away up in Mt. Vernon, just so her kids would be able to get a college education, tuition-free. Life wasn't bad for a long time, through middle school. But immediately following Jane's death, Smith's father fell into a deep depression he couldn't come out of, was institutionalized for six months, and retired from the postal service on a meager disability pension. When he died, that pension got cut in half. There had been winters, brutal, 75 below, with the wind off the plains, when his mother could barely afford the price of heating oil, living in one room, the rest of the tiny, white three-bedroom clapboard house on Blue Bird Lane closed off with plastic sheeting.

"So, tell me, Kasim," Smith continued, "what other absolute crap has Jessica laid on you?"

But the Turk, still digesting Smith's jazzed-up Iowa pedigree, didn't seem to be listening. Gypsies, their filthy clothes sewn with coins, came through the crowd on the street, playing the santour, a kind of elaborate zither, and the *kemence*, a long-necked lute stroked with a bow like a violin. A Gypsy girl, no more than six or seven, strutted around snapping tiny cymbals between her thumb and forefingers. When Vatran looked back at Smith at last, his eyes were black, murderous.

"I want you to get the fuck out of here right now," he said in a low voice, and a black something in his tone made Smith feel afraid. "Get up and get out and don't you ever call her, don't you fucking ever come to Istanbul again! If you do, I'll fucking . . ."

He rose out of his seat, about to lunge at Smith, his thick fingers curling to choke the life out of him; Smith casting about for a weapon—a bottle, a plate a fork, anything—when Jessica's voice came from behind.

"Kasim! Stop it right now!"

Smith allowed himself a sigh of relief.

The Turk looked up, glowering, as Jessica stepped back around the table.

"I want this bastard *gone!*" he said, raising his voice. "He came here from Paris on the Orient Express just to fuck you!"

"Kasim, stop it!" Jessica said, horrified. "That's out of line! John and I have known each other for years. We went to grad school together, we starved in New York together. We're always going to be friends."

Vatran made a broad, denunciatory gesture, reminiscent of an actor in a silent melodrama. Then he seized her arm in a brutal grip. "You're coming home with me!"

But Jessica pulled away angrily. "Like hell I am!" she said between her teeth. "Not when you're acting like a real Turkish son of a bitch!"

Smith smiled to himself at this, remembering the similar scene, roles reversed, at that taverna in Cihangir. One thing about Jessica—she couldn't be coerced into doing anything she didn't want to do.

"*Yalanci orospu!*" Vatran shouted and a gasp went up from surrounding tables.

Smith knew the second word meant whore; the first he didn't know, but figured it was probably bad.

With a quick swipe, Vatran knocked the remaining meze plates to the pavement in a dramatic spray of white crockery shards and olive oil, and, still shouting in Turkish, stormed off. Two waiters ran after him shaking their fists, their blue-and-white comic opera caps askew, but he was already gone and they turned around and came back. The manager, an elaborately mustachioed fellow wearing the unlikely combination of business suit and white apron, emerged from the interior and began yelling at Smith.

"What's he saying?" Smith said.

"You don't want to know," Jessica said, turning to engage the furious little man. "*Yavas, yavas...*" she began, trying to calm him. And she managed to resolve the dispute after a few minutes haggling, using a combination of personal beauty, effusive apologies, and 375 Turkish lirasi—a little under 200 U.S. dollars.

"Sorry about all that," Jessica said as they were walking away.

"Don't you think you should go after Vatran?" Smith asked, though he didn't mean it.

Jessica considered this for a moment. "He needs to cool his jets for a while," she said. "That kind of juvenile-slash-macho-slash-asshole behavior is completely unacceptable."

"I don't get it," Smith said. "I thought the dinner was his idea."

"Well, sort of," she equivocated. "I mean you can't visit a Turk's woman without visiting the Turk, right?"

Smith realized suddenly that it hadn't been Vatran's idea at all. That it had been part of some obscure scheme of Jessica's—to make the man jealous; to relieve the boredom of living a settled life in Istanbul with an hour's worth of of psychodrama.

They came down Nevizade Sokuk onto the main thoroughfare and walked along past the European-style shops with scantily clad mannequins in the windows or sleek, white kitchen appliances. And suddenly, it was two years ago. They were in Istanbul again, on vacation, with the night ahead of them. Smith closed his eyes and imagined she was his once more.

"Well, ex-boyfriend," Jessica murmured at last. It seemed she had read his thoughts. "What do you want to do with me now?"

8.

Saturday night and all the bars and clubs this side of town were packed with Westerners—the usual mix of tourists and backpackers, leavened with the occasional secular Turk. Smith and Jessica went to several popular spots up and down Istiklal Caddesi: First to the Argentine-themed Bescini Peron, which was like a bar in Buenos Aires, with vino tinto by the carafe and framed photos of Argentine celebrities on the walls (Evita, Borges, Juan Manuel Fangio, Carlos Gardel). Then to the Cafe Salonika, a Greek place where divorced, middle-aged European women on package tours drank too much ouzo and danced on tables. Then Cicek Bar, a sleek modern lounge favored by Turkish media types, all steel and glass, grafted uncomfortably into the remains of a gutted Byzantine-era chapel. The antiseptic postmodern interior, Jessica pointed out proudly, had been designed by Vatran himself.

"What do you think?" she asked.

"Horrible," Smith said. "Awful."

"You're just jealous," she said.

"True," Smith said. "But it's still awful."

Jessica turned away, annoyed, and spent a half hour talking to an acquaintance, an Istanbul television personality, a balding, shifty-eyed man who did canned government-scripted political commentary on Istanbul Dokuz. Jessica didn't bother to introduce Smith, who sat by pouring more raki down his throat. When they exited Cicek after a while, Jessica left a barely touched glass of white wine on the counter. She'd done this at each stop so far, remaining—at least to Smith's increasingly drunken perspective—obstinately sober. He was beginning to slur his words, approaching that maudlin, sodden hour after which he'd remember nothing in the morning.

"I never did get why you left me, Jess," he said, trying to keep the obvious whine out of his voice. "What happened to us?"

"Let's not go there," Jessica said, taking a dainty sip of her new glass of wine.

They were at Buyuk Londra now, a dead-on imitation of an English pub: warm bitters on tap, rugby on the tele, tasteless pub grub (broiled chicken and creamed peas) wilting under heat lamps on a steam cart.

"Come on," Smith persisted. "I just want to know. For my own peace of mind."

Jessica sighed. "Haven't you been reading my e-mails for the last two years? I thought we went through all that."

"Oh, I read them," Smith said. "Then I printed them out and stapled them to my chest."

"One thing's clear"—she couldn't suppress a grin—"you're a fucking masochist." Then: "Seriously, Johnny, you've got to move on."

"I know that," Smith said. "But I still love you."

"You don't love me," Jessica said. "You love the idea of me."

"O.K.," Smith said. "What idea's that?"

"You know—healthy, big-titted, friendly blond slut. Like Anna Nicole Smith, only with some brains."

"You're thinking of Vatran," Smith said. "That's his idea."

"So you'd still love me if I were some skinny, ugly chick with no tits at all?"

"Actually, no."

"Fucker," Jessica said, but she laughed.

"So what about Vatran," Smith persisted. "Does he love you?"

"Honey." Jessica wagged her head. "He loves every piece of me." Then she looked away, and when she looked back, her eyes were serious. "I needed a huge change, Johnny. That's what happened to us. I couldn't take that bohemian bullshit anymore. Disgusting tiny apartments and no money, no health insurance. You on the road half the time. A gig here, a gig there, nothing steady. And me, waitressing. How I fucking hated waitressing. And you know what? You can't take it anymore either. Look at yourself—you look positively haunted. You need to call it quits, go to law school, join the Marines. Anything."

"I'm an actor-singer-dancer," Smith said grandly. "That's what I am. Triple threat!"

"An unsuccessful actor-singer-dancer," Jessica corrected.

"I've got a great voice. Perfect for musical comedy—the Cleveland *Plain Dealer* said so. Hell, I've done LORT A! One step, baby, one step below Broadway!"

"How long ago was that?" Jessica shot back.

"Tell you what"—Smith put an exploratory hand on the curve of her ass, which she shrugged away impatiently—"come back to New York with me and I'll go to law school. I'll join the Marines. I'll do anything you want."

"You're completely pathetic," she said, but she leaned over and kissed him on the cheek.

9.

They emerged arm in arm from Buyuk Londra into the cool air a little before midnight, pausing for a moment at the summit of one of the narrow streets that led out to the Bogazkesen Cadesi. Across the Bosphorus hazy with low-lying mist, along the Asiatic shore, the closed summer palaces of Uskudar sat crumbling and derelict.

"Everything's spinning," Smith said, leaning his head against a shuttered garage. Its metal door showed layers of spray-painted graffiti: Islamist slogans, the hammer and sickle of the PKK—the Kurdish Workers Party—and an odd symbol, so recently done Smith could still smell the sharp tang of the paint: An eye or a fish, crossed with three dark lines.

"Take some deep breaths," Jessica said. "If you've got to puke, puke. But I don't think I can carry you home."

"I'm fine," Smith said. "Just resting . . ." Then he spun around suddenly and put his arm around her waist and kissed her on the lips. She pushed him away, but didn't seem particularly annoyed, so he tried it again a moment later. This time, she kissed him back and he felt her tongue gently in his mouth and the erection stiffening in his pants before she pushed him away again.

"Whoa! *Tamam, tamam!*" she said. "Blast from the past. If Kasim saw us now"—she shivered with genuine fear—"he'd kill us both."

"Fuck Kasim," Smith said.

"Oh, I do." Jessica grunted. "He wants it all the time, like three or four times a day. He's a fuck machine. Comes home from work sometimes in the middle of the day just to fuck me. And let me tell you something, his cock"—she made a fist—"fat as a baby's arm holding a sausage."

"Oh, shit." Smith grimaced. "Did I need to hear that?"

"You asked for it," Jessica said.

Smith deflated, sagging against the metal garage door. He felt tears of self-pity welling up from the weak place in his soul, soft as rotten wood, and didn't bother to stop them coming. His mission to Istanbul had been a failure; his dreams of Jessica, delicate as castles carved out of ice, were melting away as he stood there in the dark. Kasim was rich and exotic and he had a cock like an elephant. What could he do against such a man?

"Look, I better be getting back to the hotel," he managed. "Thanks for dinner . . ."

"Don't be such a kid." Jessica made a face. "It's only midnight. Kasim's already pissed as shit. Might as well stay out 'til dawn."

"No thanks," Smith said mournfully. "I'm tired. Just tell me where I can get a cab—"

"One more place," Jessica insisted. "I'm more or less off the booze lately, for various reasons that I won't discuss, but booze isn't the only game in town."

At that moment, as if on cue, a taxi pulled up at the curb. It was an old, rakish Citroën DS, its sleek shark nose much dented and deformed from encounters with crazy Istanbul traffic. Jessica pushed Smith into the back and slid after him across the patched leather seat. She directed the driver to Kurtulus, a dangerous, impoverished neighborhood beyond the Tarlabasi Bulvari—she wasn't sure of the exact address, she said, but would know it when they got there. Smith opened his mouth to protest, but didn't, and let himself be driven along through the steep, narrow streets to an address on the wrong side of town.

10.

Curtained booths lined the walls of the vaulted underground chamber, so full of fragrant smoke and so dimly lit, Smith could barely see Jessica's face. They waited a while in the dark, narrow antechamber, where Jessica pushed him against the wall and kissed him openmouthed, this time without being prompted.

Finally the attendant, wearing an illegal fez and striped pantaloons like an old-fashioned harem master, led them to a booth in the corner that had just been vacated. He prepared the narghile—an ornate Turkish water pipe—changing the water and replacing the ivory mouthpiece. Jessica handed over a neatly rolled wad of lirasi; the attendant secreted this money somewhere in the folds of his pantaloons, padded off into the dim recesses of the place, and returned a few minutes later with a black, pasty mixture in a small rosewood box. He kneaded the stuff into a little black ball, pressed the ball into the bowl of the narghile, and lit it with a long fireplace match. Then he withdrew, closing the curtains discreetly behind him as he went.

The only light here was given off by a small, red-shaded oil lamp, Jessica reduced to a voluptuous shade, pressed back against the high-backed divan. An unmistakable moaning emanated from the booth next door.

"You want to go first?" Jessica said, holding out the mouthpiece.

"I don't know," Smith said doubtfully. "What is that stuff?"

"Specialty of the house," Jessica said. "Dried rose petals, opium, a chunk of myrrh, and a small black pearl, crushed. The Ottoman sultans smoked it all day, then fucked their harem women all night long. Gets you high and makes you superhorny"—she leered—"it's the big reason they lost their empire and everything went to hell."

She took the first hit, taking the ivory mouthpiece between her teeth and drawing in. Smith leaned close and watched her face go slack with pleasure, eyes fluttering as she exhaled a narrow stream of gray smoke.

"Nice," she murmured. "Very, very nice."

Smith picked up the mouthpiece from where she let it fall and took a hit. The smoke was cool and flavorful, like roasted apples, like roses, like cinnamon with a pinch of something terribly bitter, an assassin creeping up behind. He felt things go loose around the edges, felt himself shedding some of the sorrow he'd been carrying around like a tight, black tumor in his heart. It floated up with the smoke and was gone; a definite prickling in his loins accompanied this lightness.

"Wow," he said, when he could speak. "If you could smoke a quaalude, that . . ." He couldn't finish the thought. A second thought flapped around the inside of his head on powdery blue moth wings and flew away.

"Lie here with me, baby," Jessica said lazily, easing herself back on the divan.

Smith lay down beside her, his head on her shoulder.

"Put your hand on my tits," she breathed.

He did so at once, gently kneading one, then the other. They felt solid, heavier than he remembered. Then he trailed down and pressed his hand firmly between her legs. He felt the dampness there as she angled up to meet him.

"Oh . . . ," she breathed, excited. "This . . . this is just what Kasim was afraid of . . . oh!"

After a while, she took his face and held it between her hands, her blue eyes dark and glassy in the dim light of the oil lamp.

"You can't fuck me," she whispered. "Absolutely not. Swear you won't try and fuck me."

"Why not?" Smith said.

"You just can't," Jessica repeated. "Swear!"

"All right," Smith said. "I swear."

"Kasim would know if you fucked me. He'd smell you on me. I could take a shower, I could take two showers, it wouldn't matter. He's got a nose like, umm—" She paused, thinking hard, but just couldn't say what kind of nose he had. "But listen, he won't . . . I mean he refuses to . . ." She hesitated. "He won't go down on me."

"What? That's crazy!"

"Yeah, he says men don't do that in Turkey, some macho bullshit. So would you . . . I mean, you know how I like, umm . . . would you please . . . I mean that's not fucking, right?"

"Only fucking is fucking," Smith said. "Look at Clinton."

"Just swear you won't fuck me. O.K.?"

"O.K., O.K.," Smith said.

"You swear?"

"Jesus! Do you want me to go down on you or not?"

Jessica smiled and arranged herself across the cushions and Smith knelt between her legs and peeled her out of the beige pants embroidered all over with paisleys and a pair of matching paisley panties underneath. She had stopped shaving down there—the way Kasim liked it, she said—and as Smith lowered himself to his task, he began working surreptitiously on the buckle of his belt. A few minutes later, he pulled up and slid out of his jeans and boxers and was inside of her in a single efficient motion. She thrashed against him, pounded her fists on his back.

"No!" she said. "Stop! Now! Get off me!" But not loud enough for anyone beyond the booth to hear her. "No! You swore! Bastard! I told you, no! I . . . ah! Ah!"

A long, violent spasm overtook her; arms flailing, she nearly knocked the narghile off its stand. Smith followed a moment later, releasing two years' worth of pent-up frustration, longing, mental anguish, sleepless nights, the dark and bitter juice of his broken heart, deep into her body.

11.

Afterward in the same battered Citroën on the way back to Beyoglu, Smith watched the faltering lights of Terebasi pass out the scratched window, feeling drained but very pleased with himself. He had come all the way from New York just to fuck her and now he'd done it, the first personal goal he'd met successfully in several years. But Jessica sat trembling with anger, pressed away from him against the far door. Tears had blurred the mascara down her cheeks into a grotesque kind of Rorschach test—showing, perhaps, a cobra eating a mouse. Smith reached for her hand but found it clenched into a tight fist. She jerked away at his touch, then brought the fist up suddenly and coldcocked him, a powerful blow to the left side of his jaw. Smith actually saw stars—

"*Oww!*" he exclaimed, and the force of the punch knocked his head against the window. "What did you do that for?" Though he knew. He looked up, rubbing his jaw, and saw the driver watching them in the rearview.

"Rapist!" Jessica hissed. "You raped me!"

"Hey, come on, Jess!" Smith cajoled. "You can't exactly call that rape."

"Bullshit! You're a rapist! I told you not to fuck me! You swore you wouldn't, but you fucked me anyway. I told you not to! That's rape!"

"Probably not in Turkey," Smith said. "Given the circumstances."

"You *bastard*!" she shouted. And she hit him hard on the side of the head and would have caught him on the jaw again had he not grabbed her wrists. They sat there like that for a long minute, tense, panting, then Smith let her go and she fell back into her corner and began to sob.

"Jessica, please," Smith said. "I love you . . ." His voice trailed off. But it wasn't exactly true—he knew that now. In the last hour his love had clearly revealed itself to be a kind of passionate narcissism—part sexual obsession, part illusion, part pride, part anger, part revenge. And now he was spent and empty and there was nothing left but the ashes and a puff or two of pale smoke drifting away, smoke that held the fragrance of rose petals, myrrh, opium, and a crushed black pearl nestled in a black shell dredged up from the depths of the Black Sea.

12.

The taxi stopped on Istiklal Caddesi, idling loudly at the bottom of Vatran's street and the steps that led up to his house. From here, Smith could just make out the aquarium glow of the third-floor window, and a menacing figure pacing back and forth inside.

"Please, Jess." Smith reached for her hand again. "Come back to New York with me. . . ." Even though the offer was no longer quite sincere.

"I'd rather go to hell."

"I really worry about you over here," Smith persisted, trying his best to sound concerned. "You don't love Vatran. That'll end too. If you won't come back with me, at least come back to the States. Don't waste too many years among strangers."

"You don't get it," Jessica hissed. "I'm pregnant."

"But . . ." How could it happen so quickly? he thought stupidly. And how could she be so sure?

"With Kasim's baby, you fucking idiot," she spat, reading his thoughts.

"Oh, shit!"

"Yeah. Shit."

"That's why Vatran didn't want you to drink."

She shook her head. "He doesn't know yet."

"Wait a minute—you're pregnant and smoking opium?"

"I checked with a doctor, a little opium's O.K. at this stage. Hell, the doctors here prescribe an opium derivative to ease morning sickness."

"Come on! That's fucked-up! You're—"

Smith stopped himself suddenly. He felt his stomach churn, a sour taste in his mouth that wasn't the aftertaste of opium at all but something else, some oestral hormone, and he suddenly called to mind the pleasant but unusual heaviness of her breasts and the rounded contours of her belly and felt sick to his stomach. He had just had sex with a woman pregnant with someone else's baby! There was a gut-wrenching, existential horror in the thought.

Jessica burst into tears again and jumped out of the car and slammed the door closed.

"Rapist!" she shouted. "Self-absorbed asshole!"

She ran up the street, stumbling once, but catching herself, painfully, palms-out against the top step. Then, the front door of Vatran's house sprung open soundlessly as if activated by an electronic eye and she disappeared inside and Smith sat there and watched her go. Now the taxi driver turned to him. He had a long, narrow face; a thick scar showed white against the dark skin of his forehead.

"We drive now, sir," he said in English. "Many peoples here know this house. The man who live there"—he shook his head—"very violent man."

At that moment a burly silhouette appeared in the doorway, a dark something clutched in his right hand. Vatran's servant, Smith guessed. He didn't want to stick around long enough to figure out what the man was holding.

"Stamboul Palace Hotel," Smith said anxiously. "Go!"

The taxi driver lurched into gear and the car bounced over the tram tracks and down Istiklal Caddesi. A second later came a small burst of flame and sharp cracking sound instantly followed by the rattle of a bullet hitting the cobbled street a foot shy of the rear tire of the accelerating Citroën.

4

THE UGLY AMERICAN

COWBOY

1.

Grainy afternoon light slanted through the steel shutters into Smith's room at the Stamboul Palace. He lay fully clothed except for his shoes and socks beneath the bedspread, farting in his sleep. The phone was ringing and had been ringing for some time, for hours maybe. He sat upright, head pounding, stomach raw, and all at once threw himself out of bed to puke in the bathroom sink. The phone was still ringing when he came out wiping his mouth on a towel and now he picked it up:

"Yeah?" he said hoarsely.

"She's dead," the voice said. "I thought you might want to know."

"Who is this?" Smith said, though he knew.

"Come down, if you want to hear the rest of the story."

"Wait a minute—" Smith began, but the voice was gone. He stood there for a long time, the empty humming sound of the line in his ear. It couldn't be true; some kind of stupid joke. But against his better instincts, he pulled on a clean T-shirt, slipped his feet sockless into his cowboy boots, and went downstairs on the creaky wrought-iron elevator that had once been graced by the evanescent beauty of Garbo herself.

The lobby was thronged with people in their Sunday best—brunch at the Stamboul Palace had been a tradition with consular staff since the 1920s—and Smith pushed through the crowd of nicely dressed Europeans waiting their turn at the buffet tables in the restaurant, and went into the dimly lit bar, long and narrow and mostly empty. An old man just inside the door handed him a dingy checked sports jacket—required in the bar on Sundays—and Smith shrugged it over his shoulders and advanced down the line of high-backed banquettes set at right angles to the wall, his eyes adjusting to the gloom. Muted afternoon sunlight filtered through the stained-glass window at the far end: This ochre and red rosette showed a streamlined locomotive going at full speed. Stylized minarets hovering oddly to one side made it impossible to know whether the train was leaving or approaching Istanbul. Pieces of colored glass set into the border reflected an abstract halo on the worn carpet.

"Over here . . ."

Smith turned to confront Kasim Vatran sitting in the recesses of the farthest banquette from the door. They stared at each other for a moment. Vatran seemed perfectly composed, calm. He wore an elegant dark blue suit, neatly buttoned, a rose-colored dress shirt and a glossy pink silk tie. A pink rosebud decorated his buttonhole. He might be on his way to a wedding or a formal reception for someone in the government.

"I don't think that jacket goes with your T-shirt," Vatran said in an affable tone.

"What did you mean by what you said over the phone? What the—"

"First, a drink," Vatran interrupted.

"No, thanks," Smith said. "A little early for me."

"If you don't mind"—Vatran made a quick gesture and the waiter brought over a bottle of very expensive whisky—Loch Lomond Single Malt, fifteen years—and set it down with two glasses.

"I thought you didn't drink," Smith said.

"Special day today," Vatran said. "I think I can be permitted a glass. Sit, please . . ."

Smith sat reluctantly. "O.K., what's the gag?" he said.

Vatran poured himself a healthy three fingers of scotch from the bottle and drained it off. Then he pinched the lobe of his ear with his right hand and whistled softly through his teeth—an old Turkish gesture that was supposed to ward off the machinations of the devil.

"Jessica told me everything," he said, his voice curiously flat. "She was very upset, you understand, even hysterical. She told me what you did to her—"

"Hold on a minute," Smith said, bristling. "Don't go flinging around the word *rape* because that's not what—"

"Please!" Vatran held up his hand, a gesture that held such authority Smith shut up. "I am not talking about rape," he continued. "She used that word, but it is not possible to rape a woman in such a position. She had already disgraced herself, utterly. Under the circumstances you did the right thing."

Smith stared at the man, aghast. Then, he noticed something odd—a slight twitch that seemed to ripple from the left eye, down the side of Vatran's cheek—then he saw the thin stream of red coming from between the fingers of the left hand, so tightly clenched the nails were digging into the palm, drawing blood. Smith gasped and began to be afraid.

"What the fuck?" he said. "What did you do to her?"

Vatran looked away, casting his eye toward the racing locomotive in the stained glass, which from his perspective, was definitely leaving Istanbul behind.

"I am a coward," he said. "I couldn't do it myself. So I called Ahmet and he did it. He is very strong, you know, a former wresting champion. He put his hands around her throat like this"—he demonstrated by taking up one of the white cloth napkins and twisting, blood from the gouges in his palm staining the fabric—"I think her neck snapped—there was a sound. In any case, it was over very quickly. She didn't suffer much."

Smith gaped. He couldn't get his head around this bizarre confession. He couldn't imagine the vibrant, voluptuous Jessica dead; his heart hurt with the thought. More, that he might have been the cause of it, however indirectly, filled him with new and painful sensations—shame, remorse. Then he rejected the possibility altogether. Of course it wasn't true. Not true. No.

"Come on, Vatran," Smith said. "Give me a break. You're kidding, right?"

But the Turk's black eyes were hard as stones. He reached into the pocket of his suit jacket and took out a small revolver and brought it level with Smith's heart. Smith recognized the weapon from the guns and ammo magazines he sometimes perused at the CVS at Astor Place in Manhattan—a five-shot .36 caliber Taurus hideaway. It was usually loaded with hollow points to compensate for low muzzle velocity and would make a loud noise and a big hole, absolutely lethal at this distance.

"W-wait a minute," Smith said, trying to sound reasonable and failing. "What's going to happen if you shoot me here, in public?"

"That doesn't matter to me," Vatran said, still calm. "You have insulted my personal honor and the honor of my family, and this insult must be avenged. I loved her. You tore her from me—"

"Hey!" Smith interrupted. "You tore her from me first, remember?"

"Jessica has already paid with her life," Vatran continued, ignoring him. "Now you will pay." And he pulled back the hammer, which made a precise racheting sound.

"Don't do it," Smith said desperately. "They've got the death penalty here. This is Turkey, remember?"

"Yes, this is Turkey," Vatran said, smiling faintly. "Honor is important in Turkey as it is important in every civilized country in the world, as it is no longer important in America, which is therefore no longer civilized. Let us suppose I am somehow convicted of premeditated murder for killing Jessica and for killing you, which is unlikely, given the current temperament of Turkish justice. You see, the private honor of a Turk is worth more than the lives of two corrupt foreigners. *Tamam*, perhaps I am convicted. So I will be given six months, a year, no more for killing a Christian whore and her American lover."

"Wait, wait if you just . . ." Smith couldn't bring forth the words he needed to keep this fanatic from pulling the trigger. Then a single thought occurred to him: "You killed Jessica," he said, bringing twenty years of acting experience to steady his voice. "You're going to kill me. O.K., maybe we were both a little guilty and who the fuck cares, right? But you also killed someone else. Someone entirely innocent, you know that, right?"

Vatran raised an eyebrow. "Keep talking if you want," he said, grinning ferociously. "I'll give you ten seconds. . . ."

"I'm talking about your *baby*!" Smith shouted this last word. "Jessica was pregnant! You didn't know that, did you, stupid asshole? She was pregnant with your *son*!"

Smith had no way of knowing the gender of the opium-addled fetus— but this speculation was just the right touch. Vatran blinked crazily for a beat, digesting this information, just long enough for Smith to throw himself backward, and the banquette went crashing over to splinter on the tile floor. Smith rolled away from the wreckage, just as Vatran began firing. He felt the warm breath of a bullet pass a fraction of a millimeter from his left cheek and pushed himself up and vaulted over the zinc-topped counter to scramble on his hands and knees along the rubber matting just behind the bar. A third shot splashed into the bottles set in even rows on the barback and shattered the huge gilt mirror brought from France in 1911, then another, closer, and Smith felt himself sprayed with liquor—rum, he thought from the smell—and splinters of glass. The alarmed shouting of men and the screeching of women now came from the lobby. Smith reached the far end of the bar, there was no place farther to go, nothing but wall ahead. Oh, God, he found himself praying—probably for the first time since his sister's death back in Iowa—Please, God, help me! Melt this wall! But the wall didn't melt and his feeble prayer came out as no more than a spiritual squeak, a transparent bubble that dissolved in terrestrial air before reaching heaven.

Another shot hissed just over his left shoulder and drilled into the oak paneling, and a sharp splinter, like a tiny arrow, gouged his cheek. Now Smith twisted around desperately to see Vatran standing behind the bar not three feet away, gun at his side, muzzle smoking. If there was something else Smith could do to save his own life, he couldn't think what it might be. As the Turk raised the gun for the last time, Smith closed his eyes.

2.

Inspektor Biryak of the Istanbul Metropolitan Police sat at his desk in his large pleasant office in the Galatasaray district on Mesrutiyet Caddesi beneath an unusual framed photograph of Atatürk: Instead of the usual head-and-shoulders stern-faced, uniformed, bemedalled Father of the Turkish Nation, this one showed a vacationing Atatürk, beer in hand, in shirtsleeves and sunglasses on a patio at somebody's villa overlooking the Adriatic, white sailboats luffing pleasantly in the background.

"I tell my superiors Atatürk did not drink this beer." Inspektor Biryak chuckled. "That it was not his beer at all, that he was just holding it for the photographer. Atatürk, you understand, is more than a human being to us in Turkey, he is like a perfect saint. But to you, I tell the complete truth. According to my great-grandmother, who was a German—this is her drinks party you see in the photo—the man who was not yet Atatürk, who was still only plain Mustafa Kemal, drank down this beer with gusto and also drank two or three more and then fell asleep with his mouth open in a comfortable garden chair in the sun. Like many ordinary Turks"—he chuckled—

"our Great Turk could not hold his liquor. Like perhaps"—he took a cigarette from a silver case and lit up—"this unfortunate Kasim Vatran."

"I don't know about that," Smith said. Somehow he couldn't keep his teeth from chattering, though it wasn't cold in the room.

"There was"—Inspektor Biryak consulted his notes—"a bottle of whisky on the table, yes?"

"That's right," Smith said. "But the man wasn't drunk during . . ." His voice trailed off. He could still hear the sound of the gunshots ringing in his ears and the screaming as he scrambled along beneath the bar.

"Excuse my rudeness"—Inspektor Biryak held out the cigarette case—"would you like one?" He was a large, broad-shouldered man, the bottom half of his face occupied with the shaggy mustache usually associated with Turkish policemen.

Smith didn't smoke, but took a cigarette just to have something to do with his hands. The inspektor offered a match. Smith managed to light up on the third try, the inspektor shaking out the two previous matches in the moment before they singed his glossy, manicured fingernails.

"Third try unlucky," Inspektor Biryak said, frowning, and he tugged his right ear with his left hand as Smith had seen Vatran do in the bar at the Stamboul Palace. Trembling, Smith fumbled the cigarette to the floor after just a few puffs. It rolled beneath the inspektor's desk, where the man crushed it with the heel of his boot.

"You are indeed rather nervous, Mr. Smith," he commented dryly.

"Y-yes," Smith stuttered. "I am nervous. The bastard almost killed me."

"Of course, I understand." Inspektor Biryak nodded. "Now please describe the unfortunate incident to me exactly as it happened. I've read the police report, but such statements can be misleading." He smiled, showing large, square, cigarette-stained teeth.

Smith took a deep breath and tried to reconstruct the sequence of events out of the painful blur of sound and image in his head—what Vatran said, what he said in response, etc. He managed to keep his voice steady until the end, when he choked with emotion and dropped his face to his hands.

"Take a moment to compose yourself." The inspektor clucked sympathetically. "Being shot at can be an exhilarating experience as long as one is not hit, of course. Try to look at it that way."

Smith wiped his eyes on the back of his hand, feeling ashamed. "There he was—" he began, gulping.

"Please be specific," Inspektor Biryak interrupted.

"I mean Vatran, just standing there with his gun. We were behind the bar at this point, he had one, maybe two shots left. There was nothing I could do. I'd already gone pretty far, it looked like the end of the line for me. Then he . . ." Another emotional pause.

"Go on," the inspektor prompted.

"He raised the gun and I figured O.K., good-bye world, and I closed my eyes. I heard the shot, the loudest thing I've ever heard in my life, and my heart jumped, but I didn't feel anything. So I thought O.K., I'm dead, maybe I'm already dead, then Vatran fell right on top of me. And there was a lot of blood."

Smith stood to show his bloodstained jeans, his blood-spattered T-shirt, and the ugly checkered jacket from the Stamboul Palace, also spattered with blood. All this was so far beyond the realm of his experience as to be scenes from the life of another man. He took a deep breath, cleared his throat. "Vatran shot himself through the heart. Right here"—he thumped his chest—"made a hole all the way through. So big you could put your hand in the back."

"Suicide," Inspektor Biryak murmured, and jotted something on the blue pad at his elbow.

"Yes."

"What I am after now, as a policeman, you understand"—he hesitated—"is at once simple, yet complicated: Why did he do it?"

Smith looked up at the man, baffled. "Well, he just killed"—Jessica, he tried to say, but found he couldn't speak her name out loud—"his, my ex-girlfriend. You know that, right?"

"I don't mind telling you we have a confession in this particular case," Inspektor Biryak admitted. "Another man, one Ahmet Kuluk, has admitted to the crime."

"Yes," Smith said. "He was Vatran's servant. Vatran told him to strangle her."

The inspektor made a stern gesture that seemed to brush this comment aside.

"You see, suicide is illegal in Turkey, Mr. Smith," he continued. "As it is in France or England or any other modern country. Here it is deemed extremely un-Turkish. Thus, if you have contributed in any way to this act of suicide, you might be yourself guilty of a crime. I shall have to investigate thoroughly, to ascertain where the blame lies. In the meanwhile"—he consulted a small, sinister-looking book, bound in black morocco and very thick—"I shall have to charge you with . . . yes . . . suspicion of encouraging suicide. And also with, with . . . ah, behavior designed to undermine the Turkish national character. That should do nicely for now."

Smith stared at the policeman, aghast. "But the dude tried to kill me! Ask anyone. He almost got me twice. He came that close . . ."

"So you insist." Inspektor Biryak nodded. "We shall discover the truthfulness of these facts presently. But for now, I must ask you to surrender your passport."

Smith reached into his pocket, withdrew the precious, battered blue document stamped with the American eagle, and handed it to the inspektor, who tossed it atop a random pile of papers on his desk.

3.

A police sergeant secured Smith's wrists and ankles with primitive-looking manacles and drew him along, hobbling, out of Inspektor Biryak's office. He was led to a spiral staircase that he descended with great difficulty and was taken to an interrogation cell, and there stripped of his clothes and his father's old Rolex and his cowboy boots and subjected to a thorough cavity search—an indignity to which he submitted with as much dignity as possible. Then he was issued a clean striped cotton shirt like a pajama top and striped cotton pants and a pair of Chinese-made rubber-toed sneakers without laces, and he shoved himself into these clothes and was manacled again and put in a gorilla-sized mesh cage set in the middle of an echoing, high-ceilinged room. He waited there, trembling, for what would happen next.

An hour later, a clamorous gaggle of media types entered through a side door—newspaper reporters, photographers, TV news cameramen—and pushed up to the wire mesh of Smith's cage. Flashes snapped in his face, these bright explosions recalling for a terrible moment the flare of gunfire; questions were shouted in Turkish and English.

"Are you a murderer, Mr. Smith?"

"Do you work for the American CIA?"

"*Namussuz insafsiz garbli!*"

"Do you revile the Prophet Muhammad, peace be upon him?"

"I didn't do anything," Smith shouted above the din. "The guy tried to kill me!"

One of the newspaper reporters, a fox-faced young man, his hair cropped short, his eyebrows arched up sharply like the eyebrows of a pantomime devil, rattled the wire mesh of Smith's cage in an aggressive manner.

"Isn't it true that you violated Kasim Vatran's wife?" the fox-faced reporter shouted.

Smith looked down at him, alarmed. "*No!*" he shouted back. "And she wasn't his wife! She used to be my girlfriend!"

"Did you not lure this woman to the notorious Klub Uyutucu Bahce, an illegal place of opium consumption, and there sexually violate her behind curtains under the influence of said illegal substance? Did you not in fact rape the poor woman?"

"*No!*" Smith shouted helplessly. "That's not how it happened!"

"And isn't it true that Kasim Vatran attempted to exact revenge for this terrible crime against his honor when he tried to kill you with a gun at the Hotel Stamboul Palace?"

Smith stared at the man, speechless. How did he get this information, by and large—he had to admit—completely accurate?

"I have spoken to the taxi driver personally who drove you to Terebasi." The fox-faced reporter grimaced. "I have also spoken to . . ."

But Smith drew away from the mesh, feeling dizzy, and the reporter's words were drowned out in the general cacophony of prejudice and recrimination.

After a while, the police sergeant returned, unlocked the cage, and hustled the overwhelmed Smith out through the media gauntlet and into a long, windowless concrete corridor. Smith glanced back and saw the pack of journalists climbing over one another to get to the table where the cops had tossed his clothes and battered cowboy boots, camera flashes snapping; then the door slammed shut behind him and he was taken down the windowless concrete corridor to an equally windowless concrete cell lit bright as day with powerful fluorescents protected from the wrath of the incarcerated by a steel box.

The cell, scrupulously clean, was bare except for a concrete slab for sleeping and a five-gallon plastic bucket for slops. The sergeant closed the cell door gently and shot the bolts home on the outside with a heavy clanking sound and Smith was alone. He slumped down on the concrete slab, bewildered, bathed in hard green light, the faint shadow of superheated gas snapping back and forth in the long glass tubes overhead. He stared up at the fluorescent tubes for a long while, his mind blank. Then he curled up in a fetal position and closed his eyes and the glowing tubes made bright stripes like luminous bars against the inside of his lids, dimming gradually to a pale green darkness as he fell asleep.

4.

The newspaper kiosks in Sultanahmet and around Taksim Square the next morning were full of pictures of Smith's battered old cowboy boots taken from various, sinister angles. It was a case of journalistic synecdochism. Smith's used Noconas (handmade in Texas, black on red, white stitchery, originally $375, but found—a coup!—at Domsey's in Williamsburg for $19) standing in for Smith himself: the Ugly American Cowboy. He in turn standing in for aggressive Bushite foreign policy in the Middle East, for Western decadence, for what was going on in Iraq, Afghanistan, for everything.

Every major paper carried a shot of the boots beneath an alarmist, anti-American headline: AMERICAN COWBOY SHOOTING AT STAMBOUL PALACE said prosaic *Hurriyet*; COWBOY LOVE MURDERS SULLY TURKISH HOMELAND said patriotic *Akit*; LECHEROUS AMERICAN COWBOY CAUSES DEATH OF BRILLIANT TURKISH ARCHITECT, this from the arsty-fartsy *Gir-Gir*. COWBOY KILLER A JEW? asked the anti-Semitic *Zir*. Beneath these headlines, each paper contained detailed and mostly fictitious accounts of the violent episode at the Stamboul Palace, where, apparently, Smith was heard calumnizing the prophet at the top of his lungs, screaming "Down with Muhammad!" and "Death to all Turks!" and "Up with Israel!" in the moments before gunfire erupted. The evening editions ran a reproduction of Smith's passport photo, illegally obtained from police files and digitally enhanced to add a touch of vicious Neanderthal to an already awful mug shot.

Ironically, the most accurate account of events appeared in the radical Islamist and anti-Western *Hakikat*, although the conclusions reached by their editorial writers (that Turkish men should beware of corrupt, sex-crazed Western women; that such women generally deserved to be strangled and raped for exposing their hair and other odds and ends in public; that Smith himself deserved to be flogged and castrated, then flayed alive), were deemed unpalatable by the other major dailies and part of a plot to delay Turkey's entry into the European Union. The government-sponsored *Cumhurriyet* even went so far as to accuse *Hakikat* of being secretly funded by the Israelis for this purpose.

Such is the subtlety of the Eastern mind: shadow puppets projecting not their own shadow, but the shadow of their shadow; betrayal leading immediately to antibetrayal, leading back to more of the same like a chameleon chasing its tail while compulsively changing colors; every motive haunted by another motive that was the exact opposite of the first, as if by an evil twin.

5.

Meanwhile, Smith malingered in solitary confinement in the brightly lit cell in the basement of the Galatasary police station. The fluorescent lights were never turned off and no one spoke a word to him; but he was well fed with platters of meze catered out of the rather good local *mehayne* frequented by members of the Galatasary District constabulary, and he was not molested in any way or subjected to any *Midnight Express*–style abuse. Twice a day, police cadets wearing sanitary masks and surgical gloves entered to remove the plastic bucket of slops. They never spoke and were even forbidden to look in Smith's direction.

Despite the brightness and constant buzzing of the fluorescent lights, Smith slept or napped lightly like a cat most of the time, dreaming vivid, half-awake erotic dreams: Jessica's body moving beneath his own in the shuttered light of their cramped bedroom back in Brooklyn; Jessica on the beach on vacation at Frisco on the Outer Banks of North Carolina three years ago in the excellent pink bikini that made her look naked; Jessica on the catwalk at the Yvan Guest show in Milan way back in her modeling days.

But after a while, these troubling images faded. In their place came comforting backyard dreams of his lost Iowa family, of Wiffle Ball played in the scrubby grass behind the old house on Blue Bird Lane in Montezuma. He saw his father, still in post office blue, fresh from work, waggling the plastic bat over a crushed cardboard box home base in a comical manner; his mother wearing a frilly apron, cooking up brats on the barbecue grill. And there was his sister, Jane, premeningitis, her hair a mess, falling out of trees or eagerly tearing the limbs off her Barbies in the pile of leaves by the utility shed. All of them dead and gone. And Jessica dead too, and himself to blame.

During waking hours, Smith paced the cell, exactly twenty by sixteen, did push-ups and sit-ups, sang show tunes loudly to himself—"I get no kick from champagne, mere alcohol doesn't thrill me at all. . . . But I get a kick out of you"—waited for the food to arrive (the main event of his day) and went slightly crazy, wavering between opposed magnetic poles—self-loathing and self-pity—constantly attracting each other and constantly repulsed. No one now alive loved him. This melancholy realization brought tears to his eyes. But the sound of his own sobs bouncing off the bare concrete block walls of the cell only made him more and more disgusted with himself. Thus, Smith wavered, a helpless particle caught in the emotional force field of a more or less unexamined inner life. Then the force field collapsed all at once and he was left with an accurate snapshot of his character for the first time in many years: He was indeed criminally self-absorbed, as Jessica had charged. Perhaps he had raped her, after all. He had certainly come thousands of miles to fuck her—mistaking, to quote the old Go-Go's song, lust for love. And fucking her, he had contributed to her death. Guilty, then. He had not loved Jessica enough for herself, but mostly for her body, for her physical beauty that, as a reflection of his own, probably represented a deep-seated masturbatory impulse that was too horrible to contemplate. Now he was filled with shame and regret over Jessica's fate, and in this bitter mood, came as close to truly loving her as he ever had in life. The poor woman, strangled by a vicious Turk! For a long time, maybe fifteen or twenty minutes, Smith, oppressed by guilt, could barely breathe. He didn't spare himself or his own personal plight a single tear. He thought only of Jessica, how she was gone from the world, which had become in her absence a less beautiful place.

Actors are often vain—one of the hazards of the profession—or at least more so than the average tax attorney. Smith wasn't a very good actor, a truth he was prepared to acknowledge now for the first time. But he did possess an excellent, flexible tenor voice, perfect for the musical theater, probably one of the best in the States. Unfortunately, he lacked the ambition, the sheer obstinacy to push his talents through the crowd of mediocre, driven people who assault the top positions in any creative field. He had allowed his good looks—his regular Midwestern features and excellent hair—to substitute for artistic conviction.

Self-examination is a torment. Despite the philosopher's exhortations to explore all inner nooks and crannies, there exist dark corners of the soul better left to obscurity. The final thought regarding these painful matters, which occurred to Smith somewhere around day three of his captivity (impossible to mark an exact passage of time with no daylight and no Rolex) was also one of the hardest for him to bear: The acting-singing thing, as Jessica had said, was over. If he ever got out of this Turkish jail, he would need to find something else to do with the rest of his life.

6.

When the police sergeant came to take Smith from his cell, he refused to go. He wanted to stay buried there, suspended like an embryo between his old life and whatever unpleasantness lay ahead.

"Immediate! You, please," the sergeant said in broken English. "Must go Inspektor Biryak."

But Smith shook his head and crawled beneath the cement slab he'd been sleeping on for a week and wrapped himself firmly around the metal supports. Swearing, the sergeant went off and returned with two burly cadets—both former wrestling champs in the All Istanbul League—and these young men wrenched Smith from his hole and, seizing his arms and legs, carried him, sagging between them like the corpse of a drowned man pulled from the Bosphorus, up the stairs to the inspektor's office. They entered respectfully, bowing their heads—it was the first time they had been in the office of such an exalted personage—lay Smith gently on the floor faceup, and exited, still bowing.

Inspektor Biryak came around his cluttered desk, hands in the pockets of his uniform jacket, and stared down at Smith staring up.

"Come now!" he said sternly. "Get up off my floor, Mr. Smith!"

Smith, who had been studying a water stain in the ceiling, met the inspektor's gaze with some effort. What he saw there—concern, amusement, mixed with a healthy dose of justified contempt—caused him to get up, dust himself off, and take a seat in the chair opposite the inspektor's desk.

"Good," the inspektor said. "Now . . ."

He turned and began shuffling through a pile of papers on his desk until he found Smith's passport, casually tossed there a week before: Smith almost burst into tears when he saw this familiar document and reached out for it as one reaches for the hand of an old friend. The inspector ignored this gesture. He leaned back against his desk, tapping his glossy fingernails against the passport's blue cover.

"I have completed my investigation of your lamentable case and have concluded that you bear no direct legal responsibility for the death of Kasim Vatran and his wife."

"They weren't married," Smith croaked, interrupting, his voice crackling with disuse. "Jessica never married the man."

"Ah, but she did," the inspektor said. "A civil ceremony performed last month at a private resort on the Black Sea. Would you like to see the documents?"

"No," Smith said, deflating. So she had married the monster after all.

"Of course, there are certain crimes I can charge you with. Adultery, for one," the inspektor continued. "Or use of banned substances, or various other anti-Turkish activities—perhaps including possession of forbidden headgear, should I by chance discover a fez in your luggage. But I have decided not to pursue any of these possibilities."

"*Teşekkür ederim,*" Smith said humbly.

"No doubt you have had some time to reflect on the damage you have caused here in Istanbul." Inspektor Biryak's tone now was deadly serious. "Is that correct, Mr. Smith?"

"Yes," Smith whispered.

"And do you regret your role in this tragedy?"

"Utterly," Smith said, with as much sincerity as he could muster. Then: "Sir, do you think I might see the body? Jessica's, I mean. To say good-bye." He felt a gothic impulse to throw himself across her strangled corpse, to plant one last kiss on her decomposing lips, to beg her forgiveness, as if dead flesh could forgive the living.

"I'm sorry." Inspektor Biryak shook his head. "Madame Vatran has been cremated along with her husband. Their ashes were spread yesterday over the sea at Ince Burun, where they were married. This was the family's request."

Smith swallowed a lump in his throat. Jessica was completely gone. Even her ashes, a fine gray powder, dissolved into the great shroud of the sea. She might have found happiness with Kasim, with her half-Turkish baby, and her plush, circumscribed life in Istanbul. She might have converted to Islam, taken to wearing the veil, discovered the peace of Allah. It no longer mattered. Jessica, Kasim, the baby—they were all equal now.

A pause. Inspektor Biryak studied Smith for a long moment, then nodded to himself, confirming something.

"Some friends have come for you," he said at last.

"Friends?" Smith looked up, surprised. He couldn't think of any friends, at least not in this hemisphere.

The inspektor tossed over the passport. Smith nervously let it slip through his fingers, then leaned over and scooped it quickly off the floor.

"I have decided to release you into their custody," the inspektor said. "But your tourist visa has been revoked. You will leave Turkey within twenty-four hours."

Inspektor Biryak turned away and resumed his seat behind a desk piled high with paperwork, with reports and affidavits, with far more important matters.

7.

The tea peddler and the letter writer stood waiting on the sidewalk when Smith, blinking, dazzled by the outdoor light, came down the steps from the Galatasary station. Smith, dressed again in his own clothes, now indelibly stained with Vatran's blood, his boots and watch returned, smelled like an animal after a week in the cell without washing, but this didn't seem to bother the waiting Turks. The tea peddler stepped up first and embraced him warmly, tears in his eyes.

"*Benim maaleseſ çocuk!*" the tea peddler lamented, wiping tears from his face. "*Benim çocuk!*"

The letter writer stood back gravely, like a concerned uncle, then reached out and took hold of Smith's hand.

"Hakim and I have been concerned," the letter writer said. "We have much found your photograph in the newspapers."

Smith had never been happier to see anyone in his life than these two relative strangers.

"Geez, guys!" he managed, temporarily reverting to his original Midwestern self. "Oh, geez! Thanks so much for coming!"

"Did they beat you?" the letter writer asked, lowering his voice. "Did they beat you here"—he gestured to the blown-out wingtip he wore—"bottom of your feet?"

"No." Smith shook his head.

"Because there exist laws against such practice." The letter writer wagged his head adamantly. "Very strict laws against use of the *falaka*, which is a small but very terrible stick to beat the bottom of the feet. We are a civilized nation, we Turks. We have been civilized for many years and such practices are no longer allowed."

"Really, I'm O.K.," Smith said. "*Tamam, tamam.*" It was the one Turkish word he had adopted into his personal vocabulary. So neat and expressive: *Tamam.* It's fine.

"Very good," the letter writer said. "We go."

The Turks each took one of Smith's arms and walked him over to the tram station at Tünel. The tram came; the letter writer dropped a handful of coins into the till, enough for all three of them, and they clambered up and clanked slowly along Istiklal on this antique conveyance. Smith stared out the window dazed, nearly terrified by the crazy swirl of pedestrians and cars, but he couldn't take his eyes away. Over the course of the week in the fluorescent cell, he had come to know every crack in its gray-green walls, every subtle gradation of color; his ears attuned to faint scraping sounds far away in the silence. All the noise and movement on the street now suggested the immediate aftermath of an explosion: He was glad for the watery hush of the Abdulhak Hamit Hamam—a dilapidated, old-fashioned steam bath—when they got there twenty minutes later.

Once again, Smith surrendered his clothes and was this time given a pair of wooden clogs and a striped towel to cover his lower half. He left the tea peddler and the letter writer in the antechamber, the peeling wood-paneled *camekan*, and followed the bath attendant into the steam room. Here he sat for a contemplative hour, sweating profusely, the foul stench of incarceration running out of his pores. At last, the attendant returned and led him to the marble *gobektasi* and laid him out facedown and went to work, slapping and kneading and twisting Smith's limbs, his joints cracking, his skin pinkening beneath the blows. When he could take no more of this beating, he was lathered, rinsed, and released, wobbly and weak in the knees, into one of the outer rooms. Here, on a wooden bench, the tea peddler and the letter writer sat waiting for him. They had in the meantime gone to the Stamboul Palace and retrieved Smith's duffel and the remainder of his clothes.

"Thank you, my friends," Smith said, once again moved by their concern for his welfare.

He sat on the bench between them and tea was brought—strong and sweet, with mint leaves crushed at the bottom like a mojito.

"*Pek parlak degil,*" commented the tea peddler, by way of professional assessment, making a face, but he drank the stuff anyway and the three of them sipped for a while in companionable silence. Then, the tea peddler set down his cup and spoke at length. When he stopped speaking, he smiled sadly and patted Smith's arm in a consoling manner. This gesture was the only thing that didn't need translating:

"Hakim says many thing," the letter writer began, after a moment. "But first he says to know you are a gentle person who is like his son to him, and he is sad such terrible events happen to you."

"Thanks, Hakim." Smith nodded. "Thank you so much."

"Also he says about how he see your picture published in *Akit* where they write that you do terrible, un-Turkish, and anti-Islamic things. That you cause the killing of a good Turk, that you spit, so to speak, on the beard of the prophet, peace be upon him. Understand, following your arrest there was very many people shouting outside the Galatasary police station, they"—he hesitated, a flush coming to his cheeks—"wanted to take you, to beat you, they want to cut your"—he indicated Smith's crotch—"your manhood away. They try to smash the door down so the police must come out with plastic shields, with helmets and clubs—but before this, Hakim comes. Hakim stands up and says how you are only such a sensitive boy brought low by the woman in the window. He tells what he has seen, the golden-haired woman almost naked there beneath a big piece of glass, but no one will believe him. They shout, they throw rocks. Finally there is a terrible fight and the police beat many people with clubs and the crowd goes away finally, some to prison, some to hospital."

"My God!" Smith said, horrified. "I had no idea. How awful!" He'd caused a riot, he'd almost caused the lynching of his good friend the tea peddler!

"Very terrible," the letter writer agreed. "So we come back four days ago to have you out of jail, because of course you have done nothing wrong, but Inspektor Biryak tells us they must keep you locked up until passions are forgot by the people, but not to worry because the people is so easy to forget—" He paused to take a sip of his tea. "The inspektor was indeed correct. Today, they shout and scream about another things, a few foolish cartoons of the prophet in a newspaper in Finland, and now you are here safe with us."

"Oh, geez," Smith began, but he couldn't say more, again moved to tears by what these two men had done for him: The tea peddler had confronted a lynch mob on his behalf; both of them had sought his release from imprisonment in a country where such an action might have been construed as sedition and landed them behind bars with no tradition of habeas corpus to get them out again.

"How can I ever repay you—" Smith began, but the letter writer interrupted gently.

"Good men must help other good men," he said. "In America, in Istanbul, doesn't matter. Else the bad sleep well." He made a gesture.

"Yes, you're right," Smith said, touched by the nobility of this sentiment—though he couldn't think of himself at that moment as a very good man.

"*Nerede gidis?*" the tea peddler asked, and the letter writer translated.

"I don't know." Smith shrugged. "Back to Paris for now. Then, New York. Or somewhere to toughen up, emotionally, I mean. I definitely need to get my shit together. Maybe I'll join the Marines," he joked. "That's what Jessica said . . ."

When the tea was done, Smith dressed quickly in clean clothes from the duffel, and the men took him on the tram to Tünel, where they transferred to the funicular down to Karakoy. From here, they walked arm in arm through the crowds across the Galata Bridge, the tower on Galata Hill receding behind. A stiff breeze lifted off the Golden Horn, whipping the blue-green water beneath the pilings into whitecaps. The wind and the water brought Smith's spirits up a notch—I have never had such good friends, he thought—and they got back on the tram at Eminonu and rode it down one stop to the Sirkeci Station.

On trains departing from the echoing interior of this tile and plaster terminus, it was possible to reach Paris via Edirne, Sofia, Bucharest, Vienna, Brussels, and points in-between, an expensive trip even at its cheapest, with four or five transfers that would take several days and consume nearly all of Smith's remaining funds. He didn't have a plane ticket back to the States, hadn't planned that far ahead. But he couldn't allow himself to think further along than Paris—a city he knew well, where he had once lived for eight months during an AID-Amicale Etats-Unis-sponsored production of *Oklahoma!* (not a great gig); he'd only been in the chorus.

Maybe in Paris it would be possible to get a temporary job, save a little money for the trip home.

8.

The tea peddler and the letter writer waited with Smith for two hours for the Thessaloníki local, which was an hour and a half late. Sirkeci Station, empty in the early part of the day, filled with commuters on their way back to the outer suburbs, to Cankurtaran and Yenikapi, to Yesilkoy, its un-kept rose gardens and tiny, cigarette-strewn beach of black sand now overshadowed with storm clouds blowing down from the Black Sea. The Thessaloníki train pulled in at last, disgorging women in headscarves and seedy-looking Balkan types wearing dingy pin-striped suits and carrying heavy briefcases full of who knows what.

"I better get a seat," Smith said, standing up. He embraced both of them manfully. Then the tea peddler spoke.

"He would like to have something," the letter writer translated.

"Of course," Smith said, slightly disappointed in this last-minute merce-nary turn. "I don't have much money left, but he can have it all." He reached for his wallet.

"*Hayir, hayir.*" The tea peddler patted the air between them, offended.

"He means a small personal item," the letter writer explained. "A souvenir to remember you. A scarf, perhaps?"

"Oh. Yeah, sure . . ." Smith searched through his duffel and pulled out a faded blue sweatshirt, nicely worn, with the motto I TOOK A SWIG AT NIGS!— WISCONSIN DELLS 1997 printed across the front in circus-style lettering.

It was from Smith's favorite bar in the world, a little hole-in-the-wall place in Wisconsin Dells, Wisconsin. As he handed over this precious gar-ment, he saw in the eye of his memory the falls glittering beyond the dusty fan-shaped window over the bar, the fat tourists from Milwaukee and Cedar Rapids filling up the stools, the putt-putt golf courses and go-kart ovals out on Route 12. He'd gone down to the Dells, to Story Book Land and the roller coasters and the water parks, every summer when he was a kid with his parents and sister before her unexpected demise and all the complica-tions that followed. And later, during college, he went back to smoke pot along the hiking trails and drink at Nigs and the other dives along Main Street and ride the amphibious Ducks drunk and high through the lime-stone gorges. He'd lost his virginity there on the morning of his nineteenth birthday in room three of the Hotel Hiawatha with a pale, pink-nippled, redheaded sorority girl from Madison. Afterwards, they'd gone skinny-dipping in the river at a secret place she knew about, the cold water as red as her hair from iron ore deposits in the soil. All this he folded into the faded blue sweatshirt as he folded it neatly and handed it over to the Turk.

"Take this, my friend," he said.

The tea peddler nodded his thanks, eyes downcast.

Smith then took out a scrap of envelope and scrawled out the address of a friend in New York who might hold mail for him and gave it over to the letter writer. "I don't really have an address right now. But you can try this. Send me a postcard, tell me how you're doing."

Then he shook their hands one last time, took up his duffel, and mounted the steep metal steps into the second-class car and lost himself in the onion-smelling interior. The best good byes are the swiftest. He hunkered down in an empty seat and watched through the scratched window as the tea peddler and the letter writer walked across the marble platform and disappeared into the forward rush of commuters. They didn't look back. Smith didn't bother to knock on the window or wave. He knew he would never see them again, would never return to Istanbul, and was filled with an unaccountable sadness at the thought, even though such terrible things had happened and he hadn't been happy there, not for a single moment.

A few minutes later, with no preliminaries, no whistles or bells, the train lurched forward and began to move slowly along the tracks through Eminonu, beneath the aqueduct built by Valens nearly two thousand years ago, past the Hippodrome and the Great Bazaar, which once brimmed with the spoils of the gorgeous East. It began to rain. Light at first, then heavy; a downpour darkening the elegant fluted columns of the Blue Mosque, the wide green domes of the Hagia Sophia, washing cigarette butts and discarded lottery tickets and orange rinds and other urban rubbish into the deep, stagnant cisterns beneath the city.

5

THE END OF SMITH

1.

In Paris, Smith looked for work and stayed two nights in the cheapest hostel he could find—a dingy flea trap in an anonymous quartier near Cité Universitaire, just beyond the Périphérique—but soon realized he was both too old and too American for such low-class digs. On the second night, the six belligerent Australian backpackers with whom he shared his dormitory-style room stumbled in piss-drunk at 1:00 A.M. They had acquired an illegal passkey from the desk clerk, a fellow Australian, thus circumventing the hostel's 10:30 curfew. And though the rules also forbade the consumption of *l'alcool* on the premises, the Australians carried a case and a half of Pelican Brun between them and continued to drink heavily for the next couple of hours, talking at full volume, lurching drunkenly between the painted metal bunks, vomiting in the sink.

Smith, outraged, protested twice. The first time the Australians ignored him. The second time they threatened to beat him senseless if he didn't shut his mouth. Still rattled from the ordeal in Istanbul, Smith was in no shape for a fight, especially not with six drunken Australians; so he shut his mouth, crawled deeper into his bunk, and jammed a musty-smelling pillow over his head. He managed to catch a half hour's tortured sleep sometime after the Australians passed out around 5:00 A.M.

First light showed pink and pale blue and exhausted in the sky above the black monolith of the Tour de Montparnasse. The Australians snored, an alcoholic cacophony every bit as loud and odiferous as a diesel-powered generator going full blast. Smith, despairing of further sleep, rose and dressed. Then he gathered up several half empty bottles of Pelican lying around the room and quietly dumped the remaining contents into open Australian backpacks. This stealthy act of revenge accomplished, he slipped out of the hostel by a side door.

Traffic was just picking up along the boulevard Jourdan. Smith felt the rumble of the métro at Cité Universitaire as a small earthquake beneath the pavement beneath his feet. He bought a bottle of mineral water and a fresh-baked baguette, still warm, at a boulangerie near the busy intersection of avenue Reille and avenue René Coty, and found a bench in the Parc de Mont-souris. Swans slept on the muddy banks of the small island in the middle of the lake, slate-colored in this early light, heads tucked beneath their wings. Munching grimly on the baguette, Smith counted out his remaining funds. The total amount came to less than he had expected—115 U.S. dollars in traveler's checks, 63 euros in cash, and a handful of useless Turkish lirasi, maybe 8 dollars' worth. Not enough for a plane ticket to New York at current rates, even on an underbooked Air India charter flight with babies screaming and nonstop Bollywood movies playing on the drop-downs.

He saved the second half of the baguette for lunch and, to economize on métro fare, walked an hour across the city, from the Fourteenth to the Fourth Arrondissement—which is to say from Observatoire to the Quai des Célestins—to the American Cultural Center in the basement of the American Methodist Church overlooking the green-brown waters of the Seine. Here the Methodists maintain what they call the Official Paris English-Language Job and Housing Bank. This grandiose moniker conceals a some-what paltry reality: five or six tattered binders with the good listings already ripped out; two computer terminals upon which, for a euro a minute, the applicant might consult craigslist France; and one overladen bulletin board covered with rarely culled three-by-five cards and myriad scraps of paper listing both employment opportunities and apartments to share. From the Job Bank's quirky porthole windows it was just possible to glimpse the tall white facades of the Isle St. Louis, anchored like the fantasy of a luxury liner in the middle of the river.

Smith spent the morning down there, sorting through the outdated listings (English Language Tutor Wanted—French required; Companion for Elderly Man—French required; English-Speaking Tour Leader—French required; Child Care Provider—French required), wasting precious resources on watery cups of coffee from an American-style vending machine, on fleeting chunks of Internet time and phone calls to numbers that had been disconnected, to jobs that had been filled six months ago.

At about two in the afternoon, as he stood dumbly studying the bulletin board for the last time, a young woman came down the short flight of steps from the Quai des Célestins and through the foyer and the glass doors into the Job Bank and stepped up and pinned a yellow scrap of paper to the board with all the other scraps. She was in her early twenties, short and a little overweight, with brown hair and a shiny-greasy complexion unadulterated by makeup. Her brown eyes held a slightly crazed, glittery look. She wore a pair of Ole Miss sweatpants and a bulky beige cable-knit sweater; the knockoff Hermès scarf knotted around her neck seemed a pointless concession to French fashion sense.

"Y'all looking for a job, or a place to stay?" the young woman said brightly to Smith, her voice drawly and Southern.

Smith turned to look at her. "Both, I guess," he said. Something about her eyes made him want to look away.

"Well, my goddamned co-loc bagged on me last week, ran off with some dude to, like, the Czech Republic. Here Czech it out"—she waved to the pinned-up yellow scrap—"get it, Czech it out? Hey, that was a joke, y'all."

"Funny," Smith said, not meaning it. But he leaned forward and squinted at the spidery, nearly illegible handwriting on the scrap: Quartier Ménilmontant-Père-Lachaise, he deciphered, on a street he'd never heard of. One bedroom; sleeping couch in living area. The rent at 250 euros per month was crazy-cheap for Paris, even for a closet or a bit of floor space in a corner.

"It's just the right place if you like dead people," the young woman said. "Père-Lachaise Cemetery is right across the street. That's where Jim Morrison is buried—"

"And Balzac," Smith interrupted. "And Oscar Wilde and Joyce. Not to mention Proust and Molière and Bizet and the great actresses Rachel and Sarah Bernhardt . . ."

But she didn't seem to be listening.

"Sounds like a deal," he admitted finally. "But really, I don't have enough cash right now. I need a job first."

"Yeah, but where're you staying meanwhile?" the young woman persisted.

Smith shrugged.

"Well, you got to stay somewhere."

"Yes . . ."

"Hey!" she exclaimed, suddenly. "Are you hungry?"

Smith admitted he was.

"Come on"—she tugged at his arm—"let's get something to eat. We'll talk it over."

"Like I said, I'm pretty broke . . ."

"On me!" she said, pulling him toward the glass doors. "Don't worry about a thing."

2.

Her name was Blaire—"You know, like the prime minister"—Smith never got a last name, though he learned nearly everything else about her in the first five minutes: She was from Atlanta; had graduated from Emory last fall with a major in communications and a minor in French. She didn't have a boyfriend right now. Sure, she'd made out with a few girls in college, but was definitely not a lesbian. She was an only child, parents divorced—father living in San Diego with a Mexican woman who used to clean his house, and that was weird; mother still in Georgia married and divorced twice more since, second time to a creepy born-again computer programmer who once tried to put his hands down Blaire's pants. Now, she was living in Paris for a while, sitting in on classes at the Sorbonne and trying to decide whether or not to pursue a master's in French literature.

"Though I got to admit," she chattered on, "I'm not really into the whole deal. Baudelaire—that guy's depressing as shit. Writes poems about chicks strangled after, like, sex . . ."

Smith winced at this.

". . . and I can hardly understand the professor. He speaks so fast and gets real excited, jumping around like a monkey when he talks about symbolism this and symbolism that and I don't know what-all. Shit, you know, I've been at it for months and I'm still not sure what symbolism is. Do you know?"

"Well—" Smith began.

"I mean I guess he's talking about Mallarmé and Verlaine," she continued, oblivious. "And Rimbaud—who is cool, don't get me wrong, *poète maudit* and all that bullshit, like a rock star . . ."

After a while, Smith stopped listening. She had no apparent need for anything from him beyond the occasional assenting grunt. They were sitting on the terrace of a mediocre and expensive bistro on the rue d'Aubigne, a row of severely cropped topiary trees in big pots shielding them more or less from the heavy flow of traffic along the boulevard Moreland. They ate *ris de veau et frites*—veal sweetbreads and fries—the special of the day, and split a large green salad. Blaire ordered a bottle of Pouilly-Fuisse, which didn't go with the food at all, then to make up for this mistake, a bottle of red. She seemed intent on getting drunk. Smith wasn't in the mood, but allowed himself to be drawn in by her enthusiasm. The afternoon wore on; soon it was dusk and the streetlights flickered for ten minutes, then illuminated themselves, glowing faintly purple along the quais, above the darkening river.

The drunker Blaire got, the more she talked about everything and nothing, her talk, so full of tangents and backtracking and non sequiturs, often making no sense at all. As it got dark, she popped a small white pill into her mouth—

"Speed." She held out a small tin pillbox. "Want some?"

Smith declined. She made even less sense after this: fast, rambling monologues about nothing followed by rants about people he didn't know. He was dead tired now, beyond exhausted, hadn't slept more than an hour in the last forty-eight, desperately needed to find a place to crash and said so, several times.

"All right, buddy, tell you what—" Blaire said at last. "Since you don't have a bunch of cash right now, I'll rent you the place by the week until you can get a job. That's, like, roughly sixty-five euros per week. So give me the sixty-five now"—she held out her hand, small and pawlike, the palms rough with eczema—"and you've got 'til next Tuesday to come up with the next sixty-five. Deal?"

Smith hesitated; she seemed crazy to him, slightly unhinged, but what choice did he have? He shook her hand—an unpleasant, damp, scaly sensation—and reached into his pocket and counted out his last sixty-three euros. "I'll have to owe you the two," he said. "Just until I can get these traveler's checks cashed tomorrow."

"Fine," she said, frowning down at the money. "But don't try and stiff me." And she hopped up and went into the bistro and came out with another bottle of wine.

3.

At ten o'clock, Smith found himself dead sober and suffering from a splitting headache at a table in the corner of a rough sort of bar called Aux Rouge Gorge, on a steep street in Buttes-Montmartre. A large, rusty red ax blade hanging from chains out front served as the bar's only advertisement. A dozen motorcycles parked along the curb bore the insignia of the French equivalent of an American biker gang: a Club Moto based in the gritty banlieu of Marly-le-Roi, known as les Barbares. At the bar inside, the French bikers, tough-looking brutes in battle-scarred leathers, stood drinking white wine from dainty glasses.

What's wrong with this picture? Smith thought, and might have been amused by the spectacle had he not been so tired. He had been lobbying for a visit to his new apartment for hours now; Blaire, determined to spend all Smith's rent money on booze, refused to head home until it was all gone or until last call, whichever came first. Now, she went up to the bar and returned with two glasses and a bottle of horrible, cheap champagne—Château d'Isigny, 2005.

"No more," Smith said, waving his hands, alarmed. "After this, we go!"

"Yeah, yeah, suck my ass," Blaire leered drunkenly, pouring two glasses. "Come on, this is fun! Aren't you having fun?"

"It's real fun," Smith lied. "But I'm extremely tired. Otherwise it would be more fun than I could stand."

"You're a bastard," Blaire pointed the bottle at him. "You know that?" Then: "Sometimes I think I should just go on back to Atlanta and get a job selling commercial real estate. That's what my mom does. She sells commercial real estate."

Smith sighed.

"Like, what's wrong with you, buddy?" Blaire said, narrowing her eyes. "Are you depressed or something?"

"Just very, very tired," Smith repeated.

"Do you smoke weed?"

"I have," Smith said, no longer put off by her non sequiturs. "I don't anymore."

"Why not?" Blaire demanded aggressively. "Got a problem with it?"

"Not really, it's just that—"

"So you got any? I'd really dig some. I mean good weed's, like, really hard to score over here."

"I just told you I don't—"

But this statement was interrupted by a commotion at the street door. Raised voices, a bottle shattering, then three men in khaki military uniforms pushed in from the outside: Two of them, wiry and pale, with blond hair and icy blue eyes, looked Swedish; the third, muscular and very dark, probably African, with high, aristocratic cheekbones. They wore absurdly spotless white military caps on their heads and dark blue sashes wrapped around their waists; huge, shaggy red epaulets hung off their shoulders. Their uniforms were pressed and starched and utterly clean—though one of the Swedes, a fresh, congealing gash down the left side of his face, had dripped blood into his shirt collar.

"Fuck'n shit," Blaire hissed. "*Les Képis Blancs!*"

"Who?" Smith said.

"*Les Képis Blancs*. The White—whatever—Caps, Hats. It's what they call those dudes, on account of their hats. They come in here all the time to fight the bikers. Y'all watch, any minute now, there's going to be a serious *bagarre*."

The three white hats elbowed their way up to the crowded bar and a space seemed to clear around them—though the bikers at the far end pretended not to notice them. The noise level in the room receded like the tide, everyone suddenly talking in subdued tones.

"Maybe we should get out of here," Smith whispered. Then: "What the hell are these guys—French Special Forces?"

Blaire shook her head drunkenly. "No French allowed," she said. "They're, like, foreign mercenaries, paid by the French. Légion Étrangère, they call them."

Smith thought for a moment, translating slowly in his head. "You mean Foreign Legion? The French Foreign Legion?"

"You got it," Blaire sneered. "Bunch of assholes."

"Wow, the Foreign Legion's still around," Smith said. "Do they still take anyone, no questions asked?"

"How the fuck should I know?" Blaire said, annoyed. "All I know is we got to get out of here. My student visa ran out about a year ago. If *les flics* ask for my papers . . ."

"*Tamam*." Smith pushed up from the table. "Let's go."

Blaire held up the bottle, still nearly full. "You got to be kidding! Come on, buddy, help me out here . . ."

"I've had more than enough," Smith said, but he sat down again. Blaire drained her glass and moved on to Smith's. Then she pushed the glasses aside and took the bottle and upended it between her lips.

Smith turned away from this disgusting spectacle to watch the Foreign Legionnaires at the bar, bottles of Kronenbourg in their hands. They possessed an undeniable swagger, a fearlessness that might be part of an elaborate pose, or might be completely real. The Foreign Legion was, he remembered reading somewhere, famously brutal, the toughest army in the world. Every year, recruits were killed during the merciless training process, or committed suicide or deserted if they could. Now he remembered watching an old movie with his mother back in Montezuma when he was a kid—*Beau Geste* with Gary Cooper. His mother singing a snatch of something snappy by Harold Arlen and popping popcorn in the kitchen. Then, rabbit ears adjusted and readjusted to bring the picture in straight on the ancient console TV, they curled up on the couch under a quilt as snow drifted deep across Iowa and the hot glare of the desert shone out from the small black-and-white screen. Smith couldn't remember anything of the plot, only a column of men marching over endless dunes and the image of Gary Cooper, sternly beautiful, taking aim at a burnoosed Arab with an antiquated rifle. And a single line of dialogue, uttered by a sneeringly cruel man with a pencil-thin mustache: "Fools! Even in death you serve the Legion!"

Blaire put the bottle of champagne down and belched. "I'd fuck that black one anytime," she slurred, indicating the African Legionnaire. "Look at them pecs. That boy works out!"

The three Legionnaires finished their Kronenbourgs quickly and ordered Ricard, snatching the bottle gruffly out of the bartender's hands when he brought it over and filling their glasses to the brim with the pernicious yellow liquid.

"*Main de Danjou!*" one of them called, bringing himself to attention. The others repeated this obscure toast and the three of them drained off the Ricard in a single swallow. Ricard was strong stuff, Smith knew, more than ninety proof; it must burn like hell going down unadulterated with water. Then, the

African Legionnaire turned away from his comrades and put a hand on the nearest biker's leather-clad shoulder: "*Z'avez une cigarette, la tapette?*"

The biker swung around, fists raised, bristling at what was clearly an insult, but the African Legionnaire took a lightning step back and knocked him down with a quick, sharp blow before he could strike. In the next moment, the brawl broke out in every corner of the bar, like something out of an old-fashioned Western. Chairs went flying, tables upended. Glasses shattered against the wall. One of the Legionnaires bit the neck off an empty bottle of Kronenbourg, and, spitting out glass and blood, slashed at a biker who had drawn a knife.

"*J'appelle la police!*" the bartender shrieked, pulling out a cell phone. "Police!"

A flung bottle missed Smith's head by inches. In the distance already, the *mee-maw, mee-maw* sound of French police sirens approaching. Smith jumped up, shouldered his duffel, and seized Blaire by the arm.

"We're going!" he said. "Now!"

She wrenched her arm away drunkenly. "Why? This is a trip!"

"Because of your papers—remember your papers?"

Blaire allowed herself to be led around the fracas and out into the street.

There, slumping over the low fender of an old Renault 4CV, she retched up half a bottle of cheap champagne in the gutter. More bikers were pouring into the bar from somewhere, as if they had been waiting in nearby alleys for the fighting to begin. The Legionnaires inside fought back to back now, embattled, vastly outnumbered, their neatly pressed uniforms torn, ruined, spattered with blood, white kepis somehow still perched, spotless, atop their heads. They looked oddly happy in there, Smith thought, watching them through the open door from the safety of the curb. As if to support this conclusion, one of them started to sing—"*Tiens, voilà du boudin, voilà du boudin. Pour les Belges il n'yen a plus! Ce sont des tireurs au cul!*"—and his comrades joined in, a strident martial chorus, and they fought on, arms flailing, fists flying, blood spattering, singing happily in the yellow light of the bar.

4.

Blaire's apartment wasn't a one-bedroom at all, but a filthy one-room studio, divided in half by a hip-high pasteboard wall. And it didn't overlook the white marble obelisks and elaborate aboveground tombs of the

Père-Lachaise Cemetery, as advertised, but gave out on one side on an air shaft, the thick smell of garbage curling up from the trash bins below; on the other, a grim, nameless street, utterly featureless.

Smith half carried Blaire up the stairs, six narrow, steep flights. Blind drunk and maxed-out on speed, she raved on, blabbering in two languages. Smith could hardly make out a single coherent phrase. He tossed her down on the bed—a stained, bare futon—where she instantly passed out. He took off her shoes and covered her with a sheet, then stepped gingerly around the divider and tried to clear a space for himself to sleep on the floor. The overhead bulb had long since burned out and, there being no lamps to speak of—she'd been using candles, with waxy residue and burned matches all over the place—he worked by streetlight reflected through the casement window. Even in this sepulchral dimness, the complete squalor of his surroundings was clearly apparent: moldy food, wads of toilet paper dark with an unknown substance, a decomposing beta fish floating in an algae-spotted bowl, filthy heaps of clothing; the kind of disorder that could only mirror a disordered mind.

How horrible! Smith thought, scraping a pasty something off the floor with the edge of his shoe. This was the absolute bottom. But he had paid for a week and at least the bottom was a place from which it was not possible to fall. He softened his duffel with a few blows for use as a pillow and laid his jean jacket over a disturbing stain on the floor and lowered himself down. He had barely closed his eyes when Blaire lurched around the divide from the other side. She was totally naked.

"Hey, asshole," she said. "What do y'all think you're doing?"

Smith stared. She was far more attractive without her clothes—that bulky cable-knit sweater had concealed nice breasts and compact curves—but she was smudged-looking, as if she hadn't bathed in some time, and her eyes were spinning mad in her head.

"I'm going to sleep," Smith mumbled, embarrassed, turning away from her. "So should you."

"Hey, *hey!*" she spat. "Y'all better fucking do me after all the money I spent on you today! And I mean you better pound my bones good, or I'll kick your ass right out into the street!"

She stumbled toward him and Smith jumped up, alarmed.

"Blaire, please—" he began, but she began to laugh, an hysterical shrieking sound. She wasn't just drunk and flying on speed, Smith realized. At that moment she was as crazy as a loon.

"That's not my name, asshole! Fucking Blaire? Do I look like a Blaire? That's hilarious!"

"O.K.," Smith said, desperately trying to stay calm. "What's your name then?"

But she didn't answer. Instead, she put her hands under her breasts. "Do you like my tits?" she said. "I've got great tits."

"Umm, actually, you do," Smith said. "But I'm really, really tired . . ."

"Oh, I fucking get it!" the woman who was not Blaire spat. "You're a fucking faggot! You're a gay fucking faggot, is that it?"

Smith didn't say anything.

"Let me tell you something! I don't want a faggot living in my flat. I don't want to come home one day and find you, like, fucking some other gay faggot up the ass. So get the fuck out of here! Now! *Faggot!*"

"Just hold on one goddamned minute," Smith said, getting angry. "I've already paid you sixty-three euros—"

"*Get out!*" non-Blaire screamed and took a step forward and swiped at him with one withered paw.

"I'm staying here tonight, Blaire," he began.

"My name's not Blaire, *asshole!*" And she jumped around him with surprising agility and knocked the casement open with the palm of her hand. The glass pane shattered from this reckless blow, and fell in gleaming shards, hitting the pavement below with a faint musical note.

"*Help!*" she called out the window, her hand bloody. "*Au secours! Viol! Viol!*" She paused and turned to Smith, grinning crazily, and made a bloody streak with the wounded hand on her forehead. "Know what that word means, asshole? *Viol?*" Then she turned back to the window. "Rape! *Viol!* Rape! *Infâme, il me viole, le salot!*"

"Oh, God!" Smith groaned aloud. "Stop! Cut it out!"

But all he could think was no, not again! and a moment later, he heard a dull thumping coming from an adjacent apartment and imagined that the police would be there soon. He had no desire to see the inside of a French prison cell, even for the amount of time it took to explain the situation, which very well might be several days. In a panic, he shoved his feet into his boots, grabbed up his duffel, kicked the apartment door open, and scrambled down six flights of narrow stairs, bouncing off the railings, nearly tumbling through an open bull's-eye window into the air shaft, but made it at last out to the narrow, nameless street. And he didn't stop running until he had reached a wide, brightly lit thoroughfare—the avenue Gambetta, as it turned out—with the high walls of the Père-Lachaise rising on his left. Though he couldn't say exactly how he'd gotten there or from which direction he'd come.

A marble breath filtered through the great iron cemetery gates, from between the jumbled alleys of tombs. The night air, cool in Smith's face, did little to quell the outraged thumping of his heart. He waited for a few pointless minutes at a bus stop and thought he could still hear, like the tolling of a distant bell, like the call of guilt itself, the faint sound of non-Blaire's voice shouting "Rape! *Viol!*" carried from afar, all the way from Istanbul, on the disquieting wind.

5.

The huge digital clock in the empty central concourse of the gare de l'Est read 2:05 A.M. It seemed much later than that. Smith trailed slowly past the closed magazine stands, the shuttered ticket windows, looking for a convenient spot to sleep. At last, he found a wide, shadowy doorway just off the columned arcade on the rue d'Alsace side of the station. It wasn't until he'd set his duffel down and prepared to settle himself in the threshold for the remainder of the night that he realized he'd left his jean jacket behind in non-Blaire's apartment. Tucked in the inside pocket of that jacket was an envelope containing the last of his cash and his passport.

A kind of deadness seized Smith's soul at this realization.

"This," Smith said aloud to himself, "is the end of Smith," and he felt the panic twisting in his gut. But the thought of his own negation gave him a little surge of energy. He would retrace his steps, he would find non-Blaire's apartment, reason with her. . . . Then he realized this option did not exist: Other than its putative proximity to the Père-Lachaise, Smith remembered nothing about the place, not the building or the street, which had been nondescript in the extreme. Not a single distinguishing detail. He could wander the labyrinthine quartier up there for a week and still not find non-Blaire's filthy studio. He didn't know her last name; he didn't even know her real first name, which might or might not be Blaire. Here he was, crouched in a dusty corner of the gare de l'Est, just after 2:00 A.M., with absolutely nothing left, not a single sou—worse, without a passport. It was a place that very much resembled despair. Smith trembled there for a while, numb and afraid, and tried to think himself out of the situation, but it was like trying to think himself off a deflating raft surrounded by sharks in the middle of the ocean. Whether you went down with the raft or threw yourself to the sharks didn't matter much in the end. And now, suddenly, he began to feel the pull of a sinister undertow, a swift current drawing him toward the vast shaggy continent of madness looming in darkness and surrounded by perilous reefs just ahead.

Smith peered at this dreadful silhouette for a long, terrible moment, felt the black winds on his face, felt himself slipping closer, closer, ashiver with it. But just as he was about to let go, give in to the current, his attention was drawn to a large rectangular billboard, illuminated by a bank of yellow lights, suspended above the arcade, just across the way. This billboard and these yellow lights were very much things of this world, the yellow lights recalling a scene from earlier in the evening—three Foreign Legionnaires fighting back to back and singing joyfully in the yellow light of the café. And the image on the billboard was exactly appropriate to this mental picture: It showed a square-jawed Legionnaire, white kepi gleaming, visions of faraway deserts in his eyes, a row of medals glittering on his chest.

LÉGION ÉTRANGÈRE, the caption read. FORT DE NOGENT—OUVERT LES 24 HEURES.

Below this, an old-fashioned-looking bomb with a seven-pointed flame blossoming from its fuse, and a motto that Smith knew enough Latin to decipher: LEGIO PATRIA NOSTRA. The Legion Is Our Country.

"I guess it's better than going nuts," Smith said aloud again, his voice echoing hollow in the high, empty hall. And he picked himself up and shouldered his duffel and marched down the central concourse and out into the cobbled *place* at the front of the station. Here he found a taxi stand, a lone Peugeot 504 waiting. The driver sat with the dome light on, reading a copy of *Paris Turf,* the frilly sound of old-time café music—the French call it *les flons-flons de l'accordéon*—playing softly on his radio. Smith rapped on the window on the passenger side and opened the door. The driver folded his racing sheet carefully and looked up. He was a sad-eyed, middle-aged Frenchman, his hair nearly white. He wore a black beret—a hat, though not forbidden by law, as rare in Paris these days as a fez in Istanbul—and a shabby corduroy jacket sprinkled with cigarette ash.

"*Excusez-moi*," Smith said. "*Parlez Anglais?* English?"

The driver shrugged. "Little," he said.

Smith drew a breath. "Fort de Nogent," he said. "*Légion Étrangère.*"

"*Mais vous êtes fou!*" the driver said. He tapped his head with a finger. "Crazy! Go home!"

"You know where it is?" Smith persisted. "Fort de Nogent?"

The driver nodded reluctantly. "*Oui. C'est loin.* Far."

"Thing is, I have no money." Smith opened his hands to show they were empty. "*Rien.*"

The driver stared in disbelief, then reached across and slammed the door. "*Fiche-moi la paix!*" he shouted angrily and turned back to his racing sheet.

Smith unstrapped the Rolex from his wrist and rapped it against the glass. His father had won it shooting craps in the army in 1951, carried it through the Korean War, timed the contractions leading up to the birth of Smith and his sister, using its precise red second hand, the lateness of the mail trucks from Des Moines, the hours leading up to and following his daughter's funeral, and his own faltering pulse in the moments before the unknown seizure that struck him down. Smith fought back sentimental tears as he pressed its time-yellowed face to the glass—but this was a sacrifice he knew he had to make, an offering to the gods for a new life.

"Rolex!" he called, rapping the glass again. "*Pour vous.* Fort de Nogent . . ."

The taxi driver looked at the watch, considering. A moment later, he unlocked the door.

6.

They bumped over rutted streets in the darkness, skirting the Arab and North African quarters at the fringes of the great city. Then the gleaming lanes of the Périphérique and lonely suburban boulevards lined with tall, narrow houses tightly shuttered against this uncertain hour. At last, they came to the massive, mold-spotted walls of an endless fortification. The accordion music played on. The cab was stifling, but Smith didn't open a window. The driver said nothing at all, not a word. I'm leaving everything behind, Smith thought, and felt that now too familiar feeling of vertigo, of the world slipping away from beneath his feet.

The driver pulled up at a drawbridge. A white metal barrier and an empty guard box prevented him from crossing. On the other side of a deep, dry moat loomed enormous gates, built to accept twelve-horse gun carriages during the reign of Louis Philippe.

"Fort de Nogent," the driver said, without turning around. He pointed across the bridge. There, a ceramic sign illuminated with a single yellow light: LÉGION ÉTRANGÈRE. An arrow pointed down.

"O.K.," Smith said, "*Merci.* Enjoy the watch." But as he gathered up his duffel and made a move to exit, the driver got out and came around and opened Smith's door. Smith stepped out and the driver tried to hand back the Rolex.

"*Pas nécessaire,*" the driver said. "You keep."

"*Non, merci,*" Smith responded firmly. "It's yours. I insist."

When the driver understood Smith wouldn't take back the Rolex, he offered a little bow. Then he drew himself up smartly and saluted.

"*Bon courage, Légionnaire,*" he said. And he got into his cab and with a backhanded wave out the window drove off into the night.

Smith reflexively checked his wrist, but his watch was gone now; he guessed it was going on three in the morning. He crossed the bridge into a warren of low barracks buildings and eventually found himself at a nondescript blue door marked with a tiny brass plaque, no larger than a coat button, in the shape of the seven-pointed bomb insignia of the Legion. He knocked. Nothing. He knocked again, louder. Nothing. It was like knocking at the door of an illegal gambling parlor in Chinatown, or some ultrahip underground sex club. At the third knock, a narrow window slid to one side and Smith found himself staring into a pair of dark, suspicious eyes. The eyes stared back. They were black and hard with a kind of existential hardness, as if the man behind them had never gotten a break, as if he'd been the scapegoat time and again for everyone else's crimes and had become innured to this terrible and ridiculous fate.

"*Oui?*"

"*Légion Étrangère?*" Smith said.

"*Vous êtes sûr?*" The hard eyes narrowed. "*Vous avez assez réfléchi?*"

"Sorry." Smith shook his head. "My French is not—"

"English?"

"American," Smith said. "I'm volunteering."

7.

The eyes belonged to a square-built, tough-looking soldier wearing the blue sash and shaggy red epaulets of a Legionnaire. The Velcro tag on his pocket identified him as Sergent-chef Evariste Pinard. Two rows of hash marks on his sleeves recorded fifteen years' service; the spidery creep of crude tattoos traced up his throat. Crossed trumpets on his collar tabs identified him as a musician in la Musique Principale, the Legion's famous military band, but it was diffucult to imagine this brute playing anything, or even humming a tune. He had the kind of face, scarred, apparently villainous, that made others nervous. Here was a man who looked guilty as hell.

Smith took a deep breath and, suddenly full of misgivings, followed the sergent-chef into a dingy waiting room no one had bothered to sweep in a long time. On the wall a map of France; blue, white, and red pushpins marked the various Legion recruitment centers. Also, a large, water-stained framed print showing a nineteenth-century battle scene: Three Legionnaires in the fancy blue and red and gold uniforms of the era, one carrying a French flag shot full of holes, charged from a ruined farmhouse beneath a burning sky into a massed formation of the enemy. Despite the cheery colors and puffy cotton-candy clouds and banners waving, things seemed to be going very badly for the Legion.

"Camerone," the sergent-chef offered, following Smith's gaze, a kind of reluctant pride in his voice. "*Le trente Avril*, 1860. *Un pitoyable douzaine contre l'armée Mexicain!* Maybe twenty men, fighting against one thousand! For days they hold out, no food, no water. Only three left"—he held up three fingers—"they fix bayonets, they charge! You remember Camerone! Every Legionnaire must remember Camerone!"

"What happened to the three men?" Smith said.

But Sergent-chef Pinard only shrugged to indicate that this question was without merit and led Smith to a metal table at the back of the room. They sat across from each other and the sergent-chef took up a blunt pencil and several multipaged forms with carbon paper between each page. No sign of a computer anywhere, not even a typewriter.

"Age?" Sergent-chef Pinard said.

"Thirty-two," Smith said.

Pinard's pencil broke as he tried to write this down and he swore—"*Tabarnak ostie!*"—as he took up another one, and Smith knew the man was a French Canadian. This curious curse—the altar, the host!—a relic of sixteenth-century French, was an archaic blasphemy against the Catholic Church that survived only in Quebec, a fact Smith remembered from an old Quebecois roommate who swore like that often and frequently. Anyway, genuine Frenchmen were not allowed to serve in the Legion.

"You're from Quebec?" Smith said.

"The Legion is my country." Pinard scowled. "That's the first thing you'll learn."

"Sorry."

The sergent-chef leaned back and studied him frankly. "Honestly, you are quite old," he said. "Not too old, officially, but physical requirements are difficult."

"I'm fit," Smith said. "I run, I lift weights."

"*On verra,*" the sergent-chef said. "We will see, Johnny."

"How did you know my name?" Smith said, surprised. Johnny was what Jessica had always called him.

"*Les Americains* are all Johnny to us," the sergent-chef said. "Because this is so often your name, John Smith, John Smith, everyone is John Smith."

"But that *is* my name!" Smith insisted. "John Smith!"

"You see?" Sergent-chef Pinard grinned. Then, serious: "Now you must answer me carefully. What are you reasons to join Legion?"

Smith shrugged. "Nothing better to do," he said.

"*Un femme?*" the sergent-chef suggested. "You join because of a woman?"

"More or less."

"*Pardon?*"

"Yes, if you like."

"I write here a woman." Sergent-chef Pinard scribbled on the form. "It is an excuse, mostly bullshit, that my commanding officer will understand. But," he added ominously, "the Deuxième Bureau will have words with you soon. And to them, I suggest to tell whole truth, because they will find out anyway."

"What's the Deuxième Bureau?" Smith said.

But Pinard didn't respond. "*Passeport,*" he said, holding out his hand.

"I lost it," Smith said.

"You must have a passport." The sergent-chef tapped his pencil impatiently. "No passport, no Legion. You must go to American embassy, get a new passport, then you come back."

"It could take weeks to get a new passport—" Smith began, horrified. "Here . . ." He scrambled for his wallet, which contained a variety of defunct credit cards, and pulled out his expired New York State driver's license and his Stage Actor's Guild card and pushed them across the table.

The sergent-chef rejected these items with a weary gesture

"I've got something else," Smith persisted desperately, and he went rummaging through his duffel and found a creased professional CV. Stapled to this, a four-by-six glossy postcard bearing a headshot from shampoo commercial days that showed his hair at its shiny best, and a theatrical still from his LORT A gig at the Guthrie. He'd packed a few of these when he left New York; never knew when you might meet, say, Barbette Schroeder on the train from Düsseldorf to Hamburg. He laid CV and postcard out on the table.

"I'm pretty famous in the States," Smith said. "Triple threat. I sing, I act, I dance. But mostly I sing."

"You sing?"

"That's right."

Sergent-chef Pinard appeared interested suddenly. He looked at the glossy and looked at Smith, then picked up the CV and read it slowly, his lips silently forming the English words.

"You sing good?" He looked up.

"Very good."

"What type of singing?"

"Musical comedy," Smith said. "Broadway. Show tunes."

"*Non, non.*" Sergent-chef Pinard waved impatiently. "Your voice."

Smith thought about this for a moment, puzzled. "Tenor," he said.

8.

A series of dusty vestibules and cold waiting rooms led to a walled enclosure like a prison yard littered with large piles of old cobblestones. Across this vacant space and up a flight of worn marble steps rose the upper regions of the fort. Here spacious corridors intersected with more spacious corridors. Rows of white doors on either side were stenciled neatly with the names and ranks of the French officers now sleeping within. More military prints hung on the walls, these illustrating Napoléon's famous victories: Austerlitz and the charge of the Cuirassiers; the stand of the Old Guard at Eylau; the Armée de l'Egypte drawn up in fearless, immobile ranks before the pyramids to meet the onslaught of ten thousand fanatical scimitar-wielding Mamelukes.

Smith and Sergent-chef Pinard came at last to a highly polished mahogany door. A gleaming silver nameplate read: COLONEL PHILLIPE DE NOYER—1ER RÉGIMENT DE MARCHE, LÉGION ÉTRANGÈRE. Hanging limply to one side, the regimental standard—a gold-fringed tricolor, its blue, white, and red bands overlaid with gold lettering spelling out the names of a hundred battles. Victory or defeat was all the same to the Legion; it only mattered that they had fought to the last possible drop of blood.

"Do you think this is a good idea?" Smith whispered. "Won't the colonel be sleeping?"

But Sergent-chef Pinard shook his head. "*Colonel de Noyer ne dort jamais*," he said. "He's never asleep. Listen."

Sure enough, from beyond the double doors now came the faint, melancholy tinkling of a piano. Smith recognized the piece; one of Satie's quirky *Gymnopédies*, which to him had always sounded like a small, sad animal daintily picking its way across the keys.

The sergent-chef pressed an ivory buzzer. The piano went silent. They waited. Smith stood there, hands at his side.

"Me, I'm about to make officer," Pinard said suddenly. "My commission arrived last week. Three months' study at Saint-Cyr, then to Africa with the NU."

"Well, congratulations," Smith said, surprised at this confidence.

"But you'll never make officer." Pinard scowled, his voice getting harder. "You'll fuck up first. Too old, too soft. And you're"—a look of disdain came across his face—"an American. Americans are too soft for the Legion. You're wasting your time here."

This, coming from a *Canadian*, Smith thought. But he kept his mouth shut.

"You're my last recruit forever," Pinard continued. "Tonight's the last night I have to take in all you shit-drunk idiots. So now I'm going to give you a piece of very good advice: Go home."

"I can't." Smith shook his head stubbornly.

"It's so bad, whatever you did?"

Smith didn't get the chance to respond. At that moment, the colonel's door opened and Sergent-chef Pinard snapped to attention.

"*À vos ordres, mon colonel!*" he announced to the pale man on the other side.

Colonel Phillipe de Noyer arched an eyebrow. "*Mets-toi au repos, Sergent-chef.*"

"*Je me mets au repos à vos ordres, mon colonel,*" the sergent-chef replied, standing at ease.

The colonel was a wiry, bleached-looking man, probably in his mid-fifties, but his hair had gone completely white. He wore a Hugh Hefner–ish smoking jacket over silk pajamas; his black velvet slippers, monogrammed in glittery gold thread, looked like a present from a wife or mistress. His white hair and fair skin made a sharp contrast with the dark circles under eyes that were almost colorless, as clear as clear blue water in sunlight.

"*Un vrai ténor, mon colonel,*" Sergent-chef Pinard said, and he handed over Smith's rumpled CV and glossy. "*Enfin.*"

Colonel de Noyer glanced through this material quickly, then Smith felt the man's colorless eyes upon him:

"*Oui, évidemment,*" the colonel murmured. "You do indeed look like an actor, Mr. Smith. But can you sing?" His precise Oxbridge-accented English suggested hours spent punting on the Cam, bank holiday weekends at country houses in Scotland. Just as there were Francophile Brits, there were Britophile Francs. The colonel was perhaps one of them.

"I'm what they call a triple threat," Smith interjected brightly. "But I would classify myself as a singer who can act and dance rather than an actor who can dance and sing. There's a distinction."

A stunning blow to the solar plexus suddenly brought him to his knees. He looked up, gasping in pain, to see Sergent-chef Pinard looming over him, gone vicious in a split second.

"*On dit, 'À vos ordres, mon colonel'! Mongol américain!*" the sergent-chef spit through clenched teeth. "*Et tenu au garde-à-vous!* At attention, idiot!"

But Colonel de Noyer intervened. "*Tu peux disposer!*" he commanded sharply.

Sergent-chef Pinard drew back instantly, saluted, and marched off. Smith, watching him go, hoped he would never see the man again. The colonel helped Smith to his feet.

"My adjutant is a highly disciplined Legionnaire," he said. "And as such can't tolerate anything less than crisp military behavior in his subordinates. I'm sure he forgot that you have yet to join our ranks officially. Allow me to apologize on his behalf for this unwarranted assault."

"No, no, it's O.K.," Smith said, rubbing his gut.

"Should you persist in volunteering, you will most certainly receive harsher treatment, some would say sadistic treatment, at the hands of other NCOs much less humane than Pinard. Compared to most of them, he's an absolute saint. I warn you, relentless and unfair punishments are usually handed out for the smallest infractions. But this is our way, the Legion way. In the Legion, brutality for the sake of discipline, for the sake of esprit du corps, is part of an honorable military tradition dating back one hundred and seventy-five years. Do you understand?"

Smith said he did, though he didn't really, and followed the colonel into his apartment.

9.

Bookcases lined the vaulted chamber, otherwise upholstered in dark green buttoned leather. Classical busts peered out sternly from niches amid the books. Family portraits, their varnish cracked and yellow, hung from braided ropes. A baby grand piano occupied most of the opposite end, by the windows. The glossy lid of this formidable instrument was strewn with sheet music, most of it—Smith saw with a glance—by the enigmatic Erik Satie. A silver-framed photograph showed a beautiful woman, very French-looking, posed in front of what looked like an ivy-covered château. Marbled notebooks thick with writing lay stacked on a small table. This was the room of a rich and polymathic dilettante, like something out of Proust or *Phantom of the Opera*. Smith gaped openly. He had never seen such a cultured space; an entire civilization contained between four walls. Only a stumpy-looking modern assault rifle leaning in the corner indicated the military vocation of the occupant.

"The FAMAS 5.56 caliber," the colonel said, following Smith's gaze. "Called by journalists *le clairon*—the trumpet—for its size, and bulldog by soldiers for its vicious bite. Standard light arm of the Armée de Terre, including the Legion. Do you know this excellent rifle?"

Smith shook his head.

"Legionnaires learn to dismantle, clean, and reassamble it in less than two minutes, blindfolded, just by touch. They love it more than they love their own pricks. There is an expression with us—'*Ton femme c'est ton FA-MAS.*' A pun that means 'Your wife is your rifle. . . .'"

The colonel nodded grimly to himself at this and sat down at the piano and drew his fingers lightly across the keyboard. Out beyond the ramparts, Nogent slept in the last hours before dawn. A damp wind washed the clouds from the sky. The moon hung low and fading just above the sinuous curves of a distant river, probably the Marne.

"Americans make rotten Legionnaires, it's true," the colonel continued after a while. "They are far too attached to the idea of personal freedom. But the purely personal is dead in the Legion. Harsh discipline has killed it. Americans always demand to know the reasons behind their orders, as if every soldier must be justified in his heart whenever he shoots someone. How ridiculous! They demand to know why they are being sent to die on futile campaigns halfway around the world in the service of a people who hate them. And believe me, all good French people hate the Legion, Mr. Smith. My wife, for example, hates the Legion. The French hate the Legion as they hate the police and their butcher and any other petty fascist who does their bloody work for them." He glanced up from the keys, an odd detachment in his pale eyes. "The American Legionnaire is the most likely of all to chuck months of expensive and rigorous training and simply"—he made a fluid gesture that meant desert, take it on the lam. Then: "You are a tenor?"

"Yes, sir."

"Have you heard of la Musique Principale?"

"No, sir."

"It is our corps of musicians, one of the most famous in the world. It is divided into two equal parts—the regimental marching band and the Chorale du Légion, the men's chorus. Like the Russian army, we maintain a tradition of choral music, of men singing together. Last year, we won the silver medal at the International Choral Society's competition in Moscow—this is our sixth silver medal, but it is not enough and my superiors grow restless. I happen to be the officer in charge of the chorale and next year, I would like to win the gold medal. The key to this victory is a really good top tenor. I am always searching for such a voice. Are you a good tenor, *mon enfant?*"

"I am, sir," Smith said.

"*Bon. Chantez quelque chose pour moi.*"

"Choral music isn't exactly my specialty . . . ," Smith equivocated. "Musical comedies. Broadway shows, that sort of thing."

"Sing," Colonel de Noyer commanded. "Anything."

Smith racked his brain for something sufficiently martial and at last recalled a number from *Cabaret,* which he'd done with Mask and Bauble in the Legacy Theater at Cornell College. Smith cleared his throat, closed his eyes for a moment, and tried to insert himself in the scene again from the distance of fifteen years.

A sweet-looking young man rises from among a crowd of jolly drinkers in a German beer garden and begins to sing an innocent pastorale that grows increasingly fervent. "Oh Fatherland, Fatherland, show us the sign your children have waited to see. . . ."

And the red and black flags go up and the jolly beer drinkers start goose-stepping around and the sweet-looking young man strips off his coat with a flourish to reveal the sinister armband of the Hitler Youth.

Smith sang, cold, off the top of his head, without the benefit of vocal exercises or scales. He stumbled on the first verse but warmed after that. His voice, crackling and frail from disuse, quickly gathered strength. Colonel de Noyer watched critically, leaning on his piano. Smith put everything he had into the last verses, as much emotion as he could summon from his dried-up heart.

"*Bon,*" the colonel said when he was finished. "Another one. Give me a range of what you can do. Stretch your voice."

Smith sang on, selections from *Brigadoon, Oklahoma!, Guys and Dolls, Finian's Rainbow,* as dawn rose over Paris, over the Sacré-Coeur, gleaming on its hill for the sins of 1870; over the Trocadero and the golden dome of the Invalides. The audition ended; the strangest of Smith's life. Colonel de Noyer gently closed the keyboard cover and rose to pace the room.

"A fine voice," he said. "*Mes compliments.* Truly professional quality. Technically perfect."

"Thank you, sir," Smith said.

"And yet—" The colonel stopped pacing. "Viva Paris!" he exclaimed.

Smith looked at the man blankly. Was he crazy too? Was everyone crazy?

"No, I'm not insane." The colonel grinned. "At least not yet. What I'm talking about is art, Mr. Smith. Viva Paris—it's a story Lorca tells. Do you know Lorca?"

Smith nodded. "I played Leonardo in *Blood Wedding* off-off-Broadway."

"Lorca was a great aficionado of the flamenco, you see. He writes somewhere of a dancer, a beautiful, determined young woman who studied for many years and achieved a complete mastery of technique. There wasn't a step she couldn't execute, her gestures were perfect, everything done with vigor, absolutely nothing that could be criticized. She toured the provinces to great acclaim and at last came to the famous Alcazar in Madrid, where all the best flamenco artists must come sooner or later and where reputations are made or broken. All the critics were there that night, the newspapermen, the theater directors, the true *aficiones.* Lorca himself was there, though somewhat drunk. The houselights went down, the woman danced. She dominated the stage, absolutely . . ."

The colonel paused, staring out the window into nothing.

"So the dance ended. This was the moment when the applause rises up like thunder to heaven, where they cover the stage with roses. There was only silence. The dancer, no longer young, had spent years of her life, forsaken lovers, friends, family, to achieve this technical perfection. But technical perfection does not lie at the heart of flamenco or any other art. The dancer stood there, breathing heavily, covered in sweat, waiting for the applause, perhaps not understanding. At last, a single critic rose to his feet and began to clap his hands very deliberately.

" 'Viva Paris,' he called out. 'Viva Paris.'

"And the entire audience took up this chant, which was the greatest insult imaginable coming from these passionate Spaniards, these lovers of flamenco. To them Paris represented all that was slick and professional, all glitter and no heart and full of false glamour—qualities Catholic priests usually attribute to the devil. The dancer fled the stage of the Alcazar, crushed. She ran to the nearest bridge and threw herself over the side. Those who witnessed this leap said it was the most beautiful thing they had ever seen. She seemed to fly like a bird, inscribing a beautiful, flaming arc in her red flamenco dress against the blue sky. One would like to think that she had finally dispensed with perfect technique and become a part of the dance she sought to master. Unfortunately this was her last act. She went under and was swept away by the waters of the Manzanares. Her body was never found."

Colonel de Noyer returned to his piano when he had finished this monologue and resumed playing his Satie. Smith remained silent, a chill running up his spine.

"Is that a true story?" Smith said at last.

"More or less."

"You're talking about my singing."

The colonel stopped playing. "Your voice is impeccable, like the flamenco dancer's steps, Mr. Smith, and cannot be criticized. But there is—how should I put it—too much ego involved."

Smith didn't say anything.

"And there is something lacking, something essential to an artist. *Duende*, the Spanish called it—the term is untranslatable because it has no precise meaning. *Joy, spontaneity, soul, passion*—all these words come close, but not quite. Maybe the Legion can teach you a bit of *duende*, I don't know. But let me ask you a question now. A very important question. Why do you want to do this terrible thing to yourself?"

"Which terrible thing?"

"The Legion, Mr. Smith."

"I have my reasons," Smith said.

"As does everyone," the colonel replied dryly. "However, it appears from your CV that you've made a reasonably successful career on the musical stage in America. For your sake I urge you to spare yourself much pain and suffering and return to it."

"Not much of a career these days," Smith confessed. "I had a few lucky breaks early on, but I haven't worked much in the last couple of years. Talent just isn't enough in New York anymore. You need to have the right connections. I don't have any connections, not really. I'm from Iowa, my family's from Iowa, for generations. And my agent dumped me and I can't seem to get another one. I've been to a dozen open casting calls since last November, but"—he shook his head—"nothing. I've failed. I'm a loser."

"And you are also an idiot!" Colonel de Noyer snapped. "The Legion deserves its reputation as an army of the damned! A home to murderers, thieves, drug addicts, sodomites! Men whose only alternative is prison or suicide. You may have failed in New York, as you say, but are you one of these?"

Smith looked away. He refused to answer.

"Ah . . ." The colonel nodded thoughtfully. "I will tell you why men such as yourself seek out the Legion. Not at all for the reasons they say—to find adventure, to escape from failure, or bury a broken heart. These things are a subterfuge. The real reason is because they wish to punish themselves for being themselves, for being a stupid drunk or for being a coward or for having done nothing of value with their lives. Or worst of all, for having no honor. Well, if it's punishment you seek, *mon enfant*, you have come to the exact right place. Your perfect voice will earn you no special treatment. You will suffer the same harsh discipline as your comrades. The Legion will abuse you as you've never experienced—physical, mental, spiritual punishment. Tell me, truthfully, is it punishment you seek?"

"Yes," Smith whispered, his eyes downcast. He could barely hear his own voice.

"And why do you desire this punishment?"

"Because . . ." There was a woman, he wanted to say. Because I caused her death. Because I was weak and selfish. Because I raped her. . . . Smith looked up. None of this was exactly right.

"Because I have no honor," he said.

Their eyes met. Colonel de Noyer nodded sadly. Then he rose and kissed Smith on both cheeks.

"Welcome to the Legion."

10.

Morning light shone through the barred windows of the Legion recruitment office at the Fort de Nogent. The hum of early traffic flowed along distant boulevards in another world. Then came the blare of a lone bugler playing the reveille over the fort's loudspeakers and the groans of belligerent, exhausted men and the clank and scrape of water through rusty pipes sounding like prison doors rasping shut forever.

Smith, his voice hoarse from so much unaccustomed vocal exercise, returned to Sergent-chef Pinard, whom he had hoped in vain never to see again, and was taken by two subalterns into a side room where, for the second time in three weeks, his possessions and clothes were stripped from him, even his underwear and socks. Nude, he was issued a pair of unwashed denim overalls that stank of human sweat and rancid French cigarettes, and the same sort of Chinese-made sneakers without laces that had been given to him in jail in Istanbul—the mandatory footwear, he guessed, of desperate men.

Sergent-chef Pinard entered and handed him a two-page contract printed on thin blue paper in French, which Smith couldn't read.

"What does it say?" Smith said, though he knew he would sign even if the contract stipulated his soul henceforth belonged to the devil.

"It says the next five years are for the Legion," the sergent-chef said wearily. "It says you're fucked, so shut up, *mongol américain*, and sign."

Smith signed in three places, then the contract was torn away from him and replaced with a large pink card with the words NOM DE GUERRE printed at the top.

"Write a new name," Pinard said. "You can be whoever you want. And a new birthday. Write it down."

Smith hesitated. This was *l'anonymat*, one of the sacred traditions of the French Foreign Legion: Every volunteer would be received into its ranks with a blank slate, name and identity taken from him, past crimes erased. Here as nowhere else on earth—such was the legend—a man would be given the chance to redeem himself. Smith knew he had been lazy, weak, and stupid, but mostly weak. He tried to think up a new name that would characterize his terrible weakness of soul and, after a long minute's reflection, wrote CASPAR P. MILQUETOAST in large block letters.

"What's today's date?" He looked up at the sergent-chef.

"Le premier Avril."

"Perfect," Smith said. "April Fools' Day."

He put down April 1, 1977, as his birthday, thus shaving off the last two and a half miserable years of his life and making himself thirty again. That should be about right, he thought, before Jessica and I went to Istanbul. He handed the pink card back to Sergent-chef Pinard, who folded it in half and put it in his pocket.

"You are an idiot," Pinard said. "You will bring the Legion no good."

"We'll see about that," Smith said, then Pinard turned away with a disgusted grunt and Smith was led away, humming a line from "Fascinating Rhythm"—Oh, how I long to be the man I used to be!—to himself for courage. The subalterns marched him out a side door and down a flagstone path into a large, decrepit gymnasium. Here, canvas and wood fencing dummies, relics from those days when every gentleman officer was obliged to maintain a thorough knowledge of swordsmanship, lay stacked in moldering heaps around the central beams. Pigeons rustled in the rafters near broken clerestory windows. Grimy green paint, probably lead-based and toxic, peeled in long strips off the walls.

A dozen volunteers of various nationalities, wearing the same laceless

Chinese sneakers and dirty denim overalls, dozed or fidgeted or stared into space in rickety wooden chairs arranged in even rows at the center of the room. This bunch looked half starved and crazy and their immediate environment stank of cheap wine, urine, sweat. One of them, a large hairy man who might be an Arab or a Turk, displayed a disturbing visible twitch—one side of his face curling into a ferocious grin then uncurling two or three times a second. A sleeping African, his face showing vivid tribal scars, snored loudly, head back, mouth wide open.

Smith sat down in the chair farthest away from anyone else and tried not to make eye contact and tried also not to think about what he was doing. Doom gathered like a cloud in the pigeon-haunted rafters. Smith knew he had just willingly thrown himself into the lower depths, like a suicide off a cliff. His nearest neighbor, a vile-smelling rat-faced kid, maybe eighteen, with a mop of uncombed red hair, suddenly leaned forward and gushed thick streams of wine vomit all over the floor. The stench was immediate and awful. Disgusted, Smith picked up his chair and moved it across the gym.

The other volunteers stared. It was as if Smith, by moving himself away from them, had committed an outrageous act. A moment later, the mop-headed kid stood, wiping puke from his mouth with the back of his hand, and approached.

"*Peut pas supporter le bordel?*" he said with a sneer.

"Sorry," Smith said, warily. "My French is not so good."

"Fock'n hell!" the man exclaimed in a thick Scots accent not much easier to understand than his French. "You fock'n U.S.A.?"

"U.S.A. all the way," Smith said.

"What's a fockn' 'merican doing here? Fock'n daft or what?"

Smith shrugged. "What are you doing here?"

"I'm fock'n mad as a hatter," the kid said. "Absolutely daft. An' a bludy fock'n dipso to boot. One more year on the outside, I'll drink m'self to death."

"Oh," Smith said.

An abrupt silence followed. The kid's eyes drifted, eerily unfocused, and Smith got the impression of a childhood head injury that hadn't been properly treated.

"Legion's bludy fock'n hell," the kid persisted. "Y'know that, right? Wors' kind o'hell yur ever gonna experience."

"I've been through a couple different kinds of hell already," Smith said. "One more . . ." He shrugged.

"Fat cunt like you . . ." The kid spit, his tone suddenly insulting, his bony hands curling into fists. "You don't know what the fock hell is!"

Smith tensed himself for a fight and felt a jolt of fear course through his guts, but was at the same time curiously exhilarated. Isn't this what men were supposed to be doing? Fighting each other over nothing?

The kid drew closer and Smith could smell the vomit on his stale breath. "We're talkin' terrible beatings," he hissed. "Fifty-k marches on an empty stomach. *Marche ou crève*—that's what they say. Forget all that Legion Is My Country shyte. March or Die, that's th' unofficial motto, an' it's the fock'n truth! You stop marching and they leave you behind for the fock'n jackals an' the bludy savages to finish you off."

"Hold on a minute," Smith said. "How do you know all this? You've been in the Legion before?"

The kid's eyes drifted again. Five long seconds later they drifted back. "I read a book," he admitted.

"A book?" Smith couldn't suppress a laugh.

"That's right." The kid seemed offended. "What's wrong with that? *Legion of Lost Souls*. Fock'n good read."

"O.K., kid," Smith said. "See you at the library."

"Listen, y'ass," the kid said. "I come over t'do y'a good turn—better move your chair back with the rest of us pissers, whether you can stand the smell o' vomit or not."

"Go away," Smith said, and he crossed his arms, closed his eyes, arranged himself as comfortably as possible and, overcome with a pleasant drowsiness, was almost asleep when he felt the chair knocked out from under him. He snapped awake in midair, just before he went crashing hard to the stone floor. He scrambled up, swinging, only to find himself knocked down again by the heel of a military boot. The next blow caught him exactly on the cheekbone and closed his left eye, swelling it shut in an instant. Another kick caught him in the ribs and knocked the wind out of him. He rolled back to his feet and found himself confronting a pock-faced Arab Legionnaire whose Velcro tag read CAPORAL-CHEF AHMAD.

"*Tête de noeud!*" the caporal-chef shouted. "*Salope!*" And he balled up his fist and brought a crashing left hook against Smith's jaw. Smith went over in a shatter of stars, then felt himself dragged across the room by the collar of his overalls and through the pool of wine vomit on the floor. Then he was heaved to his feet again and Caporal-chef Ahmad began to scream in his face. Smith didn't understand a single word of this rant, but he got the general point.

"I tried to warn ye," the kid whispered, when Caporal-chef Ahmad had turned away, wiping his hands. "You wouldn't listen. Man said Legionnaires, they eat, sleep, an' breathe in each other's puke an' shyte. Man said—"

"Just shut the fuck up!" Smith said. "All right?"

"Soot y'self," the kid mumbled sullenly and subsided into silence.

Smith could feel gobbets of the kid's puke drying on his neck, down his back. His face felt on fire, his ribs ached from the blows. This must be the beginning of the punishment Colonel de Noyer had talked about.

A few minutes later, Caporal-chef Ahmad returned, formed the new *engagés volontaires* into a line, and marched them out into the high-walled exercise yard. The hopeful morning light had faded. The sky now showed a rainy slate gray over the Fort de Nogent. The volunteers were then put to the task of moving the enormous piles of cobbles from one corner of the yard to the other. Each cobble weighed about fifty pounds. After an hour of this pointless, Sisyphean labor, Smith's fingers were torn and bloody, his back and shoulders painfully stretched. Another two hours passed. The worst part wasn't the physical pain, but the effect of mindless routine on his mental faculties. He felt himself growing dull, blunt with repetition, and he knew many months, perhaps years of such utterly grueling, deadening activities lay ahead.

He paused for an exhausted beat and found the kid panting at his side.

"Sketch," the kid murmured. "Bludy Legion sketch."

"What?" Smith said.

"It's what they do to ye," he said. "Work ye like a nigger, just to work ye, just to break your balls. *Sketch* they call it. That's the word. Means other things too—like stupid bludy incompetence, like send'n ye out t'fight with outdated equipment or no equipment a'tall. With guns that don't fire, rott'n food in yer belly. Shyte like that."

"You read all that in your book?" Smith said.

"Fock you," the kid said, turning away.

"Hey," Smith said. "Name's John Smith."

The kid looked at him skeptically. "That yer real name?"

"Yes," Smith said.

"Iian McDairmuid." The kid grinned, and they shook hands. "But I told 'em *my* name was John Smith."

Smith laughed at this and his laughter brought Caporal-chef Ahmad across the yard and a flurry of close-fisted blows to Smith's back and neck.

"*Ta gneude!*" the caporal-chef shouted, flailing away. "*Silence! On ne rigole pas! On travail ici!*"

"Work, not talk, the man says," Iian whispered.

"I got that," Smith whispered back, and he straightened, rubbing a growing knot on the back of his head, and they worked on, side by side, in silence for the remainder of the day, shifting the fifty-pound cobbles with no food forthcoming and nothing to drink except for a few sips of rusty-tasting water ladled out of an old jerry can.

At five in the afternoon, it began to rain. The cobbles became slippery, unmanageable. Smith turned his face to the sky in despair and let the rain pour down on him, washing the dried vomit from his clothes, and he knew—without a doubt—that he wouldn't long survive this ordeal, that he was too old for such harsh treatment, that he had made the greatest, the last mistake of his life. But, smiling to himself, he suddenly recalled the mildly successful musical version of Beckett's *Malone Dies* he'd done at the Community Playhouse in Utica a few years back, and humming a line from that show—I can't go on, I'll go on—he hauled up another block, slippery with rain and blood, and heaving it to his shoulder, stumbled across the yard and dropped it on the pile with the rest in the lowering dusk.

6

PUNISHMENT

1.

Not enough time to bathe, barely enough time to eat and shit, and only four hours of sleep in between; only rocks and wind and rain and no talking from darkness to darkness. The lights of Paris tinted the wet sky a sickly yellowish-green above the high walls of the exercise yard as Smith heaved the equivalent of forty tons of fifty-pound cobbles from one side to the other and back again with his bare hands. A word, a joke, the slightest pause would earn terrible beatings from Caporal-chef Ahmad. After two weeks of this gruelling labor, they were without warning marched out through the gates of the fort in the dark, put on a bus with steel mesh covering the windows, transferred to a similarly sequestered train, and shipped south. The ride ended at Legion headquarters in Aubagne, a dry garrison town in the Bouches-du-Rhône, surrounded on all sides by the arid slopes of mountains—the Garbalan, the Sainte Baume, the Douard—more prison walls!—and blasted by the Cers, a dry powdery wind. Here, the Legion had made its permanent home after being expelled from Sidi Bel Abbès in Algeria in 1961.

The hot Provençal summer passed slowly—the worst summer of Smith's life, a season once devoted to mediocre summer stock productions of *Pajama*

Game and *Cats* in Vermont—now full of more beatings, hunger, thirst, and sadistic discipline. Not even *Cats* had been this bad. October came, bringing a few days of relief from heat, then all at once, biting cold. There seemed to be no autumn in this part of the world. The miserable corps of *engagés volontaires* were marched one snowy morning into the mountains in the instant winter, over frozen trails and down trackless valleys to the Legion farm at Castelnaudray a hundred kilometers away. There, training continued in a freezing, exhausted nightmare.

In these purgatories, in Aubagne and at Castelnaudray, Smith witnessed again and again the spectacle of his fellow volunteers driven beyond the limits of endurance: fifty-kilometer hikes up steep mountain trails loaded with seventy-five pounds of gear, their feet raw with blisters, their boots full of blood. Punishing sit-ups with railroad ties balanced on the stomach. Droning hours of rifle breakdown and reassembly, the last bit blindfolded. Daily doses of *corvée* and *la pelote*—onerous kitchen patrols and penalty duties—designed to break the individual will. Men so worn out they couldn't unbutton their pants and so lay in their sleeping bags gibbering like imbeciles, pissing themselves. Men forced to hack out latrine trenches with tiny shovels in frozen ground on a blasted hillside after two relentless days on the march, only to be ordered to fill the trenches up again and start over in another location ten kilometers away.

The standard Legion training regimen included lack of food and basic supplies, little water for drinking or bathing, no toilet paper, no access to television, personal mail, cell phone, or Internet, incomprehensible French lessons, and the roughest, arbitrary discipline. Men were expected to march all day on little more than a mouthful of liquid and a morsel of bread, then present themselves in spotless, meticulously prepared uniforms—thirteen carefully ironed creases per shirt—for full dress inspection. Once, at Aubagne, Smith got himself beaten unconscious by the caporal-chef in charge of his barracks—a sadistic Polish drill instructor named Ostwronski—for neglecting to shine the *bottoms* of his shoes. To have raised a hand in self-defense would have meant forty-five days in *le trou*—a stinking metal tank buried half underground, its dirt floor covered with feces. One might forget the names of lovers and friends, but never the name of one's torturer. Smith would remember Ostwronski the rest of his life.

But worst of all were the vicious hazings and assaults perpetrated upon the newest volunteers—*les rouges*—by their supposed comrades in arms—*les bleus*—whose enlistment date gave them seniority by just a few weeks. A dozen or so Legionnaires of Greek extraction, all petty thieves and extortionists in civilian life, made up a kind of criminal gang. Called le Mafia Grec by their victims, they came to rule the rudimentary barracks at Castelnaudray through the force of collective brutality. These Greek thugs, traveling in packs, terrorized their fellow *engagés volontaires* at will, extorted money and stole food rations, all with the connivance of the sergent-chef responsible for weapons training, a hulking bruiser named Costas Melis. Another torturer, this one a corrupt Greek with an unforgettable name.

Melis and his Greek mafia quickly singled Smith out for special abuse, resentful of his handsome actor's face and the fact that he was an American. Smith was assigned thirty-six-hour guard duties (ten hours being the norm); suffered beating after beating at Melis's instigation—for a mispronounced word, a look, for nothing at all—was given horrific latrine cleaning *corvées* after Melis ordered the entire training section to piss all over the floors. Melis also forced him to shave nightly with a straight razor while wearing a dirty bucket over his head and singing "La Légion Marche." This inventive abuse went on for weeks. It stopped only after Smith was rushed to the infirmary gushing blood, a deep gash in his throat millimeters removed from the jugular. His cheek and jaw, once unblemished, actor-model perfect, now bore a dozen barely healed razor cuts, like chevrons. Whitening into scars, they added the kind of character his too-pretty face had formerly lacked.

Many of Smith's fellow volunteers deserted. They jumped off moving trains, hijacked cars and drove like mad for the Spanish border, vanished during the course of twenty-four-hour hikes across the undulating landscape of the Lauragais. Almost all were dragged back to Aubagne by military police, subjected to beatings and waterboardings and thrown into the *trou* for nine weeks. If they emerged alive from this ordeal—and some did not— they were immediately expelled from France, penniless and broken. One or two lucky individuals managed to make good their escape; the exact number of these fortunate few would never be known for sure. They were never heard from again—or at least not until publishing a memoir of the hell they'd endured for six months in the Legion. There existed a couple dozen volumes in several languages on this subject, enough to fill a modest shelf in the library: *Legion of the Damned*; *The Damned Die Hard*; *Mouthful of Rocks*; *L'Armée du Diable*; *Die Schwartzenlegion*; *El Legion del Muerte*. . . .

Smith, to his credit, resisted the powerful impulse to run. It helped to imagine the awful stringencies of Legion life as just another acting job, an extreme example of the Method in action. How hard could it be to play an idiot who gets himself stuck in the French Foreign Legion? Remember Laurel and Hardy in *Sons of the Desert*? The role wasn't difficult, merely required superhuman endurance, absolute discipline, a prophylactic dose of gallows humor, unquestioning obedience to sadistic authority, and a working knowledge of the French language.

2.

In the end, only two of the volunteers Smith had moved cobbles with that first day at the Fort de Nogent remained: a Nigerian named Mboku and the wiry Scottish kid, Iian McDairmuid (nom de guerre, John Smith), who was tougher than he looked. Over the months, Smith and Iian had become *copains*, a semi-official relationship in the Legion. A *copain* was more than a friend, less than a brother. Survival was impossible without a *copain* to watch your back and shine your shoes and polish your buckles and straighten your kit on days when you were broken down with exhaustion and in too much pain to finish these necessary tasks. Your *copain* would give you a little extra food from his own rations and lie on your behalf to the caporal-chef if necessary; you would do the same for him tomorrow.

Smith and Iian survived together. They managed to complete basic training in eight months without major injury, fits of terminal despair, or suicide attempts. Though Iian developed acid reflux and a persistent cough, and Smith broke two toes and lost forty-five pounds of the one hundred and eighty on his frame at enlistment and was now distilled to muscle, sinew, bone. The two of them graduated from *rouge* to *bleu*, suffered beatings together (what you got was often meted out to your *copain* as well), fought the Greek mafia side by side. One stumbling behind the other, they endured the required two-hundred-kilometer march through the Pyrénées in knee-deep snow without provisions or water to the abandoned village of Camurac.

This was their final exam.

On a blustery March day, Smith and Iian were at last presented with their white kepis in a theatrical ceremony on the parade ground at Aubagne, beneath the gaze of four bronze Legionnaires supporting the bronze terrestrial globe—the Monument aux Morts—raised to honor the Legion dead of nearly two centuries. A hundred gold-fringed, gold-wreathed battle flags glittered in the clear, cold afternoon. Wind nattered the leafless plane trees; the shadows of their branches made complicated patterns on the brown grass. Three generals and a cabinet minister stood in the grandstands, hands over their hearts; la Musique Principale played "Le Boudin," "La Marseillaise." Disdainful journalists from provincial papers snapped photographs; colorful Legion ceremonies always made good photo ops, despite the knee-jerk anti-Legion politics of the editorial page. As Smith inclined his head to receive the famous white hat, he felt a half-forgotten emotion swelling in his breast, something he hadn't felt in years: pride.

The whiny, self-indulgent triple threat was no more. The Legion had replaced him with a more capable understudy. The name on his name tag, Velcro and removable to preserve *l'anonymat*—Legionnaire Caspar P. Milquetoast—confirmed this astonishing substitution. Here was a newly hardened individual, able to bunk on the ground in any weather and rise at dawn to march a hundred clicks without breakfast. Trained in knife fighting and in the use of explosives. A fair shot with the FAMAS 5.56 assault rifle that he could—as Colonel de Noyer had promised—disassemble, clean, and reassemble in under two minutes, blindfolded. Trained in Savac, France's answer to the martial arts, which taught, among other things, how to kill a man in a dozen unconventional ways—bare hands, broken sticks, a rolled-up newspaper, piano wire, a rock, a ballpoint pen, a stale baguette. Prepared for any expediency in the service of France.

3.

Freshly minted Legionnaires were sent to one of the regiments stationed in Metropolitan France or the overseas departments for specialized training. They might end up in the 1er REC, the Legion's armored cavalry division in Orange; in the 1er REG, the combat engineers in Laudun; or be sent off for survival training with the 3e REI in the thick jungles of French Guyana. Or they might request assignment to la Musique Principale, though this required a special evaluation for musical ability by a committee composed of regimental musicians, both Legionnaires and officers, serving with the marching band.

In the weeks following the kepi ceremony, Smith filed all the necessary paperwork in triplicate for a posting to the Musique Principale with a pref-erence indicated for the Chorale du Légion, then headed off on his first weekend pass to Marseilles with Iian. The *copains* boozed from one end of the town to the other, started fights, got kicked out of bars, had awkward condom-protected sex with prostitutes—requisite hijinks for the Legionnaire on leave. New assignments usually took months to come down through the Legion bureaucracy, allowing time for several such binges. But to his sur-prise, Smith received his orders back in barracks in Aubagne, Sunday night.

They were not the ones he had been expecting.

The TGV blasted up through the green breast of France with Smith aboard the next morning, racing at speeds approaching three hundred kilo-meters per hour over placid rivers and through poplar-lined fields. A beauti-ful day dawned, the hillsides of the Rhône already flushed with wildflowers. It was the beginning of another spring, the first since Jessica's death. Still suffering from his binge in Marseilles, Smith dozed fitfully, drank six cups of coffee, two bottles of water, peed it all out, sweated a rank alcoholic sweat. A couple of hours later, the grimy outskirts of the capital appeared through the scarred windows of the train and he peered out at congested industrial *banlieus*, warehouses, dingy storefronts, the utilitarian backsides of apart-ment blocks busy with piping and ductwork—all bathed in bright, forgiv-ing sunlight. The meandering Seine sparkled green in the sun. North African vendors in the warren of streets below pushed bloody carts from which butchered lamb flanks dangled on hooks. Billboards splashed with the two-story-tall image of a buxom young woman in a skimpy bathing suit adver-tised an unknown product—Cosmoluxe. A detergent, a hair spray, a bikini wax? Smith couldn't say.

He caught a taxi from the gare de Austerlitz to the fort and found Col-onel Phillipe de Noyer, duffels packed and stacked in the foyer, noodling as ever on his baby grand. The rest of his once splendid quarters had been taken down to bare walls. The books and classical busts were gone; the paintings and buttoned-leather covering, all gone. Only the piano re-mained.

"Legionnaire Milquetoast reporting as ordered." Smith saluted and stood back, rigidly at attention.

"Beautiful weather," the colonel murmured. He didn't remove his eyes from a spot in the air somewhere above Smith's head, a thousand miles away.

"*Oui, mon colonel.*"

"Milquetoast—this is your nom de guerre."

"Yes, sir."

"You are something of an ironist, eh, Legionnaire?"

"I'm a tenor, sir." Still stiffly at attention, Smith felt his stomach muscles begin to ache.

"At ease."

"Thank you, *mon colonel*." Smith relaxed.

Phillipe stopped playing and lowered the lid over the keys. A moment of silence followed as if out of respect for a friend who had died.

"That's probably the last note I'll ever play," he said, half to himself.

"Sir?"

"Frankly, I didn't think you'd make it, *mon enfant*." The colonel looked up absently.

"Neither did I, sir."

"But here you are."

"Yes."

"You certainly stink like a Legionnaire—a combination of body sweat, Basta, and Kronenbourg. I take it you've been on the obligatory spree to Marseilles?"

Smith permitted himself a smile. The colonel grew serious.

"Have you requested your regiment?"

"*Musique Principale, mon colonel. Chorale du Légion.*"

"Good. But there's no need to stand for the selection committee. You're coming with me."

"Where to, sir?"

"An obscure place called the Non-Self-Governing Territory of Western Sahara. It has no legislature, no borders, its very existence is under dispute. And make no mistake, even though we will be flying the blue flag of the United Nations, we are going to war. The Legion is going to war."

A cold feeling churned at the bottom of Smith's stomach. "I didn't know there was a war."

"There's always a war if you look hard enough, Milquetoast, especially in Africa. This one's been going on nearly four decades between the Moroccans and the Saharouis—they're the indigenous people of Western Sahara—just simmering along with a handful of casualties on both sides each year and monitored by the benignly incompetent UN mission to the region, known as MINURSO. But a third party, a kind of insurgency, has thrust itself into this stale conflict and now the death toll has exploded. They call themselves the Holy Marabout Army of the Gateway to the Age of the Hidden Imam. Ridiculous, I know, but they themselves are not ridiculous. They are murderous fanatics, without remorse or human feeling, the enemies of civilization itself. France is contributing three hundred troops to MINURSO to help keep the peace, which means she is sending the Legion to fight on her behalf. I have asked for seventy-five combat volunteers from my Corps of Musicians, half of these from the Chorale. Desert air is good for the lungs and sound travels a long way out there—we will not be idle, I assure you. We will practice toward winning the gold medal in Moscow next year. In any case, I will certainly not go to war without a top tenor at my disposal!"

"Yes, sir."

"To save time I decided to volunteer you on your behalf. But I should warn you things might get difficult. Do you have a *copain*?"

"I do, sir," Smith said. "Legionnaire P.C. Smith."

"Inform him he has also volunteered for Africa."

An uncomfortable silence, in which Phillipe tapped gently on the piano lid, as if he expected someone to tap back from inside. He looked up, meeting Smith's eyes, and Smith was startled by what he saw there: a kind of chaos at the center of his gaze, a storm about to burst.

"Do you believe in God, Milquetoast?"

"No, sir," Smith said.

"Pity. You'll need Him where we're going. *Tu peux disposer, Legionnaire!* Dismissed."

4.

Paris city traffic—a bewildering variety of unknown small cars, Peugeot taxis, three-wheel scooters, motorcycles, and the vast green-and-white accordion buses of the intra-urban lines—stood at a dead stop in the avenue Gambetta. Waves of high-pitched beeping rolled through the stalled vehicles at regular intervals like breakers over a pier, but no one was going anywhere for a while: Someone had run over a young woman walking a little white dog in the pedestrian crossing at the rue des Amandiers. End of April now, almost May, but the sky showed a leaden gray over the quartier Menilmontant and over the endless alleys of crypts and funerary obelisks behind the high walls of the Père-Lachaise. It might be dawn or dusk, winter, fall, or spring. Hard to tell with the concrete chill of Paris still clinging to the sidewalks, to the intercises between the old stones of the buildings.

Smith watched the blue lights of the ambulances flashing off the storefronts, heard the mournful yip of the little dog. The accident had happened a mere ten meters from where he sat beneath the awning on the terrace of the café Tlemcen. He'd been there for a couple of hours, malingering over a single cup of espresso and a thimble-sized glass of Armagnac, watching the métro exit across the way, and trying to keep an eye on pedestrians coming along the avenue Gambetta and the boulevard de Ménilmontant and entering the rue Duris, the rue Novograd, or the rue des Amandiers, all at the same time, all visible from his well-situated table at the Tlemcen—itself located at the end of a sharp block jutting like the prow of a battleship into the Place Auguste Métivier. But somehow, Smith managed to miss the accident.

He'd heard the desperate shriek of tires, the horrified shouts of the passersby and swung toward the intersection moments afterwards to see the young woman lying there, already struck down—*descendu*—her white coat matting with blood. He jumped up to help, got a leg over the railing—he'd learned CPR and lifesaving skills, among other things, in the Legion—then stopped himself. Legionnaires were not welcome in Paris, in any situation. Parisians of every type from taxi drivers to cabinet ministers despised them as dangerous drunks, brawlers, murderers, rapists, fascists, militarists—all of which they were, to an extent. Anyway, the young woman was dead. Smith could see that now, from the way she lay, nearly bent in half, on the hard pavement. So he settled back into the cane-bottomed café chair and watched as a crowd gathered, as a doctor arrived from somewhere, as the ambulances pulled up, driving slowly along the sidewalk, as the paramedics finally zipped the young woman into a body bag and it began to rain, the rain washing her blood into the gutter.

"*Eh bien*," he heard someone behind him say, "at least they don't have far to go. The Père-Lachaise is just there!" And someone else laughed, cruelly, at this.

Smith got up and walked the neighborhood again, stalking the same streets he'd been stalking for days, but still couldn't recognize any of the buildings. It was hopeless. He'd never find the right address, all of it a blank facade in his memory, exactly like the blank facades looming up all around. At last, rush hour came—*l'heure de pointe*—and he gave up and made his way down the avenue de la République against the flow of pedestrian traffic—experiencing the distinct pleasure of having people avert their eyes and step out of his way. He wore his *tenue de ville*: the khaki shirt ironed into thirteen precise creases; the khaki pants so stiffly starched you could bounce a coin off the knee; the eye-catching shaggy red epaulets and blue sash; the desert-rated combat boots—les Rangers—polished to an impossible Legion sheen; the seven-pointed bomb insignia glinting from his collar; the white kepi perched on his head at a jaunty angle, now shielded from the rain with a clear plastic cover.

All of it marking Smith out as one of them. A Legionnaire, one of the world's violent. One of the wolves.

5.

The Bar des Bluets, a hole-in-the-wall Legion hangout off a steep street in the Buttes-Montmartre, smelled of vomit, cigarettes, and cheap beer—exactly like the basement fraternity parties Smith had attended back at Cornell College in Mount Vernon, Iowa.

The patron was an ex-Legionnaire, a battered old drunk named Claude with a glass eye, the missing orb lost fighting the Fellagha during the Algerian War in the 1950s. In Claude's day the Legion was still based out of Sidi Bel Abbès, a town the Legion built for itself in the pleasant, hilly countryside north of Oran, in what was then French Algeria. When France abandoned that colony as a result of the war, the Legion relocated every scrap, every brick, electrical outlet, and pane of glass, every memorial tablet, toilet, and statue—including the massive Monument aux Morts—to Aubagne. A large, water-stained panoramic photo of Claude's old regiment—the 1er REP posed in full dress, battle flags flying in 1956—hung in a broken frame behind the bar. Spindly palm trees swayed in the background of the photo. Farther off, the slopes of forbidding Algerian mountains, the peaks touched with snow. Later, Claude's regiment was disbanded—its men disgraced and scattered, its officers thrown into prison—for the role it played in the failed Legion-backed coup d'état that had sought to keep Algeria French. This historical photograph and an explicit beaver-shot centerfold out of a grim Spanish porno magazine nailed to the door of the water closet made up the totality of the Bluets's decor.

Smith found his *copain*, Iian McDairmuid—Legionnaire Smith—leaning on one elbow at the bar, staring up at the centerfold, twenty empty bottles of Kro lined up like a company on parade before him along the zinc countertop. He was very drunk, eyes wandering in his head like stray asteroids around a sodden moon. His white kepi was gone, his uniform soiled, its elaborately pressed tunic vomit stained and wrinkled, lacking blue sash and one precious epaulet.

"You drink too much, kid," Smith said, sitting on a stool next to him. "Look at your uniform. Two months' pay, right there."

It was true. The Legion provided each *engagé volontaire* with four complete uniforms—*tenue de ville, tenue de sortie, tenue de combat,* and *tenue de soir*— any piece of which was ridiculously expensive to replace. The shaggy red epaulets alone would cost Iian 170 euros each; the sacred white kepi, more than 500 euros.

"Fock you, lad," Iian muttered. "I told you I was a fock'n dipso. What's i' to ye?"

"How about a cup of coffee? I'll buy you one."

"I shit in your cup of coffee. Buy me another Kro."

"No."

"Buy me a Kro or I'll cut you fock'n throat."

"Don't be an asshole," Smith said. "The problem with you is your liver. Every time you drink, you turn into an idiot, then you puke. You've got the liver of a girl. Your liver is the size of a fucking Milk Dud. You know how big that is?"

Iian shook his head and Smith made a very small circle with his thumb and forefinger.

"Like this." He grinned. "About the same size as your dick."

"Go t'hell!" Iian growled, belligerence in his voice.

"You're in Paris," Smith continued, enjoying his newfound role as the voice of reason. "Go to the opera, the Louvre. See a show, see the Arc de Triomphe. All you do is sit in this shithole all day staring at that poster with those wobbly eyes of yours—"

"One of the nicest snatches I ever seen, fockface," Iian interrupted. "An' fock you!"

"Culture," Smith concluded. "A little culture might not be bad for you. Actually, it might help."

"When I hear the word *culture,* I go for my gun!" Iian shouted, outraged. "Y' bourgeois faggit!"

He lurched forward and took a swing—a vicious left hook with force behind it—but Smith, expecting this explosion, ducked away and the blow glanced off his left shoulder. The kid spun off his stool, unbalanced by momentum, and landed facedown on the unwashed floor. He was so drunk he couldn't get up. He lay in the muck of puke, spilled beer, and Paris grime, cursing loudly. The only other customers, two paratroopers from the 2e REP at the far end of the bar, their hands all over the Senegalese prostitute sitting between them, paid no attention to this fracas. Claude, *le patron*, his remaining eye fixed on a Formula 1 race on the television over the bar—Schumacher leading the pack as usual—didn't bother to turn around.

You could be your worst self in the Legion, an obnoxious drunk, an unvarnished bastard, a liar, a con man, and still count on the unwavering support of your *copain*. The fragile niceties of civilian discourse, its false smiles, phony solicitude, and calls for intervention had no currency here. Smith helped Iian back up on to his stool and bought him a shot of cheap cognac and the kid knocked it back, his hand shaking.

"Yu've heard aboot the heads," he said at last, calming down.

Smith looked at him blankly. "What heads?"

"Another UN team site wiped out last week in the Non-fock'n Territory of West Fock-all. Some place culled Om Dunka, or sumthin' wherever the hell that is. Been all over the French tele. Makes the second massacre now. Number two. And that's where we're going, laddie, in case yu hadn't heard. Right into the shyte. Th' cocksuckers over there chop off everyone's noggin, just t'—you know—put the terror to the blue helmets. Funny thing, they only leave th' heads behind. What yu suppose they do wi' all the bodies?"

"How should I know?" Smith said.

"You'll go see me dad?" the kid said, after a moment, his voice trembling slightly. "If I don't get back. He's not a bad un, good man, really. Tried to do right by me, t' keep me off th' booze and drugs—I jus wasn't havin' any."

"Sure," Smith said, keeping the smile from his face with difficulty. "When you planning on checking out?"

"Fock you," Iian said. Then, after a glum moment: "Did y' find her?"

Smith shook his head. A pause. Then Smith ordered a Kro for himself and another for the kid, who drank it thirstily, as if he hadn't had a beer in a month.

"How many days now?" Iian said.

"Three."

"Going to piss what's left of your leave, looking for some miserable bitch?"

"Yes," Smith said.

"Follow y' own perspcription, man! The fock'n Opera, the fock'n Tour Eiffel. All that tourist shyte!"

"Don't do as I say," Smith said. "Do as I do."

The kid scratched his jaw for a moment. He swayed dangerously to one side, then to the other, like a kite in the wind, gears in his mind working audibly. Then, the pilot light flared up and the alcohol fumes behind his eyes caught fire.

"You remember where you first met her?"

"Yes."

"So go back there and you'll find her again. Simple enough, heh?"

Smith grinned. Out of the mouths of drunks! Somehow, this thought hadn't occurred to him.

6.

The yellow scrap of paper, now nearly a year old, lay tucked under a heap of newer scraps on the bulletin board in the basement of the American Methodist Church on the quai des Celestins.

Smith found it the next morning after fifteen minutes digging through the various papery layers—the ride-shares to Barcelona, the telemarketing jobs that required knowledge of French and German, the group apartments looking for student co-locs who wouldn't mind sleeping in shifts on the couch. He recognized the spidery handwriting the moment he saw it and seized the yellow scrap off the board, sending other bits of ancient paper like snowy flakes sailing to the floor. Written there was a cell phone number (Smith immediately tried calling—disconnected); the quartier, which he already knew; and the street, which he did not, but which he quickly found in the pages of his *Guide Bleu* pocket map: a tiny blind alley, one of Paris's smallest capillaries, called—ironically, it seemed to him—the passage du Plaisir.

Smith hastened to the métro and took it back to Menilmontant, and quickly found the passage in question, settling in to wait in a deep doorway across from where it debouched into the rue Duris. He waited as the day waned. He did not smoke a cigarette or read a newspaper; he waited in the shadows of the doorway silently, hardly breathing, entirely focused on his prey. The blue shadows of a premature twilight engulfed the narrow passage, which only received direct sun once a day around noon and only for five minutes. A few people came and went—a couple of loud schoolkids cutting class to get high, the postman with his bulging leather bag and natty Yves St. Laurent-designed uniform, an old woman carrying a cat off to the vet in a mesh cat-carrying bag, the cat mewing with alarm all the way around the corner. No one saw, or wanted to see, the mysterious man in uniform waiting there in the doorway.

Then, nearly seven hours after Smith took up his vigil, he heard a crazy laugh from around the corner of the rue Duris, and snatches of a too familiar conversation in a drawly southern voice—

"O.K., like symbolism, what the fuck is it? I mean . . ."

Moments later, non-Blaire appeared, wearing the same cable-knit sweater and sweatpants ensemble she'd been wearing when they met a year ago. The same fake Hermès scarf, now dirty and tattered, hung knotted around her shoulder—it seemed she hadn't changed her clothes or her subject matter in all that time. Struggling along under the weight of a huge backpack, a crusty punk backpacker kid, maybe seventeen, and scrawny looking, his matted dreadlocks tied with a scrunchy bulging like ganglia off the back of his head. Crudely sewn to the left arm of the backpacker's military fatigue jacket, an upside-down patch bearing the Bear Flag of the California Republic. Smith stepped out of the shadows, blocking their path down the passage, an unexpectedly martial apparition on this nondescript impasse.

"Blaire!" Smith called.

The young woman gasped. "What the fuck?"

"Remember me?"

"Huh?" Non-Blaire blinked up at him uncomprehendingly. "What are you, a *Képi Blanc*? Why would I know one of you motherfuckers?"

"You don't remember," Smith said. "You don't remember a thing."

"Like I said." Non-Blaire bristled. "I don't fucking know people like you. Military asshole!"

Smith almost laughed, then didn't, figuring it would spoil the effect. She didn't retain any memory of the disastrous night that had sent him to the Fort de Nogent and into the rough embrace of the Legion. Of course he probably looked like a different person in his smart uniform, with his hair shorn and thirty pounds slimmer—but he knew even if he looked exactly the same, she still wouldn't remember him. He might be anyone. Just another face she'd slid past in the murky twilight on her way down.

The California backpacker shifted his eyes from Smith to non-Blaire, didn't like what he saw, and began to edge slowly back toward the rue Duris. The sounds of city traffic could not be heard from the gloomy *trottoir* of the passage du Plaisir. It seemed they were alone in the vast city.

"Hey, you—wait!" Smith commanded. His newfound authority—or the authority implied by the uniform—was such that the California backpacker stopped. "Did you pay her any money?"

"What's it to you, dude?"

"I don't really give a shit," Smith said. "But if you did, you just got ripped off. There's no room for anyone else in her tiny miserable-ass pad—and believe me it isn't a place you're going to want to stay longer than five minutes."

The California backpacker thought about this for a long minute. "I gave her a hundred euros," he said in a flat voice. "And, like, some weed."

"Give it back to him!" Smith turned to non-Blaire. "Now!"

"Fuck you!" non-Blaire spit out. "He's my new co-loc! That's rent money! And who are you, like the fucking housing cops?"

"Do what I say or I'll call them now," Smith said. "And not the housing cops. I mean the gendarmes who might be interested to hear your student visa ran out two years ago!"

Shaking with rage or fear or both, non-Blaire reached up under her dingy cable-knit sweater and pulled out a belly-pouch (the placement of which gave her an unflattering pregnant look, when in reality she was quite thin) and Smith suddenly remembered her body, her breasts, which she'd exposed to him that terrible night. She pulled a handful of crumpled bills out of the pouch with a trembling hand and thrust them at the California backpacker. He took the money and counted it quickly, smoothing the colorful bills between his palms.

"What the fuck!" he said at last. "There's only thirty left! Where's the rest of my money?"

"We ate lunch, remember," non-Blaire said. "We drank wine!"

"You said you'd pay for that!" the kid insisted. "You said you'd put it on your card!"

"Like I have a fucking card!" non-Blaire said.

"See what I mean?" Smith said.

"And where's my weed?" the California backpacker said, increasingly irate. "Give me back my fucking weed!"

"The weed," Smith said to non-Blaire, holding out his hand.

Cursing, non-Blaire reached again into her belly-pack and pulled out a transparent blue plastic Baggie printed with Chinese characters and stuffed with a dried-up green material, heavy on stalks and stems that looked more like dried oregano than marijuana, but was in fact a potent blend from the Orient called Bangkok Bag, very popular with backpackers. Smith ripped open the Baggie and shook it out on the sidewalk and the marijuana went fluttering to the gutter in the chill Paris wind. The California backpacker stood there, a stunned expression on his face.

"That was totally uncool!" he groaned. "What a fucking asshole!"

"Get out of here, you little jerk," Smith growled, curling his hands into fists, and the kid moved off toward the rue Duris, shouting "Fascist asshole!" at the top of his lungs, and was gone. Then, Smith turned his full attention to non-Blaire. She stood slumped against the grimy wall of the passage—an injunction, DÉFENSE D'AFFICHER, stenciled on the crumbling plaster behind her head—looking like she didn't care what happened next.

"How did y'all know that?" she said, her voice careful not to betray any emotion. "About my student visa and all?"

7.

The flat, heaped with trash, empty bottles, old newspapers, moldy food, shoes, dirty laundry, looked even worse than Smith remembered. Pages torn out of *L'Officiel* had been duct-taped over the window non-Blaire broke on the occasion of his last visit. The place had a peculiar stink—oddly, not entirely unpleasant, Smith thought—like the den of a small, dangerous animal. A raccoon, perhaps.

"What are you going to do to me?" non-Blaire whispered, and she sank down to the stained futon behind the pasteboard partition and drew her legs up to her chin. The posture was defensive, but Smith knew he could do whatever he wanted to her and she wouldn't necessarily ask him to stop. He could turn her over and tear off her jeans and take her from behind like that—and the thought gave him an erotic jolt that did him no credit. But he wasn't that kind of person anymore; he was a better person, a Legionnaire who lived by a code of honor, earned through enormous suffering. What he'd done to Jessica in Istanbul had been an anomaly in his life. This is what he now chose to believe.

He turned away from non-Blaire and kicked around in the rubble on the other side of the partition until he found what he'd expected to find, exactly where he'd left it, spread on the floor like a bedroll: his old jean jacket. He seized it up, felt the pockets and extracted an envelope containing 115 U.S. dollars in traveler's checks—the last remnant of his funds from the ill-fated trip to Turkey—and the precious blue booklet, its pages stamped with entry visas for Turkey and France and the countries in between: Affixed to the inside flap, the photograph of a callow, self-centered young man taken four years ago, embossed with the official seal of the United States.

"Aha!" Smith allowed himself a brief moment of triumph.

"What's that shit?" non-Blaire said sulkily, looking up.

"My traveler's checks," Smith said. "And my Get-Out-of-Jail-Free card."

"What?"

"My passport."

"How did that get here?"

"You really don't remember?"

Non-Blaire shrugged. She didn't remember a thing. Then, to change the subject: "What do y'all need with a passport, anyway?" She uncurled herself from the fetal position and rose to her knees. "Don't they make all *Képi Blancs* citizens of France?"

"That process takes five years," Smith said. "I might decide to go home before then."

"Home . . . ," non-Blaire repeated softly, and there was something about her tone that made Smith pay attention. Her eyes were unfixed, wavering a little like Iian's. She was drunk, yes, but she probably needed psychiatric care, a long stay in the country, the help of someone who loved her. Here she was trapped like a ghost, doomed to walk the streets of a city that was not her own, cadging money and sex off unsuspecting students and back-packers, living off that meager half con and a few occasional dollars from her mother, all the while falling farther and farther into an abyss of her own making with each bleary, hungover dawn. Smith had been there, it was a view he recognized, the walls of your hole looming up.

"Got any money?" he said.

Non-Blaire, sniffling, wiped her nose on the back of her hand. "No," she said. "There's nothing left. That California kid was my last hope for rent . . ." Her voice trailed off. Then: "Why are you punishing me? Will you at least tell me that?

"This isn't punishment," Smith said. "Here"—he reached into his pocket and withdrew 150 euros in cash left over from his first Legion paycheck and tossed it down to her. Non-Blaire stared at the money, surprised. Then she scooped it up and stuffed it under her sweater.

"What do I have to do for this?" she said, her manner both cold and suggestive at once.

"Nothing," Smith said.

She nodded. That was O.K. too.

"What's your real name?" Smith said.

"Margaret," non-Blaire said.

"Want some advice, Margaret?"

"*No.*"

"Paris is killing you. This place is killing you. Look around"—he gestured to the piles of trash, the broken window—"you live like an animal in a cave. Make up with your mother. Go back to Atlanta, if that's where you're really from."

And he stuffed the traveler's checks in his pants and buttoned the passport into the pocket of his tunic and, leaving non-Blaire there on her knees, went down the stairs and into the passage du Plaisir that all too quickly turns into the rue Duris. Later, waiting on the métro platform at Ménilmontant, the blue ozone smell of the third rail and the stink of decomposing rat carcasses and urine hanging in the stale air, Smith found himself smiling. He had recovered more than just a hundred bucks in traveler's checks and his passport from the detritus-covered floor of non-Blaire's pitiful flat. He had recovered a small, precious fragment of the personal dignity he'd thought irretrievably gone.

8.

The wide, beautiful streets of the First Arrondissement, nearly empty at this late hour and shining wetly in a light rain, looked exactly like a photograph by Brassai. The stern, aristocratic galleries of the Louvre rose from their formal park along the Seine. Smith came up through the Tuileries, his Rangers making no sound along the damp, sandy paths, and turned up the rue du Louvre to the main Paris post office—the only such establishment in Europe open for business 24/7, three hundred and sixty-five days a year. There he bought a padded envelope from a machine in the lobby, addressed it to himself c/o Poste Restante, sealed his passport inside, and dropped it into the dark mouth of the mail slot. They would hold it in general delivery for a year and a day; surely enough time to get to Africa and safely back again.

After this, Smith decided on a whim to head over to the Left Bank, to one of the crowded dives along the Boul' Mich. Halfway across the river on the Pont Neuf, he met Iian McDairmuid coming from the other direction. They had not planned to meet here, they had not planned to meet at all tonight, but it is axiomatic that two acquaintances set adrift in a large city are bound to run into each other sooner or later, by some mysterious law of personal gravity.

"I'll be flummoxed," Iian said, though he didn't sound surprised. "There's m' man Johnny!"

"Iian."

They stopped for a cigarette and leaned against the balustrade. The Isle St. Louis floated out there on the dark river, the homes of the rich bathed in sumptuous white light. The gargoyled towers of Notre Dame rose above its square on the Île de la Cité at the heart of medieval Paris, now awash in garish colors—pinks, yellows, mauves—and subject to the tinny fanfares of a *Son et lumière* show.

"Did y' find the bitch?" Iian said.

Smith nodded.

"Did y' wring her fock'n neck?"

"No."

"Y' fuck her, at least?"

"No."

The kid leaned over and spit into the water and watched it fall. "Then why all the trouble?"

"My passport." Smith grinned. "I got it back."

"Lucky bastard." Iian whistled. He understood: Desertion was an expediency never far from the mind of any Legionnaire. But to desert properly, you needed to get out of France, and to get out of France, you needed a valid passport, and the Legion confiscated all passports upon enlistment. These valuable documents were returned only after washing out of Basic in the first couple of weeks, or upon honorable completion of the full five-year contract. Colonel de Noyer had waived the passport rule in Smith's case, compelled by an unquenchable desire for a good top tenor. Now, Smith had the unique option of desertion at any time; he could buy a plane ticket, slip out of the country over the course of a six-hour pass.

"So yer goin over th' wall tonight, then?" Iian said bitterly. "Back to the U.S.A.?"

"No." Smith shook his head. "Not tonight."

"When ye plannin' on goin'?"

Smith shrugged. Five years was too big a chunk of his life. He would give the Legion ten more months, maybe a year.

"One of these days," he said. "But don't sweat it. Tomorrow I'm going to Africa. With you."

"Tha's just plain idiotic," Iian said. "You should get out tonight. A war, th' colonel says. You wait an' see, we're in for some punishment over there."

"Maybe."

"O, we are!"

Just then a *bateau d'ombre*—one of the night tourist boats—passed under the arches of the ancient bridge. Despite its name, lights blazed from the big observation windows. The kitschy wheeze of an accordion rose up along with the low burble of conversation and laughter and the smaller sounds of people dining, drinking. Then it passed on, into darkness, up the river. The Legionnaires watched it go. As it faded out of sight, Iian said, "Let's go get drunk."

"*Tamam,*" Smith said.

And they crossed the bridge to the Quartier Latin, where they were sure to find cheap wine and something to eat and, because of the uniforms they wore, belligerent debates with left-leaning students they would settle in the end with their fists.

7

MASSACRE AT
BLOCKHOUSE 9

1.

None of the larger desert animals roamed the remote, barren corner of the Western Sahara called Sebhket Zemmur. No fenec foxes or gazelles, and certainly none of the flamingos, riotously pink, that could be seen taking off gracefully from the brackish lagoons around Nouadhibou on the coast.

Neolithic graves have been found in caves in the nearby foothills. On their rough walls human handprints and the images of elks and wooly mammoths and flocks of migratory birds and groups of men hunting them and fighting one another with rocks and spears, all drawn in charcoal and ochre and red-iron stain, the relic of distant eons when the climate of these parts was wet and lush, the landscape a rich marshland watered by many rivers. The elks and mammoths and migratory birds were gone, their bones compressed into oil deposits hundreds of feet down. The ant and the scorpion now ruled the sands and barren salt flats, once teeming and green. But even these tiny, venomous creatures were forced into hibernation most of the year, asleep except for a week or two of frantic copulation every winter when a few drops of dew condensed at dusk on the shadowed, west-facing slopes of the dunes.

Of the Sebhket Zemmur's original inhabitants, only the fighting men remained.

2.

War came to Smith and Iian McDiarmuid in the dry wasteland of the Sebhket at Blockhouse 9, a four-square desert fort built by the Legion during the vicious French colonial struggles of the 1920s—and once again garrisoned by the Legion, now the willing tool of neocolonial UN interventionists. This was just before dawn fifteen days after leaving Paris.

Smith had been under fire twice before: first in the bar of the Stamboul Palace Hotel with a .25 caliber automatic; second during Basic when a drill instructor fired a full clip of 5.56 into the air an inch over Smith's head just to make him piss his camos, which he did. Neither experience prepared him for the relentless pounding that began with a single, exploratory mortar round from out of the darkness just beyond the rim of surrounding dunes. Smith and Iain and twenty more Legion volunteers under Colonel de Noyer's command were now blue-helmeted MINURSO peacekeepers using the blockhouse as a forward observation post. Mere observers, officially neutral.

But here they were, hopelessly beseiged.

Mortar rounds drop with a sharp whistling sound and can be avoided by the agile, quick-thinking combatant. Rockets, on the other hand, are almost completely silent as they fall, many times more powerful, and obliterate everything for meters around the point of impact. After the first mortar, a couple of rockets smashed into a stony *guelb* just beyond the fort's defensive perimeter. The unmistakable shudder and thud sent everyone scrambling in crazy darkness for their Rangers and substandard UN-issued American-made body armor.

In the midst of this chaos, Colonel de Noyer emerged from his quarters in full dress, with his uniform splendidly arranged. He had chosen *tenue de ville*, not *tenue de combat* for the coming battle. In other words he had forsaken desert camos, body armor, and boots for his fancy white evening uniform and patent leather shoes—more appropriate for an official event at the Élysée Palace than combat. The breast pockets of his white uniform jacket showed row after row of colorful ribbons and service medals; the gold braid on the crown of his best kepi shone bravely in the predawn light. The Legionnaires gaped.

"Th' Colonel's gon' fock'n bonkers!" Iian whispered to Smith. "Them's the togs y' wear to your funeral!"

"Better hope not," Smith whispered back. "Because it's your funeral too."

Phillipe ignored the uneasy whispering engendered by his gleaming dress whites, unlocked the armory, and distributed assault rifles and ammunition like a counselor handing out canoe paddles and life preservers at summer camp. According to MINURSO regulations, peacekeepers were not allowed to carry anything other than small arms. They had been issued only the standard 9mm Beretta pistols and Legion FAMAS 5.56s and a single Browning 12.7mm tripod—the famous *douze-sept*—at least as old as the Algerian War. The Browning might have been effective for a little while against a massed assault on the fort, but its firing pin had been lost somehow along the road between Dahkla and the desert and the big gun now functioned only as decor.

"We are at war, gentlemen," Colonel de Noyer announced in a calm voice to the startled Legionnaires. "Ignore that pale rag"—he gestured to the blue UN flag flapping on its pole from the battlements—"today you fight for the honor of the Legion. Remember—the Legion is your country." And he calmly ordered his men to their posts.

The next two rockets hit the perimeter wall, snaking an instant skein of cracks from foundation to battlement. Another blew a chunk of the only remaining tower into the dunes. The barrage continued as the sky brightened. A direct hit on the barbed wire and sandbag redoubt guarding the gates blew the two Legionnaires on point twenty feet into the air and destroyed the fort's first line of defense. The sun, rising, revealed the overwhelming numbers of the enemy: Blockhouse 9 stood surrounded by at least two battalions of Marabout fighters, their shoulder-mounted Oblomov 89mm rocket launchers gleaming like spearpoints must have gleamed in the smoky, desperate light of battles past.

Twenty-one lightly armed men, even if they are Legionnaires, cannot stand against an army of two thousand outfitted with modern artillery. Reinforcements, days away at MINURSO Command Headquarters at Dahkla, within sight of the blue-green waters of the South Atlantic, would never make it in time. Colonel de Noyer and the remaining Legionnaires of the garrison had the example of Camerone and a hundred other hard-fought last stands to steel their nerves for death. They might surrender, of course. Surrender, though an indelible stain on the honor of the Legion, was always an option. They discussed this matter in hushed voices, like cowards, and with the hopeful certainty of desperate men: Surely, the Marabouts would hold them for ransom? Such an outcome wasn't unheard of in this part of the world! But the Marabouts quickly rendered such discussions pointless. A large red bee banner rose from their midst, the *deguellere*, the throat-cutter that spoke a language everyone understood. Surrender or fight on—it didn't matter now—the defenders of the blockhouse would be butchered.

The next Marabout rocket barrage blew the UN flag and eight defending Legionnaires from the battlements. Scraps of pale blue cloth, khaki uniform, bits of meat and bone, head, torso, condensed into a bloody cloud before falling to earth in a kind of thick pink rain. Five more died in a series of blasts from a battery of small howitzers that shook the ground like the aftershocks of a medium-sized earthquake. Colonel de Noyer quickly separated the remaining eight Legionnaires into flying squads. These, dodging from sandbags to rubble and back again, accounted for thirty or more of the advancing foe with close-range fire, but were finally driven back and scattered.

Smith, in B Squad, floated through this desperate fight in a state of detachment that was the onset of shell shock, rendered half deaf by the concussive blasts and humming to himself in this temporary deafness one of his favorite numbers from *Guys and Dolls*: Luck be a lady tonight! Luck don't ya 'member, I'm the fella you came in with? Luck be a lady tonight!

None of it seemed real. He was watching a funny movie about a ham actor who had joined the Foreign Legion. He was thinking about ducking out to the lobby for some popcorn, extra butter, but didn't want to miss the big action sequence.

When the Marabouts came pouring into the blockhouse through the shattered gates at about one in the afternoon, blue djellahs flapping around their bodies like the dark wings of birds of prey, only five Legionnaires remained standing. Two were soon mauled by flying shrapnel: Legionnaire Achilles Argos and Caporal-chef Pantocras Constantin—a last remnant of the old Greek mafia from Basic; both pitiless bullies whom Smith despised. The operational force of the garrison was now reduced to three: Legionnaire Caspar P. Milquetoast, Legionnaire Jaime Velázquez—a dour Spaniard who played the Chinese chimes in the marching band—and Smith's unfortunate *copain*, Iian McDairmuid, Squad A's sole survivor. The poor kid had clearly hitched his wagon to a falling star.

"I told ye ther'd be fock'n punishment," Iian gasped, limping along, clutching his FAMAS—he had taken a hit to the big toe—"an' punishment there is!"

"I don't need to be remind—" Smith began, but in the next moment was knocked flat by the shock wave of an exploding howitzer shell. When he picked himself up, he found he couldn't speak.

Colonel de Noyer led this battered remnant to a sandbag-step redoubt constructed earlier against the rear wall of the latrines as a defensive position of last resort. As they hunkered down, they could hear the Marabouts screaming and firing off their weapons and whirling around in a violent frenzy in the main yard. They were out there chopping off the heads of the wounded and the dead and generally smashing and destroying everything.

"Don't fancy making my last stand by the fock'n terlets," Iian said, trembling. "Can't we call for help?"

"A nice idea," Colonel de Noyer admitted. "But our satellite phone—" He didn't finish the thought. The garrison hadn't been issued a satellite phone. An old-fashioned hand-crank shortwave was their only means of communication with the outside world—completely useless this far out in the desert. They were underequipped, undermanned, underprovisioned. The usual Legion sketch.

"Got a confession t'make," Iian said, his wandering eyes wide with fear. "I'm too young for the fock'n Legion, only seventeen. Used forged documents t' enlist"—he turned desperately to Phillipe—"you got to get me out of this, Colonel!"

"I will see that you are repatriated with an official apology to your parents," Colonel de Noyer said. "But we must first defeat the enemy and return to France. Until then you are a Legionnaire."

Smith hadn't yet regained his voice. Wasn't this the scene in the movie where the relief column arrived from Fort Tokotu?

Blood flowed from shrapnel wounds in Legionnaire Argos's forehead. He was blind. He groaned darkly and his FAMAS slipped from his blood-wet hands.

"For your wounds, *mon enfant.*"

The colonel reached into his pocket and extracted a silk handkerchief embroidered with the arms of the de Noyers—three ravens on a red ground, bar sinister—the same heraldic device his Crusader ancestors had carried on their shields in their wars against the Saracens of Outremer.

Caporal-chef Constantin, though himself suffering from a vicious-looking wound, his left trouser leg soaked in blood from the thigh down, took the silk handkerchief and pressed it to his comrade's face and spoke to him softly in Greek, and Argos's bleeding stopped, as if by a miracle. In the last moments of life these two hardcase alpha-dog bastards displayed a childlike tenderness toward each other. Argos's father and grandfather and great-grandfather—a morsel Smith now remembered from barracks-room talk—had been sponge divers in the Greek islands. How nice, he thought, his mind drifting in the current, how calm and quiet to be walking around in one of those old-fashioned diving outfits on the bottom of the sea.

"Pick up your weapon, Argos," the colonel said gently. "Be ready when they come."

But blind Argos wouldn't listen; the Greeks trembled, ready only for death.

3.

Battle, like a poorly orchestrated piece of music, is composed of hectic clamor followed by inexplicable lulls. Now a few quiet minutes slipped by. High cumulonimbus clouds trailed along the blue sky above like man o' war jellyfish. Smith collapsed, panting, against the sandbag wall, and watched these magnificent, airy constructions sail over the horizon. Phillipe removed his officer's kepi, its gold braid shining in full sun, and wiped his forehead on the now tattered white sleeve of his dress coat. Smith understood suddenly why the man had worn it: If you're going to die, die in your best clothes. Unidentified tearing sounds could be heard from around the side of the latrines. Not much time before the Marabouts found them, finished them off.

"Remember, *mes enfants*," Phillipe said cheerfully. "Always save the last bullet for yourselves."

He uttered this death sentence with a pleasant smile on his face and no more emotion than one might reasonably display while ordering a jar of bath salts from the little shop at the Legion caserne in Aubagne. He was an aristocrat, the last offspring of an illustrious line going back before the days of Charlemagne, to the origins of the French nation. His ancestors had stood at the side of Louis IX, had willingly followed that sainted king into unendurable captivity in Egypt. Such men were made for mornings like this, for the last desperate minutes of a lost battle. Phillipe withdrew a platinum cigarette case—a birthday gift from his famously beautiful wife—and offered his last smokes to the men.

"Smoking is bad for you, *mon colonel*," Smith said, forcing an actor's grin. "Causes cancer."

"I think we might risk a cigarette at this point, Milquetoast."

But Smith had no stomach for smoking. The others, livid, trembling, weren't able to bring a cigarette to their lips.

"*Permettez . . . ,*" Phillipe murmured politely and lit up.

"I know it's been said before," Iian blinked, his eyes fixed in their sockets at last. "But I don't really want to die."

Smith didn't say anything.

"That's all you've got f' me?" Iian retorted. "Nothing? You got me into this, and now y' got nothing to say?"

"I got you into this?" Smith began in anger, but stopped himself. Then he said quietly: "I wanted to die when Jessica left me, when my singing career went south—maybe that's why I went to Istanbul in the first place, maybe that's why I joined the Legion. Now that I'm going to die, I don't want to die anymore. Talk about a cliché."

"Fock'n Legion," Iian groaned. "The fock'n French Foreign Legion. What was I fock'n thinkin'?"

"You weren't," Smith said. "You were drunk most of the time."

"You could have gone over th' wall back in Paris, and fock th' Legion! Bet you wish you dun it now!"

"Maybe." Smith nodded.

"*Attention, les deux,*" Phillipe interrupted sharply. "Allow me to call your attention to the facts: Before the Legion, you had nothing, and if you died, you died for nothing, like a million other poor idiots every hour of every day. Now, though you still die for nothing, you die for nothing in the service of France and you will join on the Elysian Fields forty thousand brave Legionnaires who have already done so. *Vous avez mes felicitations.* Congratulations. *Vive la Légion!*"

"Fock France," Iian spit out. "Fock the Legion."

The colonel opened his mouth to answer this outrage but Marabout fighters surged around the corner from the exercise yard thirty meters away, driving a couple of stumbling, mangled Legionnaires before them as a human shield. Smith recognized Grabner, a German who had run a foam club

in Ibiza and was caught there dealing heroin; escaping from the hands of
the Spanish police, he'd made it to France and joined the Legion. The other
one was Pelletier, a sour Belgian about whom nothing was known, his face
now a mess of raw meat, half shot away. The Marabouts had blasted off every
available rocket and mortar and blown off every artillery round and thrown
all the grenades at their disposal in the assault on the blockhouse and were
now armed only with these hostages and their more or less reliable Indonesian-
made Kalashnikov knockoffs.

"If I don't make it . . . ," Iian whispered now.

"Don't worry. I won't either."

"You're a slippery bastard, you'll make it."

"Thanks."

"You'll find m' dad, right? You'll tell him—"

"I will," Smith said, cutting him off. But he wouldn't.

The colonel tossed aside his cigarette. His pale, haunted face gleamed
with sweat like a block of ice in the sun.

"*Voilà un joli petit coup de main*"—a nice little battle—"before the end. Fire
at my signal."

"Wha' about our guys?" Iian gestured.

"I place their souls in the hands of the Almighty." Colonel de Noyer
brought the stumpy FAMAS to his shoulder and began to fire in long, ropy
automatic bursts.

"Poor miserable fucks!" Smith murmured, but he didn't like Grabner or
Pelletier at all and was really thinking only about himself. He leveled his
own weapon and fired until his clip ran dry. Iian fired, tears streaming down
his cheeks. Velázquez fired. The wounded Greeks huddled together down
behind the sandbags, whimpering for mercy like dogs and calling on the
Virgin. Enemy rounds found them there as they cowered and they died like
that. Bullets splashed into the walls of the latrine, into the bloody dirt.
Velázquez collapsed, without so much as a grunt—though no visible entry
wound could be seen—inscrutable in death as he had been in life, the sound
of the Chinese chimes perhaps ringing his entry into the long, vaulted corridors of death. A moment later a round slammed into Iian's forehead, which
exploded like a red flower blossoming and he dropped, arms flailing; he too
was dead.

Smith tossed down his own empty FAMAS and grabbed the kid's rifle
from the dirt and kept firing. He didn't spare a moment's remorse for his

dead *copain* because he knew they would drink together soon again in hell. But, impossibly, he wasn't hit. The bullets just seemed to break away from him for reasons that had everything to do with wind shear and trajectory and nothing with the will of God—or maybe this was wrong, maybe wind shear and trajectory were the will of God made manifest. Or maybe God just loves a good tenor. Then Smith's ammunition ran dry. He and the colonel, invisible for the moment, stood safely enveloped in a billowing cloud of dust and propellant gas. They were now the last survivors of the garrison.

"You breathe still, *mon brave* Milquetoast." Phillipe nodded in his direction.

"I guess I'm hard to kill," Smith said, trying not to sound afraid.

"A good quality in a soldier."

"Where are they?"

"Patience. They're coming."

Vague shapes began to emerge, groping through the dusty atmosphere. The colonel seized an assault rifle and pulled the trigger to an empty clicking sound. Nothing left. Not a single round.

"*Merde, c'est fini.*" He heaved his spent FAMAS in the general direction of the enemy and turned to Smith with his final command. Not the expected, fix bayonets! Rather, casually: "Why don't you sing something, Milquetoast."

"You mean 'Le Boudin'?" Smith said, surprised—then, he wasn't. This is why he'd been recruited into the Legion in the first place. For this last moment, for a final song.

"No." The colonel shuddered. "Not that."

"O.K.," Smith said. "What about 'Sous le Soleil Brûlant d'Afrique'? Or 'Eugénie'?" Two more venerable Legion standards.

The colonel shook his head. "I don't want to die with the sound of that military claptrap in my ears. You'll be the first to hear the news—I now officially resign my commission in the Legion with the intention of abandoning the craft of war altogether and returning to my wife in France. Something I should have done many years ago." He smiled distantly. "What a fine woman she is, my Louise! So sweet and so clever! And so beautiful, let me tell you. I thought absence would keep our love fresh. I am a fool. The truth is simpler, absence is just absence. All those hours we could have spent together. All the children we never had."

Smith kept his eyes on the armed cloud, boiling, about to burst, just ahead.

"So what do you want me to sing?"

"Why not something from the American musical stage." The colonel put his hands in his pockets and slouched elegantly against the blood-spattered wall of the latrine. "Something perhaps a bit melancholy as befits the occasion of our death. This is your final performance, Milquetoast. Put the ego aside. Find some *duende*, disappear into the song."

"O.K.," Smith said. "*Duende.*" He took a slug of water from his canteen, rinsed the taste of grit and blood around his mouth, and spat it out again. The Marabouts inched forward through the cordite haze, pale dust settling on their robes, on the breech of their cheap Indonesian rifles. Smith switched his internal playlist to shuffle and sang out in a clear, bright voice the first thing that came to him.

"There may be trouble ahead, but while there's moonlight and music and love and romance, let's face the music and dance . . .

"Before the fiddlers have fled, before they ask us to pay the bill, and while we still have the chance, let's face the music and dance . . ."

And through the force of his imagination, disappearing into the song, he was back in summer stock years ago doing an Irving Berlin tribute at the Morris Amphitheater in the heat of an August night in Storrs, singing his heart out, a talented fresh-faced kid full of ambition and the optimism of youth, singing as moths fluttered to their deaths against the bright globes of the footlights, his voice ringing out perfectly pitched and full of emotion, the best damn tenor they'd ever heard way out there in the wilds of Connecticut, the best they would ever hear.

8

THE LOST PATROL

1.

Sous-lieutenant Evariste Pinard of the Foreign Legion, commanding the relief column from Dahkla, rode shotgun in the lead truck. He caught a close-up of the severed head through the lenses of his high-powered Épervier *jumelles* and a sweet panic gripped his guts: Morning sun, rising from behind the distant peaks of the Guelta Mountains, suddenly illuminated the vacant eye sockets; they blazed for a moment with a kind of supernatural fire. Fifteen years in the Legion band had taught Pinard much about the oboe (how to play it while marching the crawl, how to shave a good reed, how to blow the lowest low notes without excess vibrato); his duties in dingy Legion recruiting offices across Metropolitan France had taught him much about the cardboard despair of drunken young men, and a hardscrabble childhood had taught him much about violence and loneliness. But nothing had prepared him exactly for this. Death. Well, here it was!

By damping the filter of his Éperviers against the glare, Pinard was able to make out two more heads, these impaled on sharp bits of rubbish behind the smashed gates deep inside the exercise yard.

"*Tabarnak ostie!*" he swore. "*C'est un vrai bordel!*"

The driver, a strong-smelling, bass-voiced Mongolian corporal named Hehu Keh, glanced over at Pinard apprehensively from behind the wheel.

"*Mais, t'as vu quelque chose, le chef?*" he said in French flattened by the accent of Ulan Bator. Their convoy consisted of six French army-surplus Peugeot P4 LVRAs, lightly armored and painted UN blue, an excellent target for anyone who wanted to shoot at them. Caporal Keh was on loan from the 2e REP, the Foreign Legion's lone parachute regiment, based out of Calvi, in Corsica. He'd had a soft life on that rocky island, a barmaid girlfriend, not too bad-looking, Sundays at the beach. Now this bastard of a desert, the smell of massacre in the air.

"*Arrêtez le camion!*" Sous-lieutenant Pinard ordered. The Mongolian stomped the brakes with such force, Pinard went flying against the dash. "*Putain de merde, taboire!*" he swore. "*Keh, t'es un crétin d'un wanker!*" He dropped the binoculars and grabbed his walkie-talkie. "*Attention les camions! Arrêtez!*" he called urgently. "*Arrêtez immédiatement!*"

When nobody else stopped—the multilingual UN troops under Pinard's command didn't understand French, had only a smattering of Dutch in common, and probably had their walkies tuned to the wrong frequency anyway—Pinard stuck himself half out the window and began to wave his arms.

At this signal, the second Peugeot (containing two British Pakistanis, a Latvian medic, a Catalan, a Hungarian Legionnaire named Stefan Szbeszdogy, all-weather equipment, two crates of RCIR reheatable meals, and eighteen hundred liters of water) veered wildly into the dunes. The third and fourth trucks, packed with arms and ammunition, and the remainder of the fifteen-man force (a Brazilian explosives expert, two Turkish naval ensigns, and five diminutive Dyak militiamen from Borneo, their tea-colored skin covered with intricate tattoos), stampeded after the second like a couple of scrapies-maddened cows. And it was only with much swearing over the walkie in several languages and the use of more frantic arm-waving that Sous-lieutenant Pinard managed to get this rolling Babel under control again.

The convoy regrouped, engines idling, behind the cover of a sheltering dune two clicks to the southeast of the blockhouse. The Peugeots drew into a circle like covered wagons huddled against Indian attack and the men dismounted and assembled in the lee of the dune as Pinard crawled to the top. Visibility is excellent in the desert. Rock formations six or seven kilometers off can seem just a few hundred meters away. The half-destroyed walls of Blockhouse 9 could be seen clearly from here, heat-haze dancing above the ragged battlements. Shattered sandbag redoubts showed the effect of shoulder-fired rockets. The watchtower was gone, the gates blown apart.

Pinard felt a kind of déjà vu as he examined the ruined old fort through his binoculars. He'd seen dim, black-and-white photographs of similar outposts in the campaign histories he'd been forced to study during his officer training at Saint-Cyr. Too many Legion grunts had died building and defending Blockhouse 9 and many others like it during the brutal Moroccan campaigns of a century ago. In those days it was the Legion, vastly outnumbered, holding a chain of forts strung across the Sahara against the wild surge of the desert tribes. All that was gone, ancient history; now the Legion had returned to Africa in the name of peace. And yet the horrors of bygone wars—full of massacres, torture, merciless reprisals, and counterreprisals—still haunted their regimental subconscious like a battalion of ghosts.

Pinard slid back down the dune. Marabout insurgent fighters favored hit-and-run tactics, usually at night, and there was a good chance they'd find the fort abandoned. But the sneaky cunts just might be dug in behind the rocket-blasted walls.

"Many dead inside, maybe some wounded," he announced, waving in the direction of the blockhouse. "So we must—" He stopped himself. The blank look on the faces of his subordinates corresponded with their lack of French. His hold over them was slim: only the sous-lieutenant's single bar, gold on black and newly issued, pinned to his epaulets.

The sun continued to climb, searing the plain. The simoom blew from the south as if from the wide-open vents of a blast furnace. Pinard stood there for a long minute, panting—even his tongue was sweating. In such heat it was not possible to think. Then he turned to Legionnaire Szbeszdogy. The Hungarian, also detached from the Musique Principale by Colonel de Noyer, played the French horn.

"*Stefan, on a besoin des volontaires. Dites en hollandais.*"

"*Oui, le chef.*"

Szbeszdogy spoke Hungarian and Spanish and Dutch; but Dutch only if he thought it through in Hungarian first, translated into Spanish in his head, then translated from Spanish into Dutch. (He'd once lived with a Spanish student nurse for six raucous months in Amsterdam; he'd learned his Spanish from her and his Dutch from the hash bars of the Leidseplein, was good with drug lingo and sex talk and bad at everything else.) The orders emerged slowly, half Dutch, half sign language: They would uncrate the FAMAS 5.56

rifles and the big Browning Douze-Septs. They would establish a defensive perimeter. A party of volunteers would advance on the fort.

No one moved. The two British Pakistanis, childhood friends from East London drafted into the Pakistani army during the course of an unfortunately timed vacation to their paternal homeland, shifted uneasily in their rope-soled combat sandals.

"What's the bloody Frog tryin' to say?" one of them whispered. "An' why's he speaking German?"

"Bollocks if I know," the other one said. "If them Marabouts is runnin' about choppin' 'eads, I say we mutiny and run like hell back to Dahkla."

"I'm for you," murmured the Catalan, who understood English. "If the bloody officer don't like it, we shoot him first."

The Dyaks, squatting in the sand oblivious, twittered happily like a flock of small brown birds. Suddenly, they climbed back into their truck for a mid-morning nap. Pinard didn't bother to go after them. No one spoke Dyak and the Dyaks pretended not to understand anything else. In any case, UN troops couldn't actually be ordered to do something they didn't feel like doing. They could only be requested very firmly to volunteer. If they refused to volunteer, a charge of noncooperation could be brought, but only after weeks of paperwork submitted in several languages and long legal briefs filed with JAG lawyers in Brussels. Such was the state of discipline in UN MINURSO, currently under the command of the controversial Dutch pacifist general Kurt van Snetters.

"*J'appelle les volontaires!*" Pinard shouted angrily. "A patrol. For reconnaissance. *Immediatement!*"

The Dyaks could be heard twittering dismissively from inside the truck. The British Pakistanis backed away, shaking their heads. The Turks and the Brazilians and the Latvian hoped Pinard would decide to turn around and head back across the dunes as fast as possible. A deep sigh, which was the mutinous Catalan expelling breath, rose into the superheated air.

Only Legionnaires Hehu Keh and Szbeszdogy took up their FAMAS assault rifles and stepped forward.

2.

It's a female did that," Caporal Keh said, not bothering to keep his voice down anymore. An unpeopled silence hung heavily over the smashed and crumbling battlements of the blockhouse.

Pinard agreed. "Just the kind of thing a woman would do. Cut off a man's *bite* and shove it in his mouth."

"Them Marabout bitches fight alongside the men," Keh said. "Just for the pleasure of mutilating enemy corpses afterwards."

"Like the War Women of the Apaches." Szbeszdogy nodded. He had just finished reading a Hungarian translation of Evan S. Connell's *Son of the Morning Star.*

Pinard, Keh, and Legionnaire Szbeszdogy crouched in the narrow band of shade directly below the severed head almost certainly shoved into its shell-hole niche in the wall by the same band of Marabout insurgents who had attacked the UN team site at Om Durga a couple of months back. That time they struck just after midnight, killing everything alive, even the company dog and two egg-laying chickens. The proof here was the mysterious hieroglyph carved into the powdery bricks, the graphic symbol of the Marabout insurgency, their swastika, their hammer and sickle: an eye shape, crossed with three parallel slash marks meant to represent—though the significance remained uncertain—a bee, stinger attached.

"Someone take it down," Pinard ordered vaguely, at last. He looked away. The dead mouth, stuffed full of the ultimate indignity, leered at him with a rigor mortis grin.

Szbeszdogy suddenly leaned over and vomited up the few crumbs of UN protein crackers left in his stomach.

"What did you do in the 1e RE?" Keh said, amused.

"Musique Principale," Szbeszdogy admitted, wiping his face.

"Another musician!" Caporal Keh offered a derisive snort. "*Regardez comment c'est fait, les musiciens!*" And he reached up and grabbed down the head by jabbing two fat fingers in the empty eye sockets, wrapped it in a shred of camouflage meshing, and tied the meshing to his belt, the head bouncing against his thigh like a soccer ball.

"Back in Mongolia, it was my job to gut the sheep and crack their skulls." He smiled at the memory. "My mother made an excellent stew with the brains and glands. How much difference, I ask you, is there between a sheep and a man?"

"Quite a bit, actually," Szbeszdogy deadpanned. "For one thing there's the wool."

"For another thing, Mongolians prefer to fuck sheep," Pinard said. "When they're not jerking off. *C'est correcte, Caporal?*"

The Mongolian didn't find this amusing. He had been caught last year naked and drunk out of his mind on the eve of Camerone Day—the Legion's most sacred celebration—masturbating frantically in the middle of the parade ground at the 2e REP's headquarters in Calvi and had become the laughing-stock of the regiment. It was for this he'd sought reassignment to MINURSO.

The sand, blown by the simoom into little furrows, looked as white as snow in the hot glare. Flecks of feldspar glittered pinkly in the drifts. The tops of the Peugeots could be seen as a thin black line over the dunes in the heat-haze. No one seemed to be manning the Brownings, their main source of covering fire.

The Legionnaires malingered there in the narrow shade beneath the wall a moment longer.

"Could be booby-trapped," Szbeszdogy offered presently. "Or an ambush."

"Possible." Pinard shrugged. Though they hadn't taken fire advancing to the walls of the fort.

"Stop!" Caporal Keh said, nearly shouting. "Do we talk or do we go in?"

Pinard unclipped a grenade from his belt and lobbed it over the rubble blocking the main gate. The blast shuddered the old wall; a cloud of brick dust, dirt, and small stones blossomed into the air. The Legionnaires hurdled themselves through the falling cloud, over the rubble and into the block-house yard, firing their weapons. Three full clips of 5.56 exploded simulta-neously. Severed heads went spinning wildly in a rain of bullets like grotesque bowling balls. Piles of shattered debris littered the yard. Smashed furniture, plastic bits of laptops, books with every page torn to shreds, scraps of choral sheet music. The entire contents of the enlisted barracks and officers' quar-ters, even the wooden slabs from the latrine pulled out and rendered into bits. This total destruction seemed the result of a dark animal urge. A bear with a dog in its teeth, shaking until everything has been shaken apart. Gory patches of splatter in the sand indicated the places where the Legion-naires of the garrison had been decapitated. Scratched here and there glee-fully in the bloody muck, the bee hieroglyph.

Pinard moved through the mess cautiously at first, FAMAS held ready. But the fort was completely deserted. There could not be a more deserted place.

"*Ces sales chiens de Marabouts!*" the Mongolian growled. "I knew these men. True, most of them were assholes—"

"But they didn't deserve to die like this," Szbeszdogy said, kicking a head out of the way. "Butchered like pigs."

"Maybe not," the Mongolian agreed.

Working through the debris a couple of minutes later, Pinard found three more heads. He conquered his squeamishness this time and, following the Mongolian's example, took hold of the heads by the empty eye sockets. It was the easiest way. The hair shaved in the *boule à zéro* style favored by the Legion offered no purchase; the ears and nose had been lopped off by the Marabouts, mouths stuffed with withered genitalia. He thus assembled eight heads in a gruesome pile. Thirteen more were discovered by Caporal Keh laid out grotesquely, like cabbages, in a couple of rows in the dirt behind the latrines.

Pinard studied this macabre display, horror and rage boiling inside him. The completeness of the massacre brought to mind other notorious Legion slaughters—the debacle at Camerone; the rout and murder of the Forestier expedition in the Hoggar in the 1880s. But more immediately the many atrocities perpetrated by the infamous el-Krim during the Moroccan wars. El-Krim's special trick, the flaying alive of captured Legionnaires, was done in such a way that they lingered, skinless, for days. Though some he buried up to the neck in sand and covered their heads with honey, leaving ants and dung beetles to finish the work.

The head of Phillipe de Noyer, Blockhouse 9's commandant, Pinard's superior and a mentor to many in the 1e RE, no doubt lay somewhere in the surrounding mess. But it would be now impossible to identify the colonel's mutilated, sun-blackened head from all the other mutilated, sun-blackened heads by facial characteristics. Forensic specialists in Aubagne would have to rely on DNA samples, dental records. Of course the bodies were nowhere to be found, another sign the Marabouts had been at work. They'd left no corpses at Om Durga either, only disembodied heads.

"I know what they do with the bodies!" Szbeszdogy cried. "They eat them! They're a bunch of fucking cannibals!"

"*Du calme!*" Pinard said sternly. "*C'est du merde, ça, Szbeszdogy!* Psy-ops lies!"

"Ask me, a Legionnaire makes a pretty indigestible meal—" Caporal Keh began, then he paused: An unmistakable rumbling echoed across the desert like distant thunder.

"What's that?"

"What?"

"Listen—"

They raced up to the parapet to see the telltale plumes of diesel exhaust in the distance. The Peugeot LVRAs, hurriedly reloaded with all guns, ammunition, and equipment, were moving off. Pinard watched helplessly through his Éperviers as the trucks pulled out of formation and lurched in a westerly direction over the last dunes at the rim of the horizon.

"*Putains! Lâches!*" Szbeszdogy shouted. "Come back!"

Caporal Keh raised his FAMAS and got off a quick burst at the retreating trucks, before Pinard ordered him to desist.

"Don't waste ammunition!"

"*Nous sommes fini!*" Szbeszdogy groaned and slumped down against the parapet.

Unfortunately for them, the Hungarian was right: They had come three hundred kilometers and four days across the desert from Dahkla and through the Berm at passage fourteen, sector twenty-one. A massive sandstorm from the direction of the Saharoui refugee camps at Tindouf on day three had cost them eighteen hours. There is nothing to do during a sandstorm like that but hunker down and wait, the sky going purple-brown, the hot air thick as soup with flying particles, nearly impossible to breath without a respirator. It was the season of storms, another one might blow up at any time. Being left out here in le Vide—the Empty—was like being left in the middle of the ocean on a flimsy raft with no water, no food, no radio, no compass. All this gone with the trucks.

"Maybe they thought from the gunfire we were under attack," the Mongolian said quietly. "Maybe they saw something. Maybe—" But he was interrupted by the sound of the Hungarian's unmanly tears.

"Don't be a fucking woman, Szbeszdogy!" The Mongolian looked down, contempt in his voice. "Keep it up and I'll bend you over and give it to you good!"

Szbeszdogy didn't answer, his sobs echoing in the stillness.

"Take care of the poor bastard," Sous-lieutenant Pinard ordered, his voice thick. He felt like weeping himself. "I'm going down to look for the last couple of heads."

But as he descended to the exercise yard the melancholy strains of Schumann's *Three Romances for Oboe and Violin* echoed in his head. It was the piece he'd been practicing before leaving Aubagne. He had vague notions of trying out for one of the lesser-known European orchestras some day, when he left the Legion behind and was made—as was the right of every honorably discharged Legionnaire—a citizen of the French Republic.

"*J'aurais dû rester avec mon hautbois . . . ,*" he whispered to himself ruefully. Should have stuck with his oboe.

3.

Evariste Pinard was 100 percent French Canadian—in other words slightly more than a quarter Indian, in his case Abenaki—born in Ours Bleu, a mill town two hours northwest of Quebec City. He ran away from home at fourteen after smashing his third stepfather over the head with a bottle of hard cider during a drunken argument and soon found his way to the stews of Montreal. There he lived on the streets for a couple of years, then became a runner for a Jamaican drug gang selling dangerously pure heroin to Anglophone private school kids. This line of work was lucrative but risky: A couple of his clients died from overdoses; a couple more got themselves hopelessly addicted, and fell into prostitution and other vices, ruining their lives before they had begun. Pinard, caught by the Mounties at last, spent two and a half years in a detention center for incorrigible juveniles, a terrible place all the way out in the Canadian Rockies, overlooking a frozen lake. That lake, the cold mountain sky, the despair of incarceration, the savage punishments, were carved into his memory in the same way the crude tattoos inflicted upon him there with safety pins and shoe polish were scrawled across his flesh—indelibly, impervious even to the wearing away of the years.

Later, Pinard migrated to France, worked as a stevedore on the docks in La Rochelle; as a bouncer for a live sex show in Paris; thugged a bit—in other words, beat up helpless deadbeats for a Russian mafia loan shark—the only work done during those hungry years he didn't care to remember. Then he sold crystal meth and ecstasy in rave clubs in Nice for a Serbian cartel and was caught again, this time by the Sûreté Nationale. At twenty-three, he was forced by a judge wearing a funny hat to make a difficult decision: prison and eventual deportation or enlistment in the Foreign Legion.

To his own surprise, Pinard had taken well to the Legion's rigorous discipline, borne up under its famously random brutality, been thrilled by the idea that, enduring, one might rise from the ranks, redeem oneself from past mistakes through service and suffering. In return, the Legion had given him the gift of a dual vocation: war and the oboe. He had risen very quickly by Legion standards. Promotions from jeune Legionnaire to Legionnaire premiere classe, to caporal, to caporal-chef, to sergent, to sergent-chef came in the first twelve years. Then he was selected—one of three enlisted men out of the entire Legion—for officer training at Saint-Cyr, a difficult academic course that he completed successfully, but very nearly didn't, and only after many long all-nighters and much mental anguish. But in the end, Pinard's struggles exchanged resignation for hope. He had, beyond all expectations, risen to that upper world where men made polite dinner table conversation with other men's wives, where one rented apartments overlooking the sea, bought furniture. He was an officer.

Over the years of his career as a peacetime Legionnaire, Pinard had participated in many military exercises all over France. He had scaled rocky outcroppings in Brittany via knotted ropes without using his feet; orienteered his way shoeless and without food or compass through chestnut forests populated with truffle-snuffling pigs in the Dordogne. From the vantage of various sun-warmed mountaintops in Provence, he had surveyed placid vine-covered slopes for the best potential placement of imaginary snipers' nests. Once he had infiltrated a nudist's colony near Cap d'Antibes, where the crude and brutal images tattooed across much of his flesh somehow made him feel the most naked of all.

None of these experiences mattered to him now, at dusk, overlooking the empty expanse of the Sebhket Zemmur, which he knew would be his tomb.

4.

Night came on quickly, deep black and filled with pitiless stars. A nameless wind whispered down from the Gueltas, their sharp peaks black silhouettes against a blacker sky. The blackness seemed absolute, the silence complete. In the hours after dark, the temperature dropped precipitously, reaching a nadir nearly sixty degrees less than the high at midday. The stranded Legionnaires, shivering, made a fire of paper scraps and debris and huddled around it to warm their freezing hands.

"*Pourquoi les abeilles?*" Sous-Lieutenant Pinard wondered aloud. "What's the meaning of bees? There are no bees out here in the desert."

"That's exactly why," the Mongolian said. "Because there are no bees. Because the Marabouts always turn up where you don't expect them. That and the obvious, of course."

"Which is?"

"Bees." Caporal Keh grinned. "They sting you know."

Pinard considered this bit of logic. The Mongolian wasn't an idiot.

"I've been over every centimeter," Pinard said after a moment. "And I only count twenty-one."

They'd assembled the severed heads into a pile, a grisly pyramid of gaping mouths, congealed blood.

"You?"

"Didn't count them," the Mongolian said. "But looking like they do, they might be anyone."

"There were twenty-three men in this garrison, including the colonel," Pinard continued. "If my count is correct that means two heads missing."

"Maybe two hostages," the Mongolian suggested.

"Can you imagine being a prisoner of those ghouls?"

This question hung between them, unanswered. Saharoui Polisario Front Fighters—no match for the Marabouts in sheer perverse bloodthirstiness—during their generations-long war with Morocco had kept a couple hundred Moroccan prisoners locked in tight wooden cages for more than twenty years. A few of those miserable wretches had managed to survive, though their limbs, atrophied from disuse, blackened and fell off.

"They probably took the colonel alive," the Mongolian said. "That's what I would do."

"Him and someone else," Pinard agreed. "But who?"

"I was an astronomer once." Szbeszdogy's voice seemed to come out of nowhere. He looked up, turning his gaze away from the blue heart of the flames. It was the first time he'd spoken since his embarrassing histrionics that afternoon. "I mean at the university at Dunáujváros, in Hungary. I never took my degree, but I still follow the science as a hobby."

"Your problem, Szbeszdogy, is you talk too much," the Mongolian joked.

"I make a point of fixing the stars in my mind wherever I happen to be"—Szbeszdogy waved a hand toward the black sky—"I know what the stars look like in Dahkla, I know what they look like here. By comparing the two pictures in my head, maybe I could navigate—"

"*Putain de merde!*" Keh cut him off, snorting. " What have I got here? A fucking flutist and a stargazer!"

"The flute is an inferior instrument!" Pinard said. "Mine is the noble oboe."

"And you, Mongolian shit!" Szbeszdogy retorted. "You're some kind of hero?"

"I'm a soldier, me," Keh said. "Ten years in the Mongolian People's Army before this band of fucking incompetents. Fucking Legion sketch! At least I know when to die and when to sleep." He rolled over and was asleep in an instant, his snores rattling off the walls of the old fort.

"How does he do that?" Pinard said, envy in his voice.

"A clear conscience," Szbeszdogy said. "The man's a saint."

Now, the cold, west-blowing night wind, the nourmoom, gusted through the gate, crackling the embers of the dying fire. The two men sat in silence for a while, wrapped in their own thoughts.

"This is May twenty-eighth," Szbeszdogy said at last.

"So?"

"At about midnight tonight there will be a lunar eclipse that should be clearly visible from this latitude. The moon will rise full and, given current atmospheric conditions, probably red as if stained with blood—appropriate, I would say, considering our circumstances. More than enough light to start our way east, the shortest route to the Berm. From there, we might make Laayoune. There are bars in Laayoune. Hotels, a soccer stadium. Maybe we'll find a Moroccan patrol."

"Or the Moroccans will find us," Pinard said grimly. Then: "Yes—why not? What else is there? We just might make it."

Though it was impossible. A death march over burning sands. And what if they found some Moroccans? The Moroccans still hated the Legion for the reprisals of the desert wars a hundred years ago—those people never forget!—and were just as likely to shoot them as anyone else.

5.

The moon rose as Legionnaire Szbeszdogy had predicted, fat and round and red, hovering like a rotten *pamplemousse* over the southwest wall. The Mongolian slept on.

By the sinister light of this red moon, which was like the light of a blaze far away, like the faint reflection of burning, firebombed cities, Sous-lieutenant Pinard and the Hungarian moved around the fort gathering anything that might be of use—canteens, a rucksack, an empty five-gallon jug, and, unexpectedly, the regimental colors of the 1e RE, folded neatly in a clear plastic case, somehow overlooked in the rampage. Its wide bands covered with gold laurel wreaths and the names of forgotten battles spoke of campaigns in

far-flung, exotic corners of the world—some marking French colonialism's first vigorous wave (Mogador, Constantine, Madagascar); others (Dien Bien Phu, Algiers) the inexorably receding tide.

Pinard siphoned rusty water from the tank above the regimental shower, filling six canteens and the plastic jug, which he then fitted into the rucksack on Szbeszdogy's back, along with a single half-eaten package of protein biscuits—their only rations.

And he found, leaning in a corner, casually left behind, one of the Marabouts' shoulder-fired rocket launchers, a Russian-made 89mm Oblomov, one of the thousands obtained by the insurgents from the shadowy underworld of international arms traders. The Marabout bee symbol had been scratched into the wooden stock; one high-powered rocket shell, half-propellant, half-explosive charge, sausage-shaped like the boudin of the Legion anthem—had already been loaded into the chamber. A second remained clipped upright in the loading canister, like a tube of lipstick on display at the makeup counter at Au Printemps in Paris.

"*Voilà, ma belle.*" Pinard smiled to himself, examining the weapon. "Two chances more than we had ten minutes ago."

Gear assembled, he woke Caporal Keh with a well-placed kick.

"Enjoy your nap, Keh?" The Mongolian stumbled to his feet, swearing, and Pinard shoved the rocket launcher into his hands. "Know how to use one of these?"

Keh hefted the weapon to his shoulder, adjusting the sight, squinting through it with his hooded eyes. Then he tossed it into the air and caught it again with one hand like a cowboy, released the canvas webbing with a slick snapping sound, and strapped it across his back.

"*Oui, le chef.*" He grinned. "We used these back in the MPA. A very nice weapon."

Then, Pinard turned to the pile of heads, stacked like so much rotten produce in the red shadows of the yard.

"Let's do this like soldiers," he called. "*Garde-à-vous!*"

Szbeszdogy and Keh drew themselves to attention sharply.

"*Legionnaires, répétez avec moi—Code d'Honneur du Legion!*"

And they said together: "A Legion mission is sacred. As a soldier in the Legion, I will carry out my duty to the end, to the last drop of blood. I will under all circumstances act without passion and without hate. I will never

abandon my dead and wounded. I will never surrender my arms! *Legio Patria Nostra*—the Legion Is My Country!"

"*Camarades!*" Sous-Lieutenant Pinard called, addressing the pile of heads. "We will return for you. We will know your names!"

But the heads, tongueless, earless and yet distracted by the restless whisper of the unknown wind, did not answer back.

"*En avant! Marche!*"

"Where are we going, *le chef*?" Keh said as they marched single file out the main gate.

"To engage the enemy," Pinard said. "Where else?"

At this, the men laughed.

"Let's have a song, Keh!" Szbeszdogy called. And the Mongolian, the star of his regimental chorale—he possessed one of the deepest bass voices in the entire Legion—obliged.

"*Dans le ciel brille les étoiles . . . ,*" he croaked, " *. . . adieu mon pays, jamais je ne t'oublierai!*"

"*En Afrique, malgré le vent, la pluie . . . ,*" Szbeszdogy joined in the refrain with his warbly alto. In Africa, beneath these brilliant stars, despite the wind and the rain, we march . . .

And soon, all three men were singing, a strangely jolly sound echoing against the dunes.

6.

They marched on for three days, mostly at night, catching a little fitful sleep during the infernal hours, with the sun blazing down from the center of the sky; allowing themselves no more than two swallows of water every eight hours, at dawn, at noon, at midnight. But navigating by the stars is not a matter of precision: In the great era of sail, using similar means, entire flotillas found themselves wrecked upon well-charted rocks in moonlight by following unlucky stars to the wrong ends. Thus, late-afternoon day three found Sous-lieutenant Pinard, Caporal Hehu Keh, and Legionnaire Szbeszdogy utterly lost and nowhere near the Moroccan Berm.

The steep wall of sand that marked the Berm's east-facing defense rose up nearly sixty feet, easily visible for twenty-five kilometers in any direction; Sous-lieutenant Pinard's excellent Épervier binoculars extended this visibility by another ten or fifteen kilometers. But perched on Keh's shoulders atop the tallest dune they could find, he scanned the horizon and saw nothing, only more dunes rolling like the waves into an infinite ocean of sand.

Dusk coming on now, a deep, amber light leaning over the blistered landscape; night and cold seeping into it like a dark mist from the other side of the world.

"*Mauvaise nouvelles*," Pinard said, clambering down, his lips so cracked, his mouth so dry and swollen he could hardly speak above a whisper. "I'm afraid we're lost."

"Ridiculous," the Mongolian said. "The Legion doesn't get lost in the desert. Right, Szbeszdogy?"

Szbeszdogy made an exhausted gesture. "I did my best," he managed weakly. "The stars don't always comply . . ." His voice trailed off. He couldn't continue.

"You're an idiot," the Mongolian said. "That much is clear." Then, turning to Pinard, "What now?"

Pinard shrugged. "We keep going, that's all."

They paused here at the top of the dune in the dying light to share their evening meal: two sips of foul-tasting water each, and a single protein cracker, divided three ways.

"And when the water's finished?" Szbeszdogy hissed.

"That's easy," the Mongolian said. "We drink piss. And when the piss is gone, blood. When that's gone—" He shrugged.

"We'll be dead before then," Szbeszdogy said weakly. But he was stating the obvious.

They lay back in the rapidly cooling sand as the sun faded out and the stars rose. Pinard raised his Éperviers to the sky; Alderbaran hung red and low above the horizon. Sirius, the Pole Star of the ancient Egyptians, the celestial beacon that glittered enticingly—so the pharaohs once believed—above the Eternal Field of Reeds, shone faintly blue with little flecks of yellow in the corona like sparks from a tin windup toy. They dozed as the nourmoom blew over them gently—only to awake, startled and nearly frozen, two hours after midnight.

"*Tabarnak ostie!*" Pinard swore, staring into the blackness.

They had lost hours of good marching time—it wasn't possible to make much progress during the full heat of the day—and now they picked them-

selves up, cursing, and stumbled over the lip of the dune and onward, in an
easterly direction, Szbeszdogy plotting a shaky course, using thumb and
forefinger like a sextant, toward what stars he knew looked down on the
window of his barracks room in the mission compound at Dahkla. They
passed down a ravine cut like a gash between the dunes, the bed of an ancient river. Their Rangers made crunching noises on the ground, surfaced
here with a thin crust of salt and vaguely phosphorescent.

Shortly before 4:00 A.M. Caporal Keh stopped and cocked an ear to the
wind.

"Do you hear something?" he whispered.

"Nothing," Pinard said. Or only the ceaseless hush of blood though his
veins.

"There it is!" Szbeszdogy said brightly, eyes mad. "I hear it!"

"What?"

"An engine, I think. And voices!"

"*Non, les mecs*," Pinard said, shaking his head. "You're both hallucinating.
I don't hear a thing."

"This way!" the Mongolian shouted, and he cut toward the south and
jumped the ravine and disappeared over the hump of the nearest dune.

"Hey! Stop!" Pinard shouted. "*Arrêtez!*"

But the Mongolian didn't stop. Szbeszdogy dashed after him and Pinard
followed, flailing over rocks and dunes, scrambling up the inclines and rolling down the opposite side, until they caught up with Caporal Keh, who
now lay on the ground, peering over the edge of a stony elevation into a wide
depression below, a kind of circular salt pan perhaps a kilometer two or
around. A narrow track, silver in the moonlight, led into the *guelb*; another
led out of it toward the north. Down there, not fifty meters distant, sat two of
the four Peugeot P4 LVRAs from Pinard's own relief column. One of them
was in trouble, its hood raised. Marabout fighters, blue-robed and veiled,
swarmed over the engine of this stalled vehicle, as if trying to conjure from
its mechanical innards the magical spirits of internal combustion that made it
run. The second truck, idling to one side, shone its headlights on this confus-
ing work. More blue-robed veiled men and several women crouched or slept
on the ground around the second truck. They had clearly been waiting a
long time.

Pinard studied this scene carefully, silently counting the enemy. He could
guess what had happened to the other two trucks and to the deserters—and

couldn't suppress a bitter little jolt of satisfaction at the thought that they might have met a painful fate: Seeking to escape death at the hands of the Marabouts, they had driven their Peugeots directly into the arms of Death Herself.

"*Mes enfants*," Sous-lieutenant Pinard whispered. "With a truck, we can make the coast. Otherwise . . ."

"How many do you think there are?" Szbeszdogy hissed, barely audible.

"About fifty *indigènes*. Men and women. Not counting any kids asleep in the trucks."

"Kids?" Szbeszdogy said, blinking.

"That's right," Pinard said. "They bring their kids along sometimes. But, even if there are kids—" He left the thought unsaid. "With these odds—"

"Pah," the Mongolian cut in. "Twenty to one. That's nothing for us. Not with one of these—"

He unlimbered the rocket launcher, flipped up the sights, adjusted the target distance on the infrared scope. Then he set the weapon aside, primed and humming with readiness, and the three of them pooled their ammunition: Not including the nine 9mm rounds in Sous-lieutenant Pinard's Beretta pistol, there remained six fifteen-round clips for the 5.56mm and two concussion grenades.

"Plenty to go around," Caporal Keh grunted. "Six rounds per Marabout." Sums had never been the Mongolian's strong point.

"You hit the lead truck with the first rocket," Pinard said. "But only at my signal. Understand? Put the second round where you think it will do the most good. Then run like hell to catch up with us, laying down fire all the way."

"*Oui, le chef.*"

"We've got one chance," Sous-lieutenant Pinard concluded. "We've got to make them think the whole Legion is attacking. We've got to . . ." But his words were taken by a sharp and unexpected gust blowing up from what seemed like all directions at once—this was the drimoom, the wind that heralds the dawn—bringing with it the smell of blood and burnt rubber, traces of the other two Peugeots burned to the gunnels somewhere out in the dark, their occupants decapitated, slaughtered.

Pinard turned to the Hungarian. "Let's have that water. Might as well finish it off."

Szbeszdogy nodded and drew the gallon jug, now barely a third full, out of the rucksack. The three men drank eagerly, long indulgent swallows, more than they'd had in days. This polluted swill seemed like the sweetest drink they'd ever tasted. When the water was gone, they rose, adjusted their uniforms.

"*Le drapeau,*" Pinard said gravely.

Szbeszdogy nodded. He pulled out the Legion tricolor they'd found amid the rubble at the blockhouse, discarded the plastic case, and shook it out. MINURSO regulations allowed only the powder blue UN banner to troops under its jurisdiction; to display any national flag was a gross breach of the mandate, might even be construed as an act of war. To hell with that now.

The Hungarian grinned. "MINURSO no more," he said and he held the tricolor in his fist and it flapped noisily in the breeze. "I piss on MINURSO!"

Pinard tied the tricolor to the back of the Hungarian's rucksack. Unfurled by the wind, it's golden fringe and laurel wreaths flashed boldly in the half light.

"At three," Pinard said, holding up three fingers. "*Un...*"

The stars waned above. Pink flushed the sky, dawn on its way. But down here in the desert, in the Empty, there was no light except for the twin faltering beams of the headlights below. Pinard could barely see the faces of the Legionnaires at his side. Suddenly he recalled the opening strains of Mozart's Oboe Concerto in C Major, saw the notes in his head like crows swirling above a fallow field in winter, then they flew off and were gone.

"*Deux...*"

Pinard locked the first 5.56 round into the chamber of his FAMAS, set it on three-round bursts, and folded out the short stabby bayonet. His hands were shaking. What did it matter, where you died, in the desert, in France, in Canada, in your bed, in the ocean. A disturbing thought occurred to him—he had never really loved anybody in his life, not really. At least not as an adult. Certainly not a girlfriend—there had been only whores, of varying price—not his mother, another whore, or his older brother who had become a policeman in Ours Bleu after doing half the coke in Canada. Maybe he'd loved his father once and been loved, but he couldn't remember exactly; his father had died when Pinard was five, killed by a falling tree at a logging camp way up in Lac St. Chretien, near the Arctic Circle. They had polar bears up there in those days; his father sent him a postcard once, showing a huge shaggy white beast, with a red gaping mouth full of sharp teeth. The polar bears were gone now. The Legion was his family.

Out of the corner of his eye, Pinard saw the Mongolian set the rocket launcher to his shoulder. A slight nod. Ready.

"*Trois!*" Pinard shouted. "*À moi la Légion!*"

And he jumped up, shouting at the top of his lungs, and firing his rifle into the blue swirl of startled Marabouts. He heard the cries of terrified women, the hoarse exclamations of men, what sounded like an infant crying—but he kept firing. Then the Mongolian's first rocket struck the stalled Peugeot dead-on with a *whump*, and the truck blew and blue-robed men flew into the air and pieces of steaming metal sizzled by, and chunks of human flesh smacked wetly into the sand, and Sous-lieutenant Pinard, bayonet fixed, hurled himself down the slope toward the *guelb*, toward the smoke, toward the screaming, and the brightness of flame.

9

EPITAPH
FOR AN ARMY OF
MERCENARIES

1.

The Monument aux Morts glistened darkly over the parade ground at Aubagne in a driving rain. In twenty-one white coffins on twenty-one black catafalques draped with sodden regimental flags, in the forecourt of the Legion crypt, lay the heads of the Heros de la Vide—as they had been dubbed by *France-Soir*—all that remained of the slaughtered garrison of Blockhouse 9.

Generals wearing clear plastic rainslickers over their uniforms stood at attention beneath the dripping canopy of the grandstand as la Musique Principale played a familiar dirge. Politicians raised hands to hearts; journalists slouched, damp, filterless Gauloises Bleus smoldering cynically between their lips. Flocks of sullen blackbirds, feathers hunched against the rain, watched from the bare branches of the clipped plane trees up and down the parade ground. For nearly two hours, patriotic speeches echoed from the loudspeakers in waves of damp static, full of phrases like *sacrifiée pour le bien des autres* and *ces braves soldats, mort pour la France au bout du monde. . . .*

Meanwhile, the bronze doors to the crypt stood open to welcome the

disembodied heads. Down a flight of rain-slick marble steps, behind another set of bronze doors in a crystal reliquary in dimly lit silence lay the
Legion's most sacred relic: the wooden hand of the legendary Capitaine Danjou, officer in charge that famous day at Camerone, who, dying, made his
men swear to hold out until the last drop of blood, thus setting the pattern
of pointless heroics and pyrrhic last stands for the next hundred and seventy-
five years. Encircling this fabled prosthesis, on the walls of the subterranean
chamber, hung marble tablets inscribed with the names of the dead —
37,000 perished Legionnaires—the Roll of Honor. Here too, engraved on a
plaque donated by English veterans of the old 1e REP, was the following
inscription:

> *These, in the days when heaven was falling,*
> *The hour when earth's foundation fled,*
> *Followed their mercenary calling,*
> *And took their wages, and are dead.*

2.

After the appropriately rain-drenched ceremony in honor of the heads, a
luncheon was provided for dignitaries and media in the 1e RE mess:
The menu included *salade verte, poulet Marengo, légumes,* and flan, served with
a good white table wine pressed from grapes out of the Legion's own vine-
yard at Puyloubier. The half-dozen postcard-perfect Legionnaires allowed to
attend, selected for their physical beauty by the regimental public relations
officer, were ordered not to get drunk, a restraint in the presence of alcohol
entirely out of keeping with their inclinations.

But Sous-lieutenant Pinard, Legionnaire Szbeszdogy, and Caporal Hehu
Keh, those men directly responsible for the rescue of the heads from the hell
of Western Sahara and their return to France pickled in barrels of UN etha-
nol, were each for their own reason conspicuously absent from both memorial ceremony and sober, funereal lunch.

At that moment, Pinard, freshly released from the Legion infirmary, stood
painfully at attention in full dress uniform as if for parade inspection in a
small, stale-smelling room in a low-eaved building on the outer fringes of the
base. The green walls of this room were peeling, its small window covered with
a rusty steel grate like the window of a prison cell. Seated facing Pinard on

the other side of a long, graffiti-scarred table, wreathed in cigarette smoke, three lean, dour-faced men wearing nondescript dark suits. These were the nameless interrogators from the Deuxième Bureau, the Secret Service of the French Army, called *le gestapo* by those who knew it well.

"Describe what happened to the Mongolian," the first interrogator said. "His nom de guerre was"—he paused, checking his notes—"Hehu Keh, correct?"

"Yes, Caporal Keh. As I told you, monsieur—"

"No, no." The second interrogator waved a narrow hand. "Reply to our questions without qualifications and without second thoughts, even if we ask them a hundred times. We have our methods, you see."

The third interrogator, studying his well-manicured fingernails, said nothing.

They were treating Sous-lieutenant Pinard like a criminal, but he had expected this reception: In France, in the legal system enshrined in the Code Napoléon, you were guilty until proven innocent. In the Legion everyone was automatically assumed to be a criminal; this general suspicion a result of the long tradition of offering escaped convicts and various sorts of villains a refuge in the ranks. The interrogators from the Deuxième Bureau were themselves part of a long tradition: those faceless men, their identities unknown to history, who had established the service in 1871 had been educated by Jesuits in a famous Jesuit *lycée* in Paris. And after the fashion of any good Jesuit confessor, it was the aim of the interrogators to elicit a confession of guilt from Sous-lieutenant Pinard, even if he were entirely innocent of the crime in question. For which of us, they reasoned, is not guilty of something?

Pinard told them in detail all he could remember about finding the hijacked trucks in the desert, and about the firefight that followed:

Caporal Keh blew the stalled Peugeot with his first rocket, detonating mortar rounds and other ammunition stored in the bed, and obliterating an unknown number of Marabout children asleep in the back atop crates of 12.7mm shells. The desert lit up with this massive explosion, which also instantly flattened ten or fifteen of the Marabout fighters. Shards of metal flew through the air, steaming chunks of tire, body parts. As Pinard and Legionnaire Szbeszdogy charged down the slope, the head of a child ploughed into the sand like a cannonball, not half a meter off their left flank.

The Deuxième Bureau interrogators exchanged a glance at this horrific detail.

"Please, no more heads," the first interrogator said. "There are entirely too many heads in your story already."

"And what's this about children?" the second interrogator said, looking up from his notes. "You didn't mention any children in your written report."

"No . . . ," Sous-lieutenant Pinard said uneasily. "I suppose I forgot."

"Forgot about a child's head?"

"Yes, I'm afraid so."

"Tell me, where do they come from, these headless children?"

"The Marabouts are not an army in the modern sense," Pinard said, re-membering the *Commentaries* of Caesar he'd read at Saint-Cyr. "They're a nation under arms, like the barbarian invasions of ancient times. They campaign with their wives, their children, even their grandmothers—"

"We are not interested in strategic opinions or historical analysis," the second interrogator interrupted harshly. "Confine yourself to what actually happened."

"Make no mistake," the first interrogator added. "You stand before your judges."

The wound in Pinard's thigh was now beginning to throb.

"And please don't mention these supposedly dismembered children to anyone," the first interrogator added. "Think what the press would do with such a story. This is classified. *Comprends?*"

"*Oui, monsieur.*"

"Continue."

The battle for the remaining Peugeot dissolved in Pinard's memory into the flash and blur of tracer bullets, eruptions of bloody sand, the dim shapes of screaming Marabouts. Fighting back to back, firing their weapons in tightly controlled bursts, Sous-lieutenant Pinard and Legionnaire Szbeszd-ogy gained the meager shelter of a pile of flaming rubble a meter or so away from the second truck. There, just as Pinard blew off the last of his 5.56, a Marabout round ricocheted off a rock and struck him in the thigh. Another grazed his ear and left temple, releasing a blinding gush of blood and, wounded and nearly blind, he made what peace he could with the merciless deity every soldier must face in the end: the God of Battles.

"You find yourself praying," he said, his voice nearly a whisper. "Even if you believe in nothing at all."

"Surely even an atheist has belief after a fashion," the first interrogator suggested, a Jesuitical smirk on his face. "He believes in science perhaps."

"*Ni l'un, ni l'autre.*" Pinard shook his head.

"*Passons, passons.*" The second interrogator made an impatient gesture. "This is not the place for amateur theological discussions."

Pinard continued.

As a dozen of the enemy closed in, Caporal Keh came careening down into the *guelb* from his hiding place above, rocket launcher at his shoulder, an inchoate Mongolian war cry on his lips. He fired his second and last boudin into the melee; the concussive *whump* gave Pinard and Szbeszdogy just enough cover to scramble into the cab of the idling Peugeot. Pinard threw himself behind the wheel and jammed the truck into gear and accelerated, fully intending to swing back around to rescue the embattled Mongolian. But burning debris now illuminated Keh's fate: His head, eyes still blinking as if in surprise, suddenly rolled from his shoulders and the headless corpse toppled into the sand. He had been cut down with a single blow from a Marabout scimitar. Such was the end of the valiant Hehu Keh, Legionnaire, ex-private of Mongolian People's Army, masturbator, lover of barmaids, the deepest bass voice in the Legion. Marabout bullets crashed against the armored flank of the departing truck, a kind of valedictory drumroll to speed Kch's departing soul off to the Mongolian Valhalla. One of these sent a sharp piece of metal slamming into Szbeszdogy's ribs and he fell back, screaming in pain.

"There was nothing we could have done," Sous-lieutenant Pinard continued, keeping his voice steady with effort. "I've thought it over and over a hundred times and I still say there was no way to save Keh. We had no ammunition left and I couldn't see because of the blood in my eyes. Anyway, there wasn't enough time, we were taking heavy fire. The truck was pointed toward the horizon and I hit the accelerator. Before I could turn the wheel, it was too late, they'd got to him"—a lump rose in his throat—"Messieurs, I would like to recommend Caporal Keh for the Medaille Militaire. If you permit me, for the record: Caporal Keh acted with fierce courage, beyond the call of duty, with no regard for self—"

But Pinard's speech was interrupted at this point by a voice from above: "No use wasting a medal on a dead man, is there, Pinard?"

The sous-lieutenant looked up, bewildered. The voice, familiar, pompous, issued from a camouflaged speaker box in the ceiling. Up there also, the tiny lens of an electronic eye. He had been listened to, watched the whole time.

The voice belonged to General Victor le Breton, second in command of the 1e RE, a big, obnoxious man, dangerously obese and very vain, who had his unique, showy white uniforms custom-tailored at the Yves St. Laurent atelier in Paris. In full dress, a hundred golden medals pinned across his chest, he resembled an ornate, gilded ship scudding before the wind.

"Is that you, *mon general*?"

"No, it's the voice of God!" the general answered.

The Deuxième Bureau interrogators, Jesuits that they were, seemed displeased by this blasphemy.

"You are familiar with article seven, section two of the Legion Code?"

Pinard hung his head. "Of course."

"Repeat the pertinent injunction for me."

"'I will never abandon my dead or wounded,'" Pinard said in a flat voice, recalling the pledge they'd made to the pile of heads back at the blockhouse. That one at least had been honored.

"Where are the earthly remains of Caporal Hehu Keh at this moment?"

"We searched for his body, sir," Pinard said desperately. "We couldn't find anything. There was a sandstorm. It was the season of many such storms. We couldn't even find the Berm in that mess. We set out for the blockhouse in the teeth of the storm two weeks later to retrieve the heads with the wind howling around us like the devil—we had to abort that mission. It took us two more weeks to get the heads back to Dahkla. As for finding what was left of Keh . . ." His voice trailed off.

"And what about the two missing men?" the general boomed down at him. "You returned to France with twenty-one heads. There remain a twenty-second and a twenty-third head. Am I not correct, Pinard?"

"*Correcte, mon general.*"

"*Alors?*"

"The Marabouts operate out of unknown bases hidden somewhere in the Gueltas. We would need an entire division to assault those mountains, not to mention—"

"Pinard, you are an ass!" the general roared. "Another excuse out of your mouth and you're court-martialed!" Then, calming himself: "Messieurs—has the Deuxième Bureau established the identities of the missing heads?"

The interrogators exchanged a veiled glance.

"There is some new information," the first interrogator offered carefully after a moment.

The third interrogator, who hadn't uttered a word in hours of questioning, coughed gently at this—a sound that spoke volumes.

"Pinard!" General le Breton roared again. "I'll see you in my office at 08:00 tomorrow. *Tu peux disposer!*"

"*Je peut disposer à vos ordres, mon general!*" Pinard drew himself up and saluted the loudspeaker. Feeling foolish for this, he exited and found Legionnaire Szbeszdogy slumped dismally on the hard bench across the corridor. The Hungarian was reading an ancient issue of *Pif Gadget*, its childish colors faded and yellow, extracted from the dusty heap of old newspapers and magazines on the floor. Many Legionnaires had lingered there for many years, their fate in the hands of the gestapo; each had added something to this disorderly pile. Sbeszdogy looked up from the cartoon antics of Pif and Hercule with a grimace of pain. The flying metal at the *guelb* had broken two ribs and badly bruised a lung. Only in the last couple of days had he been able to summon sufficient breath to resume practice on his French horn.

"How did it go in there?" he said in a low voice.

"The gestapo loves a scapegoat," Pinard said. "And you're next."

"I'm ready." Szbeszdogy nodded. This was false bravado. "Listen, I've written something, a piece of music in memory of Caporal Keh. I want you to take a look—"

He pulled a crumpled sheaf of papers scrawled over with musical notations from somewhere and held it out. Pinard only shook his head and put on his kepi and went out into the rain to have a mournful smoke alone.

The Hungarian watched him go, thinking, *Je suis enculé.* He dropped *Pif Gadget* back onto the pile and picked up another magazine, but with a shudder of disgust flung this one aside.

It was *Képi Blanc,* the Legion's equivalent of *Stars and Stripes,* full of cheerfully fake news and PR nuggets dreamed up by advertising consultants hired by the top brass. Its chipper articles, copiously illustrated, did not mention the abusive discipline and brutal assaults perpetrated by one comrade upon another; the stealing so bad, every item of value in the noncommissioned barracks had to be kept locked in a safe. It said nothing about the drunkenness and drug abuse and stupidity; nothing about the madness of *le cafard*, a kind of fatal boredom caused by the isolation of remote posts and the endless repetition of tasks both pointless and painful; nothing about the sheer sketch of it all, about the Legion deployed with antiquated weaponry, undersupplied and outmanned as they were now in Afghanistan, as they'd been in Bosnia and Desert Storm and on every battlefield from Algeria to Tonkin since 1830. And nothing, not a word, about the whores.

3.

Soldiers have always gone to whores, there is no keeping them away. Each of the regiments of the Foreign Legion is supplied with its own brothel—which is actually two brothels in one, often housed on the same premises, with some of the whores reserved exclusively for officers and others for enlisted men. The French take an enlightened, scientific approach to venereal matters. Official Legion whores are inspected for STDs twice monthly, given frequent AIDs tests and free medical care and condoms, vacation days and birthday parties, all paid for courtesy of the French Republic.

The Legion is hidebound by tradition; it is one of the most hidebound armies in the world. The campaign history of each regiment has always dictated the ethnicity of the whores in their regimental brothels: The 2e REP, for example, though based out of Calvi in Corsica, served through Indochina, was mortared to pieces at Dien Bien Phu in 1954, and prefers Asian girls. There had been in use for the last time in history at that terrible battle one of the Legion's notorious *Bordels Mobiles de Campagne* (Mobile Field Brothels), staffed by Vietnamese whores who also acted as battlefield nurses during the desperate last days, as the French strongholds fell one by one to the Communists. Afterwards, the unfortunate whores, captured and sent off to re-education camps, denounced their former vocation and joined the people's struggle against Western imperialist aggression. This denunciation didn't stick. The official 2e REP pimp, traditionally the regiment's ranking adjudant-chef, now makes two trips a year at Legion expense to Vietnam, where his patronage is eagerly sought. He recruits there and in Thailand and Cambodia, offers travel expenses and a relocation bonus.

The DLEM—Détachement de la Légion Étrangère de Mayotte, stationed in remote Dzaudzi in the Comoros—favors Malagasy whores for obvious reasons of convenience. The whores of the 13e DBLE brothel, once located in Djibouti, are all large-breasted black Amazons from the Horn of Africa.

But the 1e RE, mustered for the conquest of Algeria in 1831, headquartered for a hundred years at Sidi Bel Abbès and now based in Aubagne, is considered the mother regiment of the Legion. The whores of the 1e RE brothel still come from the Kaybile tribe of the Algerian Berbers and are considered by Legionnaires who have much experience in such matters to make the best whores in the world. When stationed at Aubagne, Sous-lieutenant Pinard frequented a Kaybile whore nicknamed La Mogador after the long-ago Algerian battle in which the Legion seized a heavily fortified Moroccan citadel with more than 60 percent casualties, higher than the rate at the notoriously lethal Charge of the Light Brigade. There was always a whore nicknamed La Mogador in the 1e RE brothel, as a kind of ironic comment on that outrageous toll; La Mogador of the 1e RE has become a recurring character, like the temptress Angélique in those trashy books by Serge Golon.

Kaybile whores have smooth, toffee-colored skin and large, soulful dark eyes and are generally slim, with breasts like plums, and are very flexible. But it is no mere physical attribute that makes them so appreciated. They seem to have the ability, almost magical, to make themselves fall in love with their Legionnaire clients and to make the Legionnaires believe this affection is genuine—if only for an hour at a time. Thus, the paying Legionnaire is able to indulge himself in the fantasy that he is spending his combat pay on a date with a particularly energetic girlfriend, and not for an hour with a whore who will move on to the next man when the clock runs down.

Reality sometimes reinforces this fragile illusion: every so often, one of the Kaybile whores actually ends up marrying a Legionnaire, for whom she makes—it is said—an excellent wife. Others return to their homes in the Atlas Mountains after twenty years' hard service. With the money made on their backs in Aubagne they manage to buy olive orchards and farms and innocent young husbands and a high-status position in the affairs of Kaybileland, which has experienced a dramatic shift in values over the course of the last generation or so. The ancient patriarchal traditions of the Kaybiles are wearing away. The tribe has become a matriarchy.

4.

Pinard stumbled back to his quarters after the interrogation, dropped to his cot, and lay still for a couple of hours, enveloped in a blank darkness like sleep, but unvisited by dreams. He awoke at dusk, feeling uneasy and anxious, and knew what he needed to calm his nerves and knowing made him disgusted with himself, but there it was, and he put through the necessary phone call and jumped into the shower.

Stepping out of the mildewed stall a few minutes later, Pinard caught a glimpse of himself in the mirror and was momentarily startled by what he saw: Who was this ugly, cruel-looking individual? The unfamiliar face, hawkish and blunt as the face of one of his distant Abenaki ancestors, didn't look like the face of someone who found joy in the sound of the oboe. The skin of his arms, legs, and torso, slightly olive in tone, was covered with many crude and garish illustrations, some done back at the juvenile detention facility in Canada, others by professional tattooists—ridiculous to call them artists—in grimy military towns all over metropolitan France. The barrel-chested physique, toned but stocky, seemed ungainly, out of balance, thick up top, thin at the bottom, and resting on rickety legs bowed like the legs of a sailor too long at sea. The male organ dangled there in its thicket of hair, a dark vicious stump. Pinard turned away with a shudder. He didn't understand himself completely and didn't care to. His life had been hard, there wasn't much more to say than that. He was not by nature given to self-examination, avoided looking in mirrors and had learned to shave himself in the shower by touch alone, for the simple reason he was often, as tonight, startled by the man he saw looking back.

Now he splashed himself with a cheap Italian cologne called Basta, very popular with Legionnaires, though its odor, supposedly musky, called to mind a natural gas leak, and he took his *tenue de sortie* out of its dry-cleaning bag and put it on. This was the Legion's walking-out uniform, differing from *tenue de ville* in its pale khaki color and absence of shaggy red epaulets, and in the presence of braided lanyard rope encircling the left shoulder. Thus attired, Pinard marched the length of the parade ground to the caserne, humming one of the difficult sections of Albinoni's *Two Oboe Concerti*. There he drank two quick glasses of red wine at the bar and went across the hall to the little store, where he impulsively dropped an unnecessarily large portion of his pay on a very small bottle of Chanel No. 5, a pair of hoop earrings strung with onyx beads, and a copy of the latest *Paris Match*.

The 1e RE officers' brothel was located on the rue Montaigne, a side street in a quiet bourgeois neighborhood about four kilometers from base in a large house that had once belonged to the mayor of Aubagne. To make up for his foolish expenditures, Pinard decided to walk out there, bypassing the line of exorbitant taxis waiting at the main gates to take Legionnaires into the dives and clip joints of Marseilles, an hour away. Those few Legionnaires fortunate enough to have steady local girlfriends were now groping in the bushes of a little park up the street, its lamps purposefully broken with well-placed stones.

The night wind felt cool on Pinard's face as he walked. A light rain fell. Birds chirped restlessly from nests hidden beneath the boughs, tight against the trunks of the pines. It was the hour of late dinner. Military life is essentially lonely. Walking along the quiet streets of well-kept homes, families gathered inside around their cassoulets, carafes of wine gleaming on well-appointed tables, Pinard felt this loneliness acutely. He quickened his pace to a fast march, trying not to mistake the clusters of seedpods hanging from the branches of the horse chestnuts for severed heads, trying not to see the blast of the sun on the Sahara in the flare of passing headlights, and worrying out the Albioni concerti, whistling loudly now, to keep his mind off such terrible things.

The brothel's street wall, topped with razor wire artfully entwined in a tall hedge, concealed a well-kept garden and the wide veranda on which the whores sat on summer nights in transparent dresses sipping Cynar—a bitter-tasting apéritif made from artichokes that was supposed to be an aphrodisiac but wasn't. In the wide entrance hallway stood an age-darkened pier glass and a hat stand hung with a dozen kepis, both blue and white, the former allowed only to Legionnaires above the rank of caporal-chef. Madame Grasson—the tall, dignified Frenchwoman who looked after the whores—took Pinard's kepi with a graceful gesture and knelt to unlace his Rangers, which were then exchanged for carpet slippers. He mounted the stairs one step at a time like a man ascending the gallows, to the tiny room where La Mogador waited naked on the bed, reading last week's *Paris Match*. (This issue, like so many others, featured a long story on Johnny Hallyday, the aged and inexplicably popular French rocker. On the cover an image of the man at the beach with his latest starlet girlfriend—his absurd bouffant gone gray, his pecs sagging, his skin leathered by too many summers on the Côte d'Azur.)

"*Evariste, mon amour!*" La Mogador cried as Pinard came into the room. "*Oh, vien t'ens, chéri. Embrasse moi!*"

Pinard couldn't help smiling at the enthusiastic reception—her act was perfect, artfully done—and she flung herself into his arms and kissed him on the lips, which he didn't like much, not from a whore, and he gave her the perfume and the earrings and the new *Paris Match*. She made all the ex-pected enthusiastic noises over these little gifts and seemed genuinely happy to see him, but he knew this was all part of the comedy they were playing. Even their conversation—to pass the awkward minutes as Pinard removed his uniform carefully, folding everything according to regulation over a clothes chair put there for that purpose—seemed like a scene from a play about a whore with a heart of gold.

"I ached for you here," she whispered, putting a hand over her heart. "And here, even when I was with the others"—lowering her hand between her thighs—"night after night I dreamed of you!"

Pinard grunted irritably at this foolishness.

Then La Mogador moved on to a bit of cheerful regimental gossip about one of the girls, who at last retiring to marry a Legionnaire, had then promptly fallen in love with another man, and been dumped by both and was now destitute, reduced to walking the streets. After this behavior, the brothel, of course, wouldn't take her back. It was one thing to be a whore, quite another to be a faithless one. And she chattered about the weather, about a recent shopping trip to Aix-en-Provence where she bought an ex-pensive scarf on sale, about her brother in Algeria who had decided to go to trade school to become a diesel truck mechanic—and did Pinard think that was a good idea? Finally she asked about Pinard's months in Western Sa-hara.

"Miserable," Pinard responded. "Hot as hell. Nothing but sand, ants, and scorpions. Not a place you'd ever want to visit. Here's hoping I never have to go back."

"I suppose it wasn't much of a party," La Mogador said, frowning.

"Right about that."

"But you're a hero! They'll give you a medal, *mon amour*!"

"Not me," Pinard grunted. "You're thinking about Caporal Keh. He was the hero. Now he's dead."

"How did he—" But she stopped herself, sensing Pinard didn't want to explore this painful subject, and she dropped to her knees abruptly and pulled down his briefs. "Well, here's something to welcome you back, *chéri*. More fun than a medal."

As she went to work, Pinard's mind wandered.

He looked around the room, at the bright Algerian scarves strewn on the dresser, the magazines stacked on the cowskin-covered stool, the pot of geraniums on the windowsill. He looked at the framed photographs on the table by the bed: her parents and younger brother a couple of years back on the pilgrimage to Mecca. And—brilliant touch!—a shot of himself she'd taken with her digital camera last year, hastily slipped into the kind of snap-together frame from Prix Unique that could be taken apart quickly, the photograph replaced with another of the next client. Still, La Mogador had really managed to make the place comfortable, like a room in a normal house where she lived with a couple of lusty co-locs. Pinard was not by nature a sentimentalist, but for reasons he couldn't quite say, at the moment he appreciated the illusion. Then he realized he didn't remember La Mogador's real name—was it Zahra or Syeda?—and the illusion vanished.

A few minutes later she lay back on the bed with her legs in the air and Pinard went at her. He didn't last long—it had been months; the two or three ragged whores available to UN forces in Dahkla were best avoided—and afterwards they lay side by side in silence, passing a cigarette laced with hashish back and forth. Her beautiful tawny brown skin was unblemished except for a small blue tear tattooed at the corner of her left eye. Her breasts were perfect.

"You can have me again if you want," she whispered huskily through the pungent smoke. "You can do it as often as you like tonight"—and she reached for him with a lazy smile, already high—"I've made room for you, *chéri*, canceled all my other appointments."

Pinard looked at her, amazed. Could she really love me? he found himself wondering for a crazy moment, then nearly laughed out loud at the thought.

"And what would it cost me for such an evening?"

La Mogador looked away, slightly offended. Then she looked back at him, a rueful smile touching her lips.

"The money's already been advanced by General le Breton. He told Madame Grasson you were a hero and wanted us to treat you like one, because . . ." She hesitated—then blurted out the first true thing that evening—"But you're a damned unlucky bastard, aren't you, *pauvre salot*!"

"What do you mean?" Pinard said.

Then he saw the look in her eyes and knew immediately. And he felt a chill rippling along his spine that was more than the damp breath of wind from the window cracked open to let a few drops of the rain nourish the geraniums.

5.

Did you enjoy yourself last night, Pinard?"

"*Pardon, mon general?*" Sous-lieutenant Pinard felt the muscles tightening at the back of his neck.

"Don't be an idiot." General le Breton licked his fleshy lips. "I'm talking about your little Kaybile girl."

Pinard wanted to punch the fat bastard of a general in the mouth for this crack, an assault that in former days would have meant an on-the-spot court-martial, immediately followed by a firing squad—from initial blow to completely dead in less than five minutes. Even now, such an act would earn him a three-year sentence to the brutal Legion prison camp at Lac d'Islay in the icy Jura mountains. There the Legion sent the worst of the worst (multiple rapists, murderers, the chronically insubordinate, homicidal maniacs), those dangerous sociopaths who all too often managed to penetrate the ranks.

Pinard resisted the impulse. "She's not my little Kaybile girl, sir." He shrugged. "She's just another whore."

The general's expression clouded. This response wasn't in keeping with the accepted mythology of the regiment. More, he took it as a subtle challenge to his authority. He leaned back in his oversized leather armchair, big as a throne and as gaudy, done up with shiny brass upholstery tacs and red leather cushions. Big as it was, it still creaked beneath the general's ungainly bulk.

"I am intimately familiar with your personnel file," he said coldly. "Did you know that?"

"*Oui, mon general.*"

"I find your history—to say the least—distasteful. Your involvement with hard drugs, your incarceration as a juvenile, the fact that you are"—he pronounced the word with unnecessary emphasis—"a *Canadian*. Not to mention your stupid devotion to—what is that foolish instrument you play?"

"The oboe, sir."

"Well, it's a miracle that you are now a junior officer in this regiment. *Reçu,* Pinard?"

"*Reçu, mon general.*"

"At times I regret supporting your application for officer training. Without my recommendation you would not have been accepted at Saint-Cyr."

"Yes, sir," Pinard said. "Thank you, sir." But he knew the general was lying. The officer truly responsible for his elevation was now probably dismembered, dead. Or worse, one of the two unknown *miserables* suffering hourly tortures as a prisoner of the Marabouts far away.

The general picked a stray bit of tobacco off his tongue. His huge seaweed-smelling Venezuelan cigar lay smoldering in the ceramic ashtray on his desk. He paused and took several long puffs off this foul log, smoke rising in a thick blue plume, like truck exhaust. He was known for his long, strategic pauses, an interrogation technique learned from the Jesuitical interrogators of the Deuxième Bureau.

Pinard waited, stifling a yawn. The rain had stopped after a three-day deluge. The usually bright skies above Aubagne were bright again. Beyond the tall window behind the general's desk, Pinard could see a trio of Legionnaires at work wearing the gray overalls of punishment duty, their heads shaved *boule à zéro*. Backs bent, they raked with tiny plastic toy rakes the island of sand around the Monument aux Morts, which according to Legion tradition must never show the blemish of a single footprint, bird dropping, or stray leaf. Of course it was a highly trafficked area, constantly marched over by many boots. The Legionnaires would slave away at this absurd task all day long and far into the night; another example of Legion sketch.

A large framed portrait of Charles de Gaulle in presidential garb hung on the wall to the right of the window. More than his custom-made uniforms, Venezuelan cigars, and unmilitary girth, this portrait marked General le Breton out as a dangerous iconoclast, an officer, no matter how much he pretended to *be* the regiment, fundamentally at odds with it. For de Gaulle had hated the Legion and had sought to disband it after the failed putsch d'Alger coup d'état of April 1961. It was one of the most dramatic episodes of modern French history. Rebellious French generals—among them many from the Legion—outraged over what they saw as de Gaulle's cynical abandonment of French Algeria, formed a secret army, the OAS, whose purpose it was to overthrow the elected government of France. They drew up plans to drop Legion paratroopers on Paris, intending to occupy the Invalides, the Élysée Palace, the Chamber of Deputies, the major department stores. The French public might have supported such a coup—a majority of the population favored keeping Algeria French. But the generals, riven by internal dissent, hesitated, fatally, for a few days. Meanwhile, de Gaulle acted. He gave a memorable, hyperbolic speech on French television imploring the nation not to support the *putschistes*, and public opinion, ever fickle, swayed in his favor. Ringleaders were quickly rounded up, imprisoned, a few guillotined following secret trials; the coup fizzled out. After that, de Gaulle punished the Legion severely for its role, court-martialing its officers, reducing its strength by 70 percent, and divesting it of its most effective weaponry.

General le Breton, at the time an undistinguished young cadet, quickly became an ardent Gaulliste, and was one of those opportunists who rose to power in the years following the coup. He hated the Legion as much as de Gaulle had hated the Legion and the Legion hated him as much as they still hated the memory of de Gaulle. To remind himself of this mutual antipathy, the general kept de Gaulle's portrait on his wall in the spot where every other staff officer hung a photograph of brave old General Rollet, bewhiskered and quaint, his chest covered with medals earned with the Legion in Morocco and the trenches of the First World War; or Maréchal Lyautey, who had died in its service. Both men had loved the Legion more than their own lives, their own families.

Presently, General le Breton laid aside his Venezuelan log and pushed a thick dossier across the glossy surface of the desk.

"*Bon, mon petit Pinard,*" he said. "*Retournons à nos moutons.*" A ridiculous expression, favored by provincial schoolteachers, literally let's return to our sheep, meaning the business at hand. "The information I am about to share with you is top secret"—still keeping a proprietary hold on the dossier—"compiled by our friends in the Deuxième Bureau. Dental records and a process of elimination have finally given us the identities of the missing Legion personnel. Both are problematic individuals with records of instability. *Allons-y*, see for yourself."

He released the dossier, leaned back, and took up his cigar again. Pinard lifted the thick cardboard cover. Two identity card mug shots were stapled to the first page; one showed a seasoned officer, the other a common Legionnaire on his first overseas assignment.

"You're going back, you know."

Pinard nodded, a clenching in his guts, careful not to show any emotion.

"I mean Western Sahara." It clearly pleased the general to deliver this terrible news.

"Yes, sir." The whole base knew already. Even La Mogador had known last night. He was going back to hell.

"But this time, you will not be attached to MINURSO. Those miserable UN cowards have been frightened off by the Marabouts and so are drawing down their mission to the region. Apparently General van Snetters has become some sort of Buddhist monk. Doesn't believe in violence, he says, doesn't solve anything. No doubt he intends to pacify the Marabouts through the burning of incense and the use of prayer wheels. You will be acting in complete secrecy, a covert Legion mission, code name SCORPIO. You will report directly to me and only to me. Once in country, you will quickly establish the whereabouts of these two missing men. If they are dead, you will find their bodies and retrieve them. If they are alive and being held hostage, you will liberate them and bring them back to Aubagne to a hero's welcome." Here the general paused to puff on his cigar. "If they are alive and deserters . . ."

Pinard opened his mouth to deny this possibility, but the general silenced him with a gesture.

"You will bring them back to Aubagne so they may feel the lash of Legion justice. If they are alive and actively allied with the Marabouts, you will kill them on the spot and cut off their balls and send them to me in a box. These arc your orders. Any questions?"

"Assuming they are hostages—will I be authorized to make ransom payments?"

The general stared at him. "The Legion does not pay ransoms."

"Am I to be alone on this mission?"

The general laughed uproariously at this. "Who do you suppose you are, Asterix with his little bottle of magic potion? Even Asterix has his Obelix! You will take your musical comrade Legionnaire Szbeszdogy—"

Szbeszdogy's going to shit, Pinard thought.

"—and you will be accompanied by a squad of commandos from the 4e RE. So your ass will be covered, but good."

Pinard shuddered. He knew all about the dreadful commando squads of the fourth foreign regiment based out of Fort St. Jean in Marseilles. They were notorious, hard-core assassins, murderers for hire in their spare time. These were the same guys who had blown up the Greenpeace harassment ship *Rainbow Warrior* in 1985 in New Zealand. In those days the tie-dyed Greenpeacers had been interfering with French nuclear tests in the South

Pacific. The 4e RE's secret mission to sink the *Rainbow Warrior*—another one of General le Breton's unfortunate schemes and a breach of international law—ignited a terrible scandal that nearly brought down the Mitterrand government.

Mission: SCORPIO would be a similar breach, an unauthorized invasion of UN-administered territory. Pinard could refuse to go, of course. But he wouldn't refuse. The Legion rallying cry—*à moi la Légion!* Legionnaires, to me!—was tattooed on the walls of his heart. A Legionnaire in trouble could expect his comrades to fly to his aid, anywhere in the world, or else what were they but a bunch of murderers? In the end, they didn't fight for France, but for one another, for the sake of all the stupid choices they'd made to end up here, at the bottom. This was the final distillation, the essence of their sacred honor; the only honor available to an army of mercenaries.

6.

A sweet cacophony, a kind of cloud of musical notes, muddled but pure, emanated from the practice room of the Salle des Musicians of the Musique Principale. Pinard, carrying his oboe in its velvet-lined case, approached this arcaded building from the rue Bir-Hakim along an allée of gnarled plane trees and silver beech grown from cuttings clipped from parent trees once planted at the old Legion home at Sidi, back in Algeria. The Monument aux Morts stood out in dark relief in the distance against these pale trees. Clear, peaceful light flooded the landscape. The buildings, the statues, the parade ground, everything, seen sharply as if for the first time, as if enhanced by a theatrical lighting technician from a perch in the sky. On the horizon, the mottled summit of the Col du St. Baume. It was one of those common, extraordinary afternoons of Southern France.

Pinard found Szbeszdogy at his music stand playing scales on his French horn in the auditorium, surrounded by a couple of dozen other musicians doing more or less the same thing. The Hungarian dropped the horn when Pinard stepped up.

"My lungs still aren't too good," he said, coughing. "I don't have the breath I used to before the desert. *Dites-moi*, what's a horn player without breath?"

"You might try the harmonica," Pinard said.

"Go to hell, Sous-lieutenant," Szbeszdogy said.

Pinard sighed. "You've heard, I assume."

"Of course," Szbeszdogy said glumly. "The whole damned base has heard, just because it's so damned secret. Volunteers are lined up from here to Marseilles to avenge the honor of the Legion. And they pick us."

"Not that. I mean the identity of the"—he paused, searching for the right words—"missing heads."

Szbeszdogy raised an eyebrow. "Who are they?"

"Commandant de Noyer for one."

"Keh said that would be the case. That night at the blockhouse. Remember?"

"The other one is Legionnaire Milquetoast. An American."

"An American?"

"Yes."

"Doesn't seem right, Americans in the Legion." Szbeszdogy shook his head. "What do they want with this torture? Don't they have their Cadillac cars and their beefsteaks? This Milquetoast must be insane. Or a complete idiot!"

There had been a lull in the music, which just then started up again, the melodic, discordant cloud rising, each man playing his own tune. Somewhere in the cloud could be heard the deep boom of the *gros tambour*, the thunderous bass drum favored by the Musique Principale; also the melancholy tinkling of the Cochin chimes. This unusual, portable xylophone was the last remaining souvenir of the Legion's years in Indochina, their most enduring trophy brought back from the Orient.

"I don't suppose I could refuse to go?" Szbeszdogy said over the musical racket.

"I already thought of that," Pinard said. "You might as well put a bullet in your brain for the kind of treatment you'd get around here after that."

"What if I desert?"

"Now you're talking like an idiot. Anyway, it's not going to be so bad. We'll have a unit of 4e RE commandos with us to handle the hard stuff."

"Those assassins!"

"Yes, hopefully."

"A dozen assassins backed up by a couple of musicians. Who needs an army?"

"There's only going to be four assassins. That's all the 4e RE can spare."

"Four! We're dead men!"

"Apparently we're going to join Keh after all."

"Old Keh. Here's something for him." Szbeszdogy handed over the sheaf of paper covered by musical notes he'd attempted to pass the day before, after Pinard's interrogation. Its title: *Nocturne Pour Hautbois et Coronet Français.*

"You wrote this?" Pinard said, surprised.

Szbeszdogy nodded. "That Mongolian *salopard* died in the dark, right before dawn, so I thought a nocturne. Can you scan it?"

Pinard set up his music stand and began to assemble his oboe—as carefully as he would his FAMAS 5.56. He scraped the double reed with a small blade, sharp as a scalpel—oboists are very particular about the shape of their reeds, it is a serious fetish with them, and they will only use a special kind of cane grown on the east coast of Spain for that purpose. And of course the oboe's three-part body must be hand-turned from grenadaille, a rare wood that comes only from the gloomy, bloodstained forests of the Congo. Reed well scraped, Pinard screwed the body of the oboe to the base and the base to the bell, fixed his reed in the slot, tootled for a moment to be sure everything was set properly and nodded at Szbeszdogy. The Hungarian climbed onto a chair and called for silence.

"*Écoutez! Camarades!* I have written a little piece to remember Caporal Keh, who didn't make it back from Africa! *Silence, un peut de silence, s'il vous plaît!*"

Gradually the cloud of music settled, like dust from a sandstorm, but it wasn't going to be that easy. Musicians hate to be interrupted when they are practicing.

"What, you wrote a song for that masturbator?" one of the musicians shouted.

"Yeah, didn't they catch Keh jerking off all over the Monument aux Morts?" another one said.

"Shut up!" Szbeszdogy shouted. "Since you want to know, I asked Keh about"—he hesitated—"that incident when we were out in Western Sahara, before the Marabout butchers got his head."

Suddenly, silence.

"And what do you think the Mongolian said?" Szbeszdogy continued. "'I was drunk out of my skull,' that was the first thing he said! Now I suppose the rest of you bastards don't drink, but I can tell you Keh occasionally tied one on!"

At this, hooting.

"Then he told me this—'I dreamed I was making love to my mother the earth,' he said, 'and she was beautiful.' That's what Caporal Keh said!"

"*Merde!*" another musician called. "On top of everything else, the man was a motherfucker!" And everyone laughed, but at an irritated gesture from Pinard quieted down again.

"So I have written this little piece in his honor," Szbeszdogy continued, "for a comrade whose headless bones are lost beneath the sands of the Western Sahara. A brave man who saved my life and the life of the sous-lieutenant here with a couple of beautifully placed rounds from an 89mm rocket!"

At this, loud cheering.

Szbeszdogy jumped down from the chair and stepped up to his music stand. He cleared his throat, drew a breath, put the mouthpiece of his French horn to his lips, and blew the first sonorous note. The music blossomed from this simple beginning, richly complex, yet utterly natural, like a tangle of swamp grass waving in the wind, yellow and green and deep blue in the shadows of the tamarisks; like flocks of flamingos rising fantastically pink into the sky above the lagoons at Noadhibou. Then the oboe joined its plaintive tenor to the bleating horn. Pinard, surprised to find himself a better musician than he thought he was, managed to follow along very well, after scanning the notations only once. The oboe and the horn dueled with each other for a quick movement, evoking the sound of the departing Peugots, then softened into the vast night of the desert, the trackless wastes of sand, and three men, a lost patrol, small as ants, wandering hopelessly over endless dunes. Then came abrupt bleats from the horn, the sound of battle and the rocket blast, and the oboe joining in again, stridently, to evoke Hehu Keh's brave rush over the top in a flutter of notes at the uppermost portion of its range—then, all at once, nine minutes after it had begun, the nocturne was over, abruptly, as if decapitated. The music came to a dead stop in a single shrill note joined by both instruments, meant to denote the fatal blow from a flat-bladed Marabout sword.

Szbeszdogy dropped the horn from his lips. Pinard put his oboe down, a look of astonishment on his face, as if startled by the appearance of a strange creature in a wilderness where no creatures are known to exist. A moment of stunned silence, then a loud outburst of applause.

"Bravo!" shouted the assembled musicians. "*Magnifique!*" and "*Encore! Encore!*" though the experience could not be repeated, not exactly like the first time, not ever. The musicians seized Szbeszdogy and hoisted him to their shoulders and paraded him around the auditorium, then someone kicked a side door open and they carried him out along the rue Bir-Hakim, tears in their eyes.

Now it was dusk. The C 160 Transall that would fly Szbeszdogy, Pinard, and the assassins of the 4e RE under cover of night to a secret location deep in the Western Sahara, a territory now shadowed by the darkest violence, utterly beyond the rule of law, was just then undergoing routine maintenance on the airstrip of the Legion base at Calvi in Corsica. Pinard disassembled his oboe as carefully as he had assembled it, unscrewing the body from the base, the base from the bell, plucking out the carefully sharpened double reed, and repacked it in all in its velvet-lined case.

10

CAP'N CRUNCH

1.

Blackness drew like a curtain across the sky in the minutes after sunset. Cold wind from the mountain sent snowflakes whirling on the open threshold. The prisoners lay in their hovel naked and freezing, wrapped only in their chains. Enforced nakedness, an ancient trick, is one of the simplest ways to control prisoners. Psychologically speaking, the naked man is always at the mercy of the man wearing clothes.

Smith, curled into a tight fetal ball, shivered violently in his sleep just before dawn. The colonel hung motionless, chained to a ring on the other side—he was awake, of course, he was always awake. He watched silently as the girl crept in from the outer dark, clutching a pointed object in her hand. He couldn't raise his voice, couldn't bring any words out of the fog. She squatted down and poked at Smith's bare ass cheek with the object—a sharp, thorny stick.

"*Ow!*" Smith jerked upright, chains clanking, joints frozen, blinking sleep out of his eyes. "It's you," he mumbled in English. "What the fuck do you want?"

The girl shrugged, not understanding. She didn't speak English or French or Spanish. They'd always communicated in a hash of rudimentary sign language and pidgin Hassaniya. She went veiled, like everyone else in the village, male and female, old and young (the Marabouts had taken Islamic notions of modesty to their furthest extreme), and it was impossible to know what she was thinking, or her age, exactly. Maybe twelve or thirteen, maybe twenty. She widened her dark eyes and made a gesture—palm under chin, fingers fluttering: sing.

"Too early!" Smith waved her off. "Still night out there!"

She wanted a private serenade. She came in every couple of days, bringing scavenged food; the week before a minuscule, if genuine, morsel of roast goat. Smith sang to her sweetly sotto voce for an hour to pay for that excellent meal.

The girl poked him again with the pointy stick. Sing!

"You want me to sing?" Smith said angrily. "Breakfast first!" He pointed to his mouth.

I will gladly pay you Tuesday for a hamburger today. The girl managed to convey this notion in a complicated charade.

"No food, no sing!" Smith huffed. "I'm a professional. A biscuit or my mouth stays closed!"

And he pressed his lips together and would not open them no matter how much the girl poked. At last she scuttled out, waving her stick, making it clear that he was a diva, infidel trash, who ought to be tortured and skinned alive—or words to that effect.

"*Mon pauvre Milquetoast,*" Phillipe croaked when the girl was gone, his voice sounding dry and cracked and a thousand years old. "You are a performing seal. You sing for a herring. Exactly like a seal I saw once at the Cirque Medrano, in Paris when I was a kid. That seal could balance a ball on the end of his nose. Can you do such a thing?"

"Go to hell, Phillipe," Smith said. But the injunction wasn't necessary. The colonel was already there.

2.

You can learn a lot about someone naked and chained and forced to live at very close quarters, in this case a ragged enclosure of stone and dirt, no more than ten-by-ten, located in a secret Marabout village dug into the side of an unknown mountain. And Smith had learned that Phillipe de Noyer was absolutely crazy and getting crazier every day.

The man never slept, never closed his eyes for more than a blink. This chronic insomnia might be a product of his craziness or the craziness caused by his lack of sleep, Smith couldn't say which. Certainly, the harsh conditions of captivity had made things worse. Phillipe now carried on loud, crazy arguments with the shadows or whispered words of unbearable intimacy to his absent wife, Louise. Or raved incoherently, often repeating the phrase *armée, tête d'armée* over and over again. And he hummed endlessly and off key, various things by Satie, chiefly *Mémoires d'un amnésique*, but also the notorious *Musique d'ameublement*, an irritating and atonal fragment composed by the maestro to be played exactly when people weren't listening. These manic phases were inevitably followed by an abrupt collapse. After hours of whispering and arguing and humming, Phillipe's eyes rolled back in his head and his head wobbled weirdly from side to side and he fell into a silence so deep it lasted for days; mental implosions, perhaps neurological in nature, and terrible to witness. For Smith it was like watching a proud old building, already half destroyed by fire, slowly fold in on itself.

But crazy or not, Phillipe had a point. Smith *was* a kind of performing seal. His career-topping performance during the last moments of the siege of Blockhouse 9 had saved their lives: Marabout fighters closing in that disastrous afternoon stopped short of the kill and lowered their rifles at the opening lines of Berlin's "Let's face the Music and Dance." They settled themselves comfortably in the dirt and listened to Smith sing number after number for nearly two hours, like cobras mesmerized before the snake charmer's pipes. When Smith stopped singing at last from sheer exhaustion, he and Phillipe were seized, stripped, blindfolded, bound with heavy chains, and hustled into the Gueltas to await an unknown fate. Smith attributed this surprising stay of execution to his theatrical training, but there was more to it: It could be said they owed their lives to Broadway itself, to the fabulous, receding echo of all those fabulous shows, all those gone good times. To the great American songbook, to Cole Porter and George Gershwin, to Lerner and Loewe, Irving Berlin, Rodgers and Hart, Harburg and Lane. To Johnny Mercer, Hoagy Carmichael, and Jerome Kern. To every romantic melody ever played as men and women swayed into each other on the worn parquet of bygone ballrooms, comfortably drunk on bourbon old-fashioneds and the possibility of love.

Now, in captivity, Smith was forced to sing Broadway standards for the assembled population once or twice a day. He stood on a granite slab halfway up the slope where the acoustics were good, his clear tenor ringing out across the stony chasms, echoing against the steep sides of surrounding cliffs. But scratch a savage, find a critic: Marabout villagers had too quickly developed the sophisticated tastes of jaded New York theatergoers. They would jeer, throw stones, and withhold food if they didn't like a particular number—or if Smith's performance lacked *duende*—and they were getting increasingly hard to please.

Trial and error and a relentless performance schedule had given Smith the measure of his audience: Cole Porter and George Gershwin had always been his favorites—he used to perform a medley of both, a kind of musical point-counterpoint, popular during his stint at a Brooklyn piano bar back when he and Jessica lived in Park Slope. But there didn't seem to be enough room for Porter and Gershwin side by side in the Marabout's insurgent hearts. They preferred Gershwin's more strident style; they also liked Irving Berlin. Cole Porter's witty melodies drew only a lukewarm response and they were left cold by Harold Arlen—this a blow to Smith, who preferred the elegant Arlen to Porter and even Berlin. Fortunately, contemporary musicals, which Smith generally detested, held no appeal for the Marabouts. Sondheim, Andrew Lloyd Webber—*Cats, Phantom,* and *Les Misérables, Hair, Jesus Christ Superstar, Godspell, Rent*—were quickly weeded from his mountainside repertoire.

Smith found he drew his most favorable response from the big, brassy Broadway scores of the forties and fifties, though here again the Marabout villagers expressed definite preferences: They liked *Pal Joey, The Pajama Game, Finian's Rainbow,* and *Brigadoon*; didn't like *Annie Get Your Gun, Carousel, Oklahoma!,* or *Hello, Dolly! Fiddler on the Roof* drove them to rage and throwing stones. Smith chalked this violent reaction up to the Jewish-Muslim divide, rather than any problem with the score. They were crazy about Rodgers and Hammerstein's *South Pacific* and Adler and Ross's *Damn Yankees* and went gaga over Frank Loesser's *Guys and Dolls,* which worked well for Smith because he also loved *Guys and Dolls,* thought that it might be the greatest piece of musical theater of all time, and once had a great run as Skye Masterson at the Center Stage of Central Florida in Orlando.

From that show, the villagers preferred "Luck Be a Lady"—Smith's personal favorite—"Sit Down You're Rocking the Boat!" and the eponymous number, always a showstopper. After singing these three tunes back to back with particular *duende* before lunch one day, the villagers threw bits of warm bread and chunks of fresh sheep's cheese, which Smith immediately gobbled down. He considered this impromptu bread and cheese feast one of the great artistic triumphs of his career, second only to his LORT A run in *My Fair Lady* at the Guthrie—though that now seemed like an episode from the life of another Smith in a different lifetime, in Minneapolis, in the snow, on the other side of the world.

3.

The girl returned the next morning bearing a small water gourd filled with coffee and a ragged scrap of flat bread that had been dipped in last night's grease. Smith ate half the bread, drank half the coffee and offered the colonel the rest—but sunk into one of his eyes-wide-open catatonic states, Phillipe couldn't be roused, even by food and drink. Then, Smith cleared his throat and sang a favorite from *Brigadoon* in a quiet falsetto. He sang directly to the girl, as tenderly as he could make it. As if he loved her, as if his heart were breaking under the burden of his love for her. The girl's dark eyes shone in exaltation as she squatted there, watching him, listening.

"Can't we two go walking together out beyond the valley of trees . . ."

Next he sang a couple of numbers from *Finian's Rainbow* and finished with "My Funny Valentine" from *Pal Joey*.

Recital over, Smith dropped chin to chest, a mock-thespian bow. "I thank you," he murmured to the imagined applause. "I thank you from the bottom of my heart. . . ."

The girl squatted back on her heels and studied him for a long time, eyes unreadable. Smith felt self-conscious beneath this scrutiny, more pointed than her poking stick. It might be possible for someone who has gone around naked all their lives to grow accustomed to wearing clothes, but the reverse did not hold true. No matter how hard he tried to forget his nakedness, he couldn't. He'd been swaddled within moments of birth, habitually wore pajamas, and except for brief periods in the shower or in bed with a woman, had remained clothed ever since.

At last, the girl put a finger over her lips to indicate secrecy and glanced over her shoulder to make sure no spies were lurking along the path outside.

"I have news," she whispered in passable French. "Al Bab is coming and you will soon be judged. They must not hear me tell you such a thing. They will feed me to the horrible bees if they hear."

Smith gaped at her. She could speak French! Then he felt a coldness in his gut that was more than just dismay over her weeks of dissimulation. The Man himself! Mystical Imam of the Marabouts! Their Jesus, their Buddha, their Joseph Smith!

"*Al Bab, lui-même?*"

"*Oui, il vient.*" The girl nodded. "*Demain soir.*"

"You speak French well. Why did you trick me?"

"Al Bab forbids us to speak French. He allows us only to speak Hassaniya, which he says is a holy language, the language of the prophet, peace be upon him. But the kind nurses from Médecins Sans Frontières taught me French at the camp at Tindouf, which is in Algeria. Remember, many people speak French in Algeria."

"Are we in Algeria now?"

The girl shook her head. "We are in the mountains of the Galtat Zemmur. It is not Morocco, it is not Algeria. It is the land of the Saharoui Berbers."

"You mean Western Sahara. The SADR?"

"Call it what you want, *je m'en fiche*! I hate it here. I wish to go somewhere else, entirely. To Milan perhaps."

"Milan, Italy?"

The girl nodded. "The women in Milan wear beautiful clothes and are very happy without so many terrible bees. I have carefully hidden a magazine of fashion from Milan given to me by one of the kind nurses at Tindouf. There are pictures of many beautiful women with many beautiful clothes. Do you know such a magazine?"

"Yes." Smith grinned. "But I don't subscribe."

"What do you mean?"

"Never mind."

"It is a fine magazine."

"Yes."

"The beautiful women in the magazine go with their face uncovered," she continued. "Here that would mean death by so many stones, here—"

"Do you know what's going to happen to us?" Smith interrupted.

"Al Bab will decide." The girl shrugged. "You will live or you will die. Like everyone."

Smith sighed. Even the kids up here were existentialists.

Then the girl did something astonishing: She untied her veil, a coarse piece of black cloth, and let it hang loose to one side of her face; the intimacy of this act was enough to get them both killed. She was older than he had guessed, maybe eighteen or nineteen. She had a thin, sharp face—high cheekbones, narrow chin marked with tribal tattoos. Parallel blue lines ran down from the bottom of her lower lip to the bottom of her chin, and a blue tear that wasn't a tear but the bee hieroglyph of the Marabouts was tattooed on her cheek an inch below her left eye.

Smith hadn't seen an uncovered female face in months and suddenly found her outrageously beautiful and felt an embarrassing little jolt that he tried to conceal, pressing his thighs together and tucking his male member between them as best he could.

"My name is Alia," the girl whispered. "And I will pray to God Al Bab doesn't kill you. You sing too well to lose your head. And your hair is the color of the sun." She reached up and ran her fingers through the matted blond pelt atop Smith's head, now more than recovered from its last Legion *boule à zéro*. "They say Al Bab is a prophet, that he is the Gateway to the Age of the Hidden Imam, or perhaps even the Hidden Imam Himself. But I do not think any of this is true. I think he is a violent, dishonest man and not who he says he is . . ." She paused. "Am I pretty?"

"You are," Smith said.

"Like the women in Milan?"

"Exactly like them," Smith said.

Alia nodded, solemnly. Then she removed her fingers from Smith's hair, refixed her veil, and went out into the growing brightness.

4.

A religious procession climbed the zigzag trail up the ravine from the desert at noon. First came the hooded mullahs bearing blue flags emblazoned with the bee hieroglyph, a dozen of them mounted on camels richly caparisoned in studded leather, saddle bells tinkling, the animals braying loudly from time to time, lifting long ropy necks to the sky. In single file behind them trotted twenty or so undernourished young men, new disciples recruited in the Tindouf refugee camps, their dark eyes hollow from days of fasting. A thick haze steamed off the inaccessible massif of the Galtat Zemmur, it's highest pinnacle awash in a thick bank of clouds. The procession, emerging from this haze as if out of the mists of history, possessed a grave medieval splendor: camels braying, starving penitents, the blue robes of the holy men, the bold flags snapping in the wind.

Marabout villagers lined the route, watching the procession rise toward the giant hive on the plateau. Smith found a place at the back of the crowd, slouching as insolently as he possibly could while naked and shivering and in chains, which wasn't very insolently at all. Phillipe squatted on the ground, digging with broken fingernails in the dead, crumbly soil. He'd been wrapped in his fog all morning, ambling along, pale eyes fixed on the ground, looking for a grub to eat, for a worm, an overlooked root, a wild onion, anything. The two captives were allowed to wander the village during the day, pitiful figures, reduced to the level of animals; dogs clad only in their own skins, squatting to take doggie craps—a single dry turd—on the stony ground. Their nakedness, the chains they wore, and the complete isolation of the place rendered escape impossible.

The disciples reached the plateau and the crowd surged up after them. Smith helped the doddering Phillipe to his feet.

"*Allons-y, mon colonel,*" he said gently. "We don't want to miss the fun. The bastards are at it again."

He drew Phillipe along, past the lean-tos and shanties made from rough mountain stone and UN pressboard and blue UN tarps, until they stood with everyone else in the presence of the hive, which emitted a loud, electric humming. This monstrous construction, set against the western escarpment on a level pan of limestone, resembled an oversized pizza oven or a giant breast. Its rough surface of hard-packed earth glittered with many thousands of bees. A man-sized opening at ground level led to the humid recesses of the interior. A thick, sticky substance oozed across the threshold.

"I saw one of those six years ago at the Awsard camp," Phillipe said, suddenly himself again. "I was the first from the outside to see such a thing. Except for poor old Milhauz, of course."

"*C'est bien vous, mon colonel?*" Smith said, surprised—though he shouldn't be: Episodes of complete sanity came over the man without warning, sweeping down from Phillipe's upper brain across the burning prairies of his medulla oblongata like a fast-moving thunderstorm. It was as if he merely resumed aloud a conversation already in progress in some drafty corner of his mind.

"Are you going mad, Milquetoast?" Phillipe frowned at him. "Who else would it be?"

"No one, sir."

"I was talking about the bees. They're an East African species, native to the scrub country of southern Sudan. Very aggressive with a very painful sting, great builders of dirt hives, as you see there. They're scavengers, they feed off *merde* and carrion like flies, and produce no honey at all, only that red waxy stuff, which isn't really a wax and has no value to industry. The Marabouts have a Web site, you know. We traced it to a server in Morocco that later disappeared without a trace."

"Everyone's got a Web site," Smith said glumly.

"The content was very informative. Their spiritual leader, the archimposter who calls himself Al Bab, lays out the Marabout agenda quite candidly and there are excellent graphics and links to related sites. His plans for conquest extend far beyond the borders of Western Sahara. Like all dangerous fanatics, he seeks to re-create the world in his own image by plunging it into an ocean of blood. Laughable perhaps—but expressed with religious fervor and absolute conviction, half *Mein Kampf,* half Koran. Did you know the bee hieroglyph has been found scribbled on walls in Paris, in London? Mark my words, Milquetoast, soon they will invade Manhattan!"

"They can try," Smith said. "But they won't find parking."

The Marabout mullahs dismounted their camels, rolled out prayer carpets, and arranged themselves facing the eastern horizon. A rustic bagpipe began to bleat, then stopped and the twenty disciples fell to their knees. Veiled women stepped out of the crowd into the windy silence and helped remove twenty scratchy goat-hair shirts and soon the disciples, reduced to blue loincloths, were nearly as cold and naked as Smith and the colonel, though they seemed impervious to physical suffering, focused on the mysterious initiation to come. Another bleat from the bagpipe and more women emerged, these bearing horsehair whisks and white plastic buckets heaped with yellow or pink powder. Gusts of wind billowed colorful puffs of the powder into the morning air as the bucket women began dusting the disciples from head to toe. The disciples got dusted with one color or the other, two or three a mixture of both. The bucket women paid close attention to the crotch area; perky responses from beneath the loincloths in this region sent knowing giggles rippling through the crowd.

"Cover up every available centimeter of skin and anything, even the arching of an eyebrow, becomes erotic stimulus," Phillipe observed, his voice low in Smith's ear. "Really, it's an excellent reproductive strategy."

Smith didn't say anything. Long minutes passed. A bee landed on his forearm; he shook it away, chains clanking. A cloud of pink powder, taken by the wind, blew into their eyes. Phillipe turned his head away and sneezed.

"Pronounced medicinal odor," he said.

"Like antibacterial foot powder," Smith agreed.

"Strange to find such an odor among a tribe of technologically innocent Saharouian Berbers. Some age-old mixture of camel dung and piss and a bush that only blossoms at midnight—that sort of thing, absolutely. But this, this"—he searched for the word—"chemical is clearly the product of a modern industrial process. Have you understood its purpose yet?"

Smith thought for a long minute. Lack of food and constant cold had made his brain sluggish. They'd witnessed three or four of these terrible Marabout initiations in their months of captivity, all with equivocal results: Some died, some lived, as if by the magical whim of the bees. Other than that, he couldn't say.

"They're breeding a race of warriors here, Milquetoast," the colonel continued. "This is how the Marabouts rid themselves of those weaker types unfit for military service. Meanwhile, we in the West natter on about tolerance and gender equality and sleep the sleep of reason in our comfortable beds. Watch the colors—one will immediately provoke the insects; the other just as quickly sedate them."

The first recruit, completely dusted in pink, lowered himself to all fours and crawled into the waxy mouth of the giant hive. At this, the bees began an aggressive humming, like a generator flipped to high voltage. The crowd of villagers carefully backed away, clearing a space all around the thick mud walls. About ten seconds later a low, painful grunting echoed from inside. The grunting grew louder, then exploded into horrible, high-pitched screams and something, a monster wearing a writhing, stinging human-shaped covering of bees, burst from the hive and ran screaming toward the edge of the cliff, bees covering eyes, mouth, nose; bees at last choking the painful screams to a desperate gargle. The cliff here dropped off about sixty feet to a ledge covered with sharp rocks. Without breaking stride this unhappy individual flung himself off into empty air, the bees sailing up like bits of confetti as he dropped. Some things seen cannot be unseen. The image of the screaming bee-man jumping off the cliff would burn in Smith's imagination forever. But the

Marabout villagers seemed unmoved by his horrendous spectacle. Going around with faces covered all the time must have a curious effect on people, Smith thought: The covering of faces, like the wearing of masks, seemed to distance them from normal human empathy. Did they feel regret, remorse, shame? How could anyone be certain? Human emotions conveyed by facial expressions perfected over tens of thousands of years of evolution were, because of their veils, unknowable.

After a while, a second disciple, this one dusted with yellow powder, crawled into the hive. The villagers settled back to wait. At first, nothing. Then a foot could be seen through the opening, twitching. That was all. After a long time—Smith guessed an hour, hard to know without his dad's old Rolex—the ordeal passed its natural time limit. Two Marabout guards wearing gloves and bee-proof meshing cautiously approached the hive. They reached in and removed the disciple via his formerly twitching foot. He was already purple and swollen, grotesque black tongue hanging from his mouth. Dead. The few bees still crawling on his flesh were groggy, engorged, and easily brushed aside.

"Different colors and yet they both died," Smith said. "There goes your theory, *mon colonel.*"

Phillipe squinted up at the nearest peak. "That fool was clearly allergic. Death came from a single sting."

5.

The earthly dwelling place of the mysterious Al Bab, Gateway to the Age of the Hidden Imam, Beloved of God, the Stung One, Supernatural Grand Marabout, Supreme Military Leader, and General of All Generals of the Marabout Uprising, lay tucked behind a rocky protrusion at the top of the village, removed at a safe distance from the giant hive and its buzzing, stinging raiding parties of heavenly messengers. It was a modest, cheery structure built solidly of brick and cinder block, its walls painted flamingo pink, a vibrant color Smith assumed had everything to do with bee-resistant pink powder mixed in with the plaster, and nothing to do with the owner's fondness for South Florida chic. A small satellite dish sprouted off the gable end; a generator chuffed away, hidden behind a barrier of thornbushes. Yellow lights burned from within. Electric lights. This familiar glow meant much more than the promise of artificial illumination to Smith, who had come to dread the long, icy hours of darkness. It meant *heat*. The death sentence that no doubt awaited him inside might be received without bitterness if he could just sit there in the warmth for a few minutes to hear it pronounced.

Dusk was the hour allotted for private petitions and also the hour of judgments rendered. The Gateway to the Age of the Hidden Imam received his faithful now as the sun descended. Villagers assembled humbly in the waning light, peasants on their way to an audience with their king. Smith stood under guard at the end of this line of wheedlers, whispering to himself a quotation from Camus: "There is no fate which cannot be surmounted by scorn. There is no fate which cannot be surmounted by scorn.'"

He raised his eyes to the heavens and watched the stars come up, repeating this mantra under his breath, and seemed able to call the brilliant little pinpricks of light into existence just by the force of these ten words. Then he was standing on the gravel of the forecourt and the door swung open and two Marabout guards dragged him roughly by his chains into the sanctuary. The sensation of heat crept in a kind of half-painful prickling across Smith's bare skin. Driven to his knees, he was forced to crawl up a narrow hallway of rough, untreated concrete to a room at the back. The first thing he saw of the men waiting for him was their bare feet and brown toes, some decorated with silver rings, protruding from beneath Marabout-blue djellahs and set against the dark red and blue arabesques of thick Berber carpets. A calloused, bare foot forced him down and for several long minutes, Smith lay deliciously warm, nose pressed to the fragrant weave. How he wished he could stay there forever!

Then the foot lifted and a hand yanked him by the hair to his knees. He looked around, blinking, and found himself in a large, plain room, crowded with men, who, being inside the four walls of a holy sanctuary, were allowed to remove their veils. The proliferation of chins, noses, mouths, beards, mustaches—features unseen for so many weeks—unsettled him. At the center of the room, enthroned in a yellow, wingback glider that looked like it might have come from Sears, sat Al Bab. The Gateway to the Age of the Hidden Imam alone remained veiled. He was a stocky figure, round as Buddha, his hands and the rectangle of skin visible around his eyes hennaed in a complicated web pattern usually reserved for dainty young brides. A large gold bee hieroglyph pendant hung on a chain around his neck; white light from the bare lightbulb in the ceiling danced off this garish piece of bling. He alone also hadn't removed his shoes—clunky-looking leather orthopedics resembling Birkenstocks—an insult, in Smith's mind, to the beautiful, soft carpet.

To one side of the yellow throne stood a narrow-faced man, with an air of self-importance about him, Al Bab's prime minister or vizier. A scraggly mustache and moth-eaten beard drooped forlornly from the man's face. For a while, no one spoke.

"State your name, Enemy of God," the vizier said at last, in French.

"I'm not an enemy of God," Smith said.

The vizier raised an eyebrow and one of the Marabout guards smacked Smith in the head with a leather quoit and Smith's vision shattered into a scattering of light and yellow squiggles.

"Hey!" Smith said, shaking himself.

"Blasphemy is rewarded with pain," the vizier said. "Be warned."

"How is it blasphemy to say I'm not an enemy of God?" Smith managed, trying to keep his voice calm. "I like God—" Though this wasn't true. He felt nothing but bitter resentment toward the divinity that had struck down his sister at thirteen and taken his father and mother and now poor Jessica without consulting him first. Anyway, he believed himself to be an atheist.

The vizier frowned and Smith was hit again.

"Your name!" the vizier commanded.

"Legionnaire Caspar P. Milquetoast," Smith gasped. "1e RE, Musique Principale. Serial number 9938947."

"Your are an American. *C'est vrai?*"

"The Legion is my country," Smith said, stiffly. "I'm a soldier in the service of the French Republic. Currently attached to MINURSO, the United Nations Peacekeeping—"

The vizier interrupted with another gesture and Smith was hit a third time on the back of the head. Al Bab watched, his black eyes without emotion.

"An American. You are an American. Say it!"

"All right," Smith said when he had recovered sufficiently to speak. "I'm an American. Have it your way."

At this, Al Bab beckoned with a hennaed hand and the vizier knelt down and listened, nodding.

"As an American, you are an unholy cancer," the vizier translated, when he had absorbed the Hidden One's message. "America is the cancer of all cancers, infecting the world with the AIDS virus grown in a laboratory as a weapon against all brown-skinned peoples."

"That's a bunch of conspiracy-theory bullshit—" Smith began, and again he was hit.

"A cancer," the vizier continued, "corrupting the world with your iPods and your computer Web full of naked women and naked men engaging in many sexual acts and perversions, sometimes with each other, sometimes with household pets."

"I hear you guys have a Web site!" Smith shot back.

"Our Web site is holy and therefore necessary," the vizier said. "Your Web site is an abomination."

"It's not that bad," Smith said. "A buddy put it up for me. An actor who waits tables at Toast, in the East Village—this crazy place that only serves toast with various kinds of toppings, peanut butter, almond spread, Cheez Whiz, caviar, whatever. Stupid idea you say, but a monster hit with the late-night munchie crowd. Anyway, Toby does computer stuff on the side and he did my Web site as a favor. I guess it's not great, maybe a little user un-friendly, but it was free."

The vizier paused, confused, then conferred with the Holy Gateway. "Not your own personal Web site," he said after a moment. "His Holiness speaks of the Internet as a whole. Full of filthy perversions."

"Got me there," Smith admitted. "The Internet's definitely 70 percent porn."

"Aha!" The vizier wagged his head. Then: "They say you are also a singer of songs. Is this true?"

"I sing," Smith admitted. "I also dance and act. The old triple threat."

"Be that as it may, we do not permit singing here," the vizier said. "It is an affront to God. Nor do we permit the flying of kites or the eating of pork, or swimming, which is an activity only meant for fish, God be praised."

"You have a pool?" Smith said.

Al Bab crooked a finger and the vizier leaned in close for a quick word.

"Correction," the vizier said. "We will permit singing under certain cir-cumstances."

"O.K.," Smith said.

"The Holy Gateway wishes you to sing something now."

"I'm not in the mood," Smith said.

"You will sing," the vizier said. "At once."

Smith did a couple of scales, then sang "One Enchanted Evening" from

South Pacific, which he'd done at the 6th Avenue Playhouse in New Paltz and that, truthfully, is a song better suited for an operatic baritone. When finished he wished he'd sung something else, but it was too late.

Al Bab spoke aloud; the vizier translated: "The Hidden One does not like this song. He wishes you to sing another one. Something better."

"I agree with"—Smith couldn't decide what to call a semisupernatural being wearing Birkenstocks—"with His Magnitude. But it's hard for me to sing while kneeling, it's all about breathing, you know. May I stand?"

The vizier nodded. As Smith rose, chains rattling, he saw the Hidden Imam's eyes glance down for the barest moment, measuring the size of Smith's penis tucked in its matted nest of yellow hair. The old locker-room syndrome, Smith thought ruefully, even out here in a place where there were no locker rooms. He cleared his throat and decided on a whimsically comic number: "Good Old Days" from *Damn Yankees*.

"Cannibals a-munchin' a missionary luncheon"—Smith did his best to give it the old comic zing—"ha-ha-ha-ha! those were the good old days . . ."

This is the lament of Mr. Applegate, who is the devil, for the passing of the bad old days of cannibalism, pestilence, and war, which to him, being the devil, were actually the good old days. Funny stuff. It was a song, Smith always thought, that could only have been written from the high ground of 1958, when things seemed to be getting better in the world for everyone: infectious diseases on the wane, totalitarianism on the outs, the stock market up, and America a gleaming beacon of personal liberty, excellent hygiene, frost-free refrigerators, and gigantic cars with fins that got eight miles to the gallon. Mr. Applegate would be very pleased with the way things were sliding these days.

But this number also fell flat. The Marabouts exchanged confused looks, rustled restlessly in their djellahs.

Al Bab sighed and spoke again at length.

"The Gateway to the Age of the Hidden Imam, peace be upon him, does not like your singing at all," the vizier translated.

"Then I guess he's not a fan of show tunes," Smith said peevishly, crossing his arms.

"This is an accurate statement," the vizier conceded.

Just then, a door opened at the back of the room and two more Marabouts entered. Before the door closed, Smith caught an intriguing glimpse of the next room: He saw a shelf crammed with books and DVDs and what looked like a shortwave radio. And, on a small table by a bowl and a spoon neatly laid out, a narrow red-and-blue box covered with garish cartoon graphics. This box was utterly familiar to Smith, and yet so alien in this context he could hardly say what it might be. Then the door closed and the identity of the thing was gone from him.

"Someone has come looking for your colonel," the vizier said presently; his voice sounded the serious note that all men's voices have when they speak about money. "They have entered the souk at Laayoune, offering bribes for information concerning his whereabouts. Do you think"—he paused, stroking his thin mustache—"someone might also come to offer money for the sake of your head?"

Smith thought about this, his skin prickling from more than the unaccustomed warmth. The Legion was looking for Phillipe! If they were looking for Phillipe, this must mean they were looking for him too! The Legion would never abandon its lost children!

"Of course," Smith said, grinning. "Absolutely."

"Your family in America, they are rich?"

"Very rich!" Smith said enthusiastically. And he gave them the same absurd story he'd given Kasim Vatran, way back in Istanbul: He came from a family of Iowa lumber barons, rich like Rockefeller for a hundred years. They owned lumber mills, acres of property, railroads, the entire city of Montezuma. More, they held the monopoly on all of Iowa's vast lumber preserves.

"Forests," Smith said. "One-hundred-foot-tall Iowa pines. Far as the eye can see."

Suddenly, Al Bab shifted in his yellow chair and uttered a short, incredulous bark. He became animated briefly, jabbed his hennaed finger repeatedly in Smith's direction, speaking rapidly in the Saharoui Berber dialect. He seemed angry. Smith's heart sank.

"You are a liar!" the vizier exclaimed, outraged. "There are no such forests. This place you call Iowa is much like a desert. With only"—he paused searching for the word—"many fields of corn!"

Smith wasn't given a chance to explain himself or make any emendations to his fantastic tale. Someone hit him from behind so hard he fell to the floor stunned. And he was dragged by his chains across the nice soft carpets and down the concrete hallway, out of the warmth of Al Bab's comfortable pink ranch house and back into the darkness and the cold of the mountain.

6.

Smith awoke to the sound of Phillipe jabbering to himself and the usual lapping of cold night air on his bare feet and ass. Phillipe's madness always intensified in the dark. Now, an odd, tuneless snatch of Satie's *Musique d'ameublement*—Pom-pom-pom-pom; pom, pom, *pom!*—emanated from his dark corner. The colonel was mimicking the sound of his old baby grand, the piano that had kept him more or less sane through all those sleepless midnights at the Fort de Nogent. You could ask him to stop, scream at him, but it was no use. He would stop for a minute, maybe two, forget himself, and start up again.

Smith clenched his jaw to keep his teeth from chattering, and tried to put his finger on something he'd forgotten, something he needed very much to remember. Then he had it: He'd been dreaming, but more than a dream. Rather, a kind of hyper-real, color-saturated memory experienced as one. He'd been having a lot of these lately—the inevitable mental by-products of his drab captivity.

In Smith's dream-memory, an undulating countryside, the smell of a new car. His father's carefully maintained 1979 Mercury Montego, its seats covered with rich Corinthian leather, this phrase echoing down the years from a popular television commercial of the era.

And there he was, a kid again, riding in the backseat, his sister Jane swatting at him maliciously with a Wonder Woman pencil. They were headed west on 80, out across the prairies, fields of corn and wheat and sorghum extending in vivid greens to the horizon on either side, the long glittering ribbon of highway ahead. They were on their way to Muscatine to do some shopping. Or to Omaha for their obligatory biannual family visit to Great-aunt Lucy—though his mother's happy, singing presence in the front seat nestled in the crook of his father's arm suggested the former. Or maybe they were just out for a Saturday drive across the luxurious blaze of an Iowa spring. Bored, young Smith extracted something from the pocket of his pocket T—a small card printed with stickers—and he began to peel them off and stick them to the Montego's back window. First a cartoon pirate, his crooked nose and mustache cartoonishly exaggerated. Then a couple of cartoon kids in sailor outfits and a cartoon dog in a sailor shirt. Finally, a funny-looking cartoon man with a bulbous nose wearing a cartoon captain's hat and a blue naval uniform. Now, from the darkness of his captivity at the far ends of the earth, Smith watched his younger self stick and unstick and restick those cartoon character stickers to the window of his father's Montego and their names suddenly came back to him: Petey the Sea Dog. Jean La Foote . . .

"Cap'n Crunch!" he cried aloud, sitting bolt upright in his chains.

"*Non, non,*" the colonel muttered from the gloom. "I am Colonel de Noyer."

"Not you, Phillipe! Listen, I think . . ."

But the colonel had already slipped back into his miasma. Smith clanked in his chains impatiently. Those stickers had come out of a box of Cap'n Crunch cereal, the preferred breakfast food of Smith's youth, purchased by his mother at the Piggly Wiggly on North Grant in Montezuma, nearly thirty years ago. He remembered pulling the stickers out of the bottom of the box against his mother's specific orders not to extract the prize until the box was done, his small hand covered with guilty yellow cereal crumbs. He remembered munching the cereal later that morning, hunched over a TV tray while watching *Land of the Lost* in which Marsha, Will, and Holly, whilst on a routine expedition, were swept into an underworld full of slithering bipedal lizards, in much the same way that Smith had now landed himself in his current pickle.

The box glimpsed on the table of Al Bab's inner sanctum was definitely the same stuff, a box of mouthwatering Cap'n Crunch!

Smith grinned to himself, absolutely certain of the identity of that red-and-blue box. Like those other great commercial icons, Uncle Ben and Aunt Jemima, Betty Crocker, Mrs. Butterworth, and that Quaker Guy from Cream of Wheat, Cap'n Crunch—altered only slightly from a graphic standpoint over the years—abided. Having digested this fact, Smith now asked himself a couple of pertinent questions: Where could this sugary-sweet utterly American breakfast cereal be obtained in the arid waste of the Western Sahara? Surely there wasn't a Piggly Wiggly located anywhere in a radius of, say, ten thousand miles! And what sort of person would eat such a cereal, even if it could be found?

Smith's mouth watered at the thought of his own lost childhood breakfast of Cap'n Crunch, awash in milk, yellow sugary nuggets floating in his

Cap'n Crunch bowl (purchased with eight box tops and a postal money order for $2.99), lit by the overhead fluorescent light of the old kitchen back home in their house on Blue Bird Lane in Montezuma, before his sister's death, before his father's fatal depression, his mother bustling about in the background always humming a Gershwin tune. But this happy memory called up mysteries that could not be answered. As he drifted back to sleep moments later, the purple flash of heat lightning illuminated the distant peaks of the Galtat Zemmur. Thunder, answering, echoed out across the desert.

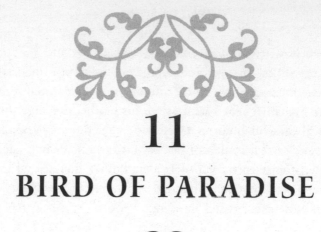

11

BIRD OF PARADISE

1.

A lone flamingo stood asleep, one leg up, at the center of the artificial lagoon in the middle of the abandoned Colline des Oiseaux—the bird sanctuary—in Laayoune, capital of the Moroccan-held portion of the Non-Self-Governing Territory of Western Sahara. Bright green algae floated on the dark surface. The early morning sky, a peerless blue and free of clouds, burned above with incipient heat. Soon, the heat would descend, making Laayoune's vast, new concrete plazas—the Place Mechouar, the Place du 27 Fevrier 1967, peopled now with a few hesitant peddlers, the sellers of feathers and dates, the purveyors of used bicycle tires and other nameless scraps—as hot and lifeless as the surface of Mercury.

The park's acacia trees and tamarisks and tall, spindly palms rustled in a warm breeze from the South Atlantic visible twenty kilometers off from the tops of the high dunes at the edge of town.

2.

Evariste Pinard followed the woman along the bare avenue du Colline from a safe distance, perhaps fifty meters back. He'd been promoted to capitaine for the duration of Mission: SCORPIO, the Foreign Legion's covert operation in Western Sahara, of which he was officer in charge. All the woman had to do was glance over her shoulder and she would see Capitaine Pinard skulking along back there, an eyesore in his tourist's tropical shirt and too-short yellow shorts: no place to hide, no concealing shade, not a tree, not a bush softening this dry stretch of road. But she seemed hardly aware of her surroundings, wrapped in her thoughts as she was in the improvised *hejab* thrown casually over her glossy, dark hair, and she did not turn around. Now she crossed the sandy verge to a gap in the fence and simply stepped inside the closed bird sanctuary.

Pinard hesitated for a long minute. A camel, tied by its bridle into the bed of an old, battered Citroën Mehari parked across the street, eyed him lazily with dark, mysterious eyes. The woman mounted the concrete steps, strewn with sun-withered palm leaves, and disappeared from sight around a bend. Pinard took a deep breath—he'd come too far to turn back now—hurried across the verge, and followed.

❦

The wire and wood aviaries were mostly empty now, the exotic birds stolen for food or sale to exotic bird smugglers—though a few survivors remained, perched on the highest branches of the artificial trees in their dilapidated enclosures. Coming past the cages along the narrow palm-lined alleys, Pinard saw the bright flash of African green parrots, heard the *chirp-chirrup-chirp* of Harbert's Finch, and the bawdy honk of flamingos. A Malian peahen, its gaudy tail feathers extended, swept along an intersecting walkway, stately as a potentate. Pinard stopped to let it pass. The place had the air of an insane asylum following some great disaster: The attendants had fled, leaving the crazies behind to fend for themselves.

He found the woman a few minutes later by the concrete shores of the artificial lagoon. The lone sleeping flamingo had just been joined by two others and these three stood side by side, resplendently pink, legs up, necks crooked into question marks, already asleep. Pinard thought he probably shouldn't speak to the woman, but it seemed pointless not to. What, after all, could be more innocuous than a French national, a businessman (his cover story), greeting another French national met by chance in an odd corner of the world?

"*Eh! Bonjour!*" he called, coming toward her, withered palm fronds crunching under his feet. "Excuse me for bothering you, but you look French."

He stopped a safe distance away and kept his hands in his pockets to show he meant no harm.

She studied him through large dark glasses that concealed her eyes, reportedly a unique shade of deep indigo blue. He didn't know for sure, hadn't been this close to her before. She was modestly dressed—a loose-fitting long-sleeved blouse and white capri pants, her improvised *hejab* actually an expensive Hermès scarf covered with clock faces and sundials—but none of this could hide her wonderful litheness, the curve of her breasts beneath the cotton fabric of the blouse, the deep ivory pallor of her skin. Below the outer epidermal layer, there seemed to be another skin, aglow, luminescent. She was like a movie star incognito or the porcelain figurine of Columbine from the Commedia dell'arte Pinard had once seen in the Collection de Sèvres back in Paris—improbably delicate yet artfully sturdy, perfectly made—though what he'd been doing in such a place, a museum devoted to china figurines, he couldn't recall now.

"I hope I'm not disturbing you," Pinard said again. "It's just that I thought you looked French . . ."

"Je suis française," the woman admitted. But she didn't offer anything more—didn't seem surprised that here, in the middle of nowhere, a Frenchman had appeared—and turned her attention back to the flamingos in the lagoon.

"You know this park is closed . . ." Pinard managed after a long awkward moment. "It's probably not safe to go walking around alone."

"Do you work here?" the woman said, the slightest trace of irony in her voice. "You are perhaps an ornithologist?" She spoke in the elegant, refined French they used to call *l'accent du seizième*, after that posh arrondissement in Paris where all the most exclusive girls' boarding schools had once been located.

"Not me." Pinard shook his head. "I'm a tourist"—then he caught himself—"and a businessman. Actually I'm here for both business and pleasure. Today, I'm doing a little sightseeing."

The woman nodded, appearing to accept this explanation, though really, there were no sightseers in Laayoune. No Westerners in the city who did not have an ulterior motive or an NGO. They were attached to UN MINURSO, or Médecins Sans Frontières, or they smuggled contraband—drugs, people, the hides and horns of endangered animals—out of Africa via the lawless Saharoui souk to dealers in China. No one came to see the sights because, despite all the efforts of the Moroccan government and all the new con-

struction during nearly thirty years of occupation, there weren't any sights
to see.

"I wanted to visit the birds," the woman said. A full minute had passed
since Pinard's last words. "I was told this was one of the finest bird sanctuar-
ies in Africa."

"That was a long time ago," Pinard said. "In the days of the Spanish."

"They said even though the park was closed now, the birds were well
cared for"—the woman paused, her lip trembling slightly. "But it's just not
true. These birds are suffering. In times of strife it is the innocents who suffer, especially the animals. No one thinks of them."

"I suppose not . . ." Pinard's voice trailed off.

Standing this close to her was disconcerting. He felt an unfamiliar squeezing sensation in the vicinity of his heart. Her lips, he found himself thinking, such beautiful lips—and a forbidden image swam up unbidden from
the depths of his libido like a dark fish: There she was, kneeling before him
splendidly naked, her bare flesh shining in the gloom of a shuttered room,
those same lips parting eagerly to take him into her mouth. A sudden dizzi-
ness sent his head spinning; he faltered, stumbled back a step or two.

"Are you all right, monsieur?" the woman asked, alarmed.

"A touch of malaria," Pinard lied. "Souvenir of a long history of doing
business in Africa."

"Maybe you should sit down"—she gestured to a crumbling concrete
bench, half concealed beneath the cascading branches of a tamarisk. "Should
I get a doctor?"

"*Non, merci*," Pinard said. "I'm fine, look"—and he hopped around on one
foot and made a lewd honking noise in imitation of the flamingos, to show
he was fine. The woman smiled at this clowning and lifted her dark glasses
as if to get a better look at him and Pinard held his breath: Her eyes were
indeed a curious shade, halfway between blue and indigo, a unique purple,
like the color of the stuff that comes drop by drop from the murex shell, the
original purple, the purple of dreams.

"Come with me," she said. "I want to show you something."

She turned on the heels of her flats and hurried up the stairs to another
long alley bordered by empty and decaying cages and Pinard followed eagerly, and would have followed her anywhere, even into a deadly ambush,
even if he knew what was coming. At the far end of the alley stood one of
the largest cages still occupied. From the top of the plaster tree in this cage,

a bird of paradise, feathers bedraggled, looked down on its disintegrating world with a mournful eye.

"You see?" the woman said. "That poor animal is clearly depressed."

"Well, it's a bird"—Pinard fumbled for words—"hard to tell . . . the emotional state of a bird . . ."

"You're not looking," the woman said sharply. "Look closely."

Pinard looked again at the bird, the bird looked down at him. Its breast feathers glistened ruby red and iridescent green in the morning light, its tail feathers a deep, funereal black. Pinard couldn't shake the sensation that the bird seemed to know something he didn't; that this creature purporting to be a bird was also more than a bird. Just then, it seemed to be saying: *You and me both, brother!* But Pinard pushed this thought aside as ridiculous.

"You see? Its wings have been clipped!" the woman said, outraged. "It can't fly away. And if it could, where would it go? Here we are so far from its natural habitat."

"Thankfully, someone's still feeding it." Pinard pointed to a bowl of water and a pile of birdseed mounded on the dirty concrete floor of the cage.

"Ah . . ."

Now Pinard screwed his courage to the screwing place that was somewhere to the left of his stomach and turned to face her.

"You don't know me," he said, trying to keep his voice calm, reasonable. "My name is Edouard Deschafeaux"—this, the absurd pseudonym bestowed on him by the Legion for the purposes of the mission. He put out his hand awkwardly; the woman shook it, with a kind of mock-solemnity—"I'm in Laayoune on business for a few weeks, perhaps a month—"

"I thought you said business and pleasure?" she interrupted.

"Exactly," Pinard said, beginning to sweat. "Which is why I was wondering if I might offer you a cup of coffee this morning? Maybe some breakfast?" His ears felt very tight against the side of his head, his heart beating wildly. He felt as if he had just accomplished one of the most courageous acts of his life so far, as much of an act of courage as attacking that Marabout column in the desert two months ago.

The woman laughed, a muted ringing sound, like a sterling-silver plate being dropped into clear water.

"*Merci, non,*" she said. "I don't drink coffee, it stains the teeth. And I've already eaten. Another time, perhaps." She adjusted the Hermès scarf over her glossy hair and mounted the steps.

"Will I see you again?" Pinard called after her stupidly.

"*Paris c'est tout petit pour ceux qui s'aime,*" she said and was gone.

Pinard didn't recognize this curious statement as a line from a classic French film, and stood there for a while clutching the wire mesh of the bird of paradise's cage, trying to puzzle out its exact meaning. He finally decided it was some sort of joke on her part, and the joke was on him. This shouldn't have happened, he thought regretfully. Why had he made contact with her in such a foolishly personal way? But he didn't stick around long enough to tell himself the answer and hurried out through the closed park, a cloud of regret and worry hovering over his head. And there was something else, something he couldn't yet put a name to, that had just started to knock around in the bottom of his heart. He paused, gasping suddenly for air like a drowning man; yes, perhaps he was drowning! As he dragged himself past the few still-tenanted aviaries, the birds inside seemed to recognize this condition. They flapped their mutilated wings and fluttered helplessly to the roofs of their cages, which, though made of rusty wire mesh and sun-rotted wood, to them was the sky.

3.

Capitaine Pinard and Legionnaire P.C. Szbeszdogy, dressed for a business meeting in cheap, ill-fitting Legion-provided suits, briefcases in hand, climbed the wide, modern streets of the Oued Bou district, late for their nine fifteen meeting with the minister.

"What am I supposed to say?" Szbeszdogy complained, panting. Sweat made dark patches on the coarse fabric of his suit jacket. "I know nothing about business."

"Neither do I," Pinard said glumly.

"At least you've been briefed."

"Oh, yes. A couple of hours' worth. Now I'm a businessman."

"You didn't answer my question," the Hungarian persisted.

"Say nothing," Pinard snapped. "Just keep your mouth shut. Start now."

They hurried on, racing against the heat and slowed by it. Below lay the new Moroccan hospital, the red-and-green standard of the Moroccan king flying from its squat tower. Farther off, the medina, the new soccer stadium, all white and pink, and the new highrise government offices under construction along the rue el-Jazouli.

Down there also, like a mud-colored stain on the white city, lay the Saha-roui souk—a crammed medieval ghetto surrounded by barbed wire trenches and machine gun towers and watched over by surveillance cameras and at night by the high-intensity spotlights of the Moroccan army. During day-light hours, the two official gates into the souk—the Gate of Dawn and the Gate of Dusk—remained open, though closely guarded by Moroccan troops. These gates closed at sunset with the beginning of curfew, and entry into the souk, officially forbidden, became an adventure: Some said there were tunnels, others secret doors open only for those who knew the password and where to find them, like those magical portals in fairy tales leading to underground realms. True, many people came and went freely after dark, all with illicit business in hand, but this nocturnal access wasn't without its perils. The undertaking, advertised by Laayoune's criminal class as routine, nonethe-less each year claimed the lives of a few unfortunates making the trip.

4.

The Minister of Tourism and Social Intercourse for the Southern Prov-inces of the Kingdom of Morocco—which is what the Moroccans called the Non-Self-Governing Territory in official press releases—sat in his new air-conditioned office in Laayoune's tallest building, the twelve-story Bureau du Tourisme et du Commerce, listening with thinly veiled skepticism to Pinard's fake business plan presentation. Pinard and Szbeszdogy and the quartet of assassins from the 4e RE that made up the covert personnel of Mission: SCORPIO were masquerading as an advance team sent out by the Club Med organization to assess the suitability of the string of dingy beaches beyond the dunes—the Playa Laayoune—as the site for a new ad-dition to the franchise.

The air-conditioning in the minister's office, set to deep freeze, blasted out of two ducts in the ceiling. The minister, a sleek, self-satisfied man with a nose like a hawk's beak and a carefully combed beard, wore a black wool djellah, usually intended for winter wear, its sleeves and neck figured with gold em-broidery. At one point during the presentation, he actually pulled the hood up to warm his ears.

Pinard, shivering, almost asked if the air-conditioning might be turned down, but didn't. He put a fake flow chart on the portable easel he'd brought and rambled on. His brief briefing back in Aubagne had been delivered by two chipper Club Med reps—Club Med has always been friendly to Legion activities in the East, their fun-in-the-sun-in-exotic-places vacation packages being, in a way, the final incarnation of discredited French colonialist ideology. Pinard had come provided with all the essential facts and figures, with reams of promotional materials, with tapes of actual Club Med presentations, which he'd listened to over and over again in preparation for this meeting today. But the niceties of business-speak now escaped him. There was a reason he'd gone into the profession of arms and not into business; for the latter, despite his earlier career as a criminal entrepreneur, he felt only the most profound contempt. Also he wasn't very good at number crunching.

". . . to be considered while calculating construction budgets," Pinard was droning now, "but not including marketing and advertising costs, which will be folded into the budgets of other divisions for accounting purposes—at least initially. We are now telling management in Paris—"

Suddenly, he drew a blank. An uncomfortable silence followed. The minister tapped his glossy fingernails on his glossy desk and waited. Szbeszdogy, sitting in a chair across the room directly beneath the air-conditioning duct, was frozen by more than a fear of public speaking.

"I'm sorry, *monsieur le ministre*," Pinard said at last. "Where was I?"

"You were talking about profit margins," the minister said dryly.

"Ah! Yes! Well, we're talking about a profitability factor of, oh—17.5 percent."

The minister raised an eyebrow. "A few minutes ago you mentioned a 12 percent rate."

"Of course I did!" Pinard blustered. "But that's not quite accurate. Allow me to recalculate—" He scratched some unintelligible figures on his pad, then scratched them off. "Let's say 15 percent," he said, wagging his head. "Yes, that's fair. Just to be on the safe side."

All this was nothing but the freshest *merde*, and the minister's *merde* detector was switched to on. He pulled down his hood and swiveled his office chair toward Szbeszdogy, freezing on the other side of the room.

"Who are you again?" the minister said.

"I am Alphonse Pique," Szbeszdogy said, thankfully remembering his covert identity. "A French businessman."

The minister grunted at this. "You don't look French."

"And yet I am," Szbeszdogy said.

"What is your role in this undertaking?"

"I am a marketing expert," Szbeszdogy said, his tone flat, robotic. "I am also his assistant."

"And what do you assist?"

"*Eh bien, tout!*" Everything.

The minister glanced at Pinard's prospectus again, this time studying it with a careful eye. This particular document had been prepared by Club Med economists years ago for a never-built resort in Honduras, along the Mosquito Coast. Pertinent sections were written in Spanish, budgets given in pre-euro French francs and Honduran dollars.

"The document we have here does not seem to pertain at all," the minister said, tossing it across his desk. "First, it's written in Spanish."

"That is intended as an example only, *monsieur le ministre*," Pinard said desperately. "It is the *type* of document we will be preparing, that is after we have concluded our fact-finding mission in your beautiful country."

The minister's expression darkened. "Monsieur Deschafeaux, is there some other reason for your sojourn in Laayoune?"

Pinard looked at him blankly. "We are the representatives of Club Med France," he said. "Would you care to examine our passports? Our documents?"

"Passports and documents can be forged." The minister shrugged.

Pinard opened his mouth to protest, but the minister interrupted.

"Suppose I agree that you are who you say you are. Then I must say that your superiors are ridiculously guilty of bad business practice. In all honesty, now is not the time for Club Med or any other European touristic concern to build one of their outposts here. In ten years perhaps, when the Southern Provinces has been more firmly integrated into the kingdom of Morocco and infrastructures have been improved—but now, with these fanatical Marabouts gaining strength and Polisario issues still unresolved—" He made a gesture, easily translated, that meant something like you people are absolutely crazy.

An uncomfortable silence followed. The air conditioner whirred away. A telex machine clattered from the next room. The minister rose from his chair to indicate the conclusion of the interview.

Pinard gathered his materials; Szbeszdogy unfroze himself and pushed up, his bones creaking with the cold. The minister ushered them through the reception area, where young Moroccan men in shiny new suits performed the menial office support jobs usually allocated to women in more enlightened societies. They crossed to the elevators and stood there for a while, waiting.

"A question," the minister said at last. "Have either of you gentlemen experienced lengthy periods of military service?"

"No," Pinard said carefully. "That is, apart from a year in the Boy Scouts."

"The military life doesn't appeal to me," Szbeszdogy said. This, at least, was the truth.

"Why do you ask?" Pinard said.

The minister scratched his beard. "There is a distinct military demeanor about the both of you—" he began, but was interrupted by the elevator, its interior all polished stainless steel. To Pinard's surprise, the minister entered with them, pressing the button for the lobby. They rode down most of the way in silence, then Pinard said, "We'll get some current numbers for you in a couple of weeks. Allow me to apologize for the disjointed manner of the presentation you just heard. Unfortunately I suffer from recurring bouts of malaria. . . ."

The minister did not respond to these lies. Then, the door opened on the glare of the lobby, all polished marble and tall, tinted plate-glass windows overlooking the blazing plaza beyond.

"Twelve floors!" the minister announced proudly. He didn't exit the elevator. "It's the tallest building in Laayoune. I like to ride up and down to remind myself of the Moroccan achievement in the Southern Provinces! When we came here twenty-five years ago, Laayoune was a miserable little town with dirt streets, nothing but a few Spanish army bunkers and that terrible souk! Yes, the souk is still here, but look at what we've done with the rest!"

Pinard and Szbeszdogy stepped into the lobby. The elevator door began to close, but the minister put out an arm to hold it open.

"Pursue your business ventures, gentlemen, whatever they may be," he said in a low voice. "Though I doubt it has anything to do with Club Med. Frankly, I suspect illegal activity."

"That is absolutely not—" Pinard began, but the minister silenced him again with a glance.

"Illegal activity, despite what my superiors might think, is also a part—indeed, a most important part—of the Moroccan economy. See to it, however, that I am personally allotted at least 22.5 percent of whatever undertaking you have in mind. If you do not remit to me this percentage and I find out about it, I will see to it that you are arrested and thrown into prison for a very long time. Good day."

Smiling, he removed his arm and the elevator door closed with a pneumatic hush and the stainless-steel box lifted him unseen to his frozen lair on the twelfth floor.

5.

A week passed.

Pinard didn't see the woman again, though he went back to the Colline des Oiseaux several times and wandered the rustling alleys there, hoping and also dreading to catch a glimpse of her slim, enticing form. She was still under surveillance, a duty he had wisely delegated to Szbeszdogy. But if Pinard came to the Colline and the woman came to the Colline at more or less the same hour, and they should happen to meet. . . .

He found himself each time stopping to visit the mournful bird of paradise in its cage, which, seemingly immobile, hadn't budged from the same spot on the topmost branch of the artificial tree. *You and me both, brother*, the bird whispered to Pinard's inner ear, *you and me both!*

6.

Meanwhile, Laayoune lay stranded between Sahara and Atlantic on its miserable, waterless peninsula of sand. It's a dull, dusty town, the kind of place that has been a special torment for the Legion for more than a century and a half. Clouds of fine, irritating sand blew through the streets when the simoom came from east to west, which it did at least twice a day. The soccer stadium was always empty, its green plastic Astroturf field nearly covered in sandy drifts. The sole movie theater, its faded marquee still advertising a notorious Saudi film involving rapacious demons in the guise of American troops, had been closed for years. Three or four overpriced hotels loomed along the avenue Ksar el-Kebir, two of them with bad expensive lobby bars, which were, in fact, the only bars in Laayoune; at one of these malingered a few local prostitutes, ugly and even more expensive than the watered-down booze. There was nothing to do in Laayoune worth doing, not for a Legionnaire.

A mysterious affliction called *le cafard* comes upon the Legion in such places, at remote outposts and mountain forts overlooking unending miles of sand and rock, in dull garrison towns. It resembles a disease of the brain and is sometimes accompanied by inexplicable fevers, but is not a physical ailment, not exactly. It is a spiritual malady, halfway between ennui and suicide, that has something to do with seeing the same old faces every day and drinking far too much of the same old bad wine and not being, in a general sense, fit company for oneself. It is a kind of madness that descends out of the hot, white African sky and has extracted its toll of Legionnaires over the years, with a mortality rate nearly twice that of syphilis or the battlefield.

In the days of the desert forts a century ago, Legionnaires with a bad case of *cafard* struck out alone into the wilderness following a glittering mirage of cool water and bathing beauties and never returned; or mutinied and attacked their CO with a Senegalese *coupe-coupe*, a deadly blade like a large butcher knife; or shot themselves in the head with their Lebel rifles, an unlucky weapon for the purposes of suicide: The Lebel must be placed on its butt, business end of the long barrel in the mouth, bare toe on the trigger, an awkward firing position, particularly for short men, and one that often caused not death, but horrible, disfiguring facial injuries. Or they simply lay down, muttering to themselves about how they'd been cheated in life and unfairly maligned at every turn, and cursing the miserable fate of being alive, turned their faces to the wall, and died.

The only known cures for *cafard* are battle, death, or an immediate transfer to Paris (the latter, it is generally agreed, can cure anything), whichever comes first.

Now, over the course of the hot idle days, with excruciating slowness, like a chicken roasting in its own juices, the officer and men of Mission: SCORPIO began to fester, to grow irritable or grow melancholy or both, increasingly unsure of their purpose. They disobeyed orders, they drank much more than they were supposed to, they masturbated, shamefully, in secret. This was the beginning of *le cafard*, which, however it ended, always first manifested itself as a violent breakdown of the famously hard-earned discipline of the Legion.

7.

Sun blasted down on the courtyard of the Hotel Agadir like a death ray from outer space. It was almost noon. The hyperchlorinated pool steamed in the heat, faintly poisonous. Anyone with any sense took refuge during these miserable hours in the dim covered alleys of the souk or in air-conditioned

Western-style rooms. Hooded brown bundles that were the indigenous male population of the city napped in their djellahs beneath the cool arcades of the Djoune el Fina and in other shadowy corners. The many cement monuments to Moroccan casualties of the Polisario war gleamed glaringly white out in the empty plazas—like a detail from one of de Chirico's mysterious urban landscapes.

The four death squad commandos of the 4e RE lay drunk off sixty bottles of Kronenbourg in European-cut Speedos on canvas beach chairs in direct sunlight on the pebbly concrete, poolside at the Agadir. They'd been drinking steadily since 8:00 A.M., despite direct orders from Capitaine Pinard not to touch alcohol until after sundown and then only in the strictest moderation. Their muscled, tattooed torsos gleamed with cheap tanning lotions; the coconut stink of this stuff, mixed with the alcoholic fumes of Kronenbourg, the sickly-sweet musty smell of Basta, and rancid body sweat, hung in a cloud more poisonous than the evaporating chlorine in the stifling air.

The waiter, a sweaty, diminutive Saharoui named Nur'din, hopped back and forth from the Agadir's wine cellar, laden with large brass trays full of more bottles of Kro. When the supplies ran dry, management sent Nur'din next door to the Hotel Plaza d'Afrique for two more cases, which he brought back on his narrow shoulders, cursing and struggling. He had made a paper sun hat out of the front pages of *Le Soir du Maroc*, the French-language newspaper from Marrakesh, and it flopped comically on his head as he raced around the pool distributing the beers. The 4e RE assassins found the hat very funny and held chugging contests with one another just to see the waiter run around in the heat, hat flopping, popping open the warmish bottles as fast as they could drink them.

"*Eh, la, l'admiral! Une autre Kro! Suis soif ici!*" More beer, Admiral. One more Kro! Hop to it!

"This fucking beer tastes like hot piss!"

"Hey, you evil dwarf—get me another one!"

"Come on, Admiral! Move your nigger ass!"

This out of the mouth of the blackest of the bunch, so black he was almost purple: Legionnaire Amédée Dessalines, a Haitian from the Cité Soleil slum of Port-au-Prince. Dessalines, once a foot soldier in a pro-Aristide militia group, had fled that miserable island as a result of his role in an atrocity so horrible it succeeded in revolting even the atrocity-jaded natives of Haiti. Dessalines bore a jagged white scar around his neck, the mark of a barbed-wire harness his executioners had trussed him with in preparation for the voodoo sacrifice he'd somehow escaped. After such an escape, cursed by the voodoo gods, reviled by all Haiti, his only refuge was the Legion.

The other 4e RE assassins were easily as tough and murderous as Dessalines: Legionnaire Hector Babenco, a former Basque terrorist, had bombed a bus full of schoolchildren and nuns on the Malaga road. Legionnaire Vladimir Vladimirovitch, a thick-skulled blunt instrument the size of a tank, was a Russian army veteran of the bloody fighting in Chechnya. But none of them could match Caporal-chef Gil Solas, in terms of sheer lethality. Solas was a slight, soft-spoken, tawny-skinned Brazilian, his demeanor almost feminine, with a fine aquiline nose and soft green eyes that glowed at night like the eyes of a cat. He played bossa nova on the guitar and never went without a girlfriend, but this smooth café Brasiliano facade concealed an unrepentant monster: In his youth, Solas had been the chief executioner for one of Rio's most notorious favela gangs. He had killed men, women, children, cats and dogs. He had killed with his bare hands, with bottle caps flattened and sharpened like razor blades, with broken car antennas, rocks, tire irons, and once with a sealed birthday gourd full of hard red candies.

Being called a nigger by Dessalines was enough to make the long-suffering Nur'din lose his temper at last.

"My nigger ass!" the waiter shouted, enraged, stamping his small feet. "Black fiend! You cannot treat a proud Saharoui with such disrespect! You are nothing but a slave! A nigger-black African! I beat you with my shoe!"

"You are mistaken," Dessalines hissed, uncoiling menacingly from his beach chair. "Now you will eat those words."

"Nigger cur from hell!" Nur'din shouted. And he tossed his tray full of Kronenbourgs into the cactus bed beside the pool—a few of them broke open and began to spew foam into the sand—seized the paper hat from his head and lunged for the white scar around Dessalines's throat. Powerful as he was, the Haitian had a difficult time peeling the little waiter's hands away. They performed a violent dance, Nur'din swearing and spitting and grappling, Dessalines laughing, making sarcastic comments—*"Regardez les mecs!* Look at the admiral! He's a real battleship!" But his demeanor, now without a trace of humor, gave off a lethal seriousness.

The other 4e RE assassins watched from their beach chairs, the whites of their eyes red-rimmed and yellow with alcohol-induced jaundice. It occurred to none of them to break up this mismatched fight; it did occur to them that

Dessalines would probably kill the waiter and that this result might make an interesting spectacle, a break from monotonous routine. Now, Dessalines caught Nur'din across the face with a backhanded blow so hard it knocked the little man out of his shoes and sprawling into the cactus bed. Then he grabbed up Nur'din by his stockinged feet and turned him upside down and shook and shook until the contents of the waiter's pockets fell to the ground: a pen knife, some keys attached to a small compass embedded in a toy rubber tire, silver coins, and a few hundred Moroccan dirhams, large colorful bills worth no more than a couple of euros. Finally, an embroidered Muslim cap worn during evening prayers.

Vladimirovitch picked up the prayer cap, put it on his head, and began goose-stepping around like a Red Army trooper in a May Day parade. Babenco knelt and scooped up the dirhams and stuffed them into the waistband of his Speedo. Dessalines kicked the pen knife and keys into the steaming pool. Solas watched, his green eyes narrowing with pleasure. Now they were going to have some fun! Nur'din, temporarily unconscious, came back to himself upside down.

"Put me down, dirty nigger African!" he managed. "Let me go! Dog! Slave!"

"The man's clearly a racist," Babenco called. "Smash his head against the wall!"

The Russian said nothing.

"What should I do with him, *chef*?" Dessalines said to Solas.

Solas smiled lazily. "Let's see how long he can hold his breath underwater."

Dessalines stepped over to side of the pool, lowered the Moroccan headfirst, and held him down there for a long minute before pulling him back up. Nur'din choked out much water, gasping for air.

"*T'as attrape un poisson assez laid!*" Vladimirovitch said, laughing.

"Put me down! Police!" Nur'din shouted. "Help!"

"Man wants the police," Dessalines drawled.

"This time try two minutes," Solas said quietly. "See if that doesn't shut him up. Here, I'll time it." And he made a point of setting the second hand on his watch.

Nur'din wouldn't survive another prolonged dunking. Already the blotches of pink in front of his eyes and the prickly shapes of upside-down cacti were mutating into green waves of oxygen deprivation. In the moment before they lowered him into the hot, ultrachlorinated water for a second time, he began to scream.

8.

Pinard and Szbeszdogy, coming up the Agadir's front steps, heard the terrified screaming from the pool beyond the lobby.

"*Putain!*" Szbeszdogy swore. "It's those assassins!"

They broke into a run. When they reached the courtyard, Nur'din the waiter had been under water upside down for thirty-five more seconds, his lungs about to burst.

"Pull him out—!" Pinard almost said Legionnaire, but caught himself since these oiled monsters were supposed to be the marketing team from Club Med Western Sahara and not a squad of covert Foreign Legion assassins. But while it is perhaps possible to turn a marketing executive into an assassin, the reverse is another matter.

"*Tiens, voilà nos petits musicians,*" Solas said, a casual contempt in his voice. The order was not obeyed.

Pinard felt a stirring in the air, sensed the subtle workings of *le cafard* and knew enough of this affliction to know the situation required careful maneuvering or mutiny would ensue and one or more of them would die. Szbeszdogy held back, a thumb on the safety catch of the .22 caliber Walther he kept hidden in the waistband of his pants. Behind him, in the air-conditioned lobby, the hotel staff slept oblivious; the desk clerk, taking his siesta, snored on a gorgeous Mediouna carpet on the floor behind the front desk.

"I gave you a direct order," Pinard said, approaching Solas and keeping his voice low. "Do you take it upon yourselves to disobey your superior officer?"

"This little *conasse* called me a nigger," Dessalines said. "I'm expected to forget about that? My feelings are hurt!"

"Release him!" Pinard said, but directly to Solas, the instigator, he knew, of this unfortunate incident.

Dessalines glanced from Pinard to Solas and down to the Moroccan waiter drowning in the pool, the last bubbles of the man's breath breaking across the surface. Pinard kept his eyes locked on Solas. Relentless malice lingered there in the green Brazilian depths.

"You will confine yourself and your team to quarters at once, Caporal-chef," Pinard said. "Drinking at this hour of the day is absolutely forbidden.

Especially"—he jerked his chin at the dozens of beer bottles strewn about— "in these outrageous quantities!"

Solas yawned and said nothing. Another five seconds passed. They might have been standing on a street corner in Rio, waiting for an electric bus. Pinard pushed his face closer; his nose now just a few centimeters from the Brazilian's.

"You're drunk," he hissed. "You're endangering this mission. That's enough to send you to the Juras for fifteen years."

"*Va te faire mettre*, Pinard," the Brazilian said quietly. Pinard made a quick sign to Szbeszdogy and the Hungarian drew out the Walther and tossed it over. Pinard snatched the pistol out of the air with a nifty backhand grab and in the same motion clicked off the safety and brought its stubby barrel to bear against Solas's forehead.

"My dedication to this mission is total and if I've got to kill you to preserve it, I will. You have three seconds to pull that man out of the pool before I blow your brains out," he said through his teeth. "*Un . . . deux . . .*"

Before three Solas nodded and Dessalines lifted Nur'din from the pool and dropped him face-first to the concrete. The waiter wasn't breathing. Pinard threw himself down and began to administer CPR. He pumped the man's arms, ballooned his cheeks with breath. Soon great gushes of pool water emanated from the man's mouth, along with that morning's breakfast of couscous and chickpeas. The battered and half-drowned Nur'din revived, sputtering and coughing, at last, and rolled over and vomited more pool water and chickpeas onto the pebbly concrete. After a long minute, panting for breath, he rose unsteadily to his feet and limped off, dripping, into the lobby.

"Arab pig!" Dessalines called after him. "Next time you will have more respect for the black man!" And the other assassins laughed.

Suddenly, Pinard balled up his fist and drove it hard into Solas's nose and felt the bone crack beneath his knuckles. The Brazilian stumbled and cried out; his nose bent unnaturally to one side, spurting blood. He fumbled for the stiletto he always carried in his pocket, but he was wearing his Speedo now, a tight garment without pockets of any kind. Again Pinard shoved the Walther against Solas's forehead, this time driving him back into the pool. The Brazilian toppled over and hit with a splash, blood from his nose billowing red in the chlorine-blue water. Then Pinard swung around and brought the Walther to bear on Solas's comrades, who had sprung up, ready to defend their chief.

"I was willing to shoot Solas and I'm willing to shoot all of you," he said through his teeth. "I'll say in my report that you were killed by Marabout spies, that we came back to the hotel and found you all massacred. Szbeszdogy will back me on it, won't you, Szbeszdogy?"

"Oh, yes," Szbeszdogy said. "Absolutely."

"Now, you, *le Russe*"—he pushed the Walther roughly against Vladimirovitch's solar plexus—"repeat article six of the Code of Conduct."

Vladimirovitch balked but Pinard only pushed harder.

"'A Legion mission is sacred,'" the Russian said reluctantly. "'A mission is worth more than the lives of individual Legionnaires. Once begun, it will be concluded. Once begun, it will be pursued without passion and without hate, until the end, at all costs.'"

"Thank you, Legionnaire," Pinard said, and he lowered the Walther. The 4e RE assassins seemed chastened by these words. They stood, eyes downcast, hands at their side, awaiting orders, soldiers again. Solas pulled himself out of the pool, dripping water and blood.

"Go take care of that nose," Pinard said. Then to all of them: "We'll forget this incident. Blame it on the *cafard*. We're all spoiling for action and I assure you, it's coming. Until then, you're confined to quarters. Dismissed!"

The men trailed off. Pinard put his gun away and began policing the beer bottles strewn around the courtyard.

"That wasn't so good," Szbeszdogy said.

"Bad," Pinard agreed.

"I'll be honest." Szbeszdogy lowered his voice. "That Brazilian bastard scares me. It's those eyes—they're like the eyes of an intelligent animal. He's going to kill you for what you did to him. Unless—" He squinted up at the hot, miserable sky.

Pinard stopped policing the beer bottles and looked at his comrade.

"Unless what?"

"You kill him first. Soon."

9.

Because of the poolside incident at the Agadir and after a visit from the local gendarmes, and even though a large illegal bit of baksheesh changed hands, the Legionnaires were forced to change hotels. Laayoune is a large city of perhaps three hundred thousand, no one is quite sure exactly;

for political reasons, the inhabitants of the Saharoui souk are never accu-rately counted. But Laayoune supported only a couple of hotels rated more than one star—the Agadir and the Hotel Palais-Maroc—the former now off-limits to the Legionnaires, the latter entirely occupied by UN personnel working out a timetable for the closure of MINURSO team sites and for the general retreat of all UN forces from the Non-Self-Governing Territory of Western Sahara, this side of the Berm and in Algeria. Indeed, from any-where the Marabout insurgency might oppose their ineffectual and vaguely benevolent agenda with terror and decapitation.

The MINURSO Mission Command Coordinator, the Dutch pacifist Gen-eral van Snetters, was one of those modern soldiers who had never been in-volved in combat operations of any kind, his only experience in the field being humanitarian in nature. He was, in fact, a recent convert to a neo-Hindu sect that preached the wearing of lavender garments, a strict vegan diet, and non-violence under all circumstances, even under imminent threat of death. It was nobler and more holy, General van Snetters now firmly believed, to let the bastards kill you than to kill the bastards—a fine sentiment for a Hindu bo-dhisattva, but not, probably, for a general. Wearing the amulets and tiny silver bells of his new theology and a fancy Dutch general's hat, van Snetters was at that moment ensconced in air-conditioned comfort in the midst of his staff on the top floor of the Palais-Maroc, arranging for the delivery of vegan meals to all UN personnel during the pullout. This, while the Royal Moroccan Army and Polisario exchanged vicious shrapnel-packed mortar rounds daily across the Berm, exactly as they have done for the last forty years. And the Marabouts prowled the darkness of the desert, even unto the outskirts of Laayoune itself, sharpened scimitars at the ready, avidly hunting the heads of all nonbelievers.

10.

The rooms of the Hotel Djinn were not air-conditioned and were unfur-nished except for metal bunk beds and a few scraps of colorful but moth-eaten Zaiane carpet from the mountains of the Middle Atlas, hundreds of miles to the north. The Djinn was an ancient no-star facility in a run-down quartier of the city. Its four stories of mud brick overlooked the Saharoui souk two streets away. Spotlights from the Moroccan machine gun towers trailed twice every five minutes across the crumbling facade.

The personnel of Mission: SCORPIO took the entire top floor, with Pinard and Szbeszdogy in one room and the 4e RE assassins across the hall in two others. At midnight—the preappointed time—with the assassins locked safely in their rooms like misbehaving children, Pinard took out the satellite phone, punched in the scramble code, and called Legion headquarters in Aubagne. Tonight, for the first time since leaving France, he reached General le Breton. Pinard stood in the tall, open window where reception was best, stepping aside discreetly whenever the Moroccan spotlights swung his way.

"Did you read my report, sir?" Pinard said. "It went out in code via Internet last Tuesday."

"I read your report. A bunch of trash. How long have you been down there?"

"Thirty-seven days," Pinard said.

"Thirty-seven days"—the general's voice quickly rising as usual to the level of a roar—"and all you've got for me is one pitiful Frenchwoman on holiday?"

"The Marabouts are impossible to infiltrate," Pinard protested. "No one on the street wants to talk about them, no one will even admit they exist. We're still trying to find a way into the Saharoui souk. We're sure the Marabouts have a presence there, but access is proving difficult, the main gates are guarded by Moroccan soldiers and off-limits to everyone who's not a Saharoui. And what do we do when we get inside? If you would allow me to make contact with the Moroccan authorities here—perhaps offer money for information—they might be willing to share some intelligence. The Minister of Tourism already suspects—"

But the general cut him off. "This is a Legion mission, Pinard! And the Legion takes care of its own. Absolute secrecy will be maintained."

"*Oui, mon general.*"

"And the Legion does not pay. Not a ransom and certainly not for information. The Legion makes *them* pay, with their lives if necessary. *Reçu*, Pinard?"

"*Reçu, mon general.*"

A pause. The signal, bouncing from earth to satellite to earth again, crackled with distance. Pinard imagined the general sitting on the side of his bed in green silk pajamas in the comfort of his quarters on officer's row in Aubagne. One of the Kaybile whores from the 1e RE brothel, perhaps La Mogador herself (the general, a bachelor, often had a girl delivered directly to his bed against regulations), no doubt now slept naked and exhausted after satisfying the fat man's notorious appetites.

"What about morale?" the general asked presently.

Pinard failed to describe the near mutiny of the 4e RE that afternoon by the Agadir's pool.

"We moved hotels," he said. "Too much alcohol at the other one. But I do think the men are getting a little restless. The *cafard*—"

"*Le cafard n'existe pas!*" the general shouted. "It's a myth, another word for failure of leadership."

"*Oui, mon general.*"

"You know, I'm beginning to suspect my confidence in your abilities was misplaced! A complete lack of nerve, that's what you've got!"

Pinard thought it best not to respond to this accusation.

"*Bon, bon, retournons aux nos moutons,*" the general huffed. "Tell me about Louise. What has she been doing the last few days?"

Pinard pictured the woman at the Colline des Oiseux, Louise de Noyer, his colonel's beautiful wife. He closed his eyes for a moment and saw her pale face in the sun and shadow of the alleys lined with empty aviaries.

"Madame de Noyer remains under surveillance," Pinard said. "On Tuesday, I detailed Legionnaire Szbeszdogy to follow her full time, but she can't be followed everywhere in a town like this without arousing suspicion. So far, she still behaves like a tourist. I believe she's seen everything there is to see in this depressing place—which is possible in a single afternoon. Szbeszdogy reports she often takes a taxi to the beach. She spends entire afternoons out there lying on the sand."

"Ah!" General le Breton exclaimed. "You see what I mean by failure of leadership?"

"*Pardon, mon general?*"

"You leave such an important matter to a subordinate! This woman might lead you directly to her husband—why else did she vanish from France and turn up in Laayoune? Certainly she's trying to locate him, perhaps she's offering baksheesh for information even as we speak. Stick close, I mean very close. But do not under any circumstances reveal your identity to her. Her politics are very far to the left, she's antimilitarist, anti-French, and despises the Legion. Wait, I've got her dossier here"—the sound of some papers being shuffled—"'Louise de Noyer; family name Vilhardouin. Illegitimate daughter of well-known radical singer—'"

"You don't mean *that* Vilhardouin?" Pinard gasped.

"Yes, imbecile!" the general bellowed. "That Vilhardouin! The one who should have been put against a wall and shot back in '68! Now do you get the picture?"

"*Oui, mon general.*"

"*Bon.* Make contact, but be careful."

"I'll relieve Szbeszdogy. I'll follow Madame de Noyer myself."

"Don't sound so glum, Pinard! It's not exactly punishment duty! She's not so bad-looking, am I right?"

"An attractive woman," Pinard said stiffly.

"And for your information, she's definitely not a nun." The general paused, chuckling. "A couple of confidential reports in this dossier make the *Autobiography of Catherine M.* look like kids' stuff. So talk to her, get to know her. If you need to fuck her to gain her confidence, then fuck her!"

Pinard bristled at this. "The wife of a fellow officer—"

"Results, Pinard!" the general roared. "I don't care how you get them! Otherwise you'll face a court martial for incompetence when the Legion drags your ass back to Aubagne!"

11.

Pinard stood in the window for a long time, smoking the last of his French cigarettes, watching the Moroccan spotlights trail over the blind alleys and covered walkways of the souk, across the pendulous nodes of cumulonimbus clouds. He, no less than his men, was in the grip of the *cafard*. In him, the ailment manifested itself as a kind of melancholy introspection, even though his better judgment told him that for a soldier, introspection is best avoided. Now sad images from his past piled in drifts like dry leaves against unexamined longings, deeply held fears.

He thought of his childhood, back in Canada, a subject as a rule banished from his conscious mind. He'd been an unhappy child. No one tending to the scabs on his knees, few friends, brutal experiences at school, the unhappiness so pervasive he'd grown used to it, aware of it only as one is aware of breathing. His mother, often drunk by ten in the morning, brought men home from the run-down taverns of Ours Bleu nearly every night. His father, the only bright spot, but always away in the far north, came home rarely (once sporting an eye patch like a pirate, the result of an industrial accident), bringing tales of polar bears and sea lions and ice floes, the arctic cold clinging to his coat, his skin. Now, after all these years, Pinard recalled a forgotten incident: His father once brought him a little scrimshaw ivory tusk, intricately carved with a battle scene between Inuits and Frenchmen. On one side the Inuits were fighting valiantly, the Frenchmen winning with guns and cannons against spears; on the other side all the Frenchmen were dead, the Inuits improbably victorious. The young Pinard studied this little tusk for hours, carried it in his pocket to school, kept it under his pillow—whatever happened to it? He couldn't remember now, the years had swept it away, but he still remembered that battle scene, bold and terrifying at once. Forget the judge's order, the official choice of deportation or the Legion. Maybe that bit of tusk was why he'd become a soldier.

The Legion had been Pinard's family for more than fifteen years now. He'd been more or less content with military life until—the thought astonished him!—last week. Until meeting Louise de Noyer at the Colline des Oiseaux. And Pinard felt the peculiar squeezing in his heart again and he knew now without a doubt that he was no longer unhappy in the way he had been unhappy before; this new unhappiness lighter, leavened by longing but more painful. He was in love. Suddenly he was sick of military life, sick of the Legion. A family? No, a collection of foulmouthed brutes, drunkards, drug addicts, fools, sadists, murderers. Pinard felt himself choking, short of breath as he'd been at the Colline the other day. Stop! This was not possible! And yet the thought that he loved Louise de Noyer filled him with warmth, filled the dusty equatorial twilight of his soul with new light and hope—though hope was the devil to a Legionnaire, who learns to abandon it during the first weeks of basic training.

Agleam, suffering, Pinard turned away from the window, from the darkened souk and all the potential complications below, and lay down on his hard bunk in the gloom, his solitary universe expanded to include one other person.

12

PINARD IN LOVE

1.

Pinard took a taxi out to the dingy little beach called Rass Malek, which lies about halfway down from Cap Juby along the Playa Laayoune. The ocean rolled against the shore, subdued today, a calm, tepid pond. Frothy yellow scum and fish heads floated in the surf, refuse from the vast commercial factory fishing ships, great black, blocky things riding the horizon. Closer at hand, on a desolate island in the bay, a castle built by a Scotsman two hundred years ago crumbled into the dirty water. The Scotsman had come down from Aberdeen to trade in slaves and ivory—the wealth of Africa for scissors and hand mirrors and wooly bolts of tartan fabric—and died there of a fever, missing the simple cottage of his youth in Scotland and regretting everything: his cupidity, his murderous adventures at an end.

Pinard picked his way through the dunes, lizards scuttling out of his way in the sand, and walked along the beach for ten minutes. He was barefoot, wearing a faded T-shirt and a pair of fatigue shorts, one of the threadbare bath towels from the hotel tossed over his shoulder, a half-drunk bottle of mineral water in his hand. Two Saharoui men, their striped djellahs flapping in a sudden breeze, stood down the beach arguing about something and gesturing angrily at the ocean. The sound of their voices carried, but not their words. Pinard was immediately suspicious of their presence all the way out here. The beaches along the Playa, even the best ones, were never visited by Saharouis from the city. Then he saw her, lying on a thick, colorful blanket reading a magazine, not far from the old Spanish bathing cabanas, half sunk in sand. She wore a stunning white bikini, her fashionable wrap tossed to one side, and might have been on the beach at Cannes or Cap d'Antibes, except in those places she would be topless. As a concession to Islam the white bikini top hugged her perfect breasts. She looked up at Pinard through her big black sunglasses as he approached.

"We meet again," Pinard said and immediately felt stupid for having said it.

"Yes, here you are," Louise said—the same enviable calm, the lack of fear or surprise she had shown that day at the Colline des Oiseaux.

"Would you mind if"—Pinard hesitated—"that is, may I join you? It's a bit lonely on this beach."

"You need to be content in yourself," Louise said, a faint smile on her lips. "Otherwise you will go crazy in a place like Laayoune."

"Usually I'm very busy with my business," Pinard said. "Only today . . ." He stood there, waiting.

At last, Louise offered a kind of regal sweep of the arm as if to say she owned the beach and was letting him have a little square of it, but only temporarily. Pinard carefully laid out his thin towel beside her blanket, not too close, and threw himself down. He didn't take off his T-shirt, suddenly embarrassed by the variety of tattoos—prison, Legion, and otherwise—decorating his torso.

Louise didn't say anything, continuing to turn the pages of her magazine, an out-of-date *Paris Match* with Johnny Hallyday on the cover, as usual. Then she closed it firmly and looked up at him.

"You're going to sit there in your T-shirt? You'll get an ugly tan that way."

"Oh, yes." Pinard slowly rolled his T-shirt up and over his head, revealing the tattoos and ropy muscles like a proscenium curtain rising for the show.

"Very interesting decorations," Lousie said. "How did you get so many?"

"Oh, you know"—Pinard shrugged—"over the years . . ." His voice trailed into silence.

"So you're lonely in Laayoune?" Louise said, watching him carefully.

Pinard slid his eyes in her direction, trying not to see the way her hip bone jutted out so sharply; how her pelvis sloped neatly to its ultimate destination somewhere in the depths of her white bikini bottom.

"Not really," Pinard managed. His throat felt dry. "I'm normally very busy. I'm here with a marketing team." He felt ridiculous saying this. "I work for Club Med, you know."

"You don't seem like the Club Med type to me."

"There's a type?"

"Of course. There's a type for everything—" Then, interrupting herself: "Where did you get that one?" She pointed to the crude, fading tattoo decorating Pinard's left pectoral, approximating the location of his heart. It showed a skull with an exploding artillery shell clamped in its jaws like one of General le Breton's Venezuelan cigars; beneath this, the motto: *Honneur et fidélité—valeur et discipline.* Honor, Loyalty, Courage, Discipline. He'd gotten that one his first year in the Legion.

"I did my national service in the Armée de Terre," Pinard lied. "One night, we were in Toulouse, we got drunk and"—he shrugged—"I woke up with this."

"Why not a naked woman?"

Pinard shrugged. There were, in fact, no naked women on his flesh. Knives, skulls, bombs, one winged devil, but no naked women.

"You're blind drunk enough to disfigure yourself and not remember in the morning, and yet in the tattoo parlor, you come up with the four cardinal military virtues?" she said, frowning. "*Drôle de type.* Perhaps your subconscious mind runs to fascism."

"It's just a tattoo," Pinard said, a little hurt.

"Of course," Louise said. "That explains everything."

Pinard looked over and saw she was teasing him. He blushed, embarrassed. The two Arabs who had been arguing had stopped arguing and now stood staring at them from some distance off.

"So you're really going to build a Club Med?" Louise said. "Here on the Playa Laayoune?"

"Actually right out there," Pinard said, gesturing to the Scotsman's castle out in the bay, its broken turrets silhouetted against the sky. He was inventing freely now. "We're going to rehabilitate that place, have speedboats, water taxis going back and forth. A restaurant right here on the beach. A casino. It's really going to be spectacular."

Louise de Noyer laughed. *"Mais c'est ridicule!"* she said. "That horrible ruin looks like the Château d'If!"

"I don't know that place."

"From *The Count of Monte Cristo.*"

"Ah, oui! Bien sûr . . . " But Pinard had never read that famous book, had in fact never heard of it, and didn't know what she was talking about. Now Louise raised her dark glasses to her hair, and Pinard was confronted for the second time with her indigo-blue eyes. Looking into them, he felt himself crumbling like the walls of Blockhouse 9 under rocket fire.

"You're not fooling anyone," Louise de Noyer said, her voice low and serious. "You're clearly not a businessman. Any more than I'm a tourist."

"All right," Pinard said, sweating. "I'm not a businessman. But what are you doing here?"

"You answer first," Louise said.

Pinard's mind raced for an answer that would not be the truth but would have enough of the flavor of truth to keep her interested, and he remembered the minister's suspicions and knew what he was going to say.

"This is my secret," he said, looking out to sea. "You can't tell anyone. You must swear. If you do, I can't answer for the consequences."

"Don't worry about that," Louise said, sounding utterly sincere. "I swear. Go ahead."

"My friends and I"—he paused dramatically—"we stole some money. In France."

"Ooh la-la!" Louise said, impressed. "Fascinating!"

"We're hiding out here in Laayoune while it's being laundered, converted into usable currency."

"So you're a criminal!"

"I'm a kind of engineer, actually," Pinard said. "I dug the hole into the vault. It was a very delicate operation. The process took two months."

"C'est du Rififi, *ça!"*

Pinard didn't catch this reference to a well-known French heist film. Cultural references generally escaped him, the end result of a life spent engrossed in military matters.

"How much did you get?"

"Enough to make it worthwhile, believe me," Pinard said, beginning to enjoy this.

"What will you do with your share?"

"I'll go to Brazil," he said, thinking of Solas.

"Why Brazil?"

"The women, of course." And he flashed what he hoped might be a roguish smile.

"So, how was it robbing a bank?"

"It wasn't exactly a bank."

"What was it then?" She was like a schoolgirl, eager to know.

"I can't tell you that."

"Was it in the newspapers?"

"Yes," he said. "And no. Or at least not in a form you would recognize. It was in the newspapers, but only as a kind of unusual anxiety in world markets noted on the business pages. In weather reports of an unquiet wind blowing down the streets of the financial capitals."

"You're a poet, my new friend."

Pinard shrugged. "I've been called worse things."

"Actually, I salute you for your criminal activities. How much difference is there between a bank robber and a revolutionary? Both are dedicated to a redistribution of wealth, both—"

"Yes, the wealth has been redistributed," Pinard interrupted, grinning. "To my own pockets."

Just then, the two Arabs down the beach began to stride toward them as if they had made up their minds about something, and the necessity for immediate action had impressed itself upon them. Pinard didn't like the look of this and rose suddenly off his thin towel and reached into the pocket of his shorts and put his hand on the pearl-handled stiletto he always carried, its ebony haft engraved with the Legion's seven-pointed bomb. He stood there for a long moment, hand on stiletto, watching them coming along. When they got close enough to see his face, they stopped abruptly, turned around, and went back the way they had come.

"Who are they?" Louise asked.

"Who knows," he said. "Interpol, maybe."

"For your sake, I hope not." Then she handed up a bottle of expensive tanning lotion. "I want a little color," she said. "But I don't want to burn. Could you please do my back?"

Pinard took the bottle and squatted on the colorful blanket behind her, and she rolled over and reached around and undid the straps of her bikini top; as they fell to each side, he saw the bare white curve of her breasts and his heart stopped. Trembling, he squeezed the bottle and squirted out a white, slightly transparent puddle into the palm of his hand and the perverse thought struck him that he had never seen anything that more closely resembled ejaculate. And slowly, with the utmost delicacy, he began to work the fragrant stuff into the soft, bare flesh between her shoulder blades.

2.

The next ten days were the happiest of Capitaine Evariste Pinard's life thus far. He couldn't remember a better time. He was happy and happiness to him, who had never felt it, was like being drunk, but without the unpleasant disorientation of drunkenness and without the hangover in the morning.

He sent the 4e RE assassins under Szbeszdogy's command on secret desert maneuvers in the sandy wastes beyond Laayoune and remained alone in the city. He saw Louise nearly every day. They didn't touch each other, they didn't kiss more than on the cheek as a greeting, they didn't make love—but they both knew it was coming, somehow, and the waiting made the prospect that much more enticing. They ate together every night, sat in the bar at the Palais-Maroc eating pistachio nuts and drinking an Algerian wine that wasn't so bad, and talking about their lives.

Pinard made up a few absurd stories about the criminal enterprises he supposedly pursued, but mostly he listened to Louise talk about herself. Like most beautiful women, she had been indulged throughout her life and thought anything she had to say inherently interesting, and now Pinard indulged her, and experienced great pleasure doing so.

She was definitely left-leaning in her politics, though not as radical as her dossier suggested, no more left-leaning than the average young French woman. She supported the Palestinian Intifada, the end of genocide in Darfur, the liberation of Tibet from China's iron grip, animal rights, sustainable energy, the right of homosexuals to marry, the eradication of AIDS, the activities of Greenpeace, and stood in solidarity with those ski-masked and dreadlocked young hooligans, the Black Block Anarchists, who disrupted meetings of the G-8 with their agitprop shenanigans, rock-throwing and bus-burning. She knew the singer Vanessa Paradis pretty well—they'd been on a housing rights committee in Paris together. She was well read and musical—Robbe-Grillet, Proust, and Bulgakov were her favorite writers; Camille Saint-Saëns and Erik Satie her favorite composers, though she also liked American hip-hop, Cap Verdean jazz, and Bob Marley. She adored the films of Max Ophuls, Jean-Pierre Melville, Godard, and—despite his archaic patriarchist attitudes—the Westerns of John Ford, so beautifully made they were hard to resist.

For his part, Pinard let all these cultural references wash over him like a wave. He didn't catch any of it, except for hip-hop and Bob Marley.

She did not mention her missing husband, Colonel Phillipe de Noyer, officer in command of the 1e RE Musique Principale of the Foreign Legion—a conservative *militaire*, an aristocrat twenty years older than herself—as far from someone Pinard would match her with as anyone he could imagine. She said nothing about marrying the man at twenty-four, or about the pampered kind of life she'd led at his remote château in Brittany and in Paris, nothing about their years of marriage. She didn't wear a wedding ring. And it appeared, from the absence of a telltale band of white skin around her ring finger, that she had never worn one.

Instead, she talked about her famous half sister, Alphonsine Vilhardouin, the actress—they'd become close only recently. And she talked about her father, the immortal Hector. She'd barely known the man, had only seen him a dozen times in her life, her mother being one of his lesser mistresses—though he had supplied enough money every year for twenty years to send her to an excellent boarding school in Switzerland and then on to a university in the United States.

Pinard was surprised by this last disclosure. He couldn't imagine Louise in the United States—the anti-Canada, a loud place full of hamburger-eating fat people who cared only for brutally boring sports and Jesus.

"*L'Amérique, alors, comment s'était?*" How was it?

"A fascinating experience," Louise said. "I went to a small college in the South called Washington and Lee, which was once only for men. Don't ask me why I went there, I'm not so sure myself anymore. It's in the mountains of the state of Virginia, very beautiful, very green and lush, and very different from Europe. Racist and conservative, to be sure, but no more so than the Faubourg St.-Honoré"—referring to a posh street in the posh First Arrondissement of Paris. "Actually, I like the Americans of the South, they say what they think and they are not as stupid as one might think, and the men are quite attractive in a louche, *après-guerre* kind of way. But they drink a lot, very heavy stuff, bourbon and whiskey, and are often absurdly drunk, so drunk they vomit and piss themselves."

"Myself, I'm a Canadian," Pinard admitted. "We're not immune to the pleasures of heavy drinking."

It was her turn to be surprised.

"I thought you were French."

"I am—well, Quebecois."

"You don't have that horrible accent."

Pinard shrugged. "I've spent the last seventeen years in France."

"Robbing banks."

"Not always," he said. "I used to sell drugs. But I got out of that."

"How many banks have you robbed?" She snuggled up to him, her voice low. "You can tell me everything."

"No, I can't. You'll be compromised."

"Compromise me."

"But you haven't even told me what you're doing here! In this miserable asshole of the world!"

Louise looked away. "I don't know you well enough," she said. "What if you're a government spy?"

"What if *you're* a government spy?" Pinard said, and they both laughed at the thought.

Then, Louise took a sip of her wine and her mood grew serious. She looked away, looked back, her beautiful indigo eyes narrowing, and made a quick decision: "I'm waiting for something," she confided, her voice a whisper. "Information from the souk. I'll tell you that much."

"What kind of information?" Pinard said, the back of his neck prickling. "Is it illegal? Because there I might be able to give you some good advice."

"I've already said too much," she said. "Here's something else for you to think about. . . ."

And she leaned over and kissed him on the lips.

3.

The narrow balcony outside Louise de Noyer's room at the Palais-Maroc looked out upon the Friday Mosque, white and crenelated as a wedding cake, across the hot, empty Place el-Hedime. By a trick of perspective, you could lie in the double bed in front of the half-shuttered window and it seemed you were hanging directly over the mosque itself. The clear, hard light of the desert amplified vision as a coliseum amplifies sound and you felt that the solemn men in their djellahs and fezzes and the equally solemn veiled women draped head to toe in black, drawn along by the nasal intonations of the muezzin over the loudspeaker from the minaret, were not a hundred meters away, but directly below. If you threw a shoe out the window, no doubt you would hit one of those devout Muslims on the head.

Now Louise de Noyer, standing with her back to the half-open shutters, reached around in that awkward elbow way and unhooked the straps of her white bikini top—they had just been to the beach again—and let it fall to the floor. Then she stepped out of her bottoms and stood naked in a hard pillar of brilliant light. Pinard lay on the bed watching her, speechless.

"How do you like my little striptease?" she said in a low, enticing voice.

Pinard, grinning like an idiot, couldn't say anything. They'd been making love for three days now, they hadn't stopped. Only for an occasional small bite to eat and one trip to the beach.

"Do it for me now," she said, her hands on her breasts. "Just a little. Please."

Pinard hesitated, embarrassed by this request, one of her little kinks. "Why don't you come over here and help me out?"

But Louise shook her head. "I want to see how hard you can get yourself. Please . . ."

He complied, reluctantly at first, then with some enthusiasm, and when he was ready, she knee-walked onto the bed and settled herself on top of him. This time, he lasted until she cried out and fell across him, gasping; then he seized her fiercely by the hips and let himself go. A few minutes later, he turned her face to the sheets; and again after an hour, face-to-face, as dusk came in vermillion streaks and green flashes out of the east and the men emptied out of the Friday mosque below, followed after a while by the women from their separate doorway.

Louise lay still beside him, her hand flat on his chest covering his Legion tattoo, and they dozed, awakening to the utter darkness of a desert city at night.

"This is when I'd like a cigarette," she said. "But I've given up smoking. Anyway, it's a cliché."

Pinard, savoring his happiness, didn't say anything. The sound of a toilet flushing came to them through the plaster walls.

"Louise," he began, hoarse with emotion. "I've wanted you since . . . what I mean to say is I think . . ." He tried to keep his voice steady, but couldn't. She put three fingers over his mouth.

"No," she said sharply. "Do *not* fall in love with me. Don't even use the word. Everyone falls in love with me, every man I meet, and they don't know who I am, they just see someone they want to fuck then they think it's more than that. So please don't. I'm —"

"Married." Pinard finished her thought.

"How did you know?"

Pinard shrugged. "Anyone could guess. You're beautiful. How could a beautiful woman like you not be married?"

"Not only married," Louise said. "I love my husband. I'm sorry. I do."

"Then why this?" Pinard said, genuinely perplexed.

She laughed softly. "You talk like a schoolboy. People sleep with people they are attracted to, but don't love. It happens all the time, especially in France."

"So you don't love me?" Pinard said, feeling, despite himself, a lump in his throat.

"No, my friend," Louise said sadly. "I love my husband. And there you have the tragedy of the situation."

She pushed off the bed and walked over to the window and opened the shutters and stood against the greater darkness, exposed to the cold night air, her skin gleaming faintly, staring out at the empty square below, at the darkened mosque.

"My husband is a wonderful man. He actually saved my life, stopped me from committing suicide. That's how we met—he grabbed my arm as I was about to drown myself in the sea. Don't ask why I was about to do such a stupid thing—I was young and depressed—Phillipe understood that. After he pulled me out he took me to his hotel room and made love to me that very night, and that saved my life more than anything. He's also very talented—a musician, the piano, you know, nearly concert quality. And this is going to surprise you, I mean for someone with my political convictions, he's"—she paused—"in the military. Worse than that, actually. The Foreign Legion."

"But they're notorious!" Pinard exclaimed. "Vicious brutes! Murderers!"

"You're right," Louise agreed. "I hate the Legion for its violence, for how they abuse the volunteers, how they turn young men into the worst kind of killers. And for what they've done in the past to the Arabs and the Africans, the Vietnamese, the Mexicans, even the French—remember what happened to the Communards of 1870? Forty thousand shot in the streets and buried beneath the cobblestones of Paris. Legionnaires did that, Legionnaires following orders! I hate them because they are an army of mercenaries, the tool of neo-imperialist oppression. But they do have a wonderful military band, one of the most famous in the world, called la Musique Principale. My husband is in charge of that. And he's not one of the enlisted men, you understand, he's an officer, a graduate of Saint-Cyr. Only the top officers in any graduating class may choose the Legion. They consider it a great honor. Did you know that?"

"I didn't," Pinard said. He could barely keep the smile off his face.

"But you're right. When you add it all up, music or no music, that's just what they are, a bunch of assassins who murder for pay on the orders of the French government. I made a terrible officer's wife. I refused to attend social functions, I never went down to Aubagne for any of their stupid ceremonies—not for Camerone Day, for Christmas, or le Quatorze. I demanded that Phillipe request a posting near Paris, which wasn't at all good for his career—he ought to be a general by now. He indulged me in all these things without complaint because he loved me, and because he was so strong, he didn't care what anyone thought of him. I don't know, maybe because of my father, I've always been attracted to strong men, like Phillipe."

Pinard grunted irritably at this. Suddenly he hated Phillipe de Noyer more than he had ever hated anyone. Images of that crazy bastard playing his piano all night long came into his head unbidden. Playing that damnable Satie when he could be lying in bed, fucking his beautiful wife. The bastard.

"Please, don't get upset with me," Louise said, sensing his anger.

"I'm trying not to," Pinard said.

"I want to talk about him. Do you mind so much?"

"Talk," Pinard said, though he didn't want to hear another word. "Go ahead."

"He has a disease," Louise continued, after a moment, her voice trembling. "He's dying. It's in the blood, I mean inherited, in the genes, but sometimes it doesn't develop, it stays dormant, or it develops later in life, which it did in his case. We used to make love all the time, every day, and it was wonderful and we talked about having children. But his *métier* took him all over the world, often to dangerous places, and we never seemed to have the time. About five years ago, he went to Algeria as an inspector for the UN, to report on conditions in the Saharoui refugee camps. Something terrible happened out there in the desert that he wouldn't talk about and this disease, apparently, can be triggered by a traumatic event. When he came back, suddenly, he was sick. But it was a very strange sickness, a kind of incurable insomnia. He just couldn't sleep anymore. I mean he couldn't sleep at all, not even for a few minutes. He took a leave of absence and went to doctors in Paris, in Germany, in London, and they prescribed sleeping pills, meditation, magic potions, acupuncture; they did CAT scans, brain tests, everything. But still, he couldn't sleep. Finally a doctor at le Clinique du Sommeil in Lucerne tested his DNA and figured out Phillipe had a rare hereditary condition that attacks the sleep centers of the brain."

Pinard remained quiet, listening.

"This disease is a type of CDJ—think of mad cow, scrapies. It's what they call an autosomnial dominant disease and is spread by horrible little particles called prions, which are abnormal proteins that inhabit the brain and blood—I quote here from the medical texts that I have read and reread many times—and it is characterized by severe untreatable insomnia and cognitive disorders. In other words it is a species of madness, complete with hallucinations, manias, paranoias, everything. In some rare cases it is passed down through families—fatal familial insomnia, FFI they call it—and in this form it is like a curse, borne through the generations. The condition goes back hundred of years with the de Noyers—there are diaries, medical records, court documents, military reports. Phillipe's grandfather was killed at the Battle of the Somme in the First World War, he charged the German guns with a toilet plunger in his hand—they gave him the Medaille Militaire, they had no idea he was sick in his head. Others in his family went like that, jumping off cliffs on a whim, or attacking policemen with bricks—one of them even tried to assassinate Léon Blum, the famous socialist. But first, all of them, all of them, quite suddenly stopped sleeping."

She paused, her voice choking with emotion, her eyes filling with tears.

Pinard sagged back into the pillow, a bit stunned by this information: It certainly explained a lot about the colonel's odd nocturnal behavior; and the way he appeared to haunt his own life, the ghost of a former self. Louise wiped the tears from her face with the back of her hand and continued.

"As it turns out, there is another terrible side effect to this terrible disease.

You see, the sleep centers of the brain are quite near those parts that control sexual functioning. So when my husband stopped being able to sleep, he stopped being able to make love to me. This is why I . . . I like to see you hard, first. I'm paranoid, but just to make sure, you understand? Toward the end, Phillipe would get hard only a little, then die inside of me. And he tried over and over again, he got very desperate and finally, it didn't work at all. This was horrible, crushing to me as a woman. Do you understand?"

"Yes," Pinard said. He could barely speak.

"He offered me a divorce that I refused because I love him. But I am a very physical woman, very sexual and I can't"—she paused—"I'm weak, maybe, but I can't endure not experiencing physical pleasure, and so I've pursued many affairs, I can't help myself. Phillipe ignored my behavior for a while, he is a very understanding man, then he couldn't take it anymore and volunteered to go again with the UN to Western Sahara—to die, I think—and there, here—he disappeared. His superiors told me about an attack on a UN outpost in the Sebhket Zemmur, he was probably taken by the Marabouts, they said. But there's been no ransom demand, no trace of him. In any case, the French government refuses to pay ransoms—this is official policy—and the Legion will certainly pay nothing, so I have come to look for him and to pay myself. I've been to the Saharoui souk, I spoke to the emir, and he has agreed to help me. I'm waiting now for more information. I have been waiting weeks for a word. This is why I'm in Laayoune. I shall ransom him back, my Phillipe, so he may die in my arms. This is the last comfort I can offer him. So do you blame me"—she came away from the window, and Pinard saw the tears streaming down her face—"if I forget my sadness for a little while with you, with your—"

She stopped herself and bit her lip, watching him. He was ready again. He would never get enough of her, enough of her body, he knew now, not in this life. Best take it while he could. He gestured imperiously, and she came over meek and willing, head bowed, and knelt on the bed beside him, and he pushed her down.

4.

The Australians—five or six of them, it was hard to tell, one or another kept falling down—had somehow managed to get very drunk on the watered-down whiskey they served at the Casbah Bar in the Hotel

Palais-Maroc. They had been drinking all day, celebrating the fact that the NGO they worked for was closing up shop in Laayoune and sending them back to Sydney in the morning, and they were singing Australian songs off-key at the top of their lungs—much to the annoyance of Legionnaire Szbeszdogy, sitting at the opposite end of the bar with Capitaine Pinard and Caporal-chef Solas. Szbeszdogy's finely tuned musical ear was wounded by this racket; the boozy, Australian singing gave him a pain deep in his gut.

"These Australians are driving me insane," he hissed. "One more song and I'm going to start a fight. So help me I'll smash the next one who opens his mouth with this bottle of Kro!"

"Control yourself, Legionnaire," Pinard said, amused. "You're on duty."

"Why can't they just shut up?"

"Because this is what they do."

"What—sing horribly?"

"They travel the world, drink excessively, and regret Australia. Apparently, it's the kind of place you miss only when you're away from it."

"Ah." Szbeszdogy nodded, understanding. "Like Hungary."

"Like most places. What about Brazil, Solas?"

They turned to Solas, but he refused to join the conversation. He hadn't spoken a word all night, and would only respond to a direct order and only with a grunt. His nose, formerly straight and aquiline, now swollen with an ugly purple bruise, showed a bump in the middle and hooked to the right. His murderous hatred for Pinard, and by association Szbeszdogy, and perhaps the Legion itself, drifted off his otherwise smooth café au lait skin like a powerful body odor.

The Australians kept up their raucous singing and drinking, and a few minutes later one of them ran out of the bar and vomited in a potted palm in the lobby, another one fell on his face, yet another slid unconscious to the floor, and the two or three remaining, feeling bereft, ordered more whiskey.

"You want to know why I picked you for this recon duty tonight, Solas?" Pinard said.

Solas didn't say anything.

"First, you're the deadliest bastard we've got. Your comrades of the 4e ER are blunt instruments compared to you. They're hammers, especially that bull-headed Russian and that Haitian idiot, but you, my friend, you're a straight razor. Thin, concealable, deadly"—Pinard chuckled, pleased with his metaphorical power. "Second, I want to give you a chance to kill me. I'm quite serious."

Solas looked up. "Permission to speak freely, Capitaine," he said, his voice a low growl.

"Granted."

"I will kill you. You are already a dead man. But at a time and place of my choosing. You don't mark Solas like this"—he gestured to his nose—"and live."

"You're nose is much improved if you ask me," Pinard said affably. "Makes you look less like a girl."

"How about we settle this outside immediately," Solas growled. "I propose knives. I will cut your throat."

Pinard reached under his shirt and pulled out the .22 caliber Walther and pressed it discreetly against Solas's kidney. The Walther was now fixed with a short, stubby silencer of the latest design. It could be fired right here and the shot would go unheard by the Australians halfway down the bar, now singing a pornographic version of "Waltzing Matilda."

"Understand something," Pinard said, keeping his voice pleasant. "Your chance to kill me is only tonight, in the darkness, and only when my back is turned. But then you've got to kill Szbeszdogy too and you've got to beat it out of Laayoune without getting caught. Think you can do it?"

Solas didn't say anything. Pinard pressed the gun harder into the Brazilian's kidney.

"If you don't kill me tonight, I'll kill you, Solas, I swear it. Tomorrow, the next day. Doesn't matter, you will be dead."

"You can try," the Brazilian said through his teeth.

"I will have an easy time of it too," Pinard continued in the same affable tone. "I'm an officer now, and what's another miserable Legionnaire more or less to the Legion? Tens of thousands have died for nothing, marched directly into the mouth of the guns, cannon fodder. And you, *espèce de merde*, you're worth less than the least of them."

Solas made a gesture meaning talk all you want, we'll see.

"You know something"—Pinard released the little gun's safety catch—"I think I'll shoot you now. Szbeszdogy and I will be out the door before the Australians realize you're dead."

Heat from Solas's fingertips melted the ice in his glass.

Szbeszdogy watched them both, increasingly alarmed.

"But before I kill you, I offer another way, a counterproposal. Are you listening?" A little jab with the gun. "If we emerge from tonight's adventure alive, which we might not, let's be honest, you will come to me and you will acknowledge that I did what I did to your nose for the sake of the mission. And you will recant your threat to kill me forever."

"That's fucking stupid," the Brazilian said, his voice hoarse. "So I tell you I'm not going to kill you now. What's to stop me from killing you later?"

"Your honor as a Legionnaire," Pinard said. "I've read your dossier. You had no honor when you joined the Legion—you were a punk, a favela murderer—but you have it now, because the Legion has given it to you. So I will accept your word as a Legionnaire and a man of honor." And he laid the Walther carefully on the bar next to Solas's drink. "Use this on me if you want. Frankly, I don't care much one way or the other. But remember, if you don't kill me tonight, you will come to me tomorrow and tell me the vendetta is forgotten. Or I will definitely kill you. I swear it."

The Brazilian stared down at the gun. "If you think I won't—"

"Shut up, you idiots," Szbeszdogy interrupted. "Look!"

Pinard looked. Just then, a figure wearing a Saharoui djellah, hood up, crossed the lobby toward the front doors. Another hooded figure, stooped, ancient, waited outside in the penumbra of reflected light at the edge of the darkened world.

5.

The two djellahed figures hurried along, shadows against the encompassing shadows of Laayoune, illuminated in silhouette by the headlights of a passing delivery van. Then they turned a corner into the run-down neighborhood abutting the Saharoui souk, on the eastern end, and there was no more traffic and no streetlights, and they moved ahead silently through the black. The trick, as always, was to follow close enough, but not too close. A puddle of urine reflected faintly from the gutter. Heavy storm clouds, full of an ocean darkness, piled high above the city.

Pinard couldn't see a damned thing. Just when he thought he caught a glimpse of them, they disappeared into the gloom. But Solas's cat-green eyes could see in the dark; they actually glowed with a kind of strange tropical luminescence.

"This is nothing," he said. "When I was a kid, in the favelas, I could see every turn, every alley, and the nights were blacker than this. One night the federal police chased a bunch of us down with machetes, because they didn't want to waste any bullets. Bullets cost money. They hacked to death ten or fifteen kids and left the pieces lying around like rotten meat. Just to teach a lesson to the gangs. But me," he grunted, "I got away because I can see in the dark. Later, I chopped one of those lousy cops that did it to us, and while he lay there bleeding to death I pissed on him, and shoved a broken bottle up his ass!"

"He's not a man at all," Pinard said to Szbeszdogy, "but some kind of supernatural Brazilian tiger."

They passed along the barbed-wire trench that enclosed the souk on three sides. For a brief moment, the desert moon shone through the clouds and the effect was startling, a bulb switching on. Behind them, the spotlights of the Moroccan machine gun towers trailed like fingers across the Gate of Dusk and the Gate of Dawn. Solas, leading the way, motioned for them to keep back. Here the trench ended and they came face-to-face with the improvised walls of the souk—a series of barricaded houses and cement and cinder block reinforcements topped with broken bottles and iron spikes.

"Shh," Solas whispered. "They've stopped, they're not far."

Pinard couldn't see anything, but he took the Brazilian's word for it. The Legionnaires pressed themselves against the rough surface of a cement barricade. The yelping of a dog somewhere out in the night sounded for a moment like a child crying for help. Then, from out of the shadows, came the barely audible sound of knocking, a code: one, two. One, two. One. And the soft creak of a door opening, a faint line of yellow light and a few inaudible words. The hooded figures folded into this light, the door closed, and all was blackness again.

"Now what?" Szbeszdogy said.

"We do the same."

"There was a password," Solas said. "Did you hear it?"

"*Merde,*" Pinard said. "I couldn't hear a thing."

"Ah." The Brazilian chuckled softly. "But I could."

"You've definitely got the eyes and ears of an animal," Szbeszdogy said, grudging admiration in his voice. "*Mais rassurez-vous,* I mean that in the best way possible."

They crossed a gully and came to a wooden construction, heavy beams dried out and petrified by years of exposure to the sun. It didn't look like a door at all, but part of the sturdy system of barricades separating the souk from the rest of Laayoune. Solas stepped up and knocked out the code along one of the beams. A pause, then three of the beams creaked open an inch on concealed hinges, revealing a faint sliver of light.

"Polisario," Solas said. "*¡Libertad para todos!*"

"*¿Quién es?*" came a faint growl from the other side.

"We are those who know the password," Solas replied in Spanish. "Now let us in before the Moroccans take a shot at us."

Pinard was surprised to hear Spanish spoken, then he wasn't. Many of the urban Saharouis preserve that language from the days of Spanish colonial rule. There were still Saharoui immigrant ghettos in Seville and Cádiz, a last remnant of the diaspora of the 1950s and '60s.

The door creaked open wide enough for the men to step inside, then closed behind them. They found themselves standing in a dark corridor. At the far end an archway opened to a lattice-covered alley faintly illuminated by a smoky, yellow-green light.

"What do you want here?" The voice came from a small boy, about eight years old. He was wearing a dirty soccer T-shirt advertising AC MILAN and a Saharoui kilt. He was barefoot.

Pinard reached into his pocket and withdrew a couple of butterscotch hard candies he'd lifted from a bowl on the front desk of the Palais-Maroc.

"Here, kid," he said in rudimentary Legion Spanish. "Suck on one of these."

The boy hesitated, but he took the candies and sat back on a broken crate half hidden in a niche beside the door and began unwrapping them.

"A woman, a man, not five minutes ago," Pinard said. "Do you know where they went?"

"The woman has gone to see the emir," the boy said, his mouth already full of candy. "Everyone who enters the souk of the Saharouis who is not a Saharoui must go see the emir. You are going to see him, aren't you?"

"Naturally," Pinard said.

The boy told them the way and they headed for the opening at the far end and entered the narrow alley, no wider than four feet across. The smoky light came from primitive lamps, little more than bowls of baked mud upon which sat burning some foul-smelling substance.

"Dried camel dung," Szbeszdogy said, pinching his nose. "God, what an awful stench!"

"Try not to breathe," Pinard said.

They followed the narrow alley though a series of twists and turns until they came to a wider street, parts of which were open to the sky. This seemed to be the souk's main drag. Camels, knees folded, slept on the ground in pens fronting the tumbledown houses. The big animals groaned and huffed in their sleep, dreaming perhaps of the limitless desert. Farther on, an area lit with flickering electric lights off juice illegally diverted from the Laayoune grid.

A group of Saharoui men sat on threadbare carpets beneath the awning of a rude café, drinking sweet tea. Many of them wore piecemeal military outfits—the ragtag castoffs of a variety of North African armies; this was the thrift-store motley that passed for Polisario uniforms. A portable radio, tuned to a Moroccan station from Fez, played whiny Arab music at top volume. Dark eyes followed the Legionnaires as they passed. No one spoke.

"What's to stop them from cutting our throats?"

Just then, as if in response to Szbeszdogy's question, one of the Saharouis detached himself from the group at the teahouse. He came striding up and blocked their way forward.

"*Qu'est-ce que tu fou ici?*" he demanded in French, pushing a finger in Pinard's face. But before Pinard could answer, another man followed the first, then another and another until the Legionnaires were surrounded. One of the Saharouis began shouting in his own language and pointing at Solas.

"He is one of those who tortured our cousin in the swimming pool at the Agadir," the first man said to Pinard. "He must pay for this humiliation. Violence is traded for violence, so it is written. We will take him and you and the other can go on your way."

"We have come to see the emir," Pinard said, his voice calm and reasonable. "Do you dare detain guests of the emir in the Saharoui souk?"

Solas's hand crept toward the Walther, visible as a square bulge beneath the silk of his gaudy shirt.

"Steady," Szbeszdogy whispered.

"You will observe my friend's nose," Pinard continued. "I broke it with my fist. This was his payment for the crime of humiliation against your cousin."

"Not enough." The first Saharoui shook his head emphatically. "He must pay with his life. My family has been too greatly dishonored."

"We might conceivably let him off with a severe maiming," said the second, scratching his beard. "Perhaps we will only take his manhood. It's not so bad, we do it very quickly."

Solas twisted his mouth into a kind of smile. Threats like these he'd heard all his life, in the favelas of Rio, in the Legion, in the places between. He was calculating now how many he could kill with the gun, how many with his hands, and with the razor blade he kept always concealed in a small pocket inside of his shorts. After that it was *sauve-qui-peut.*

"Your cousin is not dead," Pinard said in the same reasonable tone. "A little roughed up, his clothes probably ruined. For this, my friends apologize. What if I offer you twenty thousand dirhams for the ruined clothes?"

The bargaining went on for nearly a half hour. The Legionnaires pooled everything they had in their pockets and promised to pay more to a boy who would show up the next day at the hotel. It was extortion and it made them sick, because, being Legionnaires, they would rather fight than pay. From nearby, from some hidden recess in the crumbling walls of the souk, as the big, gaudy bills were counted out, came the mocking hoot of an owl.

6.

The emir of the Saharouis sat playing a Nintendo Game Boy in the middle of a beautiful Zemmour carpet in an opulent tent pitched in an open area at the epicenter of the souk. The tent was spread with more beautiful carpets and hung with chandeliers of lacy, filigree silver. The emir, alone among his people, was permitted to live in a tent, a reminder of the glory days before the Moroccans and their Berm, before the Spanish and the French and the Portuguese, before the Foreign Legion came to Africa, before even the Arab invasions of the seventh century: a time of peace and freedom when the Saharouis had wandered their desert uninhibited, sailing across the dunes which were like the ocean on magnificently caparisoned camels, each man his own sheik.

The emir, a thin, spindly teenager, looked twelve, but was probably fifteen or sixteen. He wore a pastel pink polo shirt, spotless white trousers, and a crocodile-skin Hermès belt; his narrow brown feet were bare, the healthy toenails buffed and glistening. A pair of heavy gold hoop earrings hung from his long delicate lobes. He seemed utterly engrossed in his Game Boy and oblivious to the charms of his harem, which consisted of three plump, languid women, veiled but dressed in flimsy robes that exposed a good portion of their ample anatomies.

"I could have you killed for sneaking into my souk!" he said without taking his eyes off the tiny screen. He spoke in a clipped, nasal British-accented English—a product of Harrow, the exclusive boarding school in England, where he spent half the year playing polo and hobnobbing with royals.

Pinard, Szbeszdogy, and Solas lay prostrate before him, face to carpet, asses in the air, shoes off, like supplicants before an Oriental potentate, which in fact they were.

"Give me one bloody reason I shouldn't have you flogged and thrown into a pit full of vipers," the emir said, thumbs busy working the game.

"Mercy, Star of the East," Pinard replied in English. "We have come to ask your help."

"First you need to obtain my bloody permission to come and ask my help. Got that?"

"But how could we obtain your bloody permission, excellent sir?" Szbeszdogy spoke up. "Because here you are, hidden in your marvelous souk, and you do not go out."

The emir snapped his Game Boy shut. His face, though young and still softened by baby fat, was already hardened by the unchecked exercise of hereditary power.

"There are ways," he said coldly. "You have to know the right people, make inquiries, find a sponsor, that sort of thing. Rather like getting into a Mayfair club."

"Might we not now obtain your permission?"

"I don't suppose you brought any game chip software?" The emir tapped his Game Boy. "That would be a much appreciated bit of baksheesh."

"Unfortunately not, excellency," Szbeszdogy said.

"Bollocks!" the emir exclaimed. "I'm getting damned tired of Baby Kill Zone, let me tell you. I've breached all the levels, all the babies are dead, absolutely splattered. And Mossad Versus Jihad is downright boring. The damned Jews keep winning no matter what I do—and don't tell me Jewish domination of the electronic games industry has nothing to do with that outcome!"

Szbeszdogy and Pinard exchanged a confused glance.

"Listen, if you promise to send me some new games, and I mean a box full of them, I will overlook the fact that you were caught sneaking around my souk."

"Of course," Pinard said. They were suddenly speaking French. "When we return to France. As many as you like."

The emir spit in his hand and wiped it on his pants, Saharoui shorthand for done deal.

"*Alors, qu'est-ce que tu veux?*" He yawned. "Be quick. I'm busy."

"A Frenchwoman entered the souk about an hour ago," Pinard said. "We would like to speak to her."

"She is quite safe," the emir said, frowning. "We Saharouis aren't bloody white slavers, you know. She came here of her own free will and is free to go any time she likes and right now she wants to stay and she doesn't want to see anybody. Is that all?"

"If we could speak with her for a moment," Pinard persisted. "We are all here in your souk for the same purpose. A bit of coordination might save everyone a lot of trouble."

The emir scratched at a few wispy follicles of hair on his chin. For him, at least, the beard of the prophet was a long way off.

"You're talking about the Marabouts, I suppose."

"Yes," Pinard admitted. "About the men being held captive by them. We are here to help negotiate their return to France."

"What makes you think I have any dealings with those bloody fanatics?" The emir's voice rose to an outraged squeak. "That's damned impertinence!"

"You are the emir of the Saharouis," Pinard said soothingly. "Could anything occur in your country without you knowing that this thing has occurred? In the souk, in the desert, everywhere, your eyes are like the eyes of God."

"You have a very good point," the emir said, accepting this ripe piece of flattery with obvious pleasure. Then, he clapped his hands and one of the plump harem women heaved herself up and disappeared behind a curtain at the back of the tent. She returned a few minutes later with bowls of honeyed dates and glasses of sweet tea on a shiny brass tray that she set down on the carpet. The men drank the tea and ate the honeyed dates, which looked like shrivelled camel *crottes*, but which tasted much better than they looked—sweet and gritty, but gritty in a pleasant way.

"Excellent source of fiber," the emir said, his mouth full of the sticky dark fruit. "Watch out for the pits . . ." He opened his mouth, exposing on his tongue a moist black object, which he then spit onto the Zemmour carpet for one of the harem women to scoop up. "Now, on to business—"

But another one of the harem women interrupted, reaching up to wipe at the emir's mouth with a damp cloth, a maternal gesture the haughty teen found intensely annoying

"Excuse me, gentlemen," he said. "As civilized men, you'll agree business matters are unsuitable for female ears." Then he unleashed a stream of harsh-sounding invective at the woman in his own language and she stalked off angrily, ornate *babouches* flopping.

A tactical error, Pinard thought grimly. The kid was now alone with the hard-bitten Legionnaires of Mission: SCORPIO.

"Tell me something," the emir said, leaning forward. "Who are you exactly?"

"We are French businessmen," Pinard said.

"I'm young, but I'm not an idiot. Why don't you tell me the truth?"

"But we are businessmen," Pinard said. "Our business is to find the two men I mentioned. Will you help us?"

"That depends how much you're willing to pay for information," the emir said, a crafty gleam in his eye. Then he wagged a finger. "Think carefully. Do not insult me."

Though the air in the tent was stifling, the emir didn't sweat. Pinard glanced over at Solas. The Brazilian also looked cool as an eel, impervious to the heat. It was a question of metabolism; of natural selection and the influence of weather on body type.

Pinard, himself dripping with sweat, drew his men together, as if for a financial consultation.

"I should tell you right now, we're not authorized to pay anything, not one fucking sou," he whispered. "So this one's going to be all bluff, like playing American poker."

"More like Russian roulette," Szbeszdogy said.

"It is the Legion way." Pinard shrugged. Then, to Solas: "Is the safety off on the Walther?"

The Brazilian nodded.

"All right, ready?"

Szbeszdogy hesitated. At moments like this, in the lull before the fighting, a curious cacophony filled his ears. It was the sound of all the notes from all the songs he'd never written jangling together before they fell off, one by one, into the great uncreated void.

"Stefan?"

"Yes," the Hungarian said. "Why not?"

Pinard turned back to the emir. "Thirty-five thousand," he said, pulling the figure out of the air.

"I hope to Allah—peace be upon him—you mean pounds sterling!" the emir said, genuinely insulted by the offer.

"American dollars," Pinard said, just to confuse the issue.

"You're joking with me. I can spend that kind of money in a fortnight in London, just on gin and whores."

Pinard was beginning to hate this arrogant little teenager.

"In any case, the Frenchwoman has offered me five times that amount. And something else, something without price."

"What's that?" Pinard felt his ears burning suddenly.

"Her exquisite body," the emir said, smiling broadly. "For me to use as I please."

The tent got very small all at once, and Pinard felt a kind of hot pressure in his guts. Without thinking, he lunged across the carpet and caught one of the teenage emir's golden earrings and pulled down hard. The earring came off with a wet, ripping sound and the emir cried out in pain, but the sound of his voice was almost immediately stifled by Pinard's hands around his throat. Pinard squeezed hard and kept squeezing; the emir's eyes bulged, his tongue came lolling out, his face went purple.

"Stop!" It was Szbeszdogy's voice. "If you kill him, we'll never get out of this warren alive!"

Pinard let go, his hands trembling. The emir fell back, half strangled but still breathing.

"Give me the Walther," Pinard growled.

The Brazilian drew the gun, but did not immediately hand it over. Instead, he held it level with Pinard's heart. Their eyes met.

"Quite right," Pinard said calmly. "This is your chance, Solas. Kill me now and this officious little bastard will reward you with a fortune and you can spend the rest of your life here in the souk. Go ahead."

The Brazilian hesitated for two terrible seconds. Then he grinned and tossed over the gun. "From one man of honor to another," he said.

"Welcome to the fight," Pinard said, and he pressed the Walther's silenced end against the emir's forehead. "Where is she?"

The emir rolled his eyes in fear. The whites were flecked with pink where a couple of blood vessels had burst.

7.

Louise de Noyer lay on a low Turkish couch in a blue-tiled room in the emir's harem complex in her blue French underwear, attached by an iron collar and chain to a ring in the wall, as two more harem women, their clothes cast aside, applied perfumed pomade to her glossy blue-black hair. This exotic scene, reminiscent of Gérôme's *Bain*, was interrupted violently when the door to the room slammed open and the three Legionnaires entered, dragging the young emir along with them.

The harem women screamed and went scrambling for their clothes. The corridor outside was already filled with the dark shapes of the emir's myrmidons, and the harem complex—indeed, the entire souk—came alive with shouting and the urgent tromping of many feet.

"You're going to ruin everything!" Louise shouted at Pinard from her place on the couch. "Let the emir go!"

"I let him go, they cut our throats!" Pinard said.

"You don't understand! He's going to help me find my husband!"

"I understand too well," Pinard said. "Slut!"

The word came too quickly to his lips, but this wasn't the place for a lover's quarrel: Pinard shoved the Walther into the back of the emir's head and swung him around by the scruff of his pink polo shirt until he faced the door. Two big-boned Mauritanian eunuchs blocked the threshold: These bulky, emasculated henchmen carried the traditional symbol of their vocation—a heavy, curved scimitar, straight out of *The Arabian Nights*.

"Tell your dogs to piss off," Pinard growled.

The emir spoke in rapid Hassaniya, fear rattling his voice. The eunuchs—purchased in a slave market in Nouakchott the old-fashioned way, with a rawhide pouch full of silver coins and a couple of goats—backed off down the corridor.

"Let's get out of here," Pinard said. "Now!"

Solas seized Lousie de Noyer's chain and yanked hard and the chain came out of the wall in a shower of plaster and tile.

"Pardon me, madame," Solas said. "But you're coming with us!"

"No!" Louise pulled back against the chain. "I won't!"

"How you want me to handle this, *mon capitaine*?" Solas said.

"With prejudice, Legionnaire!"

"I don't want to smash your pretty face," Solas said grimly. "But if I have to, I'm going to enjoy it!"

Louise gasped in disbelief. "Liar!" she shouted at Pinard. "You're not a bank robber at all! The Legion sent you!"

"The French Foreign Legion?" The emir went pale.

"You've heard of us," Pinard said.

"You have no right to be here!" the emir cried, outraged. "This is a clear violation of national sovereignty!"

"It's not a question of national sovereignty at all," Szbeszdogy countered. "Western Sahara is a non-self-governing territory."

"I protest in the strongest terms! I shall inform MINURSO of this violation—"

Pinard, losing patience, backhanded the kid hard across the mouth. "Shut up or I'll crush your Game Boy!" he growled. "*Petit con!*"

"Brute!" Louise shouted. "Leave him alone!"

Pinard couldn't look at her. Anyway, there wasn't time now. They moved quickly out into the corridor and hustled along through several twists and turns until they found themselves in a courtyard open to the sky. Pinard glanced up and saw stars and wondered if he would live to see the dawn. They pushed through a wooden gate studded with iron nails and stumbled out into the labyrinthine alleys of the souk, now moving at a fast run through the darkness: Solas with his catlike eyes out in front, dragging Louise by her chain, then the emir and Pinard, with Szbeszdogy bringing up the rear.

"You're so stupid," the emir managed, panting. "You're all dead men . . ."

"Then so are you," Pinard said grimly. "Count on it."

The sound of voices and shouting followed them on a parallel course from a few streets over. Then they seemed to move beyond their pursuers and there was no one ahead of them, no one behind. They came to a narrow turning; here a sound like the humming of a large electric motor echoed against the mud-brick walls. Solas hesitated, slowed, the cat hairs on the back of his neck tingling.

"That's not so good," he murmured.

"Keep going," Pinard urged. "Forward!" This had always been the Le-

gion way. Over the top and straight at the impregnable bastion; the defini-
tion of that indefinable military quality peculiar to the French, through a
thousand years of victory and defeat, but mostly defeat: *élan!*

They debouched at full speed into a shabby square dominated by a structure like a giant breast or a pizza oven—its packed earthen surface glittering
strangely. This glitter was the smoky light of burning camel dung flickering
off the wings of an uncountable multitude of bees; the electric motor sound
was their insidious buzzing. Hooded figures appeared out of the gloom on
either side of the hive. They wore blue djellahs the exact color of Madame de
Noyer's stylish underwear, their faces veiled. Pinard smacked the emir hard in
the back of the head with the Walther.

"Miserable little shit!" he shouted. "You said you had no dealings with
the Marabouts!"

"But it's true!" the emir sobbed. "They consider me unclean. They will
not even speak to me. They have invaded my souk and taken half of it for
themselves and will not leave!"

"Tell those freaks to get out of our way or I blow your head off!"

The emir complied tearfully. One of the Marabouts brought up a Kalashnikov and fired two quick, sloppy bursts in response. Bullets sprayed all
around, chewing into the dirt. No one was hit and Pinard and the emir
scrambled back into the darkness of the alley.

"What will you do now, imbecile?" Louise said, her chain still firmly
grasped in the Brazilian's fist. "I told you to leave me where I was!"

"Too late," Pinard said.

"It's never too late for negotiation! Compromise—"

To a Legionnaire, the word was an insult.

"Yes, yes!" the emir bobbed his head. "Shall we go back to my tent and
sit down and discuss matters in a business fashion?"

"Hard to fight Kalashnikovs with a pistol, *mon capitaine*," the Brazilian
interjected.

"*La ferme*, Solas!" Pinard barked.

"Stop, look at these"—Szbeszdogy lifted his baggy, colorful tourist shirt
and unzipped the stomach pack he wore there and withdrew two black metallic objects, shaped like avocados, their cast surface bisected by a thick
metal seam. Complicated pins protruded from the smaller end.

"Bombs?" Louise sounded frightened.

"Very beautiful bombs." Szbeszdogy laughed.

They were concussion grenades, packed with C4 pilfered from the secret Legion arms cache in the desert.

"Stefan, you're a genius—" Pinard began, but now the emir saw his opportunity. He jerked out of Pinard's grasp and made a break for the little square.

"*Allah, il Allah!*" he shouted, as if expecting to find sanctuary with the hooded fanatics standing guard by their monstrous hive. A crack rang out, the single report of an assault rifle, and the emir pitched forward, pierced by a bullet, which exiting blew off the back of his skull.

Louise screamed and covered her face.

"Prepare yourself to run as fast as you can," Pinard commanded. "But for God's sake, stay calm!"

"That poor kid!" Louise sobbed. Then bitterly: "You murderer! You monster!" As if it had all been Pinard's fault from the beginning, as if he had purposefully gotten her crazy husband captured and placed this hive in their path and shot the emir with his own gun. But it was true: He had a guilty-looking face.

Pinard looked over at Szbeszdogy.

"Ready?"

"*Nom de chien!*" Solas swore. "Now!"

Pinard tossed the Walther to the Brazilian and plucked one of the grenades from Szbeszdogy's hand. He pulled the pin with his teeth, darted out into the open, and hurled it at the hive, bullets raining all around. He threw himself down in the dirt just as the grenade exploded with a roar and the hive blew apart like a giant pumpkin. Smoke and flames blasted into the air; great chunks coated with goopy red wax and dead bees splatted down wetly all over the place. The Marabout guards lay flopped out on the ground, dead or dying, though one managed to fire off his rifle before Solas caught him with a couple of quick pops from the Walther. Then, Pinard grabbed up one of the Kalashnikovs and, followed by the others, dashed across the square and down another narrow alley on the other side, this one ending abruptly at the high exterior wall of the souk.

"Down!" Szbeszdogy called, heaving the second grenade.

The explosion knocked them flat and blew a hole through the mud bricks. When the dust cleared, fresh air from the outside world poured into the foul-smelling souk, air that held the tang of the sea. An electric streetlight winked at them from the near distance. Out there, the wide, empty streets of Laayoune, peaceful, faraway, watched over by the paternal machine gun towers of the Moroccan army. The Legionnaires and the woman, her chain dangling freely now, clambered through the smoking hole and crossed a ditch and tangle of barbed wire into the city. Pinard was the last, dropping back and firing every few meters to make sure no one followed. The time-honored tactic of *décrochage*, a fighting retreat.

But now Moroccan spotlights were trailing anxiously over the souk. An alarm siren whined in the clean desert air. Yellow flames shot up to the sky: Houses had caught fire in the neighborhood of the exploded hive. As Pinard and the rest came around the massive supports of the nearest machine gun tower, the spotlight above swung down and caught them all in its beam. The Moroccan guards up there, shouting and gesticulating, thought they were under attack. Now, after so many months, so many years of restraint, they let loose wildly with their big guns. The blazing streak of tracer bullets ripped through the darkness, the big 12.7mm rounds smashing emphatically— *Thump! Thump! Thump!*—into the earthen walls of the souk, into the dry, stony ground.

8.

Head down, hair hanging over her face, Louise de Noyer emerged from the minister's office still barefoot and wearing her charming blue underwear, a Moroccan police jacket shrugged over her bare shoulders. She didn't look up as she approached the bench where the six Legionnaires sat handcuffed and immobilized with leg irons—everyone asleep after forty-eight hours of interrogation, hunched against one another, snoring, mouths open. Except for Capitaine Pinard. He sat there, preternaturally alert, awake as an animal in a trap, waiting for her.

Now, here she was, walking free down the long, institutional hallway at 3:00 A.M. No doubt she had told the Moroccans everything she knew.

"Louise!" Pinard called as she passed. "Louise!"

The uncharacteristic tone of supplication in his voice made her pause. She turned to look at him.

"What did you tell them?"

"The truth," she said. "That you caused the death of that boy."

"Boy?" Pinard said, coloring. "He was old enough to want to fuck you—"

"You disgust me," Louise interrupted, turning away.

"*Wait!*" Pinard called to her, desperate now. "I need to s-say something to you," he stuttered, though he had never stuttered in his life. "F-forget this stupid m-mess. Something about us, now that it's too late, I—"

"Stop." Louise's face twitched with horror, but Pinard wouldn't be stopped.

"I love you. You're the only woman I've ever loved. Maybe the only person other than my father, and he's only a vague memory to me. . . ."

A single frigid look silenced him. She didn't give a damn about him or his father or anything he had been or would be, anything he thought or did or might do. He could save the whole world from destruction, win the Croix de Guerre and the Medaille Militaire in the process and it wouldn't matter one bit to her. She lowered her startling eyes again and turned away from him for the last time. Pinard watched her go, watched her back and legs and ass, her bare feet paddling along the corridor until she was gone. He slumped down again, broken. Thus passes—he thought, though not in these words exactly—my happiness forever.

A few minutes later, two swarthy, mustachioed policemen came and took him off to see the minister.

9.

The minister had exchanged the native djellah he wore in his capacity as Minister of Tourism and Social Intercourse for the neat khaki uniform of a colonel of the Moroccan National Police. Vivid red Moroccan pentacles decorated his green collar tabs. His tie, neatly knotted, was also vividly green, meant to represent the true nature of Islam, always growing, eternally alive and like a hardy weed, impossible to eradicate.

Pinard was dragged in by the two policemen and handcuffed to a chair bolted to the cement floor. At a signal from the minister, one of the policemen reached down and ripped open the front of Pinard's gaudy tourist shirt, its panels bedecked with red and white orchids, revealing the Legion tattoo on his chest, the skull eating the artillery shell and the motto *Honneur et fidélité—valeur et discipline.*

"How do you explain this garish decoration?" the minister said.

"It's a tattoo," Pinard said.

The guard who had ripped his shirt open smashed Pinard across the face with the back of his hand, not hard enough to knock out any teeth, but hard enough to raise a fat lip.

"Insolence is frowned upon by this office," the minister said dryly. "Your tattoo—the motto of the French Foreign Legion, is it not?"

"No," Pinard said. "The motto of the Foreign Legion is *Legio Patria Nostra.*"

"How do you know that?"

"Everyone in France knows that," Pinard said.

The minister sighed. "How can I help you, Monsieur Deschafeaux, if you do not tell me the truth? Clearly you are lying. You are a Legionnaire."

"I'm a businessman," Pinard insisted. "A French businessman. I work for the Club Med organization." His cover was utterly ridiculous, but Pinard was bound to maintain it to the bitter end. He had his orders: The sacred name of the Legion must be kept out of this foolhardy mission at all costs.

The minister leaned back in his chair. He sat on the other side of a plain metal desk upon which there was absolutely nothing, not a piece of paper, not a pen, not a rubber band.

"You deny being a Legionnaire?"

"Because I'm not a Legionnaire," Pinard lied.

"Good for you," the minister said, a faint smile on his lips. "So much the better that you are not a part of that terrible group of murderers and perverts. They have quite a bad reputation here in Morocco, you know, from the period of French colonial misrule. Bloody bandits masquerading as an army, that's what they were. Despoilers of virgins, killers of children."

Pinard didn't rise to the bait.

"My grandfather fought with the great el-Krim against the Legion in the 1920s," the minister continued. "Have you heard of el-Krim, Monsieur Deschafeaux? He was a great Moroccan patriot and hero."

"Yes, I've heard of him," Pinard allowed. "In France he's also known as great. A great and vicious murderer of the Frenchmen who were here irrigating fields and building roads and schools for you bastards to use and that you still use."

The mustachioed policeman standing behind Pinard raised his hand to strike at this insult, but the minister stopped this violence with a glance.

"There is no such thing as murder in a war to throw off the yoke of colonial oppression," he said.

"Murder is murder," Pinard said, "whatever the reason for it. Your precious el-Krim used to bury captured Legionnaires up to the neck, cover their faces with honey, and let the ants devour the rest. Not exactly a humanitarian, you must admit. For this and other brutalities he was eventually brought to justice."

"French justice," the minister said.

"Enough history." Pinard leaned as far forward as his handcuffs would allow. "I have a more modern proposal. Something better discussed in private."

The minister nodded and the mustachioed policemen left the room.

"Well?"

"What would you say if I offered you one hundred thousand euros to let us go?"

The minister frowned, drumming his fingers on the desk. "In my capacity as Minister of Police for the District of Laayoune"—he waved at a map on the wall showing the so-called Southern Provinces of the Kingdom of Morocco with the Moroccan-held areas between the Berm and the sea shaded in green—"I could have you shot for an attempt to corrupt a public official. However, as Minister of Tourism and Social Intercourse, which is more of an honorary appointment, and therefore, shall we say, semiprivate—" He stopped himself, then made a gesture that seemed abruptly dismissive of their conversation up to this point.

"As you suggest, Monsieur Deschafeaux, time to discuss practical matters. The Marabouts are the enemies of Morocco, as they are the enemies of civilized people everywhere. Religious lunatics, mystics who, from what we can tell, worship bees more than God, and are not good Muslims. Can we agree on this?"

"Absolutely."

"Good." The minister nodded. "We have common ground, then. The presence of a Marabout hive in the Saharoui souk came as much of a surprise to us in the Ministry of Police as it did to you and your"—he smiled faintly—"business associates. Might I ask, by the way, where you innocent businessmen found those marvelous grenades?"

Pinard opened his mouth to deny the existence of any such grenades, but the minister interrupted, "Louise de Noyer has told us every detail of what happened the other night. In other words, your denials are stupidly useless."

Pinard closed his mouth. Just hearing her name spoken aloud caused the breath to leave his lungs, a painful clenching of his heart. He longed for the day when this pain would cease, but it never would.

"You are an obstinate man," the minister continued. "Obstinacy is a necessary trait in—in business. *Mais soyez raisonnable*, obstinacy has its limits." He rose and came around the desk and unlocked Pinard's restraints, then sat back down again.

Pinard's hands, cuffed for nearly forty-eight hours, felt dead. He gritted his teeth as the blood returned to them with the prickly sensation of stinging nettles.

"In my capacity as Minister of Police," the minister said, "I am in the position to share information that might be of interest to the Foreign Legion. This information concerns the whereabouts of two Legionnaires, one an officer, who are at this moment prisoners of the Marabouts. Would you be interested in hearing this information, Monsieur Deschafeaux?"

Pinard, flexing his dead fingers, paused before he answered. "The concerns of the Foreign Legion have always been the concerns of France," he said carefully, "and as I am a citizen of France, yes, I would be very interested in such information."

"Ah, very good!" the minister said, and he rubbed his hands together like a shopkeeper, a dry papery sound. "Now we may revisit the one hundred thousand euros you mentioned earlier—a sum far too low for information leading to the delivery of two innocent men from the mouth of Satan."

10.

The negotiations continued until first light.

At last, the amount of the bribe was decided upon, including a second, smaller but significant amount to ensure the cooperation of the Moroccan army at the Berm. The minister agreed and the two men shook hands. There was no shame in this exchange; it was merely baksheesh, one of the time-honored traditions of settling difficult matters in the East. Some might call it corruption but this would be imposing alien cultural traditions on such a reasonable transaction.

Of course, Pinard was cheating on the deal and risking his freedom and the freedom of his men as surety. He had managed to convince the minister to accept payment only after the liberation of Colonel de Noyer from the Marabouts—a tidy bit of subterfuge—and had no authorization to pay any money to anyone. He would figure out the rest as they went along, muddle through somehow. This was the Legion way, and it was also the French way: they have always been a nation of *débrouillards*, an untranslatable word meaning, more or less, that every Frenchman has inherited a natural ability to make do with the meager resources at hand.

Unlike the rule of law, the workings of baksheesh are efficent, prompt. There is no paperwork to fill out, nothing to sign, no witnesses. Eight minutes following the end of negotiations, just after dawn, Pinard and the men of Mission: SCORPIO were released and ushered down the freshly cured cement front steps of the Prefecture de Police into the Oued Bou district, its white facades still retaining the blue shadows of the westering night.

13

À MOI LA LÉGION!

1.

Alia held out her arm, usually mocha-toned and sinewy-smooth, now a dull purplish color and swollen and covered all over with large angry-looking bee stings.

"Look what they did to me!" she cried. "I go to the water tank this morning with my jugs and they swarm and bite, these accursed bees!" Angry tears sprung to her eyes. She stamped her foot on the bare earth: "I want to smash them all!"

Just then, from the ominous pink bungalow up the slope, seemingly in response to the girl's blasphemous exclamation, came the first syllables of the rantings of Al Bab, also known as the Gateway to the Age of the Hidden Imam and Munificent Signpost of Heaven. It was the beginning of one of the Birkenstock-wearing theocrat's lengthy harangues—some sort of religious indoctrination, Smith supposed—delivered via public address system at top volume three or four times a day. Everyone in the village was obliged to stop what they were doing, squat down in the dirt, and listen. Now, Al Bab's shrill intonations and harsh consonants rang off the surrounding mountain peaks like a hammer against steel.

"Oh, God," Smith groaned. "Son of a bitch's at it again."

"You don't care about my pain, 'ti Blanc." Alia pouted. 'Ti Blanc was what she called him now, literally, Little White Boy. "You care about only the food I can give for you."

Smith focused on the girl with effort. The verdict had been handed down from the holy crew in the bungalow the day before: The Marabout insurgency had no need for music. They were going to sever his head from his body and feed the resulting headless carcass to the bees. His head would be tossed onto a pile with other heads or maybe impaled on a stake. The same fate awaited Colonel de Noyer, hanging in his chains, emaciated, sleepless, saintly in his silent endurance across the room. Phillipe hadn't spoken in a couple of days; occasionally, he'd blink or wheeze. His hair, now falling out in patches, revealed a shrunken, yellow scalp. For him, death would come as a mercy.

"Do you not love your poor Alia?" the girl persisted.

Smith didn't say anything.

"Oh, how my life is terrible for me in this terrible place!"

"Maybe you could leave me alone now," Smith managed. "I've got a whole lifetime of mistakes to pick over before I go."

"You have many regrets?"

Smith nodded grimly. "As many as if I'd lived a thousand years." It was a line from—he couldn't remember where—Cole Porter? Gershwin?

"Weakling!" the girl hissed. "Where is the courage to resist your fate?"

Smith looked at her, hope suddenly burning like the acid in his empty gut. "How am I supposed to resist, exactly?"

Alia leaned close, her peeling lips barely an inch from his ear.

2.

The moon rose over the highest peak of the Galtat Zemmur just before midnight. Smith waited, his hollow stomach still churning. The moon dimmed slowly and fell with his dwindling hopes. Of course the girl didn't show—how stupid he'd been to believe her crazy promises! In the silence he could hear the persistent grumble of Al Bab's generator and the subtle buzzing of the hive. Suddenly, he became aware of Phillipe staring at him through the darkness. The colonel blinked, his pale, sleepless eyes like the eyes of some ancient owl, wise but infinitely melancholy.

"Is that you, Phillipe?" Smith said.

"Why do you always ask such a stupid question?".

"Because mostly you're not there. Mostly you've been replaced by a raving lunatic."

"Your tone borders on insubordination, Legionnaire!" The colonel frowned. "Watch yourself."

"I've had it up to here with the military shit," Smith said. "How about we just forget it?"

"You're insubordinate and a fool. The military shit, as you call it, gives us the courage to endure. It is like those Englishmen, African explorers of the nineteenth century who even in the middle of the jungle, bothered to dress for dinner."

"What?" Smith said, not understanding.

"Structure. Traditions. These things stand between us and the chaos of unbeing."

"Whatever," Smith said glumly. He wasn't in the mood for philosophizing. "It's too late anyway. We're dead men tomorrow morning."

"An end to this dirty business!" The colonel lifted a chained arm and let it drop. "We've lived long enough, eh, Milquetoast?"

"Speak for yourself," Smith said.

"But not yet, I'm afraid, not yet—to paraphrase Augustine. A bloody piece of work needs doing before the end."

"What work?" Smith said, puzzled.

The colonel folded himself back into himself once again like a large bat folding its rubbery wings and didn't bother to elaborate.

3.

Hours passed.

Smith felt despair as a sour nausea for which there was no remedy. He would be decapitated at dawn, not long now, and no one alive would give a damn. Try as he might, he couldn't believe in a personal God and couldn't pray for his own soul and didn't believe friends and family would be waiting for him happily on the other side—anyway, what would Jessica say?—and he found himself washed up naked and helpless on the barren shores of his own nihilism and self-contempt. The nourmoom blew through the ragged doorway. Distant peaks gleamed like polished tombstones in the oblique light of a fallen moon.

Somehow, at last, he slept. The dreams of imprisoned men are vivid enough (those bright colors missing from the bare walls of prison cells produced instead by the subconscious mind); the dreams of condemned men on the eve of execution explode will psychedelic intensity. Now, Smith's dreams were full of outrageous colors and loud slamming noises like the sound of a body falling to earth from a great height over and over again. There he was, an amoeba preserved on a glass slide, every intimate flaw magnified as if seen through the lens of a microscope, and he felt the weight of a scrutiny that was coldly scientific and relentless, and in his sleep uttered a loud, fearful cry:

"*No!*"

A hand over his mouth pulled him from this nightmare.

"*Mais, taisez vous!*" It was Alia's voice. "You must not make so much as the smallest noise!"

Smith squinted up at her, his eyes adjusting. She carried a dark bundle under her arm. From one end of the bundle protruded a short, stubby barrel Smith instantly recognized—the good old FAMAS 5.56 assault rifle, standard issue to the Legion, no doubt a souvenir of the killing ground at Blockhouse 9. Smith's hands reached for the gun, but were restrained by his chains, which rattled alarmingly in the stillness.

"Clumsy idiot!" the girl hissed.

She withdrew a key from somewhere and unlocked the large, primitive iron padlocks that bound Smith's ankles and wrists, catching the links so they fell quietly. Smith stood up, giddy, relieved of the weight of the chains for the first time in nearly four months. He rubbed his neck, he probed the sores on his wrists. He felt like Christ resurrected. He thought he knew the jubilation of slaves given their freedom after many years.

"Wonderful," he gasped. "Thank you."

Alia unrolled the dark bundle—a hooded djellah, stinking of body odor, that Smith shook gratefully over his head. Clothes! Then she handed him the rifle. He turned it over lovingly in his hands, released the safety mechanism. The clip held the standard combat load of twenty-five rounds. He slotted a round into the chamber and at this slight mechanical sound, Phillipe looked up, instantly aware.

"Unlock my chains," he croaked.

Smith hesitated.

"I forbid it!" Alia shook her head. "I don't have clothes or a weapon for that crazy old man. He will get us killed!"

"Listen to me, Milquetoast," Phillipe said. "You eat, you shit, you sleep, you fornicate. You are born an animal and you die an animal, that is unless you do something in between to raise yourself above this condition. I had hoped that in the Legion you would find the personal honor you never possessed." He coughed, a dry reedy sound. "I was wrong. You remain selfish and a coward. Now you are planning to escape this hell alone, without your commanding officer."

Smith bowed his head. The colonel, in his emaciated and weakened state, would be nothing but a liability. How could you scramble over steep rocks and cross immense deserts with a man unable to walk at any pace faster than a shuffle?"

"Article seven of the Code of the Legion," Phillipe said, his voice suddenly stern, commanding. "Repeat it."

Smith remained silent.

"We must go now," Alia said, tugging anxiously at the sleeve of Smith's new garment. "You will take me to Milan, so that I might wear beautiful dresses and jewels, like you promised."

"I've given you a direct order, Legionnaire!"

"I am a volunteer serving France with honor and fidelity unto death," Smith said begrudgingly. "Devoted to my commanding officers, courage and loyalty are my virtues—"

"Enough," Phillipe interrupted. "Unlock my chains."

Smith looked from the colonel's calm pale eyes to the girl's anxious dark ones and back again.

"Phillipe, I'm sorry . . . ," he began, but his voice trailed off. What was the point of attempting to excuse himself from yet another crime?

4.

They came out of Laayoune more like prisoners on a work detail than Legionnaires on a search-and-rescue mission. They were given Moroccan air force jumpsuits of coarse denim with nothing to distinguish rank or regiment, and placed in the custody of a demibrigade of the Moroccan army commanded by a fox-faced major named Abduljemal Rabani, said to be a distant cousin of the king's. They were not allowed to carry weapons and went unarmed except for the concealed blade a Legionnaire always carries. Though for Szbeszdogy, this weapon of last resort took the form of no weapon at all, only a narrow file for picking handcuffs tucked into the lining of his pants; in Solas's case, two razors and a garotting wire hidden in the hollow heel of his boot.

From Laayoune, the demibrigade struck out across the desert in a southeasterly direction, always keeping the snow-capped Gueltas to the right, their narrow peaks just visible above the horizon. Fifty rank-and-file Moroccan soldiers and the personnel of Mission: SCORPIO were crammed into the backs of two Bulgarian-made Grushinka AT troop transport trucks, baking hot and airless, without windows or ventilation. A stock 1982 Jeep Cherokee 4×4, originally Detroit red, now Marrakesh green, possessing air-conditioning and optional cassette player, carried Major Rabani, his second in command, and the two Moroccan non-coms in frosty comfort.

The major refused to reveal the exact location of the *fashula*—the hive—a word that had lately come to signify any Marabout camp—where intelligence indicated Colonel de Noyer was being held. Specific information, he told Pinard curtly, was secret property of the Moroccan government. He wore silver-lensed aviator glasses, his hair slicked back. He looked like a movie star, a swarthy matinee idol of the silent era. He pursed his mouth daintily when he spoke, as if sucking on something sour:

"I will absolutely not allow questioning, not of myself or my troops on this or any other matter," he said on the evening of their first day out. "We will get there when we get there, but we will get there. . . ." Waving airily toward the horizon, across the desert where there were no roads, where it was like navigating at sea.

The major's coyness bothered Pinard, but he did indeed seem to know where he was going, consulting laminated field maps, figuring vectors and longitudes with an old-fashioned slide rule and protractor. Pinard had no real reason to be suspicious. His Legionnaires were being well treated, supplied with food, water, and cigarettes. The Moroccan troops seemed friendly enough. And yet . . .

⟨⊙⟩

They progressed across the desert in slow zigzags, in exasperating fits and starts. The entire demibrigade, officers and men, stopped five times a day, an hour at a time, for obligatory prayers to Mecca. The major established the direction of this super-holy city using his orienteering compass, rolled out a small square of carpet, and settled himself down face forward in the sand. His men, pious or not, followed his example.

Pinard, Szbeszdogy, and the assassins from the 4e RE watched disdainfully from the shadows of truck or tent through these hours of enforced idleness, smoking foul Moroccan army-issue cigarettes and talking in low voices as fifty Moroccan foreheads touched the hot sand and fifty corresponding Moroccan rumps bumped heavenward.

"Ridiculous spectacle," Solas muttered. It was now the third day out from Laayoune, just before noon, and the Moroccans had commenced their prayers once again in the 120° heat. Visible off to the east-northeast as a bluish brown line, indistinguishable from the horizon, the infamous Berm.

"Someone give me my FAMAS," Vladimirovitch said. "I'll rip them a second asshole."

"What do they do if they're in the middle of having sex?" Dessalines wondered. "Do they stop and pray?"

"They move the boy their fucking toward Mecca and keep at it," Vladimirovitch said, and everyone laughed.

"At least they believe in something." Szbeszdogy tossed his weedy cigarette into the sand. "Which is more than I can say for you filthy bastards."

"Oh, I believe in something," Solas said grimly. "I believe in my FAMAS, my razor blade, and my own right arm."

"I don't care what anyone believes," Capitaine Pinard interjected. "So long as you men shut up and don't cause any trouble. Every day we spend kicking around this miserable desert . . ." He didn't finish this thought. "We need to get there soon if there's going to be anything left of the colonel. Understood?"

A reluctant mumble of assent followed his statement, echoed by the pious murmur of Moroccans mouthing their prayers in even rows in the blazing sun.

5.

The Moroccan Berm was pierced every hundred kilometers or so with a fortified, gated passage through to the wilderness on the other side. Out there, beyond the great wall of sand, lay unmapped territory nominally held by Polisario rebels, but now mostly under the mysterious influence of the Marabout insurgency. The gate at sector fourteen, passage seven followed the pattern of every other gate along the line, garrisoned by a dismal bunch of a hundred or so Moroccan troops, sullen and slovenly, suffering from bad morale and their own version of the *cafard*, a condition that affects not only the Legion, but any army billeted in extreme and isolated conditions. The passage formed a rough circle a hundred meters in diameter, surrounded with barbed wire and a trench five meters deep. Inside, a haphazard arrangement of tents, Quonset huts, broken half-tracks, and a few pieces of poorly kept ordnance, sunk to the breech in the sand.

The gate—a mere rolling obstruction, more chicken wire than barbed and set between two rows of sandbags—rolled back to admit the convoy from Laayoune. Behind them now, the desert all the way to the coast. Ahead through the opposite gate, more desert all the way to the mountains where the Marabouts held absolute sway. The convoy drew up in a ragged line not far from the garrison commander's igloo: a round, thickly plastered white building with no windows, only a huge square air-conditioning unit protruding from an aperture above the doorway and a couple of satellite dishes sprouting like mushrooms out of the roof.

The major exited his air-conditioned Cherokee and disappeared quickly into the air-conditioned igloo to confer with the garrison commander, a vampirish figure who only emerged once or twice a week and only for a few minutes, at dusk. Captain Pinard and the Legionnaires and most of the Moroccans jumped down from the trucks to stretch their legs. Windblown and flea-bitten garrison troops clustered around these new arrivals from cosmopolitan Laayoune, speaking a polyglot of Hassaniya, Arabic, and French, seeking any news from that faraway city, a paradise considered from the blighted perspective of the Berm.

A few soldiers approached Pinard and the Legionnaires.

"Vouz avez des cigarettes les français?" one of the garrison troops asked Pinard. He identified himself as Corporal Hassan; he was older, early fifties probably, and like many Moroccans of that generation still spoke the precise French he'd learned in parochial schools administered by French nuns, long since raped and murdered or deported.

"Non, malheureusement," Pinard said. *"Seulement des cigarettes marocaines.* And we're not French. All of us—Foreign Legion." Corporal Hassan shrugged and took several of Pinard's Moroccan cigarettes, putting one between his lips and the rest in his breast pocket. For some reason, he wore a blanket over his shoulders, despite the incredible heat.

"We have heard about you Legionnaires," Corporal Hassan said, lighting his cigarette with expert ease in the steady desert wind.

Pinard shrugged.

"My grandfather fought against the Legion in the Rif wars."

"So did everyone's grandfather in Morocco."

"El-Krim—"

"Please," Pinard said, holding up his hands. "Let's not start talking about el-Krim!"

Corporal Hassan chuckled. "Perhaps you are right," he said. "Anyway, from what I've heard, el-Krim was a bastard."

Then he made an odd little gesture, a subtle movement of head and shoulder to indicate discretion. He took a few steps away from the truck, blowing smoke into the air. Pinard followed, hands in his pocket. Nothing could be more natural than two soldiers sharing a cigarette and a few words in the waning light of afternoon.

"You seem like a good fellow," the Moroccan said darkly. "So listen to me—from one soldier to another. Your situation is about to change for the worse."

"Is this a joke?" Pinard said, careful to keep a smile on his face.

"No," the Moroccan said. "It's not funny at all. My *copain* is the colonel's communications subaltern. He runs the radio and the telex and sees every message that goes between the Berm and Rabat, Layoune, Marrakesh. Everything, you understand. And he knows almost every code."

Pinard leaned forward against the wind, trying to conceal his interest. "So what does he tell you, this friend?"

"Nothing is free on this earth." The corporal shook his head. "The free stuff you only get in paradise, where seventy-two virgins bring it along on silver trays."

Pinard pulled out the pockets of his coveralls. "No money," he said. "I've got nothing."

"You must have something to barter," Corporal Hassan insisted. "Even a trinket. It's the principle of the thing."

Pinard canvassed his men and came up with a small pile a few minutes later: Two silver earrings—both from Szbeszdogy, part Gypsy on his mother's side—a silver pendant of the Virgin Mary from Dessalines, who was at least nominally Roman Catholic, and a vintage Zippo lighter from Vladimirovitch, its worn, nickel-plated case engraved with the insignia of the 4e

RE and a blunt personal motto, probably mistranslated from Russian into French, because it didn't make much sense: Try to kill me but I will kill you. Pinard presented these objects to Corporal Hassan as a bundle wrapped in a handkerchief.

"This is all we've got," Pinard said.

The Moroccan picked over the loot in the handkerchief and gave everything back except the Zippo. He pressed the button and the blue flame shot up on the first click.

"Good," he said, smiling. "Americans made this, when Americans knew how to make things. Did you know one of their spaceships blew up not long ago?"

"Well?"

Corporal Hassan glanced over his shoulder to make sure no one was listening. "There are rumors of peace talks, a treaty," he said in a low voice.

Pinard and Szbeszdogy exchanged a worried glance.

"Between who?" Pinard said.

"Between Morocco and the Marabouts," the corporal said. "That psychopath Al Bab is negotiating to make a common cause with the king against the Algerians, against Polisario, against the UN, and against all foreigners in Western Sahara. Morocco wants no interference, you understand, with its plans for this wasteland—which is to dig up all the phosphorous and sell it to the Chinese. What is now Polisario territory would become a satellite state of Morocco, evenly divided between the king and this Al Bab. This would put you and your men in a very awkward position, don't you think? The enemy of my new friend is my new enemy, yes?"

6.

The Moroccan demibrigade and the Legionnaires exited passage seven through the eastern gate into Marabout-held territory soon after dark. Great clouds of sand and dust billowed up in the last red light. They drove through the cooling hours, the beams of their headlights falling across the emptiness, and reached a Moroccan supply depot just west of the Algerian border at 3:00 A.M. Here, at the edge of the Hoggar, previous expeditions had set up a semipermanent camp, with crates of RCIR reheatable meals, parcels of powdered soup, and plastic barrels of water buried in the sand in shallow trenches.

The Legionnaires helped the Moroccans set up their tents in even rows, tap the barrels of water, and dig latrine trenches. It appeared, to Pinard's dismay, that they were preparing for a long stay. He asked the ranking Moroccan non-com, a grizzled sergeant named Muhammed Ladjal, a couple of questions about when they could expect to move on and was immediately summoned to Major Rabani's tent for the answer. This elaborate shelter, more Ottoman splendor than military austerity, was made from a kind of stiffened linen, the breezy fabric covered in tasteful pale blue stripes. Large, comfortable pillows covered the carpeted floor inside; a tea service of polished brass glittered from a deep Moroccan tray—all gently illuminated in the shadowy light cast by the same sort of pretty filigree lamp that had hung in the tent of the late Saharoui emir in the souk in Laayoune.

The major sat directly beneath the lamp cross-legged on a scarlet pillow like a sultan, bare to the torso, wearing a pair of silk pantaloons. His subaltern, a youth of seventeen whose only garment was a loincloth, massaged oil into the major's back and shoulders. The major gasped, as the youth bore down hard with the balls of his thumbs.

Capitaine Pinard stood at attention, unsettled by this oddly charged scene. Major Rabani ignored him for a long while, grimacing and sighing and arching his neck like a turtle as the youth worked him over. At last he looked up, and appeared both surprised and annoyed by the capitaine's presence.

"I ordered you not to question my soldiers, Frenchman," he said. "Not for any reason."

"I'm not French," Pinard said. "The Legion is my country."

"You're a rotten bunch of French mercenaries as far as I'm concerned," Major Rabani growled. "Paid killers. You should have been shot as spies back in Laayoune."

"Thankfully, the minister had a different opinion," Pinard said, trying to keep his voice neutral, cool.

"The minister!" Major Rabani laughed unpleasantly, showing a row of expensively capped teeth. "The minister is a corrupt politician and a marked man. He will be replaced by the royal procurator as soon as I am able to make a full report."

Pinard's neutrality immediately extinguished itself. Clearly, the corporal back at gate seven had been correct about everything and the joint

Morocco-Foreign Legion expedition to rescue Colonel de Noyer had fallen
afoul of politics. It felt more natural this way. Morocco and the Legion had
been enemies for more than a hundred years; the notorious atrocities committed by el-Krim had never been completely forgotten in Aubagne and vice
versa. Pinard glanced around for an object he might be able to use as a
weapon, and his eyes fell on the filigree lamp. He pulled it down on the
major's head, but what about the subaltern? This question was answered a
moment later when the young man reached into his loincloth and pulled out
a neat nickel-plated automatic.

"Private Jalal is my bodyguard," the major said. "He won the regimental
marksmanship competition last year for pistol shooting, didn't you, Jalal?"

"Yes, sir," Private Jalal said, grinning. "Got a nice gold medal for it too."

"In other words, Capitaine, you and your men are under arrest."

Pinard didn't move, his eye on Jalal's pistol.

"We were promised assistance—" he began, but stopped himself. The
deal had been impossible, a cheat from the beginning. Things might have
worked out differently with cash in hand, but the absence of cash gave
people too much time to think about their integrity. He wondered now if
Major Rabani would have felt such outrage with his pockets stuffed full of
euros, but there was no time to answer: Pinard felt a breeze on his back and
the tent flap swept aside and a dozen Moroccan soldiers entered, rifles in
hand, wearing Kevlar vests.

"You and your Legionnaires will be taken to Fez," Major Rabani explained, his voice cold. "There you will become witnesses in the minister's
trial for high treason. Accepting bribes is a crime. Soliciting any such bribes
is also a crime. Attempting to corrupt a Moroccan official is a crime. Allowing operatives of a foreign government to pursue covert action in the kingdom of Morocco is more than a crime—it's an outrage to be dealt with as
severely as possible by the magistrates. I can't say exactly what will happen
to you and your men, but I can promise you will spend a long time in prison,
many years, before the French government finally gets you out. Maybe you
won't survive that long; I admit conditions in our prisons are not ideal. But
before you condemn my actions, consider this—what would your people do
if they discovered a covert team of Moroccan mercenaries on the loose in
France?"

Pinard could see the major's point, but didn't give the bastard the satisfaction of a response. The Moroccan soldiers formed a tight circle around him and escorted him out into the night.

7.

A l Bab, Gateway to the Age of the Hidden Imam, He Who Dispenses Justice to the Unjustified, Thirteenth Eye of God, Beekeeper to the Hive of Paradise, etc. etc., lay on his back on a futon covered with a plush Narguiz carpet in the secret sex room of the pink cinder block bungalow that was his Holy See, getting a blow job from one of two skinny, naked young women, their brown skin pricked out with bee stings. Still wearing his voluminous djellah, its skirts coyly thrown over his head, the prophet revealed his modest package and fat, hairy white legs and the soft pink bottoms of his feet, hennaed to the ankles, which gave the effect of a pair of cheap Italian socks.

The other young woman kneeling above the two on the futon, her eyes wide with horror or lust or both, fanned the lurid action with a paper fan made to resemble a large tropical leaf. A red lightbulb covered with a shade confabulated out of another paper leaf added a further note of bordello depravity. The only missing elements, it seemed, were fuzzy velvet wall coverings and mirrors on the ceiling.

Smith pressed himself flat against the outside rear wall of the bungalow, next to a small window. He registered the scene inside with a single scalding glance, suppressing a mixture of disgust and vertigo. A little to the left, no more than an arm's length away, the terrain abruptly dropped two thousand feet. Al Bab's bungalow was perched on the edge of this precipice. From the village side one had the impression that the bungalow's western facade opened only onto empty air. This was not quite true. A goat track, no more than thirty inches wide, twisted up the cliff face from below, leading to this unguarded metal door at the back of the house that was the door to Al Bab's private playroom. By this route women and girls from the village came and went, serving their prophet's earthly needs—a secret known only to a few of the Gateway's closest lieutenants and the entire female Marabout population.

"Not a pretty sight," Smith whispered, grimacing. "Asshole's got three girls in there with him."

"One of them is my sister." Alia frowned. "I have been asked to join these unpleasant activities, but I have not."

"Don't," Smith said.

"Those who join are given extra food, warm clothes. You must not judge."

Smith nodded sadly. He understood. Men sought power for many reasons, all of them having to do with getting more sex than the next guy. Women went along with powerful men for the candy bars and nylons and jewels and summer villas on the Riviera, all of which might translate, just maybe, into an edge for their offspring, genetically speaking. It was downright Darwinian and certainly uncomfortable from an ethical standpoint and yet a part of the very weave. But where were those disinterested individuals, the selfless, the incorruptible, those heroes and patriots and reformers who did what they did with no thought for the excellent blow jobs they would receive or the shiny nylons they would wear at the end of their travails? All betrayed by the relentless dictates of evolution, caught in the entangling strands of their DNA like shrimp in the tentacles of a squid.

"What are we waiting for, Milquetoast?" Phillipe crawled up the path behind them, out of the shadows, on his hands and knees. His patchy balding scalp shone dangerously in the reflected red light of the hidden room. He was still unclothed but wore his ribs, starkly visible beneath a thin, yellowing layer of skin, like the armor of Don Quixote, whom he now resembled.

"Stay down!" Smith whispered. "You're a walking lightbulb." Suddenly, he couldn't stop the trembling of his hands upon the FAMAS assault rifle.

"Calm yourself," Phillipe said. " 'Courage is a virtue essential to the character of the happy man.' I quote now from La Rochefoucauld."

Smith put a finger over his lips and drew back to the window:

Al Bab was now in the process of struggling out of his djellah, ready for some flesh-on-flesh action. The plush white mound of his belly emerged first, his tiny erection sticking up from beneath his ample thighs, then his face— round, babyish, pale except for the hennaed square around his eyes, which resembled the mask on a raccoon. His features were set very close in a large, round Charlie Brown head. What an ugly fuck, Smith thought, like a fat albino seal! But that face! It was the face of the fat kid on the playground, a spoiled middle-class science nerd kind of a kid, prodigiously clever but socially limited. Someone who secretly felt entitled to all the riches and all the beautiful women of the world, but at the same time suspected himself entirely unworthy of the smallest crumb. Who hated himself for his desires and for the darker desires that fed his desires. He was, Smith saw immediately, some-one he knew well: an American!

He gestured and Alia drew close, her eyes large and sad.

"Now's the time," Smith said.

"I do this because I love you," she whispered. "And because I love the music you sing. Not just because you will take me to Milan someday and buy me beautiful clothes."

"You saved my life," Smith said. "Get yourself to Dahkla. Can you do that?"

"Dahkla is far away," the girl said.

"But not that far," Smith said. "Go to MINURSO command. Tell them what happened, request refugee status. They have to give it to you, it's in the mandate. I will meet you there in Dahkla if I survive this mess. I will take you to Milan."

"I'll do what you say." The girl nodded earnestly. "But first you must kill him. Promise me."

Smith nodded, and she thrust forward suddenly and pressed her chapped lips against his and held them there for a long moment, without moving—a clumsy adolescent kiss that nonetheless had fire and need behind it. Then she pushed him away and scratched at the door. Her blunt fingernails marked out a kind of password well known to the women within.

"God go with you," she whispered, a sob catching in her throat. And she turned and ran off into the darkness down the narrow trail, agile as a moun-tain goat. Smith watched her go. She was tough, hardened by life in the moun-tains; she might actually get to Dahkla. From there it was anyone's guess.

Presently, he heard rustlings, murmuring voices. The door scraped open, a shaft of light fanning into the night. He put his foot against the red metal and shoved hard and in the next second was inside the room, the barrel of his FAMAS pressed firmly against Al Bab's forehead. The two naked young women, startled or secretly pleased at the turn of events, didn't scream, didn't make a sound. They stood back motionless, watching.

"Get out," Smith said to them and they gathered their threadbare robes and exited.

Colonel de Noyer stepped inside and bolted the door and there they were, the three of them—the Legionnaires and the enemy himself, the Gate-way to the Age of the Hidden Imam. Smith looked down at him. The Gateway looked back up, flesh quivering, eyes rolling in fear, lips working but no sound coming out, his small erection instantly shriveled. Almost immediately there came a pounding on the door leading to the interior of the bungalow.

"Your pals better not come in here," Smith said in English. "Better let them know it now, you son of a bitch!"

Al Bab pretended he didn't understand. Sweat rolled from his forehead onto the pale paunch of his belly.

"Don't give me that me-no-sabe bullshit," Smith said. "I've seen your fucking Cap'n Crunch!" And he lifted the barrel from the pressure point and delivered a rattling blow to the Gateway's forehead.

"Ouch!" Al Bab cried. "Goddamn it! That hurt!"

Smith raised the rifle for another blow, but the Gateway shouted a few quick words in Hassaniya and the pounding ceased immediately. Only the play of shadows seen beneath the crack of the door indicated anything moved out there. It was liked being locked in a house in the jungle with wild animals prowling outside.

"Your plan won't work, whatever it is," Al Bab said. He spoke American English with a flat, annoying accent that Smith instantly identified as Californian.

"We'll see about that, asshole," Smith growled.

"I don't think you've thought it through—"

"Shut up!"

Smith tossed the FAMAS to the colonel, grabbed Al Bab by his greasy black hair, and dragged him across the room to a long, heavy table against the wall. On this stood the Gateway's public address system; a microphone and receiver and the tangle of many wires. Also a couple of Dell laptop computers, an ink jet printer, a mess of papers, unopened mail delivered to an address in Marrakesh, a box of 9mm ammunition and a long, sharp-looking knife. The piles of books scattered here and there in English, French, and Arabic included admiring studies of Islamic culture published by Harvard University Press, an Arabic-English-Berber dictionary, Howard Zinn's *A People's History of the United States*, and several works on apiary culture and global warming. On the wall to one side hung a framed photo of Che Guevara shaking hands with Gabriel García Márquez and a diploma from Brown University whose florid calligraphy listed Ralph T. Wade III as the recipient of a Bachelor of Arts degree awarded in 1997, which made him exactly Smith's age.

And stacked on a shelf above it all, a dozen unopened boxes of Cap'n Crunch.

"You like your cereal crunchy-sweet, don't you, you little shit?" Smith said as he tied the blubbery, naked man to the table leg, hands and feet as hard as he could, using the printer cable.

Al Bab responded with a painful grunting.

"Shut up!" Smith said. "Not a sound!" And he stumbled back to the futon, feeling dizzy and weak. Not enough food, too much adrenaline. He put his head in his hands and tried to think himself around this situation, but could only think he could use a plate of French toast, a pile of breakfast links, and a beer. When he looked up again, he saw that Phillipe had folded himself into the far corner, enveloped once again in the personal fog of his madness. No advice would be forthcoming from him, not for the near future. After a while, Smith got up and took the gun from the colonel's lap and brought it to bear once more on their new captive.

"O.K., Ralph," Smith said, through his teeth. "Confess!"

"How do you know my name?" Al Bab said, surprised. "Are you CIA?"

Smith jabbed the FAMAS toward the prophet's Brown diploma on the wall. "You're such a fucking idiot!"

"Oh, yeah," Ralph said.

"What's up with the Cap'n Crunch?"

The mysterious prophet known as the Gateway to the Age of the Hidden Imam and also, apparently, as Ralph T. Wade III, shrugged to the extent his bonds would allow:

"Tastes good? Reminds me of home? Listen, you think you could loosen these a little? My hands are falling asleep?" He had that annoying California tic, a kind of Valley Girl mannerism that turned statements into questions, that left the end of sentences floating belly-up like a fish in polluted water.

"Where do you get Cap'n Crunch out here in the desert, anyway?" Smith persisted. "The local Safeway?"

"Big care package from my mom a couple of times a year," Ralph said, trying to work his fingers and not succeeding. "We go over to Marrakesh to pick them up."

"What are these mountains called?"

"If I tell you, will you untie me a little?"

"If you don't tell me, I'll crack your skull—" Smith wielded the FAMAS again.

"The Gueltas," Ralph said hurriedly. "Officially SADR, but the SADR doesn't really exist, does it? This territory belongs to me now." He couldn't resist a self-satisfied smirk at this.

"How far is Marrakesh from here?"

"About seven or eight hundred miles. Rough country. We go by camel train to the border and take ATVs from there."

"Long way for a bowl of Cap'n Crunch."

"It's not all I eat, you know," Ralph said sullenly. "You probably still eat some junk from your childhood? Barbecued chips? Pop Tarts maybe? Moonpies? Ding-Dongs? What about Little Debbie?"

"They'd tear Little Debbie to pieces in the Foreign Legion," Smith growled—and it hit him at the mention of all this junk food that he was starving. So hungry he'd almost forgotten how to eat.

Presently, he grabbed a box of Cap'n Crunch off the shelf and found a bowl and a spoon and a paper carton of Parmalat. The first yellow sweet taste of the stuff did indeed remind him of home—brought back winter mornings in Montezuma with his sister and his parents at the kitchen table before school in the morning, before everything went sour and everyone died. All gone, a whole world gone. And it struck him how strange it was to be sitting here at the top of a mountain in the middle of the desert munching away at a bowl of Cap'n Crunch in the presence of a monster who had, without remorse, brought violent death to thousands. But he had learned by now not to marvel at the appalling strangeness of life. It was the other things—getting up, going to work, watching television, traffic lights, bank accounts, real estate, the rule of law. Normalcy. That was the surreal part.

8.

The flap tied open revealed two Moroccan soldiers standing at attention in full battle dress, Kalashnikovs at the ready. Six more stood guard around the tent, relieved every three hours by fresh troops. The rest of the demibrigade went about their business in the camp in the slanting yellow light of late afternoon. Some squatted over the latrine trench, chatting amiably among themselves as they did their business, their bobbing heads just visible over the nearest dune. Others smoked in front of the tents, or got busy making the evening meal out of packets of dehydrated soup and freeze-dried vegetables, peeling back the tinfoil coverings of RCIRs.

Just beyond the dune, at the northern edge of camp, an endless field of stones spread evenly to the horizon. Some stood so closely jammed together there wasn't more than a few centimeters of space between them. The stony plain reminded Szbeszdogy of the old Jewish cemetery in Budapest where he used to go to smoke pot back when he was an unruly and bewildered youth—so thickly planted with grave markers as to present a solid wall to the observer from the sidewalk along Nagy Street. Beyond the stones, in the blue, rose the line of snowy peaks Pinard now identified with certainty as the Algerian Gueltas.

The Legionnaires of Mission: SCORPIO, handcuffed back to back, to one another, and to the tent poles, stared longingly out the tent flap at the prospect of distant mountains. They hadn't been given anything more than a cup of weak tea in two days; had only been allowed to use the latrine trench once in that time, which was against Geneva Convention regulations governing prisoner access to toilets. They faced years of such maltreatment, incarcerated in some deep, underground dungeon in Marrakesh or Fez, the pawns of international politics. No help would come from the Legion; General le Breton had been clear about that. As far as France was concerned, Mission: SCORPIO didn't exist. Officially, they were rogue Legionnaires, acting without orders on their own behalf.

"How is it you always find yourself in such situations, Pinard?" Solas said bitterly.

"He's just lucky," Vladimirovitch said.

"That's enough," Pinard said, but this time his voice lacked conviction.

"First there's that crazy story about Blockhouse Nine," the Brazilian went on sourly. "Everyone in the Legion heard about that disaster. Who was it you lost there? Ah, yes, the Mongolian jerk-off artist from the 2e REP. Then we get trapped in the souk and have to blow our way out and voilà, we end up at the mercy of the Moroccans. And now here we are again!"

"Shut your face, Solas," Szbeszdogy said wearily. "It's not Pinard to blame, but the Legion. Who else would send six men to do the job of a battalion?"

"The question is not who?" Pinard muttered. "But why?"

Dessalines offered a mirthless snort. "Even I know the answer to that one," he said. "Same reason we joined up in the first place, eh, *les gars*?"

The answer, unspoken on all their lips, rang out like a funeral bell. Painted over the old artillery gate at Fort St. Jean in Marseilles was a quote from General Negrier, one of the Legion's dark heroes: *You have joined the*

Legion in order to die; I am sending you where you can die. You may already congratulate yourselves on no longer being alive.

The sun disappeared at last and the moon rose, thin as the filament of a lightbulb. The blistering heat of the desert dissipated instantly at dusk, leaving the Legionnaires shivering with cold, so cold no one could sleep, except Vladimirovitch. The big Russian snored placidly, his head slumped against Dessalines's shoulder, like a stranger on a bus.

"What if we could get out of these cuffs?" Szbeszdogy whispered at last. "Did anyone think about that?"

"No," Dessalines said. Then: "Can we?"

"So we get out," Solas said. "And we're shot to death by our Moroccan allies. Even if they miss, where are we? In the middle of a desert, without water, without food."

Pinard lifted his head. Drifting off for a moment, he'd seen wandering the borderland between sleep and wakefulness, a slim, elegant figure whose face would haunt him for the rest of his life. Then, to Szbeszdogy: "Well, Stefan, can you do it?"

"I'm not Houdini, but I've got my little pick tucked away"—the Hungarian indicated the pants seam of his jumpsuit. "Not going to be easy."

"They'll kill us," Babenco said. "They'll leave our carcasses to the desert. What can six do against sixty?"

"Think of Camerone."

"They all died at Camerone," Babenco said.

"Wrong." Pinard said. "Three survived."

"But which three?" Vladimirovitch sat up, suddenly awake. "That's the question."

"A Moroccan prison might give us a better chance," Babenco said. "We could tunnel our way out, bribe guards. The possibility of immediate death in this place makes a democracy out of us! I say we vote."

"Nothing makes a democracy out of the Legion," Pinard said. "But go ahead. I'll listen to opinions, this once."

Silence. Each one considered the possibility of escape, calculated the odds, reluctant to speak first. Before they could make up their minds, Pinard cleared his throat.

"Let me ask you assholes a simple question," he said. "What are we?"

"Legionnaires," Vladimirovitch responded automatically.

"Exactly," Pinard said. "And the enemy?"

"Moroccans," Babenco said.

"Correct again," Pinard said. "And one Legionnaire is worth twenty of those bastards, so I consider them outnumbered, not us."

"Very nice!" Solas interjected. "It's a great comfort to know we'll die outnumbering the enemy."

"Some of us will die," Pinard said. "Maybe we'll all die. But won't we die, in any event, on the last day of our lives? Better to die now as a Legionnaire facing the enemy. Or do you really want to rot for years in some rat-infested Moroccan sewer? So what if we escape, or survive until France buys us back for the price of a couple of used Mirage jets. What's the best that can happen then? Do you really want to wind up a miserable old bastard at the Legion farm in Puyloubier and die in a hospital with feeding tubes sticking out of your guts and only a gay male nurse to sit by your bedside? I for one am glad I'm not back in Aubagne right now, safely marching up and down the parade ground. I say to hell with all of it! Life is for cowards. Come now, oh death!"

The men were silent following this little speech, but it was clear they had accepted Pinard's way, whatever that might be. After a long moment, Szbeszdogy said, softly, "*Bravo, Pinard. Vous êtes Valéry!*"

"What? Who's this Valéry?"

"A French poet."

Pinard suddenly remembered Louise's comment to the same effect on the beach that first day and the memory caused him pain. "Don't insult me," he said harshly. "I'm no poet. I'm the opposite thing."

"Ah!" The Hungarian grinned. "Then you're a man of action! But with you action is in its own way a kind of poetry."

"Fuck off, Szbeszdogy. Now, can you get to that pick?"

"I'll need my hands. Next time they take us out to the latrine."

"*Bien,*" Pinard said. "We are all in agreement. But understand, consensus is not the same thing as democracy. Well, Solas, any last words?"

The Brazilian had none and hid his face in the shadows. For the first time in many years, since those terrible days of running from machete-wielding police in the stinking, unpaved favelas of Rio, he was afraid.

9.

Marabout fighters appeared at the little square of window overlooking the ravine. Smith sent a couple of 5.56 rounds crashing in their direction and they dropped out of sight. But they weren't gone: Marabout fighters at the window, against the door, pressed around the bungalow in an ever-tightening noose. So close, Smith imagined he could hear their hearts beating through the cinder block and plaster. One rush would do it—only a question of when that rush would come. They only needed the right moment and a single, carefully placed round. Meanwhile, he held them all at bay with the barrel of his FAMAS jammed for hours at a time into the ear of the Mullah of Mullahs, Al Bab, the Gateway to the etc., Ralph T. Wade III.

This stalemate persisted for a day and a night and a day, then began to wobble, gently, like a skyscraper in an earthquake.

Colonel de Noyer still crouched without moving in his corner, sleepless, immobile, lost to reason, unable to find his way back out of the fog—a vague, cloudy landscape his soul inhabited no doubt scored by Satie's haunting *Messe des Pauvres*. Maybe Phillipe was finally gone for good this time. Smith craved sleep, needed a backup. Damn you, Phillipe! He screamed, spit in the man's face, pummelled him. Nothing. Desperate to keep awake, Smith clawed at the flesh of his arms until it bled, sang at the top of his voice, running the verses of a half-dozen great American songbook standards into a crazy, discordant musical collage: "You've got me in between the devil and deep blue sea. I've got music, I've got rhythm, I've got my gal, who could ask for anything more? This is the story of a very unfortunate colored man who got 'rested down in old Hong Kong. Now when I hear people curse the chance that was wasted, I know but too well what they mean. It was just one of those things, one of those crazy flings. Who could ask for anything more!"

Meanwhile, Ralph T. Wade III snoozed, snoring comfortably despite the painful nature of his bondage to the computer table. Smith, delirious with exhaustion at last, dropped off for ten minutes around noon on the morning of the third day. Waking up with a gasp, he surprised three Marabout killers already in the room, creeping toward him, muffled in their blue djellahs. Perhaps they had wafted under the crack of the door like genies out of a bottle. Panicking, Smith pushed the barrel of his rifle as far into the ear of the Gateway as it would go without splitting the man's skull.

"I die, he dies," Smith shouted. "Make your move!"

But the Gateway uttered a single word and his minions backed out, closing the door quietly behind them.

"How long you think you can keep it up, dude?" he said to Smith.

"Fuck you," Smith said halfheartedly.

Ralph shook his head. "You're not going to make it, my friend."

"And you're a dead asshole."

"Kill me now, get it over with?"

"I will," Smith muttered. "Don't rush me."

But Smith couldn't say what he was waiting for exactly. Then it occurred to him, an idea born out of delirium and lack of sleep: He was waiting for the Legion to appear over the crest of the hill like the cavalry in a Western. But how would they know where to find him? He stood up in a kind of daze, switched on the PA system, and took the microphone in his hand.

"*À moi la Légion!*" he called into the emptiness of the mountains. "*À moi la Légion!*"

Again and again for the next couple of hours. This was the Legionnaire's famous distress call—to me, the Legion! To me! Four words echoing down the years since the rainy day they mustered for first inspection on the Champs de Mars in 1831—the cry of any outnumbered Legionnaire in any tight spot around the globe for the last one hundred and seventy five years: drunk and alone in a cutthroat saloon in Algiers in 1875 with just a broken knife against fifty pissed-off Spahis; the last survivor of an outgunned garrison cut off in the heart of the Rif in 1902; lost in the weird primordial forests of Madagascar in 1890, or the malarial swamps of Cochin China in 1900. There he was, our Legionnaire, pinned down beneath a murderous barrage at the Somme in 1917 with twenty thousand casualties in a single afternoon; there he was at Bir Hakim in 1942 fighting former comrades gone over to Vichy; at Dien Bien Phu in 1954, the wily Viet Minh creeping along hidden trails through the bush, each soldier bearing on his back an artillery shell aimed directly at the Legion's beating heart.

"You're going nuts, all right," Ralph said, chuckling as Smith switched off the microphone.

"Maybe," Smith admitted.

"Like, who's going to hear you all the way up here?"

"I don't know," Smith said. "But I've got to keep myself awake somehow."

"Face it, you're going to fall asleep sooner or later."

"No. Keep talking. Say something."

"No."

"Talk or I kick your teeth in!"

"What do you want me to say?"

"What's the T. stand for?"

"Theodore."

"Ralph Theodore Wade. The Third."

"That's right."

"Enlighten me, Ralph."

"No."

"How did it all happen?"

"What?"

"How did you go from Cap'n Crunch to . . . ?"

Smith made a wild gesture, encompassing the mountain hideout, stinging bees, pointless slaughter. And the Marabout hordes waiting patiently
just the other side of the metal door for their best chance to kill him and cut
off his head.

10.

In the end, the best plan was to have no plan at all. At a signal from Capitaine Pinard just before moonrise, the Legionnaires, freed from their cuffs,
exploded from the tent and into the darkened camp like snakes out of a
bag.

Solas cut a slash in the back of the tent with his razor blade, threw himself through this aperture, and disappeared into the darkness. Pinard and
Szbeszdogy went together out the front and vaulted over the backs of the
sentries as the latter fumbled with their Kalashnikovs. Babenco, Dessalines,
and the Russian, howling like Indians, quickly followed Solas, but as they
rounded the southwestern corner of the tent were instantly cut down by a
12.7 Browning hidden under a heap of camouflage netting. Solas, out of
blind favela instinct, had gone the other way. Suddenly, there remained only
three, as at Camerone.

Pinard and Szbeszdogy reached the perimeter wire, round after round
chopping into the sand all around them, the machine gun biting at the heels
of their boots. They vaulted over this low divide and scrambled into the
field of stones as the entire personnel of the Moroccan demibrigade emerged
and began firing their weapons into the night. Bullets went flying everywhere,
exploding into the air, into the desert, aimed at nothing in particular. This
random firing went on for the next ten minutes, the Moroccans expending
entire magazines of ammunition to no effect: Safely wedged between boulder

and rock, heads down beneath the storm of steel, Pinard and Szbeszdogy were hit by nothing more deadly than a few stone chips. At last, the guns fell silent. Dense clouds of smoke, a mixture of propellant gas and cordite, hung in the dry, cold desert air.

Major Rabani appeared from out of the smoke, a resplendent figure, like a god of the desert, sleek and muscular, wrapped in a beautiful robe of figured silk. A gleaming new Kalashnikov, its hardware all gleaming chrome, its stock inlaid with the Moroccan star in silver filigree, dangled from his shoulder by a patent leather strap. He stood just the other side of the wire, shaking his fist and bellowing incoherently as the shot-up corpses of three dead Legionnaires were dragged out into the open, not ten meters from where Pinard and Szbeszdogy were hiding.

"Who did they get?" Szbeszdogy whispered. "Can you see?"

"Can't make out," Pinard replied. "Doesn't matter. Now they're the honored dead."

"Nicely put," Szbeszdogy said. "You are a poet."

"Go to hell," Pinard said.

The wind shifted. Major Rabani's words wafted in their direction like an evil smell.

"What do you think of your Legion now, Frenchmen!" he shouted. "We Moroccans have fought you many times and we have beaten you many times! When we catch you we will bury you to your dirty necks in sand and I will personally piss on you as you die! Like this! Like this! Watch me now!"

He opened his robe and pulled down his silk pantaloons and began to relieve himself on the bodies of Babenco, Vladimirovitch, and Dessalines.

At the sight of this outrage, Pinard felt a scalding heat behind his eyes. Something broke loose inside, bare wires crossed, releasing an electric charge, a surge of pure, violent energy, unusual in a Canadian. Pinard's hand found a rock, round and perfectly balanced for throwing. It fit exactly into the warm scoop of his palm. Suddenly, without thinking, he rushed forward, winding up like a pitcher on the mound. He reversed abruptly a meter or two short of the wire and hurled the rock with all his might. The major turned just then, and as he turned the rock, spinning end over end, caught him directly between the eyes. Pinard heard a thick, ugly, cracking sound and the the major's eyes rolled back and he dropped face-first into the sand, dead. Moroccan troops peered through the gunpowder haze, not quite sure what had just happened. Pinard jumped back over the wire and grabbed up the major's fancy chrome Kalashnikov, turned it on them, and squeezed out the full magazine. The Moroccans scattered in disarray into the shadows at this unexpected attack or fell down, dead.

"Surrender!" Pinard screamed between bursts. "I am Pinard of the Legion! Surrender!"

At that moment, Solas appeared from the opposite direction, the hidden Moroccan 12.7 wrenched from its tripod and its nest of camouflage and in his hands. He opened up with this formidable weapon, spraying the tents, the trucks, the supply dump, cutting the tents to shreds with the big, flaming shells. He fired until the ammunition ran dry, as the Moroccans had done earlier, but without their lack of restraint and in a cold, controlled manner. This very control is what makes the best assassins, for death is a cold business.

When Solas stopped firing, Pinard heard the wind and the sound of moaning. The open space between the tents was now strewn with the bodies of at least a dozen Moroccans—among them all three officers and all but one of the non-coms. They had gone to join Dessalines, Babenco, and Vladimirovitch in that blood-drenched paradise reserved for men who die on the battlefield. Pinard shouldered the Kalashnikov and stepped up, hands in his pockets. He might have been out for an evening stroll.

"Report, Caporal-chef."

Solas dropped the big Browning, red-hot from firing, his fingers burned. Sweat had stained his jumpsuit black.

"The rest ran off," he managed, gasping. "Out there somewhere—"

Pinard turned to face the field of stones and rubble stretching off to the horizon where the Gueltas rose against the fading dark.

"Soldiers of Morocco!" Pinard called, cupping his hands. "You won't survive in this desert with nothing. You'll be dead from lack of water two hours after sunrise. Submit yourselves to my authority and live!"

A minute passed quietly. Pinard put his hands back in his pockets. Then something waved from among the stones, a small scrap of white cloth.

11.

Men locked up at close quarters for more than twenty-four hours will either strangle one another or get to explaining themselves.

Smith and Ralph T. Wade III were, after all, Americans of roughly the same age who had, each in his own way, shared the experience of a culture in decline. Ralph, his hands bound tightly so as to prevent him from strangling anyone, began instead, at Smith's insistent prodding, to explain himself. He spoke in great, gusty bursts—sometimes in a kind of half rhyme and with the intensity of a televangelist preaching to a nation of idiots. Always, he was utterly certain of his own righteousness.

The best lack all conviction, Smith thought, listening, while the worst are full of passionate intensity. Ralph Wade, surely among the worst, ranted passionately—the perfect demagogue—his opinions all over the place, completely outrageous, often contradictory, but never unalloyed by a sad grain or two of truth.

He was from Marin County, California, the sole offspring of wealthy, long-divorced parents: His father, once a talented aerospace engineer at Lockheed Martin with many lucrative patents to his credit, turned to alcohol and pot when his wife left him; later, sober but crazy, he became a disciple of the neo-Hindu guru Rathan Ram, and bought that charlatan a mountaintop retreat outside of Seattle. His mother was briefly a snippy, disgruntled housewife, then, successively, an animal rights activist, Napa Valley vintner, meditation coach, cocaine addict, big wave surfer, radical lesbian. After a string of abusive husbands and a variety of inadequate boyfriends—some far too needy, others much too self-possessed—she eventually fell in love with and married a plain, forceful woman twenty years younger than herself with whom she now operated a successful whole-grain bakery in Carmel.

"At least Mom's happy now," Ralph said. "I mean with Amy. She deserves it after what she's been through. What about your parents?"

"Dead," Smith said. "Both dead."

"What did your dad do?"

"U.S. mail, Montezuma, Iowa. But we're talking about you."

"Whatever, dude." Ralph shrugged. "I'm just not that interesting."

"We were talking about your father . . ."

"Yeah. Well, one of my dad's first jobs was designing some gadget for the Apollo mission that went to the moon. That seems like it, right? The high watermark. Hard to believe we actually put a man on the moon."

Smith agreed.

"Hey, how about you loosen these cords a little? My ankles—"

"Can't do it," Smith said curtly. "You'll try to escape, I'll have to shoot you. And shooting you at this point is like shooting myself. Work your fingers, your toes. Maybe that will help."

Ralph worked away for a while, shifted himself uncomfortably, continued to talk: The Marabout uprising began as an undergraduate term paper written at Brown in 1995, for a seminar called "The Great Satan's Hungry: The West Eats the Rest." This seminar was taught by Abu al-Sani, the controversial academic, ex–Weather Underground, and convert to Islam. Al-Sani, formerly an upper-middle class Protestant New Jerseyite named Fred Cook, was then known fondly to his Brown students as Professor Jihad.

"Professor Jihad had the most incredible dreadlocks," Ralph said. "Longest dreads I ever saw on a white man, I mean down to his knees. And my God he stank, never used deodorant or soap. Thought deodorant and soap was, like, a wickedly ingenious capitalist conspiracy to sell deodorant and soap."

Smith grinned at this. "Maybe it is."

"It was from Professor Jihad that I came to understand, among other things, the power of smell," Ralph continued. "Americans take too many showers, we divert entire rivers for the purpose, we've got a million scrubbing bubbles and all that crap, but it doesn't stop the dirt from sticking to your skin every day, from oozing out of your pores. Filth is power, dude! The powerful people in the next hundred years will be the people who can live without the scrubbing bubbles, without antibiotics and plastic surgery, and round-the-clock access to, like, sushi and Diet Coke. Who can live on nothing, on dirt in the desert, like my beautiful Marabouts right here on this mountaintop."

"Maybe your beautiful Marabouts *can* live here," Smith retorted, "but they don't really want to. They'd rather be in Milan. They told me so."

Ralph shook his head. "You obviously don't understand. You're blinded by the whole narrow bourgeois ethic thing."

True, Smith didn't understand. He was addicted to order, though he never would have put it this way. A lover of neat Midwestern streets intersecting at right angles in a spotless Midwestern town, of musical notes arranged in a grid on a page alongside other musical notes that added up to an aria, a symphony, an opera. *Guys and Dolls.* All this was sheer perversity to Ralph. Chaos, he insisted, was the true mode of the universe, anarchy the only viable political system.

"Professor Jihad opened my eyes!" he exclaimed, still fired by the memory. "The man showed me just how repressed and miserable we are in America— and, because misery begets evil, how completely evil! We try to control nature with our dams and our state highway systems and our CAT scans and our erectile disfunction drugs, but a hurricane comes and blows everything away and New Orleans floods and the housing market collapses and every inbred redneck in fly-over country is running a meth lab and we just can't get it up anymore, our Viagra isn't working, and we realize suddenly that we can't fucking control anything, not one bit, not even our bowel movements. We realize that control is an illusion of an illusion and that really, really pisses us off, and worse, scares the absolute shit out of us. What did Thoreau say? 'You think you're riding on the railroad, but, hey, shithead, the railroad's riding on you!' So yeah, the railroad's riding our ass, and we're on massive doses of an- tidepressants just to carry on with the old day-to-day, just to get to, like, Tar- get and back without slitting our own throats. Misery is the air we breathe, dude! But there comes a point we've just got to unload or explode, and so we export our misery to the whole fucking world and end up destroying beautiful indigenous cultures in, like, Papua New Guinea, with our Big Macs and our cell phones and our iPods, with our Batman and Spider-Man and widescreen digital, hi-def flatscreen TVs. Well fuck you and your Batman too! And dude, absolutely do not dare breathe a word about all the fucking porn you're watch- ing, blasting like a gusher full of shit and piss and cum out of every computer screen in America! Like 75 percent of all traffic on the Internet is porn, you know that right?"

"We've already been through the porn thing." Smith sighed. "Your point?"

"My point? Like, everyone's pornified, absolutely everyone, even the little kids! Twelve-year-old girls shoot videos of each other getting off and make a fortune selling their snatch on eBay to good old pedophile U.S.A. Profes- sor Jihad was a genius about all this stuff, just the complete and utter badness of bad America. He saw it coming years ago, way before YouTube, rolling down on us like an avalanche of shit! Before I took his seminar, I used to think like you, dude. I actually believed we lived in a pretty good country, that America was a pretty good place. Some problems, yeah, some homeless- ness and inequality and all that, but hey, steadily getting better, steadily better. Man, what a crock! A nightmare built on the backs of slaves and butchered Indians and it's only gotten worse in three hundred years. The story of America is the story of mass murder and slavery!"

"Wrong!" Smith interrupted hotly. "The story of America is the story of more and more rights accruing to more and more people."

"You're an optimist, all right. Your glass is half full of bullshit!"

On and on, he went. The picture of the world Ralph drew was an exact negative version of the one Smith saw. A dark mirror image of the things Smith had been taught were good and true from childhood, which were actually, according to Ralph, false and bad. Ralph had grown up in his father's house overawed by the idea of the moon walk and his father's role in it; Professor Jihad made him face the bitter truth hiding behind this lie: The moon walk was just another massive crime. An oppressive act of colonialist trespass perpetrated upon the pristine, ash-gray dust of the moon.

After a while, Smith wanted to put a gag in the prophet's mouth, could have, but didn't. The outrage he felt at Ralph's words was keeping him tense and awake.

"Enough about the fucking moon walk," Smith interrupted at one point, nearly shouting. "That's obfuscation! Let me hear about your tribe of fucking bee-loving murderers! Why?"

Ralph acquiesced. And seemed to enjoy talking about what he saw as his life's great work, sprouted from a seedling planted in Jihad's seminar fifteen years ago. The great man had urged all his disciples to become practicing revolutionaries, to reject progressive liberalism as a false doctrine and to live like those hippie saints who had been his comrades in the Weather Underground. Urged them to throw bombs of their own making at "the Bad America, beneath the western sky." Ralph chanted this last bit, smiling. "Not his exact words, actually a tune by Gun Club, remember them? But you get the idea."

Professor Jihad's quirky brand of New Age Islam—hopped-up with the odd dose or two of old-fashioned Puritanism and wired together with strands of New Age pseudoscience—was one such bomb: Its strict behavioral codes, its emphasis on the enforced modesty of women and on the necessity of violence to achieve holy ends were the very antithesis to the corrupting ideals of personal liberty and pursuit of happiness enshrined in the U.S. Constitution. Ralph's chance to act out Jihad's startling, contradictory ideologies came after he left Brown, and matriculated as a graduate student at the New School in Manhattan.

"I met a bunch of other righteous dudes at the New School," Ralph said. "A few of them Jihad's kids. We got together and pooled the resources of our trust funds to form an arts-based activist organization with cells in Greenpoint, Brooklyn; Madison, Wisconsin; and Berkeley. Our mission statement at that time was a little vague. We were trying to subvert the consumerist-fake-Christian-pornified-Western-bullshit U.S.-despotic-regime-nation through agitprop street theater, free seminars on how bad everything was, and performance art. One year we recruited at Burning Man and got matching funds from the NEA!

"We did have a few successes in those days—remember that art student who blew up mailboxes in the shape of a smiley face all over the Midwest? One of us! Remember John Walker Lindh? A fellow traveler! But 9/11 really put the lie to all that artsy crap and showed us the true way. Street theater and blowing up mailboxes was nothing compared to the Twin Towers coming down in a massive toxic cloud of burning investment bankers! If only we'd thought of that first! What a brilliant stroke! So we decided to trade in the soft stuff for something new and massive. We would out-terror the terrorists and use the excellent tools of modern culture—science, advertising, marketing—to achieve our political goals, which aimed at the destruction of the very things they were a product of. Then the fucking Patriot Act came along and things got a little oppressive for us. Suddenly, the FBI was reading our e-mails, tapping our phones. So we dissolved our homegrown cells and formed an NGO and decided to focus our resources overseas.

"One of our international studies guys came up with the Western Sahara, a country without a government, always teetering on the edge of anarchy. Great place to grow a terrorist organization from scratch like sea monkeys in a jar! We quietly moved into the refugee camps out here, first Awsard, then the others. We started slowly, learning the language, devising an ideology, a brand-new religion, blending folk stories and myth and the Koran and just some totally made-up shit and then preaching it to the people with absolute sincerity. It's a fact that desperate people will believe anything that promises them a way out—"

"Tell me about the bees," Smith interrupted again.

"The bees are excellent, don't you think?" Ralph grinned. "Our consultant at Ogilvie in New York gets the credit for that one. Every great belief system needs a visual symbol, he said, something that can be scratched into the dirt with a few quick strokes. Bees because they sting, you know, because they hurt and no one forgets a bee sting, and because raising bees is good for the environment. We're very green, you know. And because bees produce honey, which is an excellent protein that indigenous people can eat to survive."

"Except your bees don't make honey at all," Smith said. "All they do is sting!"

"My bad," the Gateway admitted. "We picked the wrong species, you can't be all right all the time. So once we had our bees, we invented a myth to go along with them, some bullshit about a messianic figure called Al Bab—Gateway to the Age of the Hidden Iman, right?—being asleep in a cave for a thousand years, then there's a swarm of bees sent by Allah to sting him awake, to wake his ass up to get busy saving the world. And man, what a beautiful synergy! We had our initiation rites. Every religion's got to have an initiation. You know, baptism, circumcision, whatever? Like show me the madman who dreamed up slicing the foreskin off some poor little kid's dick so he'll be more pleasing to God! Makes our bees seem like an eminently reasonable alternative."

"What about cutting off people's heads?"

"That was my idea," Ralph said, pride in his voice. "Heads are very primal. Like the Aztecs and that wall of a million skulls Cortés saw when he marched into the Valley of Mexico. And the Dyaks riding around on motor scooters in Borneo a couple of years back slashing off people's heads like cantaloupes left and right. And shrunken heads in the Amazon, and headhunters in New Guinea, you know, stuff like that. Puts a chill right up your spine. Throw a couple of severed heads into any mix and you've got what? Fucking absolute beautiful terror!"

Smith didn't want to listen anymore. Disgust and horror rose up like bile. "Shut up, you sick fuck!" he shouted. "Just shut up!"

"Face reality, dude," Ralph said, sounding hurt. "The planet's overcrowded with people, literally crumbling under the weight of billions of feet, billions of tons of human shit. The human footprint's got to be smaller. What did Trotsky say? The revolution must be watered with blood!"

"*Non*, Robespierre said that . . ." It was Phillipe's voice, sounding dry and dusty, as if it came from beyond the tomb.

Smith spun around to see his commanding officer standing there, more or less steady on his feet, lucidity once again shining from his watery blue eyes.

"You will permit me, Milquetoast," Phillipe said. He took the FAMAS rifle from Smith's hands and flipped up the stubby bayonet affixed to the stock.

"Do you remember a little man named Hanz Milhauz?" he said to Ralph. His tone, though conversational, calm, contained an explicit threat.

Ralph blinked up at him and began to tremble.

"Ah, I see." The colonel nodded. "You don't remember him. But then, you probably never knew his name. You murdered him at the Awsard camp six years ago. You cut off his head and subjected his body to indignities. Does this sound familiar to you?"

"If you kill me now, you won't"—Ralph's voice crackled with fear—"won't get out of here. Think about that?"

"Something very important is missing," the colonel said, his eyes carefully searching Ralph's face. "Not even Hitler or Stalin could murder so many innocent people simply for a few stupid, abstract ideas. Hitler genuinely hated Jews. This was not an abstract idea with him. He hated them personally, each and every one. Just as Stalin hated the kulaks because he envied them their beautiful farms and plump, pretty wives. All politics is personal, don't you agree?"

A tear squeezed out of Ralph's close-set eyes and rolled down his round cheek.

"I offer you here a last chance to explain yourself," Phillipe said gently. "Try again, please."

"I have been explaining," Ralph said. "You weren't listening."

"I heard every word," Phillipe said. "You weren't explaining. You were preaching to a fool. And I'm afraid Legionnaire Milquetoast here is a fool, otherwise he wouldn't be in this predicament. Try again. Speak to me. One man to another."

Ralph Wade moved his lips desperately, but this time no words came out.

"As I suspected." The colonel nodded. "You do not have a genuine personal life. You're not really a human being, only a sack full of foul air. Through some terrible oversight you were born without a soul. *Hélas*, there is only one thing to do with such an abomination—"

Smith lunged, not fast enough. The colonel stabbed down hard with the bayonet and buried it to the stock deep in the stony heart of the Gateway to the Age of the Hidden Imam, once known as Ralph T. Wade III, who coughed painfully, a bright mouthful of blood spilling down his bare chest, and died.

Smith began to weep. From exhaustion, from fear. It was dark now. With the morning light the Marabouts outside would get a good look into the room and see their precious Al Bab lying there dead.

"When you meet the devil you must not hesitate, you must kill him," Phillipe said, sounding perfectly reasonable. "I swore I would claim my revenge for the murder of poor Milhauz and now I have. But to finish the job I must cut off his head."

Smith watched as the colonel began sawing away with the blunt edge of the bayonet, ill suited for such a purpose. It was, after all, a stabbing weapon. They would be clawed apart for this, eviscerated by the blunt fingers of an enraged Marabout mob, their lifeless carcasses fed to those horrible stinging bees. But soon, Smith's fear gave way to another sensation. He felt the relief of the traveler who at last comes within sight of the friendly porch of his own house after many hard years on the road. And now, overwhelmed by weariness, he lay back on the futon and fell instantly asleep.

12.

In the morning, they counted the bodies. Legionnaires Dessalines, Babenco, Vladimirovitch, and twenty-two Moroccans, all laid out side by side, equals in death. A Legion victory but a very costly one—casualty rate, 50 percent. Corpses decompose rapidly in the desert heat; in some cases, gases trapped in the viscera can lead to the most gruesome explosions. Immediate burial is a necessity.

Solas, still toting the large caliber Browning, supervised the burial detail, one long narrow grave for everyone. The surviving twenty-seven Moroccans, now prisoners of the Legion, worked with their entrenching tools for two hours as the sun rose over the desert. When they were done, Sergeant Ladjal and the rest rolled out their mats and prayed for their dead comrades in the first flush of heat.

Pinard ordered the mass grave to be filled without further ceremony, but Szbeszdogy intervened.

"You've got to say something, Capitaine," he insisted. "The Moroccans have their prayers. We need a few words for our dead."

Pinard agreed reluctantly. He stepped up on the mound of displaced sand and took off his borrowed Moroccan cap. The men, both Moroccans and Legionnaires, squinted up at him.

"I can't tell you I knew these three all that well," Pinard said. "Dessalines was a big brute, tough but superstitious as a woman. Babenco—who knows?—the man never said much of anything, but he was from Uruguay, which I understand is a quiet sort of place. And Vladimirovitch, thick-skulled and dumb as an ox. I didn't like them and they didn't like me. But none of that matters now. They are at last, officially, heroes. Their names will be inscribed on the black walls of the Legion crypt in Aubagne along with the names of forty thousand others, men from every nation in the world and every profession and all walks of life. Princes, doctors, chimney sweeps, artists, drunks, marshals of France. I don't know if there's a god and frankly, I don't care. But if there is, for these three, it's the God of Battles. So to this fierce and pugnacious being I say receive the souls of Dessalines, Babenco, Vladimirovitch. They were Legionnaires: They did their duty and are dead. Now bury them."

Pinard stepped down off the mound and put his cap back on and the Moroccans went to work filling the grave.

"See what I mean?" The Hungarian chuckled. "One would think you'd spent your whole life shut up in a library."

"Shut up, Szbeszdogy."

"In all seriousness," Szbeszdogy said. "You have a kind of natural elo-quence. If poetry displeases you, what about politics?"

"Don't insult me!"

A delegation of the Moroccans, led by Sergeant Ladjal, approached. Solas stood guard warily, 50-caliber rounds ready in the breech.

"A word, your honor," Sergeant Ladjal said in French. He bowed deeply, nearly bending himself in two at the waist, then squatted in the sand.

"*Alors?*" Pinard said, looming over him.

"What do you plan to do with us?"

Pinard thought about this for a moment. "Nothing," he said. "We'll take some supplies and a truck and your weapons and you're free to go back to Laayoune with the rest."

The sergeant nodded thoughtfully. "It is as I feared," he said. "I beg you not to do this thing."

"I don't understand," Pinard said, baffled. "You wish to remain our pris-oners?"

"Yes, of course."

"Why?"

"The major was a cruel man," Sergeant Ladjal said. "He was a bad officer and interested only in his own comforts. So it doesn't bother us that you killed him. But if we return to Morocco with our commanding officer dead and our weapons confiscated, and you and your men escaped, it will go very badly for us. I will certainly be shot for cowardice, as will the two surviving corporals. The other men will be thrown into a terrible prison for a very long time. We are not very good soldiers, but soldiers are only as good as their officers allow them to be. We could become very fine soldiers indeed and you, monsieur, seem like a very fine officer. And so, my men and myself, we would like to volunteer with the Foreign Legion."

"I see." Pinard nodded, suppressing an urge toward hilarity. But Szbeszdogy, lacking Pinard's naturally restrained temperament, broke out laughing.

"This is not a joke," Sergeant Ladjal insisted, wagging his head sourly. "Please understand we do not come to you with nothing. Our pockets are full, so to speak—we have something to trade. Some very valuable information."

Szbeszdogy stopped laughing.

"Yes?" Pinard said.

"The Marabout hive, their citadel is well known to us"—Muhammed Ladjal gestured at the distant peaks, now covered in snow—"not far from here, in the Guelta range."

The word *citadel* conjured for Szbeszdogy visions out of *The Arabian Nights*: crenelated towers, moats, invisible castles inhabited by djinns and ogres and an enchanted princess or two. You would need an army of knights to assault such a place. Pinard, who had never read any tales of djinns, ogres, or princesses, thought only of stone walls, barbed wire, and gun embrasures. In either case, a formidable obstacle.

"On a plateau between two peaks," the Moroccan continued. "Lightly held. Not a job for a brigade, not even a company. Ten men, perhaps twelve. A patrol. The element of surprise."

Pinard drew the sergeant to his feet and kissed him on both cheeks.

13.

An absolute stillness hung over the mountain redoubt of the Marabouts. Smith snapped awake in the predawn darkness, immediately aware of the absence of sound. He opened the interior door a crack. The large room beyond stood deserted. Phillipe took the Gateway's severed head by the hair and without saying a word to each other they walked through the bungalow, also deserted, down the long corridor and out the front door unmolested. No one stopped them because there was no one to do so. Even the bees were gone, their massive hive silent.

"They cleared out," Smith said, not believing the empty village, the hovels denuded of every last scrap. "You really think they're gone?"

"Oh, yes." Phillipe smiled through broken teeth. "They're gone."

"Why . . . ? Did they . . . ? Where . . . ?"

Dazed, Smith couldn't frame the right questions. But Phillipe seemed temporarily revitalized. Killing Al Bab had sent a jolt of energy through him. Perhaps he had consumed, like a hero out of ancient myth, some of the life force of his vanquished enemy through the blade of his sword.

"Marabout fighters surprised me while you were asleep," Phillipe said. "They had their guns on me, they were about to shoot. I merely showed them this—" He offered Ralph's severed head to the pale inspection of dawn. "And they got a good long look and went away quietly. An hour later I heard them all moving out, a kind of sad creaking as they took off their belongings that was the sound of the archimposter's schemes falling apart piece by piece. This happened yesterday. You've been sleeping for twenty hours. I didn't want to wake you."

"Thanks," Smith mumbled.

"The Marabouts believe Al Bab is immortal," Phillipe continued. "Always dying, always resurrected. This head represents just one of the forms of their prophet. Killing him only released his soul to inhabit a higher form. We were the instruments of that release, you and I, Milquetoast. Perhaps the Marabouts think we're a couple of angels and, like their bees, sent by heaven. In any case, I imagine they're relieved. New belief systems are generally very demanding. Now they can go back to the relative luxury of the refugee camps. Free logs of UN cheese and so on."

Smith and Phillipe wandered slowly through the darkened town, the former stumbling a little, freedom an unfamiliar taste in his mouth; the latter swinging Al Bab's severed head jauntily by the hair, like a lantern. Halfway down the slope a man in a dirty denim jumpsuit, camouflage grease smeared across his hawkish features, stepped out of the shadows. In his hands a gleaming chrome Kalashnikov, its stock inlaid in silver with the Moroccan star.

"Where did you get that ridiculous weapon, Pinard?" Phillipe said.

"Colonel de Noyer?" Pinard cried, squinting into the gloom.

"Yes, I'm afraid so."

Pinard could hardly conceal his dismay at the sight of this walking skeleton, otherwise known as Phillipe de Noyer—remembering the elegant officer, accomplished pianist, and Satie fanatic, second in command of la Musique Principale. The treasured husband of the woman he loved. To this vigorous, talented person the present emaciated toothless apparition bore no resemblance. For his part Smith, astonished, couldn't help gaping at Pinard. One thought kept running through his head: He had cried out from the darkness of captivity—*à moi la Légion!*—and, damn, if the bastards hadn't come for him.

"You remember Legionnaire Milquetoast," Phillipe said, gesturing to Smith. "Smith, my former adjutant, Sous-lieutenant Pinard—"

"That's capitaine," Pinard corrected. "Field commission."

"Congratulations." The colonel nodded. "Well done."

"*Mon capitaine.*" Smith saluted. Pinard eyed him coolly.

"So you made it this far, Milquetoast," he said.

"I did, sir," Smith said. But meanwhile, he thought, cocksucker, I never wanted to see your ugly face again! Between the two of them there was, and would ever be, the kind of natural antipathy that goes beyond personality and upbringing, that is rooted somewhere deep in the blood.

Pinard offered Colonel de Noyer a foul-tasting Moroccan cigarette from a requisitioned pack; as an afterthought he offered one to Smith. The men lit up and smoked for a long minute without speaking. It seemed they were standing on the parade ground at Aubagne in full dress, not exposed on a frozen mountaintop in the expectant moments before dawn, targets for snipers, an ambush.

"By the way, Milquetoast," the colonel said, blowing a cloud of cigarette smoke into the brightening sky. "I'm recommending you for the Croix de Guerre. You could have escaped without me, you didn't. *Eh bien, bravo!*" Then to Pinard, "Should anything unfortunate happen to me, please make a note of this commendation."

"*Oui, mon colonel.*"

Cold wind swept down from the peaks above, redolent with snow. Phillipe was on his feet and lucid, even garrulous—but the last fires of his life were clearly extinguishing themselves as each second gave way inexorably to the next. He faltered suddenly, and put his hand on Smith's shoulder to steady himself.

"Are you able to walk, Colonel?" Pinard asked anxiously. "They're waiting down there, ready to take this place by storm. If I don't get back soon we'll be caught in our own firefight!"

"Who's waiting?"

"Legionnaires Szbeszdogy and Solas." Pinard grinned. "And a few new volunteers."

"Good. Shall we go, *mes enfants*?"

Phillipe removed his hand from Smith's shoulder and took a step forward unaided, then another, and soon they were moving down the slope.

"Glad you showed up, Pinard," the colonel said. "I didn't want to carry this ugly relic all the way back to Aubagne." He raised the head, an expression of terminal horror fixed to its fat cheeks. "Meet the great and terrible Al Bab. Strangely, he was an American. What was that name again, Milquetoast?"

"Ralph T. Wade III," Smith said, "of Marin County, California."

"Half the trouble in the world seems to be caused by Americans." Phillipe shot Smith a critical glance.

Smith didn't say anything to this, but he thought, what about the other half?

Presently, Phillipe tossed the severed head of the Gateway to the Age of the Hidden Imam to Captain Pinard as casually as someone might toss a soccer ball to a fellow player after a game. A few minutes later, Pinard tossed it to Smith and a few minutes after that it went back to Phillipe again. And carrying this grisly trophy between them, first one, then the other, digging their fingers into the greasy, blood-matted hair, into the sockets of the eyes, they walked together down the trail and came to a narrow switchback that rose and fell sharply down the course of the ravine. The sun rose to the east as they descended. Dawn touched the heights, but not the desert below.

14

BRIDGE OF THE
REQUITER

1.

Phillipe lay a long time dying in the hospital in Ceuta. The windows of his room, arched in the Arabic fashion and subtly tinted with gold-colored glass like an expensive pair of sunglasses, looked out on the white city, on the fortress of Monte Hoche, on the waters of the Mediterranean, wine dark, touched with whitecaps. The room was air-conditioned and clean. He was still in Africa, that is to say on the African continent, but actually in Spain. Ceuta is Spanish territory, as it has been for five hundred years, one of the last footholds of a vanished empire.

Toward the end of Phillipe's final struggle with death, an old-fashioned gentleman wearing a pair of pinc-nez spectacles and a velvet suit, his beard neatly trimmed, came to sit by Phillipe's hospital bed on an odd, rickety-looking stool. The legs of the stool were needle-thin, but carved up and down with demonic little figures like gargoyles on a Gothic cathedral.

These gargoyles grimaced and screamed, their screams making no sound at all, and they spit out a vicious black poison that was their deathless malice, the same terrible stuff that had afflicted the de Noyers down through the generations. The gargoyles would spit this poison into anyone who came near them with an open wound, and had found the de Noyers especially receptive hosts. They had penetrated Phillipe's ancestor, Thibault, Conte de la Tour Grise in the following manner: This pious and valiant knight had gone on crusade to Egypt with St. Louis in 1277, was shipwrecked off the Egyptian coast, taken prisoner after a desperate fight, and thrown into the dungeons of the caliph of Damietta, no more than a damp hole cut deep into the earth and full of pestilence. In the caliph's dungeon, Thibault sat down on a filthy, rickety stool just like this one, a sword wound on his thigh. From the contaminated stool, and through Thibault's wound, the gargoyles entered his blood, chewing their way with their sharp teeth into his very marrow, into the fibery thickets of his most intimate material, where they then laid their poison like maggot eggs.

But the gargoyles could not infect the blood or the marrow or the intimate material of the Velvet Gentleman, who was incorporeal and far beyond such terrors and who could not be touched by anything in this world, and who found the stool quite comfortable. He took Phillipe's hand.

"You recognize them, of course," the Velvet Gentleman said gently. "I mean these malefic little demons."

"Yes." Phillipe shuddered. "They're horrible."

The Velvet Gentleman nodded. "They have been hiding inside your body, inside the bodies of your family, generation after generation, since the days of the sainted king, as a poisonous snake hides in underbrush. Sometimes they lie quiescent, asleep for fifty years, for a hundred years, and do not disturb the host. Other times"—the Velvet Gentleman offered a gesture—"we have your sad case, my dear de Noyer. They have gnawed away great gaping holes in the precious fabric of your brain like moths going at a suit."

"Where do they come from?"

"Where indeed?" The Velvet Gentleman shrugged. "I could say the East. That's where such things come from, generally. Plagues, new ideas, new religions. Before that"—he shrugged—"they inhabited a universe that is not our own, that is infinitesimally small, so small that it exists and does not exist at the same time."

"Your paradoxes hurt my head," Phillipe said. "I'm very tired . . ."

But the Velvet Gentleman demurred. "We have fought them long and hard together you and I," he said. "My music played through your fingertips made them quiet, made them slow their ceaseless gnawings, and so you have lived much longer than any of your ancestors. Think of it—six years without sleep! Who can claim to have experienced the same torment and lived!

Now, granted, your body has reached its physical limits and you will die. But your death cannot be their victory. They feel your death coming and are getting ready to jump into a new host. We can't let this happen. They must die too, this time, once and for all when your body dies. Understand?"

Phillipe nodded.

"Good. There's not much time left. So you must tell your beautiful wife how to dispose of your corpse. You must keep enough strength in reserve to tell her everything, understand?"

"All right." Phillipe smiled weakly. "When I see her in Paris."

"But she is right here!"

Phillipe turned his face to the window and saw someone, a woman, curled up in a hospital chair, asleep.

"My love . . . ," Phillipe rasped, barely louder than a whisper. Louise didn't hear him, she didn't stir. He tried to raise his hand but couldn't. It was tied to the bedrails with plastic ties; tubes ran from the vein in the back of his wrist to a clear bag of fluids hanging above. He summoned what remained of his will: "Louise!"

Louise awoke, alarmed. "I am here, my darling."

She came over to the bed and sat on the stool where the Velvet Gentleman had been sitting, but it was, fortunately for her, a different stool and the Velvet Gentleman wasn't there anymore. She took her husband's hand, though the touch of his yellow, papery flesh made her tremble with revulsion. Once a debonair, aristocratic Frenchman, her Phillipe was now nothing but dry skin and bones lacking even teeth. He reminded her of a mummy she'd seen once in the Louvre. He looked like he'd already been dead for a thousand years.

"I was just talking to Satie," Phillipe said.

Louise smiled indulgently, the way you would smile at a child telling a crazy story. He could see she didn't believe him.

"I tell you he was here," Phillipe insisted. "Right where you're sitting."

"Yes, of course," Louise said. Then, because she didn't know what else to say: "I love you."

This wasn't exactly true anymore. How could any woman made of flesh and blood and still full of life love a dried-up old mummy? But she had done what she had sworn she would do. She had found him after many hardships and strange adventures and was here with him now, during his final hours.

"Then listen," Phillipe continued. "Satie showed me the terrible things living inside me—like goblins, like gargoyles—what do they call them?"

"You're talking about," Louise said, beginning to understand, "your disease. You mean the prions?"

"Call them what you will. Prions, devils, gargoyles, hereditary infectious proteins—all the same thing. They're cunning, they have a kind of brutal intelligence. They must die with me. Make arrangements to incinerate my body. I must be cremated immediately following my death. Then my ashes must be treated with lime and thrown into the sea."

Tears welled up in Louise's eyes. Suddenly, the thought of not being able to visit her husband's grave struck her to the core. She was already planning to pay her respects once a year, dressed in the most elegant black.

"But you always told me you wanted to be buried in the vault," she said. "In Honfleur. With your ancestors. You're a Roman Catholic. Isn't cremation against—"

"None of that matters now," Phillipe interrupted. "We must kill them. Swear you will have me burned. Swear!"

Louise swore.

Then her husband's hand slipped out of her own and he faded into unconsciousness, sinking back into the desiccated yellow husk of his flesh. She pushed herself off the stool and hurried out of the room, tears in her eyes—though her tears were as much for herself as for him: With Phillipe dead, her life would be her own again, for the first time in many years. She had once almost thrown it away. What would she do with it now?

2.

Louise wandered the whispery, high-ceilinged corridors of the hospital for an hour, thinking about the future, which seemed to yawn before her like a giant mouth ready to swallow her up, and feeling an emptiness reminiscent of the despair she'd felt in the days leading up to her trip to Mont-Saint-Michel to drown herself in the sea.

At last, she came out onto the wide loggia, its balustrades entwined with sweet-smelling, flowering vines. A lone figure sat in the courtyard below, in dappled sunlight by the fountain: It was the American Legionnaire, Caspar Milquetoast—besides her husband the only other survivor of the Massacre at Blockhouse 9, his comrade in captivity among the Marabouts. Milquetoast was reading an American newspaper, the *International Herald Tribune.* He had arrived at the hospital nearly as emaciated as Phillipe, been carefully nourished, and was recovering nicely from the hardships of his ordeal.

Concealed behind the flowering vines, Louise watched him there for long minutes, almost without breathing, her heart drumming beneath her ribs, as he quietly turned the pages of his newspaper: He was an attractive man; actually, very attractive. About her age, his hair wheat-gold in the sunlight. He looked like a movie star, she thought, like the American actor Brad Pitt. Or perhaps a little like Gary Cooper—he had that sort of long, ropy, Western look. She dried her eyes, straightened her dress, and came down the stairs.

"Ah, Legionnaire Milquetoast," she said, trying to sound casual. "Do you mind if I join you?"

Smith dropped his paper and looked up, squinting into the sun, which was behind her head.

"Madame de Noyer," he said, surprised, and made to push himself up off the bench, but she gestured for him to stay put and sat down beside him.

"I hope I'm not disturbing your reading," she said.

"*Non, non—je vous en pris.*"

"It's this heat," she explained awkwardly. "Nice and cool here by the fountain . . ."

For a while, they looked at the water without speaking, the bright spray of droplets reflecting a rainbow against the Spanish tile work of the basin. The murmur of traffic came to them faintly; the muted bleat of cargo ships entering the harbor. Smith felt himself acutely conscious of Madame de Noyer's presence—he hadn't been this close to a woman in a long time. She wasn't his type, really, too French and too small, almost birdlike. He preferred the big, brassy blondes of his Midwestern youth; beautiful, hungry, amoral farm girls like Jessica. And yet this woman was undeniably attractive—in fact, very attractive—and it was very pleasant sitting there with her. Then Smith experienced a sudden, powerful jolt, like an electric shock, to the psychosexual preceptors in his brain. All at once a vivid series of erotic images, an entire scenario, appeared on the movie screen of his imagination: A large bed, the sheets rumpled. There he was with Madame de Noyer—what was her name? Louise!—locked together, legs akimbo, one inside the other, through the length of a drowsy Sunday afternoon. New York? Paris, of course. They would fuck, talk, laugh, eat, walk in the Bois du Boulogne at dusk, then back to bed for more of the same. Erotic, companionable, intellectually matched, all the necessary components of a good marriage.

No, impossible!

Smith quickly shook off this self-indulgent daydream. Such a woman could have no interest in a common Legionnaire.

"So how's your husband?" he asked at last. One of them had to speak first.

"Oh." Louise made a sad gesture. "He's delirious, I'm afraid. He raves about demons and Erik Satie."

"He had long talks with Satie up in the mountains too."

But she didn't want to talk about her husband. "Tell me, where are you from in the States?"

Smith told her.

"I went to college in Virginia," Louise began, and she told Smith about her years in Lexington, about the outrageous, drunken parties in the big antebellum fraternity houses there, lit up like ocean liners in the dark night of the Blue Ridges, the passengers, dangerously inebriated, hanging off the wrought-iron railings of the balconies, off the roof gutters. She had been terribly out of place, she said, but it had been exciting, like being a character in a novel by Faulkner. Didn't Caddy from *The Sound and the Fury* somehow end up in France during the Occupation as the mistress of a Nazi staff officer? In Louise's case, so to speak, it was the other way around.

"Wow," Smith said, laughing. "Hard to imagine you at Washington and Lee. Were you in a sorority?"

"Chi Omega," Louise admitted. "Only for one year. The girls were very Southern and all very stupid. But I did organize the first Fraternity-Sorority *Tournée de Pétanque*. You know this French game? With balls. Also called boules or bocce—"

"Yeah, sure," Smith said.

"I understand they still play, that it's become a college tradition . . ."

They talked on for a long while as the shadows moved slowly across the courtyard and the day edged from morning to afternoon. They talked about America; then about what would happen next to both of them. She would tend to her château, she said. Maybe she would open a small, artisinal restaurant in Honfleur, which at this moment lacked a really good restaurant; she would specialize in hearty Breton dishes using produce and livestock from her husband's estate. Smith supposed he might go back to the musical stage some day in supporting roles. Or get his Ph.D. in dramaturgy and teach at a small Midwestern school, like his alma mater, Cornell College in Mount Vernon, Iowa. And he told Louise about his previous life as an actor-singer, about some of his greatest triumphs, about the LORT A production of *My Fair Lady* at the Guthrie, and about doing *Damn Yankees* in summer stock in Vermont with the mosquitos so bad the entire audience was gone by the second act, and she laughed.

After a while, they found themselves sitting closer to each other on the bench, almost touching. Louise suppressed an urge to run her fingers through his thick yellow hair, to kiss his face, which was both sad and handsome and still showed the marks—a series of thin white scars—of his recent ordeal. And Smith felt a genuine stirring, a reawakening—God, I'd like to fuck her! he thought—no, more than that: God, I'd like to fall in love! And these acknowledged desires sent a powerful surge, familiar but nearly forgotten, coursing through him.

It was dreary being in the hospital. Drearier still waiting for someone to die. After their first hour together, Louise and Smith forgot the dying man upstairs. And the last promise Louise had made to her husband, that she would arrange for an immediate cremation and mix his ashes with lime and throw them into the sea, slipped completely from her mind.

3.

At about three in the afternoon, Satie returned to Phillipe's room. He had abandoned the Velvet Gentleman costume of his Monmartre period and wore the tail coat and stiff white dress shirt of the years of glory, when he had become a national treasure, celebrated by *le tout* Paris; when he had outlived the eccentricities that had made him famous and become, at last, perfectly himself.

As Satie sat back down on the prion-infected stool, Phillipe glimpsed a pair of pink, feathery wings neatly folded between the maestro's shoulder blades at the back of his tail coat and knew suddenly that Satie's presence in his hospital room was an illusion, a figment of his dying imagination. Phillipe wanted Satie to be real, to be there, and if Satie had pink wings, well, this had to be a good sign about Phillipe's ultimate destination. But he was a soldier and had learned to be utterly hard-hearted when necessary.

"You're not Satie at all," he said, with some bitterness. "You're only a product of my diseased brain."

"Don't put it like that." Satie sounded hurt. "Of course I'm Satie. Look at me."

"You do resemble Satie," Phillipe admitted.

"That's because I am Satie. Exactly as I was in life. Ah, that word"—Satie interrupted himself—"Life! Such a beautiful word, don't you think? Implying as it does, sunlight, a field full of flowers, etc., etc. Streetlamps shining through the leaves of a tree. Wine. Glasses of beer. Stumbling home after a good long drunk—'Good-bye, my friends, thank you for an excellent party! Yes, I'm fine, I know the way. . . . What's this? Ah! I've fallen over the curb!' . . . The sea, naturally. The wonderful, precious, inimitable sound of a nicely tuned piano. And the white arms, the breasts of women."

"Very nice," Phillipe interjected. "But . . ."

"Beautiful, eh?" Satie smiled charmingly. "*La vie, quoi!*"

"Yes. But you're here to tell me something."

"I am."

"Go ahead then."

Satie hesitated. He folded his long, delicate, spiritual hands in his lap, as fine as that famous pair engraved by Dürer, and his mood changed.

"I must ask you a question, *mon enfant*," he said, his voice serious. "And you must be absolutely truthful. The question is this: What kind of life have you led?"

"How can I answer that?" Phillipe exclaimed.

"As best you can," Satie replied. "Everyone must try. You see that structure there? Look—"

The hospital in Ceuta had vanished and they were walking on a narrow path through an unfamiliar forest, wildly tangled. Up ahead, stretched over a deep chasm, a suspension bridge, very delicate looking, nothing but ropes and thin pieces of wood. In the middle of the bridge stood a dim figure. At the apprehension of this person Phillipe was filled with foreboding.

"There's the bridge now," Satie said.

"Yes . . ." Phillipe was surprised by the tremor in his voice.

"It has a name. The Bridge of the Requiter. Sooner or later everyone must cross it."

"Where does it lead?"

"That . . ." Satie shrugged. "You see the bridgekeeper in the middle?"

"More or less," Phillipe said. "He's hard to make out."

"You'll see him clearly soon enough," Satie said. "You will explain your-self to him, at length, then he will tell you where you're going. Not an easy process, I'm afraid. Why don't you practice a little. Let's start with the basics—name, age, place of residence, occupation."

"Phillipe Auguste Balthazar de Brusset de Noyer," Phillipe said. "Fifty-six years old, of Honfleur and Paris. Lately Colonel, Armée de Terre, serial number 884877367, serving as second in command of the Corps of Musi-cians of the Foreign Legion and officer in charge of the Chorale."

"Impressive." Satie nodded. "But not all that important. Any children?"

"No. There never seemed to be time."

"Have you loved, been loved?"

"Yes," Phillipe said emphatically. Then, uncertain, "At least I think so."

"You've got to be sure. It's a very important point."

Phillipe thought for a long moment. "I loved my first wife at one time, but probably not enough. Her name was Celeste. She had red hair. She played the violin; she was a very good musician, actually, though too timid for professional success. She taught me to love music, to really concentrate on perfecting my piano. She wanted me to quit the army, to take up music full time. We had many terrible arguments about that. She was the one who first made me listen carefully to Sa—to you."

"Ah!" Satie smiled. "Wonderful taste, this woman!"

Phillipe closed his eyes and saw something he hadn't seen before—his first wife, Celeste, weeping bitterly on a bench in the Jardin des Palmes in Paris twenty-eight years ago, moments after he left her for the final time. She was so pretty, her hair was beautifully red, redder than he remembered it. He was surprised by this vision, he'd never seen her cry like that, never knew. . . .

". . . how much she loved you," Satie finished the thought. "It broke her heart, you see, when you threw her over for—what was her name again?"

"I can't remember, actually," Phillipe said. "No one, really. *Une fille de pas-sage.* Just because I didn't want to be attached then, in my life."

"You destroyed your Celeste. Rather thoughtlessly, I might add. And for nothing. She died recently, did you know that? In a charity hospital in Gre-noble. Complications relating to alcoholism. She'd been living on the street, in train stations and shelters."

"I didn't know," Phillipe whispered. "We haven't spoken in ten or fifteen years."

"She was very proud. She loved you. She never told you how much."

"Poor Celeste," Phillipe whispered.

"Yes." Satie nodded. "You'll be answering for that to—" He indicated the figure on the bridge up ahead.

"But there's got to be—" Phillipe hesitated, afraid suddenly. "Is there nothing on the plus side of the balance sheet?"

"There's Louise. You loved her, I think."

"From the first moment I saw her." Phillipe nodded. "Standing in the middle of all those fat American tourists, her eyes wild, on the Mont."

"You saved her life."

"Yes."

"At the risk of your own."

"Well, not really—"

"This is no time for modesty, *mon enfant*. It was dangerous, you might have drowned, the tide was rushing in, but you jumped down off the rocks and saved her. You are not a coward. You have never been a coward. In this, you resemble your stalwart ancestors, the knights and lords of la Tour Grise. That's got to be worth something."

They had passed out of the wood and were walking now in a melancholy park beneath a light drizzle. Somehow, the bridge, still there ahead, didn't seem any closer. In the park, it was quiet and sad. Moss-covered urns on pedestals seized by the branches of unclipped topiaries, the flower beds overgrown, the prize rosebushes in tatters. A nearby ruin falling in on itself looked alarmingly like the château de Noyer after a couple hundred years of neglect. Then, they were at the foot of the bridge—now transformed into an imposing structure resembling the Pont d'Alma in Paris, though devoid of the usual city traffic.

"You see where we are," Satie said gently.

"I do," Phillipe said, his heart sinking. Then desperately: "I meant to finish my monograph on your work."

"Don't worry about that. What's the point in writing about music, anyway? One has only to play it. Or merely listen."

A pause. The bridge looming.

"It's time for the final assessment," Satie whispered. "Take a few minutes. Be thorough."

Phillipe couldn't bring himself to look at the figure waiting in the middle directly. He peered around him, into the shadows on the other side of the bridge. Nothing. Or only a kind of roiling fog out of which came random episodes from his life.

There was his father, ashes dripping off a cigarette tucked at the corner of his mouth, driving Phillipe's eight-year-old self to the Lycée Louis le Grand in the old Delahaye, the worn leather-tobacco smell of the car's interior, Charles Trenet on the crackly tube radio and the crazy gearshifter—electromagnetic!—that never worked properly, and his father cursing at it in his good-humored way. There was Phillipe a couple of years later, sitting on his mother's bed, watching her put on makeup at the ornate vanity in her bedroom in the high-ceilinged old apartment on the Isle Saint-Louis: the diamond and pearl drop earrings, a dab of perfume here, there, and that memorable strapless black dress. Getting herself ready for an evening out, supposedly to a restaurant with friends, but really to a not-so-secret rendez-vous with her lover, everyone knew where she was going, even the cook! Looking glamorous and tragic and—how was it he hadn't seen this before?—strikingly like Louise. The same beautiful indigo eyes inhabited by the same foolish, unanswerable questions. The same weak, sensual lips.

And there was Phillipe years later in desert fatigues, on maneuvers with the Legion in Chad, when the 1e RE rescued that kidnapped busload of schoolchildren. He'd risked his life that time too for those kids, and without a thought.

And there he was with Celeste the first night they'd made love—they were both nineteen!—in the spare bedroom of her parents' ugly house in Soissons, desperately trying to keep the bed from squeaking. And, of course, with Louise in that tiny hotel on the Mont. And the darkening cliffs of Corfu seen at dusk from the deck of a friend's sailboat. And the parade ground at Saint-Cyr on a crisp winter morning, cadets marching in splendid lockstep in their sparkling blue uniforms. And the terrace of a favorite bar in Montparnasse at closing time, the waiters whistling as they added up their accounts. And a field seen at midnight through the sidescreen of a Citroën 2CV along the route National, light of an August moon falling hard across freshly cut grass like slabs of marble. And hours and hours and hours bent over the piano at Nogent playing Satie, his fingers working the keys, through all those torturous nights he couldn't sleep. And a streetlamp throwing its glow through the leaves of that poplar tree at the corner of the rue Lyautey and the avenue Rollin in Aubagne. How he'd loved the look of streetlight through the branches of a tree, with the wind up and the leaves rustling subtly like the voice of God! And a bottle of good Rhône wine and a nice plate of veal chops prepared *à l'Anglais* at Aux Singe du Pape. And the white arms, the breasts of women . . .

All of it reeling away, unwinding until there was nothing left, until it was all played out; the word *fin* appearing on the screen to a melancholy finale by Georges Auric, which then faded, abruptly, to black and to silence.

Phillipe turned to Satie in a panic. "But I haven't been given enough time!" he exclaimed.

"That's what they all say, *mon enfant.*" Satie put a calming hand on Phillipe's shoulder. "That's what I said when I died in 1924. But you see, I was lying to myself. I'd had plenty of time, days and days of it. Months, years. It's just that I wasted so much."

"You? Not possible! You were a genius!"

"I wasted the better part, I'm afraid. I could have done so much more with what I'd been given. Honestly, I was too often drunk. But too late now. Look—"

Satie pointed to the figure in the middle of the bridge, which wasn't so dim anymore, who stood there, clearly immovable, solidly blocking the way to the other side.

"He is the Requiter," Satie whispered. "You will be weighted against the Feather of Truth. And—this is the tricky part—the scales must be balanced against the weight of your deeds. Don't tremble so, Phillipe! *Bon courage!* One can never be absolutely sure, of course, but I have a good feeling about you. As long as you've been honest with yourself. You'll have some work to do, a little bit of *la pelote*, a *corvée* or two. Some punishment duty, but who doesn't?"

Phillipe turned and embraced Satie, careful not to crush his pink wings.

"Thank you for your wonderful music," Phillipe said. "It was a great comfort to me, at times everything. Especially when I couldn't sleep."

Then he straightened his uniform tunic. He was dressed as a common Legionnaire now, with the name tag removed; apparently he was going to attempt the passage under cover of *l'anonymat*, which was the ancient and peculiar privelege of the Legion. And so he put his hands in the pockets of his pants like a Legionnaire strolling out of a battered fortress following a siege that had almost gone the wrong way; like a Legionnaire impervious to life, to death, to what might or might not come after.

And he stepped onto the bridge. And crossed.

15

THE SMELL OF
STRONG CHEESE

1.

One month passed.

Smith recuperated fully from the malnutrition and abuse suffered during captivity and—to his great surprise—returned to France a hero. The Élysée Palace had changed hands during his absence; left-leaning President Mitterrand gave way to right-leaning President Sarkozy and suddenly, the Foreign Legion had become fashionable again—or at least no longer reviled by the public as an army full of drunken barbarians, murderers, and rapists; no longer attacked by the press as a last regrettable vestige of French colonial imperialism.

"These ten thousand men [so wrote an editorialist in *Le Matin*] have come in perilous times from every corner of the earth and from all levels of society to shed their blood for France. Isn't it time we show some appreciation for their willingness—whatever the motive, some shameful, granted—to sacrifice their lives on our behalf?"

The mission to rescue the late Colonel de Noyer and Legionnaire Milquetoast from the Marabouts, once so secret it existed only in the mind of General le Breton, was suddenly featured in all the newspapers and magazines—though it appeared, from the media accounts, that Smith and Phillipe had somehow rescued themselves. Smith's handsome face appeared on the cover of *Paris Match*, displacing Johnny Hallyday and news of President Sarkozy's supermodel fiancée. Smith was decorated with the Croix de Guerre as Phillipe had requested, and also the Medaille Militaire as he had not. The glittering awards ceremony, awash with gold-emblazoned battle flags, echoing with many speeches and the martial fanfares of the Musique Principale, and heavy with all the traditional pomp that is a Legion specialty, was televised prime-time on the ORTF as part of the Sarkozy regime's new *Fierté Française* PR push: his era would be a time of order and progress, of renewed "Pride in Being French." And one of the things of France, a relic dredged up from its glorious past—many had thought it disbanded long ago!—was the Foreign Legion.

Pinard and Szbeszdogy—both unfortunately not as photogenic or presentable as Smith—attended the ceremony only as members of the regimental band, their part in the rescue almost entirely overlooked. Legionnaire Solas was also ignored, having hastily rejoined the ranks of his fellow assassins in the 4e ER. Still, the Legion was not unappreciative: A two-paragraph piece of filler in *Képi Blanc*, under the slug MP OBOE RETURNS FROM AFRICA, featured a photograph of the rueful Pinard posed with his slightly ridiculous wooden instrument. The brief text mentioned in passing that he had played "an important part" in the success of the now celebrated Mission: SCORPIO, and that he would immediately resume his job as first oboe in the marching band, a talent for which he had been very much missed by his fellow musicians.

"*Je me félicite d'avoir encore mon hautbois!*" Pinard remarked bitterly to Szbeszdogy upon reading this chipper, dismissive little article. At least he still had his oboe—which responded with beautiful music when he put his fingers upon its glossy body of polished grenadaille, pressed down firmly on its silver keys and blew through the freshly shaved double-reed. Here he was, once again, loveless and underappreciated, his field-command promotion to capitaine officially rescinded by General le Breton, on the grounds that it had been offered only for the duration of the mission. And anyway—the general had said tersely—Pinard's military conduct had as yet failed to justify a captaincy: Had he not lost four men in the desert and failed to bring Colonel de Noyer back alive to France? He was now a lieutenant. A one-half grade promotion from the sous-lieutenant he had been at the start of the pointless adventure in Africa—but not what he had hoped for.

"You're a poet, Evariste," Szbeszdogy said, shrugging his shoulders. They were in the caserne at Aubagne, at the bar, splitting a carafe of mediocre red wine from the Legion vineyards at Puyloubier. "When will you believe me? Poets suffer at the hands of society, they are generally misunderstood. And they definitely do not fare well in the military. Look at Kleist, who shot himself in a fit of despair. Or the great Lermontov, who was murdered by the czar merely for writing the wrong kind of poems. At least you're in good company."

"Quit this little joke of yours or I'll knock your teeth in," Pinard growled. "I don't even write!"

"You don't have to write to be a poet," Szbeszdogy continued, doggedly and at the risk of his teeth. "You can be a poet of things, of events, of gestures. You can even be a poet of the oboe."

Pinard wasn't listening. Every time he closed his eyes, he saw Louise's pale, beautiful face, which hung over the landscape of his soul like an enchanted moon. This was his life. There would be no other. He drained his glass, his eyes drifting to the window. Out there, in thin winter sunlight, the 2e section of the Musique Principale drilled along the parade ground at their usual solemn pace, followed by the Chorale du Légion. At a signal the drilling stopped, the instruments fell silent. Then, the tall, broad-chested Legionnaires of the chorale raised their voices in a song about war.

2.

Smith and Louise de Noyer found themselves often in each other's company in the weeks following his return to France. They were thrown together at official functions, which Louise attended with great reluctance, and only to honor her late husband's memory. They were interviewed by the same journalists, appeared on the same news programs. They sat side by side all through the course of two or three long, memorial dinners.

At the last one, given as a benefit for military widows on a chilly spring evening on the lawn at Malmaison—former home of the Empress Josephine—somehow, during dessert (later, he wasn't quite sure how he'd summoned the necessary guts) Smith reached under the table and put his hand on Louise's knee. An anxious moment passed in which Louise did nothing; Smith began to sweat, his hand trembling where it lay. He couldn't look at her—she might shove him away, slap his face. Instead, she took his hand gently and tucked it between her thighs and squeezed hard, and when she turned to him it was with a smile on her lips—half amused, half relieved. As if to say—well, at last! All this under the suspicious eye of Hervé Morin, Sarkozy's new Minister of Defense, seated facing them.

On the way back to Paris, Smith and Louise pawed at each other in the rear compartment of the limousine, tugged at each other's clothing. They fucked for the first time that night in her plush hotel room at the very plush Georges V and woke up late the next morning, having slept no more than ten or fifteen minutes, wrapped in each other's arms, one inside the other, already deeply in love just as in Smith's fantasy. They were perfectly matched, both intellectually and physically—so Louise asserted over an English-style breakfast delivered to the room at noon. Smith, nearly swooning, agreed and leaped across the small table to kiss her and they fell back into bed for the rest of the day and most of the night, exploring in detail the newly discovered territory of each other's bodies.

But, in love or not, Smith was obliged to report back to Legion headquarters in Aubagne the following afternoon. Louise rode with him in a cab to the gare d'Austerlitz, nuzzling his neck, his ear, his collar wet with her tears. Oh, she didn't want him to go! They had to be together! It was fate! Smith agreed. He would request a transfer to the Fort de Nogent, he said, and they would be able to see each other every weekend, but this change of address might take months, even years to go through—the Legion moved very slowly when it came to administrative matters of any kind. Louise couldn't wait that long. She followed him down to Aubagne a week later and rented a furnished apartment near the base, just a few houses down from the regimental brothel, and they managed to see each other for an hour or two a couple of nights a week, Monday through Friday, half a day Saturday and all day Sunday.

In this apartment one Sunday evening after making love, they formulated the plan: Smith would claim his unclaimed passport from Poste Restante, 1e Arrondissement, Paris. The Legion was a military hell, a punishment he didn't need anymore. He had been punished enough for poor Jessica's death and for everything else. He would desert and Louise would come with him. They would go to the United States together and make a life for themselves, maybe in California; maybe Smith could apply to the M.A./Ph.D. program in dramaturgy at UCLA.

"I'm sick of France." Louise sniffed. "Sarkozy is a terrible fascist, like a French George Bush. And everyone's too tired to do anything about it, especially in Paris. But you can really accomplish things in America, in New York or L.A. You can be whatever you want to be. You've just got to try."

"You can also be a bum," Smith countered. "A homeless bum. Or murdered by hip-hop gangstas in your own apartment. Or shot in a drive-by—"

"Don't be morbid, my sweet!" Louise said breathlessly. "Let's think about this a minute—" The details solidifying in her head. "I've got plenty of money. There's Phillipe's estate. I'll have to sell a few things—but not the château, not yet. Many years ago, he bought a tiny but important Pissarro, now worth at least a couple of million euros, and there's an old Delahaye—it's a famous French car, a very fine car—stashed away in one of our barns. It used to belong to his father—even in pieces worth two or three hundred thousand. I'll get rid of those things first!"

Smith, giddy with possibility, leaned over and kissed her.

"You're happy?"

"I don't deserve all this happiness!"

"Oh, you do, *chéri*! You do!"

The thing was, he didn't.

And the thought that he didn't deserve any of it, not really, that he hadn't yet paid his debt to the merciless Furies or to France nagged at Smith all through the next two months as Louise contacted lawyers, sold paintings and cases of rare vintage wine from the cellars of the château, assembled a substantial bankroll and wired it to her new account established at a Credit Lyonnais branch in Manhattan.

At last, all arrangements in place, plane tickets bought, passport retrieved from Poste Restante, Smith obtained a two-hour pass—ostensibly to do a couple of quick errands in Aubagne—and instead snuck aboard the local for Paris, where he changed out of his expertly creased Legion uniform in the cramped bathroom of the café car. During a twenty-minute stop at Chalons, he tied it all into a bundle—the sacred kepi blanc, the stiff, spotless shirt, the neatly ironed trousers, and Ranger boots—and threw the bundle into a nearby canal, sticking around long enough to watch it sink to the bottom. And he disembarked in nondescript civilian clothes six hours later two stops short of the capital, at the Aeroport Charles de Gaulle.

3.

A major international airport is like a medium-sized city in microcosm— without permanent residents but with a city's worth of people coming and going. There are shopping districts, bookstores, cafés, better and worse neighborhoods, out-of-the-way corners. The underlit extremity of CDG Terminal 2, Spur 6, the Air Martinique Terminal, currently under renovation, with many of its fluorescents knocked out by an electrical glitch and its storefronts and departure gates closed with yellow tape, was the perfect place for a rendezvous of conspirators.

Louise found Smith there, slumped furtively over a glass of red wine at one of the three concourse tables at a small restaurant called Chez l'Auvergnat. The strong scent of the rich, aged cheeses of the Auvergne region curled out of the glass counters inside to assault the nostrils. Just now, Smith felt nervous, queasy—a sensation made worse by the stink of the cheese. It seemed what he was about to do—his desertion—had its own rancid smell, something the bomb-sniffing dogs at the security gates would surely be able to identify. He could see it now: He would be sniffed out before he boarded the plane for New York, cut from the crowds of tourists like an errant sheep and chased down the concourse by a pack of braying hounds.

Across the narrow spur just beyond some electrical scaffolding, an arched window, half covered with plastic sheeting, overlooked the tarmac. The blue and white Air Martinique Airbus liners, absolutely massive machines, were parked out there along the spokes of the wheel beneath a lowering sky. A dark line above the horizon in the distance indicated approaching rain. A Legionnaire caught trying to desert was subject to a variety of terrible punishments—beginning with beatings and solitary confinement in *le trou* and ending with a six months' stay in that frozen prison camp in the Jura Mountains. Louise took Smith's hand and put it between her thighs and held it tightly there for a moment—a potent reference to their first night together.

"*Mon amour*," she murmured. "Are you ready?"

Smith looked up from his wine with some reluctance. It was impossible to think clearly when confronted with those large, wonderful indigo eyes. She looked beautiful today wearing a simple, expensive pale blue dress, delicate blue jade hoops in her ears, her skin glowing like pearls beneath a black light, as if her blood and viscera were slightly radioactive.

"What's wrong?" She flinched beneath his scrutiny. "Something's wrong!"

"No, nothing," Smith said and finished his wine in two swallows and signaled to the waiter. "Just let me pay the bill—"

"I know you're nervous," Louise said, as Smith put the last of his heavy euro coins onto the waiter's tray. "But your passport is valid. Yes, the visa stamp isn't current, but you're going home, back to the United States. Why would they—"

"Stop it, Louise!" Smith interrupted sharply. Then, more gently, "Please. I've been thinking about all that for days. I've considered all the angles, I even talked to someone at the American Embassy. We'll be all right. Let's go, let's just get it over with."

Louise bit her lip. She looked a little hurt. "Kiss me first," she said. "I love you."

"I love you too," Smith sighed, and he kissed her and they shouldered their carry-ons and passed from Chez l'Auvergnat's pungent, shadowy corner into brighter neighborhoods—a post office, boutiques selling Hermès ties and Montblanc pens, restaurants specializing in seafood nearly as good as some in Paris—and from there into the elevators as big as railway cars that descended to the security checkpoints below.

4.

Thousands of passengers stood waiting to go through the metal detectors to the gleaming spurs and the departure gates where the planes were being fueled and cleaned for transatlantic flights. The lines snaked around, six deep, between strap-and-pole barriers, the whole area patrolled by tough-looking soldiers with bomb-sniffing dogs.

Smith watched as a team of three soldiers and two dogs came up between the barriers, the claws of the dogs—big Belgian shepherds—clicking against the hard floor of polished aggregate. They nosed along the ground, panting and sniffing at the bags and at the shoes of the wary travelers. Smith recognized the soldiers' identifying shoulder patch—these men had been detached for airport security duty from the 1e Montagnard, Armée de Terre—a mountain regiment based in Haute-Savoie, with whom Smith's training section had once participated in a twenty-four-hour joint maneuver back during Basic. They wore the Armée de Terre black beret with the mountain-peak patch of their regiment on the right side, and carried the ubiquitous FAMAS 5.56 slung over the left shoulder. Smith felt himself sweating profusely as they passed. What if one of them recognized him? But they didn't stop, their dogs trained to sniff out plastic and dynamite, not deserting Legionnaires with anxious hearts.

"Once we're at the gate, we'll get a drink in the first-class lounge," Louise whispered. "Who would ever suspect a Legionnaire of flying first class?"

Smith didn't say anything.

"It's too bad they got rid of the Concorde," Louise continued after a moment, just to make conversation. "We'd be in New York in under three hours . . ." Her voice trailed off. She was beginning to catch some of the nervousness evaporating with the sweat off Smith's skin. The metal detectors looming far ahead seemed an impossible goal, the gates to heaven.

We'll never make it. Smith peered into the distance, shading his eyes from the fluorescent glare. The dogs will get me first. In the seconds following this disturbing thought, one of the Belgian shepherds began to bark two rows over and Smith held his breath. But the dogs had found a woman wearing a colorful headscarf—probably a Gypsy or maybe Turkish—and were now snarling at the large, black vinyl bag at her feet and pointing to it with their snouts. The soldiers of the 1e Montagnard drew around the woman menacingly; she stepped away from the bag, terrified, and put her hands on her head. One of the soldiers unzipped the bag and rummaged around and after a few perilous seconds withdrew a large salami. He gestured with it crudely and the others laughed. Then, to the disappointment of the dogs, he zipped the salami back into the bag and tossed it back to the woman. Shaken by the ordeal, she burst into tears. The soldiers moved on.

"Oh, c'est affreux!" Louise said, shaking her head. "Poor woman. You would call that racial profiling in the United States!"

Smith shrugged, distracted by the crowds, the loud humming of the fluorescent overheads. He had a headache. The line inched forward.

"Those planes were tearing up the sky . . . ," he muttered, distracted, as they came up to the X-ray machine, as they lay their bags on the conveyer belt. He was talking about the Concorde, a subject that hadn't been mentioned for at least ten minutes. "Something about making a hole in the ozone layer . . ."

Louise looked at him, puzzled. "What's that, chéri?"

"Never mind."

Their carry-ons rolled into the maw of the machine, then Smith and Louise took off their shoes, their belts. Louise removed her jade and silver hoops and a heavy-looking platinum bracelet and placed it all in a plastic bowl provided for that purpose. Smith unstrapped his watch apprehensively—it had a military-style black web band and a black face with glow-in-the-dark numbers, distinctly of the type issued to the Legion. He went through the metal detector first; Louise followed. More soldiers of the 1e Montagnard waited on the other side.

But the deserting Legionnaire and his lover passed through security and the gauntlet of soldiers and down the long corridor to the departure spur without being stopped or questioned. Smith found their gate—112a Air Martinique Vol/Flight 3387 Non-Stop—CDG Paris–KIA New York, departure almost two hours off, but business class already lining up. Across the way, through a pane of etched glass, first-class passengers could be seen drinking quietly and nibbling at snacks on comfortable chairs in the lounge. One storefront down, the cheery facade of a duty-free shop gleamed with bottles of fine perfume and expensive cognac, all displayed on pedestals draped with watered silk in the window. Louise turned to Smith, and kissed him.

"*Et voilà!*" she announced triumphantly. "*Nous sommes libres.* I told you we'd be O.K.!"

Smith managed a smile.

"I'm just going to go in there"—she gestured to the duty-free shop—"I want to have a look at the perfumes. And I might get a magnum of good champagne to celebrate, enough to get us both really drunk. We'll swallow the whole damned bottle when we get to New York. Wait here a minute—"

She dropped her bag and kissed him on the cheek and went into the shop.

Smith waited. He watched her through the window, sampling perfumes, holding little cards up to her delicate nose, trying a little squirt of this or that on her slim wrist. He turned away. Two more Montagnard soldiers stood on guard close by, at the top of the escalator that led down to the departure gate. Smith tried not to look at them, but couldn't help himself. One of them was tall and very black, probably an African; the other, thin and loose-looking, all pink and white with colorless eyes set oddly far apart in his head that made him resemble a fish.

The decapitation of Al Bab had not finished the Marabout insurgency. The soul of their leader had migrated into the body of a ten-year-old boy discovered by Marabout mullahs among the refugees of the Awsard camp— this according to the latest UN reports from Western Sahara. There was talk of the Legion returning to the Hip of Africa to keep the peace until MINURSO could effectuate its final withdrawal from the region. If caught deserting now, Smith could be charged with desertion in the face of the enemy. The penalties for this infraction—in the old days death by firing squad—were still too horrible to contemplate.

The judder and scream of jet engines could be felt as a dull rumble through the soles of Smith's new civilian shoes. Suddenly, he heard Colonel de Noyer's voice, a ghostly whisper in his ear: "I am a volunteer serving France with honor and fidelity unto death. Devoted to my commanding officers, courage and loyalty are my virtues . . ."

And he saw for a moment that grim, familiar view of the peaks of the Galtat Zemmur, the bleak escarpments out the doorway of his old prison hovel, and felt the mountain chill along his bare skin and he knew that some part of himself would always be chained there, naked, waiting to die. He turned back toward the duty-free shop, a sudden feeling of despair clutching his heart. He wanted to cry out to Louise, wanted her to stop him from doing what, suddenly, he knew he would do next. She was at the register now, paying with a credit card as the smiling clerk wrapped a large bottle of champagne in colorful paper. He didn't have much time, he wouldn't have the strength to act once she returned. Now! He turned smartly on his heels and marched up to the two soldiers standing guard at the top of the escalator.

"Legionnaire Milquetoast, serial number 02294897," he announced, and drew himself up and saluted, palm out, Legion fashion. "Reporting as a deserter. I ask to be returned to my regiment in Aubagne under arrest!"

The soldiers looked at him blankly. Was this some kind of joke?

"*Mais t'es fou?*" the African soldier said. You crazy? Then, "Move on before I call security."

"Once again, I ask to—" Smith began.

"Want me to go for the sergeant?" the fish-eyed soldier interrupted. "I'll go for the sergeant!"

"This one's a big joker." The African shook his head. Then to Smith, in a low voice. "Move on, I said. You have a valid ticket and a passport or you wouldn't have gotten this far. Just get on your plane and go!"

"I can't do that," Smith said. "If you'll please call your duty officer."

"I'll get the sergeant!" the fish-eyed soldier interrupted and he turned and hurried off down the concourse.

"Get out of here!" the African soldier said to Smith. "Before it's too late!"

"Legionnaire Milquetoast," Smith began again. "Serial number—" But this time he was interrupted by the sound of breaking glass from the direction of the duty-free shop—Louise had dropped the magnum of Veuve Clicquot.

"*Non!* Stop!"

And she was at Smith's side, pulling on his arm desperately, pulling him toward the gate.

"Don't listen to him," she pleaded with the African soldier. "He hasn't been well. We're going to America, you see. We're going to start a new life . . ." But she choked on her words, tears running down her face. Smith wrenched his arm away.

"I demand to be placed under arrest," he told the African soldier insistently. "I demand to be returned to my regiment."

"*Non, non . . . !*" Louise, sobbing now. "He's crazy. John, please. Please! I'm begging you. I love you! Look at me! Johnny!"

Smith couldn't look at her, he needed all his strength for this. The African soldier shook his head.

"Idiot," he said.

A group of soldiers and five or six security guards were now approaching quickly from the far end of the concourse.

"You know what they'll do to you in Aubagne?" The African soldier leaned forward, his voice low, urgent. "They'll cut your balls off and feed them to you on a plate. Me, I'd rather go to America"—he shifted his eyes to Louise—"especially with her! Listen, I'll tell them that you're a little drunk, that it's all a funny joke. Go! This is your last chance!"

Smith shook his head and turned to face Louise.

"Darling," Smith said, resolved. "I'm sorry. I signed on to serve France for five years. I've got to finish my enlistment. I'm so sorry."

The tears on Louise's face dried suddenly, her eyes went cold. "Then you are a fool!" she hissed. "A moron! The Legion is a madhouse, perfect for people like you! Everything was arranged! How can you do this to me?"

"Come down to Aubagne," Smith said. "We'll rent the apartment again. I swore to your husband I'd—"

Suddenly, Louise put her hands over her ears and screamed at the top of her lungs—a shrill note, pathetic and enraged at once and far more expressive than words. This was the one eventuality she had refused to contemplate: Now her lover, like her dead husband before him, had chosen the Legion over her! Very quickly, in mere seconds, all the tenderness she felt for

Smith died inside her like a miscarried embryo. How could she have been so stupid to have fallen in love with this American buffoon? She stepped around him, picking up her feet carefully as one might step around a fresh piece of roadkill, and walked quickly to the escalator.

"Louise!" Smith called. "Wait—"

"I will not be some Legionnaire's bitch!" she shouted over her shoulder and she didn't turn around and was halfway down the escalator on her way to New York without him, drawn by gravity to the departure gate as rough hands pulled Smith to his knees, as his arms were drawn back, cuffs snapped over his wrists.

"I've never seen anything so absolutely idiotic!" the African soldier said now, disgusted. "You're really in for it now, *putain!*"

Smith didn't respond, trying not to think about the consequences of what he had just done. And he tried not to think about it throughout the course of the vicious beatings administered in the holding tank at the Fort de Nogent two hours later; tried not to think in the back of the prison van taking him, cut and bruised and poorly bandaged, to the Legion prison camp at Lac d'Ilay in the Jura mountains the next morning. (The hastily convened military court had sentenced him to three months' hard labor, three less the usual six, inclined toward leniency on account of his medals and the fact that he'd turned himself in.) And he tried not to think at all for the first ten days of icy solitude in his tent, or later as he broke rocks in the sleety mountain rain with a twelve-pound sledge, wearing only a thin T-shirt and a pair of shorts, his hands and feet freezing.

But when thought returned to Smith's numbed brain at last, he began to regret his impulsive decision to remain a Legionnaire. Yes, what an idiot he'd been! Why hadn't he gone off with Louise into the golden future? A house in Malibu or maybe San Francisco, bought with her money; his Ph.D. from UCLA, then the soft life of an academic. There might even be children someday. No. All gone.

5.

Back in Aubagne after completing his sentence, restored to the austere, monotonous, and brutal life of the Legion, reduced to eating Legion slop and drinking mediocre wine from the Legion's vineyards and sleeping with whores in the Legion's brothel, Smith's regret became acute, like a sharp pain stabbing him in the heart. Why had he done this to himself? And he wrote letter after letter to Louise, telling her he still loved her, begging forgiveness, pleading for a face-to-face meeting to explain himself more clearly to her—though their conversation would have to be brief and could only take place at the visitor's center on the base in Aubagne, since, because of his desertion, he'd lost leave privileges for at least a year.

Smith wrote twenty-seven letters in total. Some of them more than thirty pages long, with copies mailed to each of her several addresses—to the town house in the Sixteenth Arrondissement in Paris, to the château de Noyer in Brittany, to the little beach house she'd bought with Phillipe at Saint-Jean-de-Luz in the Pyrénées Atlantique. He never received a single response, though a few of the envelopes mailed to the town house in Paris came back scrawled over with NOT AT THIS ADDRESS!! in what was certainly Louise's own handwriting. Eventually, Smith stopped writing. He consoled himself with the thought that their relationship would have ended badly sooner or later, probably wouldn't have lasted more than a few months. Because a man, no matter how handsome or talented or good or deserving of happiness, simply cannot live off a woman for long.